V

THE CHRONICL

By

J. R. Knoll
Vultross@aol.com

Artwork is the amazing talent of
Sandi Johnson
goldenSalamander.deviantart.com

This is a work of fiction and comes solely from the imagination of the author, J. R. Knoll. Any similarities to any persons, living or dead, is purely coincidental. This work may not be reproduced in whole or in part without the express written consent of the author. No animals were injured during the making of this novel, but some of the humans got the crap kicked out of them! Enjoy.

A few dedications…

This one goes out to my boys!

Chail

The namesake for the hero in ***A Princess in Trade*** and a big old, powerful bruiser of a lad who lives up to that reputation.

Clifton

The unfortunate one who inherited his father's creative mind and has great ambitions of being a veterinarian and novelist.

Kyle

The serious sports nut of the bunch who enjoys a good game of football, basketball, or killing bad guys in his video game.

Ryan

The lucky one who gets to see the world in his own way and through eyes that will never be too old to curb his curiosity.

CHAPTER 1

Middle Summer, 989 seasons

I'm certain that few unicorns ever lived who would actually enjoy finding themselves embroiled in matters not involving some issue with their herd or finding food. To date, I know of only one, myself. Whether it was something born to her or the result of a chance run-in with an enemy of her kind would never be known. One can guess, but this little unicorn had an adventurous and mischievous side long before that encounter with the Desert Lord that fateful spring day. Many not of her kind would dare call her friend while many of her kind would consider her tainted and a threat to all they knew.

Narrow minds often accompany long life and unicorns would prove to be no exception. I have encountered many a unicorn myself. Almost all of the younger unicorns I have encountered fled upon first sight or scent of me. Older unicorns always regarded me as an enemy, a threat. Many stood their ground, determined to fight. In my youth I obliged, but with age comes wisdom. I learned that a unicorn that stands its ground will almost never attack, and the best course for those who do not wish for a confrontation is to just ignore the challenge and let the agitated unicorn calm himself and go about his way. So long as I was not a threat, they had no wish to fight, and this would be a lesson that many unicorns and dragons alike would do well to learn.

The judgment of the young is often clouded with the inexperience of new eyes, but when abandoned by fear as well they have no path that can end well.

Generally, when some large predator ventures into the forest a unicorn's instinct is to hide, to conceal themselves and do what they can to tell that predator that there is no game to hunt, and that they should just move on. Unicorns are not those who thrive on confrontation or seek adventure, and for the most part they avoid it. Shahly was to be a rare exception.

Summer mornings so deep in the forest were not without

discomforts. Moisture would hang in the air. Some mornings it would be seen as low fog and others it would just be felt as the day grew hotter, giving one, especially humans, a close, sticky feeling.

Unicorns do not seem to be bothered much by their climate no matter if it is winter or summer, but a cranky old forest cat with an empty belly would not be so comfortable.

Almost the size of a horse, the forest cat crept noiselessly toward what he hoped was an easy meal. Black spots against his light brown and tan fur made him difficult to make out in the denseness of the forest. Amber eyes were unwavering as he followed movement ahead of him, a shadowy form he had been stalking for some time. What he did not know is that he was being watched himself.

In a place where the trees were not so thick, a young unicorn, merely a season old if that, had wandered from his mother to nibble on the sweet clovers that grew in the spotty sunlight. At this age he was still oblivious to predators, as he had never encountered one. He was a light brown with a tan belly and dark brown mane and tail. His horn was not as long as a human's hand and was ivory with sparkling glints of copper within the spirals. With his nose in the deep clover and his thoughts oblivious to the danger that stalked him, he would be an easy target for the big predator that watched from only a few paces inside the trees and underbrush.

With one mighty leap over the concealing brush the forest cat would be upon his prey before the young unicorn even realized what was happening and the end would be mercifully quick.

An old silver unicorn was not far away, his eyes locked on the big cat as he prepared to spring a trap of his own. Noiselessly moving through the shadows of the trees, the big unicorn approached to within only a few paces, watching the body language of the big cat intently as he planned to make his move.

The cat's haunches tensed and his eyes were wide. His ears laid flat against his head as his claws dug into the ground. He was ready to pounce.

So was the big silver unicorn.

A sharp, young whinny drew the little unicorn foal's attention, and the cat's, and the silver unicorn's.

A white unicorn, about the size of a pony, leaped over the brush on the other side of the clearing and in two long bounds was between the forest cat and the unicorn foal. With ribbons of gold within the white and ivory of her horn glistening in the sunlight, her gold cloven hooves found the forest floor beneath her solidly and she stopped to face the threat with narrow eyes and flattened ears. Very horse-like in form, she also shared the fleet characteristics of a deer, though her upper legs were thicker and clearly stronger than a deer's. Her snow white tail swished back and forth and her mane settled evenly to the sides of her neck. Brown eyes bored into the forest cat, still hidden in the underbrush of the forest.

The silver unicorn slowly raised his head, his eyes now on the white unicorn.

Looking back to the foal, the white unicorn whickered to him and he turned and trotted away. With him no longer in danger, the white unicorn turned her attention back to the big forest cat. Lowering her head, she approached and looked him right in the eyes, whickering in a challenging tone as she stopped only a couple of paces away.

The forest cat bared his teeth and growled. He was larger than the unicorn and could easily take her, especially so close, but her posture and fearless approach put pause into him. Surely a meal like this would not be taken so easily. It couldn't be! Surely there was a deadly threat there. But there was also a glint of recognition. He knew this unicorn, and could remember chasing her before.

With an impatient sigh, the silver unicorn emerged from his hiding place among the trees and stalked toward the forest cat from the other side. He was seen immediately and the forest cat suddenly found himself outnumbered, and slowly crept backward.

Quite unexpectedly, the white unicorn leaped toward him, over the bushes that had concealed him, and planted all four hooves onto his back.

Roaring in pain and anger as the white unicorn vaulted from him, the forest cat wheeled around and launched himself after the fleeing unicorn.

The silver unicorn rolled his eyes up and heaved a heavy

sigh, showing just a little annoyance as he began to canter forward in pursuit.

So nimble as to make any deer jealous, if they felt such things, the white unicorn bounded carelessly and very fast through the forest with the cat only paces behind her. She had no plan and her heart thundered as she was pursued through the forest. Any unicorn in her place would have been racked by terror, a horrible fear of being caught and eaten, clawed to pieces and strangled by the jaws of this mighty predator of the forest, but such thoughts were not in her mind at all, only the exhilaration of the chase was, the beating hooves, the trees that blurred by, and the racing of her own heart.

Soon, she would tire and she knew she would have to end the chase. She had done this many times and now knew right where she was going. She could run nowhere that the cat could not follow, but she had outmaneuvered such predators before, and had in fact outmaneuvered this one more than a few times. While the cat was learning to better pursue her, she constantly learned better ways to elude him.

Still, long chases bored her after a time and she turned her flight toward the heart of the forest, toward a river there where she could lose the cat and get herself a drink.

Some distance later she found a human made road and ran down it for a while with the tiring cat right behind her. His paws swiped at her twice here but were just barely out of reach, and each time he swiped he lost a little ground.

Unexpectedly, she turned hard back into the forest, ran across a clearing, through the trees and leaped over some thorny underbrush, and as she turned to continue her flight, she stopped suddenly, her mouth falling open as her eyes found the three other mare unicorns all with their new foals! She had led the forest cat right to them!

The other unicorns, two brown and one tan among the mothers and one black, one blond and one gray among the foals, lifted their heads and looked right at her, their wide eyes betraying a start. They all nervously backed away as they knew the sudden appearance of the white unicorn meant there was a hungry and no doubt angry predator pursuing her, and the white unicorn seemed to have a gift for leading them right into the midst of those who did not want to be chased.

Only a second or two passed as the white unicorn stared back at the mothers and foals, but it was all the time the forest cat needed to catch up and pounce, and the white unicorn could not move in time.

Right before he reached her, the silver unicorn bolted out of nowhere, turning his head and slamming his shoulder hard into the forest cat's side. As the cat rolled to the ground some paces away, the silver turned to the white unicorn and ordered, "Shahly, lead it away! I'll take care of the families."

She looked to him and answered with an enthusiastic, "Right!" Turning toward the forest cat as he got his paws under him, she charged right at him, jumping over him as before and she kicked him on the top of the head this time as she passed.

For the forest cat, this was now more or less personal and he charged after the white unicorn again.

Knowing she would have to lead him a good distance from the other unicorns, Shahly found a quick pace to the south, wanting to put a good league between this big cat and her herd. She did not know how long she had run, but she knew this part of the forest and was well aware of where she was going. She found a path perhaps two paces wide for the most part and ran hard down it. The land inclined slightly for hundreds of paces and she tired quicker running up it, but she knew the cat would as well. She also knew what was at the end of this path.

Ahead, the shadows of the trees gave way to sunlight as the forest opened. She could see bigger, moss covered rocks ahead, and as she got closer, the land seemed to just stop. Her eyes narrowing, she knew right where she was going: There was a cliff ahead, one that was three men's heights high.

She never broke stride and hurled herself off of the cliff, whinnying all the way down to the deep water of the creek below. She hit the water flat on her belly with a big splash and fought her way quickly to the surface, not for air quite as much as to see the frustrated forest cat standing on the edge looking down at her.

And there he was, his eyes narrow, his jaws agape and his tongue hanging out as he struggled to catch his breath.

Treading water in the middle of the deepest part of the creek,

Shahly smiled as she stared back, and she began the short swim to the shore on the other side. As she scrambled up the bank, she looked up the cliff again to see the forest cat still staring down at her. They both knew she would be long gone by the time he found a way around and across the creek, and they both knew he would not follow her off the cliff. Water was not his friend.

Turning toward him, the white unicorn violently shook herself and the water exploded from her in all directions, and as she stopped and her still wet mane fell to one side of her neck, she looked back up the cliff and whinnied at the forest cat.

He bared his teeth and sent a screaming reply back.

Shahly smiled again and took a short drink, then turned to just walk away, flicking her tail at the angry cat as she paced back into the forest.

She circled back toward the creek and wandered north along it toward the river and the late season fruits she would find there.

She was nearly there when something touched her mind and she stopped. She raised her head, her eyes shifting to one side and an ear twitched that way. This would not be another chase, yet she felt uneasy. It touched her mind again and she knew it as the essence of another unicorn.

A dark gray unicorn with a white mane, tail and long beard appeared from the forest and approached her. He was a big unicorn, as large as an average horse and he appeared to be very old. The white in his horn had turned to ivory streaked with silver. His dark eyes were locked on her in an intense and frightening stare.

Shahly turned toward him and raised her head, not trying to give away that she was nervous, though he seemed to already know.

He stopped and stared back at her for long seconds, then ordered, "Follow me, Shahly." Not another word did he utter as he turned and led the way down the forest trail toward the river.

Her ears drooping as she paced behind him, the white unicorn lowered her head, not daring to speak.

What seemed to be a long journey ended near the river where a wide grassy plain perhaps a hundred paces across and following the river for three hundred more lay open in the sunshine. They followed the tree line, then veered back into the forest. The old unicorn found a stream and followed it away from the river, toward denser forest.

Shahly's uneasiness grew more with each step.

Dense forest gave way quickly to a glade that was irregular but appeared to be about forty paces wide. On the other end there was a cliff perhaps two heights high that surrounded a third of the glade. Mosses and ferns grew from it and a little pool that fed the creek was fed by a small waterfall from one side of the cliff. Surrounding the entire glade was dense, lush forest. The grass was short here, as it was often grazed by forest animals and unicorns. The sun was high and the glade was bathed in its bright light. This was one of the most enchanting places in the forest, a place held sacred to the unicorns.

Eleven of the herd elders were there, assembled in a circle in the center of the glade. There was an opening in the circle that the old gray unicorn would close, but he paused and looked back at Shahly, motioning with his head for her to enter first.

Hesitantly, she crept past him, her eyes darting about at the other unicorns who stared at her with a mix of expressions. As she got into the center, she looked behind her to see that the old gray had closed the circle behind her.

Often, when a unicorn was called to the center of the elder's circle it meant that something was horribly wrong or that a new foal was expected. Many seasons ago she had seen another unicorn called to the circle, and after that he was not seen again.

Silence gripped the forest, but for the waterfall.

The old gray finally spoke. "Shahly, the elders have watched you this season. Ever since spring you have been different. You have befriended known enemies of our kind, enemies who pose a danger to the herd."

She turned toward him, protesting, "Ralligor is no danger to the herd!"

"And the other predators you have led into the forest?" the gray demanded. "What of the drakenien? What of the forest cats that chase you into the heart of our herd? What of the humans you have repeatedly approached? All of them pose a danger to the unicorns of the herd, especially the youngest. You have been approached many times on this matter by herd elders, and yet you continue."

Her ears drooped and she defended, "But many of them needed my help."

An older brown mare with a tan mane who stood to Shahly's right pointed out, "Humans and these other creatures do not need the help of the unicorns, especially those creatures who would hunt us. We are not their guardians. The fates they forge for themselves are theirs to live with."

Shahly looked to the old mare and asked, "If we aren't here to help them, then why are we here?"

A black unicorn with a silver mane and beard on the other side of the circle answered, "We are the guardians of the forest, not those who would invade the forest. Humans have no place here, nor do dragons."

"The elders have decided," the old gray informed. "You are a danger to the herd and you must leave at once."

Shahly gasped and shook her head, backing away from the old gray.

A big bay unicorn with a black mane, tail and beard and ribbons of copper within the spirals of his horn snapped, "Not all of the elders agree on this!"

The gray looked to him and countered, "Vinton, we have been over this. The matter is settled."

Stepping from his place in the circle, the big bay unicorn glared across the circle at the old gray as he said, "We also settled a matter a few seasons ago with another unicorn. Do you remember when we decided that Bexton was a danger to the herd? How did *that* turn out?"

The old mare answered, "Circumstances were different with him, and yet we cannot ignore the similarities. Shahly is young and the ideas of vengeance are not a part of her, and yet like Bexton she has been tainted by the humans. She *became* one of them and now she seeks out adventures and predators that put this herd in jeopardy."

The black unicorn added, "She brought a dragon into the middle of the herd during the spring gathering. Do you remember that?"

Vinton looked to him and fired back, "Do *you* remember that the dragon you speak of drove away the drakenien *and* the humans who were hunting us? Do you remember that it was that dragon that rescued Shahly and me from the humans this spring?"

An old silver unicorn raised his head and took a step in from the circle. "I myself considered that. I also warned her about the dangers of humans. When this decision was made I reflected upon the actions of that dragon that came into our herd. I remember well that he drove away a group of humans and a large predator that we could not defend ourselves against that day, and yet he took no aggressive actions against the herd. None at all." He looked to Shahly. "Let the memories of all show that I disagree with this decision, and I denounce it."

"That dragon has become her friend," the bay stallion said straightly. "Few of us have ever had the courage to even approach a dragon, much less befriend one who would one day defend our herd."

"It was that dragon that made her human," the mare pointed out. "It was also decided that you have abstained from the decision to banish her. I'm sorry, Vinton. I know she is your mate, but we must consider the safety of the herd above one individual who has repeatedly endangered us. This must be."

The black unicorn added, "You yourself have approached her many times about her actions, and yet she continues."

"I have also helped her in these actions," the stallion pointed out. "Am I to be banished as well?"

"The decision is made," the gray insisted. He looked to Shahly and added, "I am sorry. You must leave at once."

She lowered her eyes and whimpered, "I—I can never come back?"

"Not so long as you are a danger to the herd," he replied. "I'm sorry. We all are, but this must be. I can only hope you will understand."

Shahly looked around at the unicorns of the circle, seeing a tan unicorn with a black mane and tail and a white beard staring back with pity in his eyes. Slowly, she approached him and whimpered, "Ahpa?"

He stared back at her for a moment, then he turned his eyes down.

Even her own father thought she was a danger to the herd.

Her mouth quivering, she turned and paced toward the old grey, who backed out of the circle and moved aside as she passed. She left the elders there in the glade and followed the creek all the way to the grassy field near the river. Pausing at the water's edge, she lowered her head for a drink, then she turned and wandered along the bank for a time. Eventually, she turned and paced into the forest, slowly making her way to a trail that would take her west. She found the trail, one that was about four paces wide for the most part, and she just walked. Her heart was heavier than it had ever been and she finally allowed tears to roll from her eyes. Memories of all she had done since spring assaulted her. She did not know how she could survive outside of the protection of the herd. She would miss the companionship of the other unicorns. Mostly, she would miss her Vinton.

Without destination, she just wandered for a time and wept. She had never felt so alone. She had no one else to turn to, nowhere to go and she was filled with a horrible emptiness. She had befriended many outside of her species, but most of them lived within a forest she now must leave. Somewhere north of her home were others who would welcome her, and others with them who would see her killed.

Alone was a horrible feeling, and after a while she had cried all she could.

She did not know how much time had passed when she raised her head, finally realizing there was one she could still depend on. Following the course of the sun, she went west, toward the scrub country.

As it had that spring, Shahly's journey into the desert felt like a long one. This time she did not worry about finding Vinton. As he had told her once, her heart would lead her right to him when she returned to the forest. The sun was ahead of her, in her eyes more and more as she neared the mountains and she found herself squinting against it. Summer days in the desert were far hotter than those of spring and she found her need for water far greater than it had been before. She knew right where to find it, but there was that large problem awaiting her once she reached it: The giant scorpion.

Once she arrived at the pool, she stopped some fifty paces away from it, scanning the sand with her essence to see if she could find the creature. There, under a weathered mound of sand only a few paces in front of her it patiently awaited the arrival of its next meal.

Shahly backed away, her eyes on the mound as she gingerly stepped backward a few paces. At a safe distance, she turned and paced wide around it, never taking her eyes from it. Once up on the rock ledge, she was careful not to kick any pebbles off this time that might alert the scorpion to her presence.

Looking into the pool of water which shimmered in the shadow of the mountain, she almost smiled, remembering the sweet taste, and she plunged her nose into it, drinking ravenously. Once her thirst was quenched, she nibbled some of the fruit from a few of the many trees that surrounded the pool, then she turned and went on her way, glancing back to make certain she had not disturbed the scorpion.

She paced down the box canyon for some time, not remembering it being so long. The last time she was being chased and was running as fast as she could, so naturally she got to where she was going quickly. She quickened her pace, finally rounding that familiar bend and finding what she sought.

Ahead of her was a huge black mass of reptilian power, sprawled on the desert floor on his belly in the shade much the way a sleeping forest cat would lay. His body was stretched out in a straight line from his snout all the way to the end of his long tail. He faced away from his cave, seemingly to spring into action as soon as some foolish challenger woke him. His thick arms were outstretched, his hands reaching nearly to the end of his nose, each about three paces away. One wing was folded to his back. The other was extended and partly enveloping the scarlet dragon who lay in much the same fashion at his side, sleeping soundly.

Shahly stopped and just stared at them for a moment, and she smiled. They looked so cute lying together like that. Falloah's head was turned slightly away from the black dragon's and she seemed to have herself as close to him as she could. Much of her body was concealed beneath his wing.

Hesitantly approaching him, the unicorn paced noiselessly to his head, which was about as large as her entire body, and she just stared at him for a moment. He was a natural enemy of the unicorns. He was also one of her dearest friends. The elders of the herd just did not understand. In the absence of their council, she would turn to his.

Slowly lowering her mouth to his ear, she whispered, "Ralligor." He did not stir, so she repeated in a whisper but just a little louder, "Ralligor."

He drew a deeper breath, and replied in a growl, "I'm asleep."

She blinked, then bent to his ear again and whispered, "If you're asleep, then how is it you're talking to me?"

He finally half opened his eyes, staring down the canyon. "Let me guess. You've done something foolish again."

Shahly took a few steps back, a little hurt in her eyes as she confirmed, "Yes. How did you know?"

His eyes shifted to her.

She stared back at him for long seconds, then looked down to the sand, kicking at it as she reported, "I got banished from the herd today. They think I am a danger to the other unicorns."

The dragon countered, "I keep hearing that you're a danger to the forest predators."

"I guess so," she agreed softly, still kicking at the sand. "Vinton kept warning me not to... Oh, I don't know what I'm doing anymore. He says it is your fault, but I don't believe that. I just am who I am."

"And your experiences this season have not affected who you are?"

"I guess they have."

"Do you remember when you went into RedStoneCastle as a human?"

"Yes."

"Do you remember how you felt once you were unicorn again?"

She nodded.

"Has it occurred to you that you take these chances because some of that human might still be in you?"

"Bexton said it would nibble away at me until I was human again. I didn't believe him, but I guess it's true, isn't it?"

"No, Shahly, it isn't true. You experienced things that no

other unicorn has. Now, being just unicorn isn't enough for you."

She turned her eyes to him.

"Your little adventures," he went on, "your crusades, your pestering of dangerous predators... You simply crave the excitement that you experienced before, the same kind of excitement that the rest of your kind avoids. You find yourself bored if you aren't in some life and death struggle."

Shahly felt anxious and this showed in her eyes as she whimpered, "That makes me dangerous to the herd?"

"I suppose it can," he agreed. "If something you did put the other unicorns at risk, then of course your elders are going to do what they must to protect your herd."

Looking to the ground again, Shahly suddenly felt pangs of guilt for the first time in many months—and she finally, truly understood. "I guess I *was* dangerous to the herd. I can never go back, can I?"

"That all depends on you," was the dragon's answer.

She nodded. "Vinton kept trying to tell me. Why wouldn't I listen?"

Ralligor raised his brow slightly. "Because he's not as wise as I am. Will you listen now?"

The unicorn nodded.

"Is he waiting for you somewhere?" the dragon asked.

"He's still with the herd," she answered softly.

"Sounds like you two have a lot to talk about."

"But I can't go back. The herd doesn't want me back in the forest."

"I don't think they would object if you are quiet and not being pursued by some predator that could get the rest of them. Just see if you can find him and talk over these issues and work on a plan to rejoin your herd. I'm sure they would welcome you back if they don't feel you're a danger."

"I suppose so."

The black dragon closed his eyes. "Then I shouldn't keep you."

"Okay," she agreed. "Thank you for talking to me."

"You're welcome, Shahly."

She turned and paced down the canyon. Half way to the

open desert, she raised her head and looked around her. The mountain's shadow was very long, stretching far into the desert, and the light of day was fading fast. She would have to take a good, long drink before starting this journey which meant braving the scorpion again. Strange sounds and smells began to reach her. Creatures she was not familiar with were wandering about out there, many of them predators that she would not be able to see in the darkness. Looking up, the desert sky was filling with high clouds. That meant no moonlight or starlight to guide her way back to the forest.

Something shrieked ahead of her and she jumped, her heart pounding as her eyes shifted back and forth. When it shrieked again, she slowly backed away, then turned and ran back the way she had come.

Breathing in shrieking gasps, she finally reached the dragon, her eyes wide as she stopped only a couple of paces from his nose.

Ever so slowly, his eyes opened and fixed on her. "Is there a problem?"

She looked behind her, then back to the dragon and informed, "It is getting dark."

"That's when I usually sleep," he said straightly.

Shahly nodded, looking behind her again.

Ralligor drew a calming breath and looked toward the sky. "You're afraid of the dark, aren't you?"

"No," she replied, "I'm afraid of the things in it." She cringed as she heard the shriek again. "Um, Ralligor, I... Uh, is anything out there...."

He growled a sigh.

Looking back at him, she asked in a begging tone, "Can I stay here with you tonight?"

His eyes found her again, then closed. "I suppose. There's a soft clump of grass behind you that you can sleep in."

"Thank you," she offered, her eyes darting around as the canyon grew darker. She turned and paced slowly to the grass near the canyon wall, grass that was unusually lush for the hard lands. Gingerly stepping into it, she turned in a circle a few times to flatten it out, then laid down to her belly, staring down the darkening canyon with wide eyes for a time. At this point she was actually very tired, but nerves were taut and alert. Finally shifting half way to her side, she laid her head down, still staring down the canyon. Ever so slowly, her eyes grew heavy and began to close.

Something down there buzzed very loudly, right on the canyon wall not far away!

Shahly sprang up and backed away, looking hard for the horrid creature that made such a terrible sound.

It buzzed again, so loud it hurt her ears.

Wheeling around, she ran back toward the dragon, tripping over his hand and tumbling into his snout.

Ralligor raised his head, his brow low over his red glowing eyes as he looked down at the little white unicorn who struggled to right herself.

Once she was standing, she backed into the crook of his arm and whinnied, "There's something out there!"

The dragon glanced down the canyon. "It's a bug, Shahly."

"It sounds loud and angry and huge!" She cringed as it buzzed again and whinnied, "It's coming to get me!"

"Shahly, it isn't coming to get you. That noise it makes scares away animals that would eat it and calls to other bugs. Just go lay back down."

The scarlet dragon raised her head. "*Unisponsus,* is everything okay?" She looked to the unicorn and greeted, "Well hello there. I didn't know you were coming tonight."

"Hi," Shahly nervously replied, her wide eyes boring into the darkness.

The dragoness looked to him and asked, "Is she staying the night with us again?"

Ralligor snarled in an exasperated tone, "Yes."

The dragoness smiled. "I see. Since my lair is in the forest she feels secure there, and it really isn't safe for her to travel through the desert at night, anyway."

"I suppose," he growled. "Shahly, go lay down and try to go to sleep."

The unicorn glanced up at him, finding some reassurance in those menacing eyes that glowed so brightly red. Hesitantly, she went back to the grass and laid back down, her wide eyes still looking for whatever was so loud in the darkness. When it buzzed again, closer this time, she raised her head and bayed. Breathing was in short gasps and she finally called out, "Ralligor, it's coming closer!"

"It won't hurt you," he assured in a growl from the darkness. "Go to sleep."

Shahly nodded and laid her head back down. Just as her eyes began to grow heavy again the thing buzzed even louder and she leaped to her hooves, whinnying, "Ralligor!" She jumped as a blast of fire slammed into the canyon wall and exploded with a thunderous boom and a bright flash, a storm of flame and fleeing sparks. Loose sand and pebbles fell to the canyon floor in the darkness after. Little glowing embers slowly faded from sight, then all was quiet. She listened intently in the silence after and swallowed hard.

"Do you think you can go to sleep now?" the black dragon snarled.

She listened a few seconds longer, then finally nodded and said, "I think so."

"Good night, then," Ralligor growled.

Shahly lay back down and this time allowed her heavy eyelids to close. Sometime later she had just drifted off to sleep when she awoke with a shriek, raising her head and looking out into the night.

Something moved!

She gasped, desperately searching for whatever was out there.

Footfalls in the sand drew closer. It sounded huge! She could smell it on the breeze, something reptilian. Trembling, she reached out with her essence and found it there in the darkness. It was a predator!

Springing to her hooves again, she backed toward her dragon friend and whinnied, "Ralligor!"

A red glow bathed the canyon as the dragon opened his eyes and raised his head. "Shahly, what the hell is it now?"

"Something's coming!" she whinnied. She backed into something and jumped half her height into the air, then slammed hooves first down on something solid, something that moved! Leaping sideways, she whinnied in terror, looking back to see that it was the black dragon's hand illuminated in the red glow of his eyes. She calmed a little and looked up at him. He looked angry, and hopefully whatever was out there would see him and flee for its life. She found her heart pounding as never before.

Ralligor looked down at his hand and balled it into a fist, then flexed his fingers, repeating this a few times before he turned less than pleased eyes on the unicorn.

Falloah raised her head and brushed her snout against the bottom of the black dragon's jaw, then looked to the agitated unicorn and explained, "Shahly, many of the desert creatures are nocturnal."

She gasped again. "That means they have really big teeth and eat unicorns, doesn't it? Can you scare it away so that it doesn't get me?"

Ralligor growled and turned his eyes down the canyon.

There, illuminated in red was the predator she feared, a lizard perhaps as long as Shahly's hind leg. With a forked tongue, it tasted the air and sand looking for food.

Laughing softly, the dragoness corrected, "No, it means they are awake at night when the sun is down and the air is cooler. That is when they look for food."

"But what if they think I'm food?" Shahly was beginning to sound hysterical.

The black dragon growled again and his head slammed into the desert sand. "Shahly, I really don't think that lizard is big enough to eat you, but if you lay down right beside me and don't make another sound for the rest of the night then I'm sure it won't bother you. It won't come too close to a dragon so you'll be safe."

"Do you promise?" she asked desperately.

"Yes, I promise."

She paced to him and laid down right behind his head, pressing herself against his neck. Laying her head down, she continued to stare down the canyon, looking for anything that might wander from the darkness.

The red light that bathed the canyon slowly faded as the black dragon closed his eyes.

Shahly heard Falloah lay back down. She swallowed hard again against a very dry throat, still a little afraid, but feeling much safer with the black dragon right beside her. Her eyes slowly closed. She tried to swallow again, but between fits of terror and the hot dry air of the desert her mouth and throat were horribly dry. She raised her head and complained, "I'm thirsty."

All of Ralligor's claws curled and dug into the sand and he drug his hands toward him, leaving deep ruts in the ground. He slowly pushed himself up and opened his eyes, the red glow from them shining even brighter to illuminate the canyon almost like it was dawn. He growled again as he slowly turned those eyes to the little unicorn.

Falloah slipped from beneath his wing and stood to all fours, raising her head to stroke her snout against his again. "I'll take her, *Unisponsus.*" She stood fully and turned her eyes to Shahly, a blue glow overtaking them and illuminating the unicorn as she said, "Come along, Shahly. Let's go get a drink."

As the dragoness turned, her eyes cast that warm blue glow to the canyon before her, lighting the way as she strode slowly toward the open desert.

Shahly stood and trotted to her side, then looked behind her as Ralligor slammed his head back onto the ground and closed his eyes, another growl escaping him. "He seems grouchy tonight," she observed.

Laughing softly, Falloah agreed, "He sure does."

CHAPTER 2

As the black dragon lifted his head, the sleeping unicorn rolled to her side and plopped down on the packed sand, waking with a start. She looked up, seeing that the sun was already climbing from the rim of the canyon, then she struggled to her hooves and turned toward the dragon.

He sat up and stretched, his spine making a succession of cracks and pops as he did. He blinked, then looked around him, his eyes finally finding the unicorn.

"Good morning, Ralligor," she greeted. "How did you sleep?"

He raised a brow, then looked down the canyon and raised his head.

Shahly also looked, seeing the scarlet dragon just landing about thirty paces away.

The dragoness strode to the black dragon and stroked his snout with hers, saying, "It's about time you two awoke. I just got back from the lake. The water is wonderful and there are some really big fish coming to the surface."

He grunted.

Falloah looked down to the unicorn, smiling slightly as she softly informed, "He wakes up grouchy, too."

Shahly whickered a laugh. Her heart felt heavy again as she saw the two dragons together and she realized how much she already missed her Vinton.

Ralligor looked down to her and informed, "It looks like we're going to the lake. Do you know where it is?"

Shahly turned her eyes down and nodded.

"It is a few hours away at your speed," he continued, "or I can fly you."

She turned her eyes back up to him and offered, "Thank you, but I want to go see Vinton one more time."

The black dragon nodded. "Very well. That's where we'll be until dark so that's where you'll find us if you want to come. Bring Plow Mule if you like."

"Okay," she replied. "Thank you for letting me stay the night."

"You're welcome, Shahly."

She looked to Falloah, then whinnied and bolted down the canyon.

After a stop at the pool of water, she set out at a fast pace toward the forest.

Half the day passed and her pace really did not slow, and before she realized, she was deep in the forest and heading north along the paths to the river. The herd would not like her returning so she had to make sure she was not noticed.

Emerging on the flood plain, she paced to the water's edge and lowered her head for a drink, then she paused and looked across the river. Memories found her again. Right across the water is where Vinton had chosen her that spring, or rather attempted to that first time. "*Two hearts are two hearts until they become one,*" he had told her. She lowered her eyes again and drank a little before looking across to that place once more.

Shahly stared for some time, remembering that last happy moment before the humans found them, before the dragon had made her human, before her simple life had taken that sudden and catastrophic change. Before she realized, she galloped into the water and swam the forty paces across, emerging on the other side and cantering to the field, the very place that would have marked the best moment of her life had her insecurities not interfered. That spring Vinton had insisted on returning there to make it the place where he would choose her, and he formally did in front of the entire herd. She never thought she would feel so alone here, or so sad.

Something bit her haunch and she whinnied and leaped half her height in the air. Coming back down, she wheeled around to see what had gotten her.

Vinton was smiling. "You know, I never get tired of that."

Shahly backed away a step, then whinnied, "Vinton!" Lunging to him, she nuzzled his neck and found herself weeping again. "I'm sorry, Vinton. I'm sorry. I should have listened. I should have done as you said. I'll change, I promise. Just tell me what I should do."

The stallion backed away from her, giving her that authoritative stare that he did when he was about to give her a good scolding. This was a look she was all too familiar with and she laid her ears back as she saw it.

Looking away from him, she admitted, "I know. I've been horrible. But I promise I will do as you say and change so that I can be a unicorn who you can love again."

"You can't do both," the stallion informed.

She turned her hurt-filled eyes to him.

He took a step toward her. "Shahly, I don't want you to change."

"But I'm a danger to the herd," she argued. "That's why I was banished. I don't want to endanger the other unicorns anymore."

"And you can't rejoin the herd," he informed coldly. "The elders won't trust that you can change some of these dangerous habits that got you banished to begin with. I'm sorry. That's just the way it must be."

She loosed a painful breath and nodded. "I understand, Vinton. I won't be a bother to the herd anymore. Just know that I'll always love you." With a heavy heart, she turned and paced down river. She would mercifully not look back to her stallion as she did not want him to feel as horribly as she did. When she raised her head, she noticed the stallion pacing at her side, his eyes on her.

Shahly stared back, feeling horrible shame for tearing them apart. "Are you going to escort me to the edge of the forest?" she asked hopefully.

"No" was his answer.

She turned her eyes forward again, craving his company and yet wanting to be alone with the horrible feelings that plagued her. She was hurting, and did not want to share that pain with the one that she loved the most. "I'll be okay, Vinton. Please don't worry over me."

"I will always worry over you," he countered.

"I'll always think of you and have you in my heart," she replied in a soft voice. They paced along in silence for a while and she finally suggested, "I guess you should be getting back to the herd, now."

Vinton veered in front of her and made her stop. "Shahly, you *are* my herd."

She raised her eyes sheepishly to his, just looking back as he stared at her for a time, then tears filled her eyes.

Vinton turned fully to her. "Two hearts are two hearts until they become one, remember? I can't live with half a heart, and you are the half that I need the most."

She let the tears go and they streamed from her eyes. "Vinton, I've been banished."

He raised his head and countered, "Then *we* have been banished."

"The herd needs you."

"I think you need me more, and since we'll be together forever that makes us our own herd. Now quit arguing with your elder."

Shahly looked away and whickered a laugh, then something serious occurred to her and she turned her eyes back to him. "Vinton, if I'm such a danger to the whole herd then I must be even more dangerous to just one other unicorn, even you."

He smiled and assured, "I'll keep you in line. Do you think I'm letting you out of my sight from now on?"

"I—I just don't want anything to happen to you."

"As much as I don't want anything to happen to you?"

She had no answer for him and turned her eyes down.

"You almost sound like you're trying to talk me out of going with you."

"I am just so afraid," she admitted.

"I think you would be less afraid with me at your side."

"I love you so much, Vinton."

He nuzzled her. "And I you, more than you can realize. I'll never leave you, I promise."

Shahly closed her eyes. "What if I can't... What if..."

"What if you continue to act like a maniac?" he finished for her.

She nodded.

Vinton backed away, meeting her eyes. "Shahly, you have an adventurous side that no other unicorn I know has. I'll admit I had a difficult time getting used to it, but it's become something I adore about you."

She blinked and asked, "Really?"

"How could I not? I love everything about you."

Looking to the ground, Shahly took a deep breath and said, "Ralligor told me that this adventurous side is something left over from when I was human. He said being just a unicorn is not enough for me anymore."

"I *knew* this was his fault," the stallion grumbled, looking away. When his little mare turned a very hurt look to him, he quickly added, "I mean your habit of taking risks. Stuff like that. I saw you do many things that were dangerous simply because you wanted to help someone else. That's a kindness within you that I would never change."

"What if I keep wanting to help them, Vinton?"

He raised his head and confirmed "Then that's what we'll do. Oh, let's face it. You were an adventurous scamp from the time you were a foal. It's one of the things I've always loved about you." One of his ears twitched and he looked toward the forest, his eyes narrowing slightly.

Shahly also looked, seeing a tan unicorn with a black mane and white beard approaching them. His ivory horn glistened with silver as he paced toward them.

As the old unicorn reached them, Vinton turned fully, raising his head as he greeted,
"Dosslar."

The tan unicorn looked to him and nodded, replying, "Vinton." He turned his eyes to Shahly, saying, "I'd hoped you hadn't gone too far." He had a deep voice, soft like a breeze and brown eyes much like Shahly's.

Tears filled her eyes again as she greeted, "Hi Ahpa."

Dosslar turned his eyes down. "These crazy times of humans hunting us seem to have all unicorns on edge."

"I know," she offered softly.

"So naturally," Vinton cut in, "the elders elect to banish her from the herd, even you."

"I had the whole herd to think about," he admitted. "My feelings had to come second. Perhaps when you are older—"

"I'm plenty old enough to realize that we don't banish a unicorn in her greatest time of need," the bay interrupted. "Remember what happened to Bexton? Do you remember what happened after he was banished?"

"I know," the old unicorn confessed softly.

"He sent the humans to hunt our kind," Vinton continued. "It was because of him that she encountered that dragon to begin with, all because he was banished from the herd during his greatest time of need. How did *that* protect the herd?"

Shahly stepped between them and pled, "Please don't fight. What's done is done."

A tear slipped from the old unicorn's eye and he said, "You remind me so of your mother. She is adventurous, and so caring." He looked to Shahly. "Not quite as reckless as you, but I definitely see her each time I see you. I'm sorry this happened, Shahly. I will try to get the elders to welcome you back to the herd soon."

She turned her eyes down and offered, "Thank you, Ahpa."

Vinton raised his head. "You can tell the elders that they will also be without me. I'll not go back to the herd until Shahly does."

The old tan looked to him with strained eyes. "I would only ask that you protect her, Vinton. Care for her and guide her."

"I will," the big bay confirmed.

Dosslar nodded to him, then nuzzled Shahly once more before he turned and paced back into the forest.

Shahly watched him disappear into the trees. Feeling a great weight on her heart once again, she turned her eyes down and turned away from Vinton, pacing slowly toward the West.

Her stallion caught up to her quickly, bumping her with his side. "Don't be sad, Love. This should be just another adventure to you."

She nodded.

"You don't want to talk, do you?"

Hesitantly, she shook her head.

"We don't have to," he assured. "As long as we're together everything will be great."

Shahly glanced at him and could not avoid a smile.

***

Unicorns do not keep track of time. These are creatures of very long lifespan, creatures considered immortal to many other creatures.

Shahly and Vinton would not know how long they traveled or how far. Banished from their herd, they paced south and west, and eventually the little mare's spirits lifted. In the presence of the stallion at her side, she could not help but feel happy.

Exiting the thick of the forest into a large field of grass, one that was near a river, half a league long and half of that wide, the stallion stopped and raised his head, testing the air. Something ahead bothered him.

Stopping at his side, the little mare looked to him, then out into the field.

Close to the tree line half way across, a huge, long haired form lay motionless in the tall grass. The brown hair moved slightly on the breeze. Much of the carcass was gone, eaten by something very large. Vultures swarmed everywhere and a few wild dogs and even a bobtailed forest cat fed on the bounty left to them.

Shahly squinted at the horrible smell, then lowered her head. "Vinton, what happened?"

"It's a grawrdox," the stallion answered. "Looks like it's been killed by a dragon. We'd better stay upwind of it." He turned and led the way toward the creek.

Following, Shahly asked, "Who do you think killed it? I don't think Falloah would attack something that big. Do you think it was Ralligor?"

Vinton glanced back at the dead grawrdox and shook his head. "No, there's too much of it gone, and what is gone was eaten all at once. That was a bigger dragon."

"Agarxus," Shahly said. "He's the biggest dragon in the land."

Vinton's eyes snapped to her. "In the world, Shahly. Please tell me you aren't going to approach him."

She glanced at her stallion. "Well, I might not have mentioned that I've seen him already."

Vinton lowered his head, his ears laying flat as he grumbled, "Shahly."

"I—I'm not going to approach him! He is huge and scary and I don't think he likes unicorns."

"I've always heard he doesn't like anyone. But, it sounds like you're coming to your senses in that respect."

"Vinton, have you ever seen Agarxus?"

"No, Love, not up close. I once saw him flying but that was thankfully at a great distance and I got to the safety of the forest as quickly as I could." He glanced at her. "You saw him up close?"

Shahly would not meet his eyes. "Well, closer than most would be comfortable with. I thought at the time I was helping. I don't know if I really did or not."

They trotted down a shallow slope toward the river. The grass was tall and lush here and topped with many various seeds. Clumps of bushes were heavy with ripe berries, some blue, some red and some black. The edge of the creek was rocky and not much grew there except for the tall trees that kept it shaded, and from a stone shelf that jetted out into the creek a couple of paces the unicorns lowered their heads for a long drink.

Drinking faster than the stallion, Shahly finished and turned to sample the berries halfway up the slope. For reasons she could not yet know, she was not interested in the grasses all around her. She stopped at one of the bushes and nibbled some of the berries. They were very sweet and she ate more. Up the slope where the bushes were more in the sun the berries were a brighter blue and seemed to be more appealing, so she trotted up further to taste them.

Movement near the dead grawrdox drew her attention and she looked that way, seeing the dark green wings of a dragon outstretched on the other side of it. Leaning her head, she looked closer.

Hesitantly, the dragon approached the carcass, looking down on it curiously. This was not a large dragon, perhaps four human's heights tall as it stood upright with black horns that swept back from its head. From the front this dragon was a light green in color, but its scales grew darker near its sides. As it turned to circle around the carcass she could see that the scales on its back darkened more and its dorsal scale ridge was almost black. Though much smaller than Ralligor, it did not have Falloah's lean female build. It was rather well muscled and Shahly guessed that this one must be male. Despite its muscular build it appeared too thin, especially below its chest and the outlines of ribs striped his sides.

She sniffed the bush once more and nibbled a few more berries from it, then turned up the slope again and trotted toward the dragon, slowing to a casual walk about half way there. She leaned her head as the dragon lowered his nose to the carcass. Drawing closer, she grimaced as he opened his jaws and tore a piece of the rancid flesh from the grawrdox.

About twenty paces away, the breeze shifted and she got a good whiff of the odor that Vinton had wanted so to avoid and she stopped, snorting as she shook her head.

The dragon grunted and swung around to face her. His piercing green eyes locked on her in surprise.

Shahly coughed and looked up at the dragon, declaring in a whinny, "Wow! That thing really stinks!"

His wings jetting outward, the dragon lowered his head and body, roaring at the little unicorn. He was clearly unwilling to leave the carcass.

Raising her head, Shahly assured, "It's okay. You don't need to be afraid of me."

The dragon also raised his head, his voice betraying youth as he roared back, "I'm not afraid of you! I fear nothing!"

Shahly glanced at the dead grawrdox. "You'd have to fear nothing to eat that. My name's Shahly."

He seemed perplexed and his wings slowly drew back toward his body. Leaning his head slightly, the dragon asked with a suspicious tone, "You aren't afraid of me? You don't wish to fight?"

"Why would I want to fight you?" she countered.

"You're a unicorn," he replied. "Unicorns and dragons are enemies. It's your instinct to try to kill every dragon you see."

"It is?" she asked. Looking aside, she could not help but whicker a laugh before looking back at him. "That's a myth. One of my closest friends is a dragon."

The dragon took a step back. "That doesn't make sense, and yet I've always heard that unicorns don't lie."

"We don't," she confirmed.

Vinton galloped to her side, a ruby glow enveloping his horn as he angled himself between his mate and this dragon. His eyes bored into the young dragon as he snorted and directed the tip of his horn toward his foe.

The dragon seemed to know that Vinton was a more experienced and powerful unicorn and backed away a step. Baring his teeth, he roared back and opened his wings as before.

Even as Vinton turned fully to drive this menace off, Shahly pushed past him and gave him a patient look. "Vinton, he hasn't come to fight."

The stallion's eyes shifted to her, then back to the dragon as he growled, "That isn't what I just heard. Shahly, you need to back away."

Shahly touched her spiral to his, tenderly saying, "My stallion, I know how you want to protect me, but please trust me. He doesn't have wicked intentions."

"He roared at you," the stallion reminded.

"I startled him. It's okay. He has a good heart."

"He has a dragon's heart, Shahly."

"Well so does Ralligor."

Vinton's eyes narrowed.

"And Falloah," she added.

He finally looked away, then back up to the dragon, who stared back and seemed to be even more perplexed. "Okay," the stallion conceded in a sigh. "What do they call you, dragon."

Raising his head, the dragon answered, "Linnduron."

The stallion nodded, replying, "Vinton. What brings you here?"

Hesitant to answer, the dragon replied, "I'm hunting."

Vinton glanced at the carcass and informed, "This one's already dead."

Shahly gently butted the stallion's nose with hers and whickered a laugh. "It must have been really easy to catch, then." She looked up at the dragon and asked, "Where did you come from? I haven't seen you in the forest before."

"You two are very curious," Linnduron observed.

Vinton informed, "No more than the dragons who inhabit this part of the forest."

The dragon's eyes widened slightly and his dorsal scales grew erect as he raised his head. "Other dragons? What other dragons?"

Shahly nodded and said flatly. "You are definitely new here."

Linnduron's eyes darted around. "There are other dragons close by?"

"Don't worry," the white unicorn urged. "They are friends."

Looking down to her, the dragon mumbled, "This is a strange

place." His eyes shifted to the stallion and he asked, "So, you haven't come to fight, either?" He nervously looked behind the stallion as he spoke.

Glancing at Shahly, Vinton replied, "I suppose not, as long as you don't pose a threat here. Contrary to what you may have heard from others of your kind, unicorns don't go around picking fights with dragons. If you think about it, that wouldn't make sense."

Nodding, the dragon seemed to relax a little and he folded his wings to him. "I suppose it wouldn't, since your kind is so much smaller." He turned his eyes away and seemed to feel a little shame. "Perhaps what the elders have said all this time does not have the same truth it did when I was younger."

Vinton agreed, "Perhaps not. I came up here expecting you to be a threat. I can see you aren't." He turned a sharp look to the little mare and snapped, "This time!"

Her ears drooped and she lowered her head, her eyes locked sheepishly on her stallion's.

The stallion abruptly raised his head, looking skyward as he whickered, "Oh, no."

Shahly also looked, and backed away a few steps.

Ralligor slammed into the ground only about thirty paces away, sweeping his wings forward as he crouched and roared through bared teeth.

Linnduron spun to face him and opened his wings, roaring back as he backed away.

The Desert Lord advanced on the smaller dragon, but only made it a few steps before Shahly bolted forward and reared up in front of him, whinnying as loudly as she could and kicking to draw his attention.

Stopping only a few paces from her, Ralligor turned his eyes down to the little unicorn, his jaws slowly closing as he saw her. He glanced at the other dragon, seeing him also looking down at the unicorn. With an impatient, growling sigh, he stood fully and folded his arms, growling, "What now?"

Shahly came down and slammed her front hooves onto the soft earth and grass before her, looking up at her huge friend as she insisted, "Ralligor, he hasn't come to fight anyone. He's new to the forest and—"

"He doesn't belong here," the black dragon snarled, turning his eyes to the smaller dragon.

His brow low over his wide eyes, Linnduron heaved for each breath, more from fear than the expected battle with a much larger foe.

"Ralligor," Shahly implored, "he's hungry and just wants to eat something. Can't you see how thin he is?"

"That isn't my concern," the Desert Lord growled, his eyes boring into the smaller dragon's. "He needs to be on his way. Now."

Taking another step back, Linnduron lowered his head and crooned back, his wide eyes still locked on the big black dragon.

"But that isn't fair," Shahly argued.

Ralligor growled back, "Not everything is a matter of fair and unfair. He simply doesn't belong here and it's my duty to ensure that dragons like him stay away from this territory."

"But why can't he stay?"

"Because we have enough dragons in this area, especially enough drakes."

Shahly huffed an impatient breath and argued, "But he has a good heart."

"It's the dragon way," the Desert Lord snarled, his eyes narrowing. "He knows that as well as I do. Now move aside."

"It isn't fair," she pressed.

"Shahly, why do you want him to stay?"

"He's my friend," she replied, "and he has a good heart."

Ralligor's attention shifted to Vinton. "Her friend?"

The stallion's eyes narrowed. "As I've said before, this is your fault. Thanks to you she has no fear of your kind and tries to befriend every wandering dragon who comes her way."

With a growl, the black dragon turned his gaze to the clouds above, then shook his head and looked down to the white unicorn. "Shahly, how long have you known this dragon?"

"He just got here," she answered.

"So you've known him only a few moments."

She nodded. "He has a good heart. Unicorns know these things."

Vinton added, "He really hasn't come to cause trouble. He's just landed to eat something."

Ralligor glanced at the dead grawrdox. "It's been there a few days and I think it's Agarxus' kill. That means feeding off of it is simply not wise." He looked back to Shahly and straightly informed, "Letting him stay is not up to me. He has to go."

She snorted and looked away from him. "That just isn't fair."

"I know," he conceded patiently. "You just have to understand..." He abruptly jerked his head up and looked over his shoulder. "You two need to get yourselves into the forest." He looked down to Vinton and snapped, "Now!"

Backing away, the stallion looked behind the black dragon and ordered, "Come on, Shahly."

"But he doesn't want to fight," the white unicorn protested.

"Now, Shahly," the black dragon urged. "Right now. Get back to the forest!" He looked down to her and snarled, "Go!"

She did not seem to understand why he suddenly wanted her to go and just stared up at him for long seconds with hurt eyes, then she saw movement skyward, a huge, dark form that she had seen before. Now she understood and her eyes widened, her mouth falling open as she retreated a few steps.

Vinton also looked toward the approaching form and mumbled, "Oh, this isn't good," as he retreated with his smaller mate. "Shahly, lie down and don't move."

Finally realizing the danger, Shahly gasped and did as her stallion commanded, her eyes locked on the huge dragon that descended toward them. As Vinton lay down beside her, she felt him fold his essence around them both. She could also feel his fear and she knew very little could cause him to be so afraid, but her big brown eyes were locked unwavering on one of the few things that could.

A shadow fell over them, a shadow that swallowed much of the surrounding meadow.

The massive dragon descended quickly and with purpose, but he did not seem to be in a terrible rush. Dark, metallic green in color and nearly twice Ralligor's size, this dragon was not one to be considered easy on the eyes, even to those of his own kind. White tusks protruded from his heavy lower jaw. Very dark green eyes were turned toward the ground where his deadly talons settled, the tips of his claws easily penetrating the topsoil. Black horns shined in the sunlight as he raised his head.

His wings stroked forward in air-hungry sweeps as he stood fully, filling the dark blue webbing with the wind, then he casually folded them to his back and sides. His black dorsal scale ridge was laid interlocked to his back.

Ralligor was careful to keep his wings tightly to him and his own dorsal scales down as he stared up at the massive Landmaster.

Slowly, the giant dragon's attention turned to the Desert Lord.

Raising his snout, the black dragon growled softly in greeting.

Without responding, the Landmaster looked to the dead grawrdox, then to the smaller green dragon.

Linnduron also wisely kept his wings tightly to him and his dorsal scales down. Further, he dropped to all fours and raised his snout, crooning submissively and showing as little of his teeth as he could.

The huge dragon stared at him for long, terrifying seconds, then he turned his cold gaze back to the black dragon.

Ralligor raised his brow.

Shahly grew more and more nervous as she watched them, and swallowed hard.

"Shh," Vinton ordered.

The Landmaster's eyes turned back to the smaller dragon, who crooned again under the attention of this enormous dragon. Another long stare and the Landmaster looked back to the black dragon.

Ralligor also glanced at the small dragon, then he asked, "I suppose you are wondering about him?"

One of the Landmaster's eyebrows cocked up slightly.

The black dragon looked back to the smaller drake, then his eyes shifted to where the unicorns were lying as still and unnoticeable as they could. He could see them, but he hoped his Landmaster could not.

"Well?" the huge dragon boomed.

When Shahly's big brown, begging eyes found his, the Desert Lord's heart crumbled just a little and he growled a sigh. "I... I found this young drake here...."

The Landmaster folded his thick arms, his eyes on the black dragon.

Ralligor glanced about, his mind scrambling. "You know, Agarxus, your northern border really has no eyes watching Mettegrawr's activities there."

"I have three dragonesses watching that border," the Landmaster corrected with a thunderous voice.

His eyes finding the huge dragon's, Ralligor informed, "But no drakes."

"I need no drakes watching that border," Agarxus corrected sharply. "He's near my kill, he's not fleeing, he's still alive and you are doing nothing about it."

Linnduron crooned again. Fear was evident in his voice.

Ralligor turned his eyes away. "I thought he might be useful."

"Another drake hunting in my territory is not useful, Ralligor." Agarxus leaned his head slightly. "Why does this one seem to have your favor so?"

Growling, the Desert Lord could not answer.

The Landmaster nodded. "I see. Kill him or drive him away."

As he turned toward the carcass of the grawrdox, Shahly's instincts and judgment abandoned her yet again and she sprang up and sprinted toward the huge dragon, whinnying as she veered into his path.

"Shahly!" Vinton whinnied in a panic as he sprang to his hooves to pursue her.

Agarxus stopped and looked down at this puny enemy of his kind.

"Please," the white unicorn begged in a whinny as she backed away. "He has a good heart. Ralligor will tell you he does. He has a good heart and doesn't want to be a problem. He just wants to eat something. You can see how thin he is. Please, can't he stay?"

Ralligor was already on his way and stepped between the unicorn and his Landmaster, looking up at the huge dragon as he quickly said, "Never mind all of that. This unicorn's clearly out of her mind with some kind of fever." He reached down and turned Shahly, then pushed her along by the haunches with one hand. "Go on, now. Get back to the forest and do whatever it is you unicorns do."

Looking back at the black dragon as she was pushed out of the Landmaster's way, she did not resist, though she did protest,

"But Ralligor, he has a good heart. He doesn't want to be a problem for anyone, he just wants to eat."

"Okay, unicorn, we all heard you. Back to the forest and don't bother the Landmaster with your ramblings."

Agarxus' brow slowly arched as he watched the mighty and powerful Lord of the Desert gently push this bothersome unicorn out of his path. Most dragons, especially those of Ralligor's size and status, would not bother. They would just have killed the grazer and been done with it. Today was a confusing day for the Landmaster. Not long ago a dragonslayer had been sorely defeated by the Desert Lord. Ralligor had brutally killed many of his enemies, including some unicorns. Now, he was shepherd to a unicorn. Feeling a presence to his side, he looked down and saw the big bay standing about forty paces away and watching anxiously as the black dragon pushed the white unicorn along. Venting a sigh, the huge dragon shook his head and looked back to his lieutenant. "Ralligor, attend to your pet later and the drake now."

Shahly swung around and snorted, glaring up at the huge dragon as she spat, "I am *not* a pet!"

Agarxus bared his teeth and strode the two steps toward her, shoving Ralligor out of the way as he dropped to all fours and brought his nose within touching distance of Shahly's.

She sucked a hard breath and dropped to her belly, laying her ears flat against her head as she stared up at the huge, murderous teeth that were less than a pace away from her.

Vinton bolted forward, but stopped a few paces away, not wanting this dragon to think he was a threat as he whinnied to draw his attention.

As the Landmaster's jaws drew closer, Shahly swallowed hard and laid her head to the ground between her hooves, her wide eyes locked on the bottom of the huge dragon's jaw. She cringed as his nose drew around her side and flinched as he sniffed, then sniffed again. He butted her with his nose and she rolled to her side, trying to remain as flat against the ground as she could.

Agarxus sniffed her again, then backed away and stood, his menacing eyes boring into her. "So you are no pet. What business is this dragon's fate of yours?"

"None," Vinton answered for her, daring to pace between the Landmaster and his little mate. "Shahly's heart clouds her judgment. She meant no insult to you."

Cocking an eyebrow up, the Landmaster observed, "This one has a fire I've not seen in a unicorn before." He looked to Ralligor and asked, "Your doing?"

The Desert Lord raised his brow and drew his head back, countering, "How would it be my doing?"

Grunting back at him, the Landmaster looked back to Vinton and assured, "I'll not kill it today, but you'd best teach it that it has a place in the natural order, and to stay there."

"I will," the bay assured, then finished under his breath, "Somehow."

Agarxus' eyes found her once again. "That's twice you've challenged me. Most creatures do not survive the first. The Dragon Lord himself must watch over you."

Even as he turned to leave again, good judgment abandoned Shahly still again and she sprang up and darted to him, asking, "Can Linnduron stay?"

He stopped and turned his eyes down to her.

"Please?" she added timidly.

After a long stare, the Landmaster turned and strode with long, heavy steps toward the cringing young drake, who lowered himself all the way to the ground as the huge dragon approached.

Shahly gasped as the massive dragon reached the smaller drake and slammed a foot onto his back.

Agarxus' jaws gaped as they descended toward the smaller dragon's head and Linnduron shrieked as the Landmaster's teeth closed around his head and neck.

"No!" Shahly whinnied.

A thunderous growl rolled from the Landmaster's throat, then he opened his jaws and lifted his head, staring down at the unmoving dragon beneath him. After a moment, he turned to the grawrdox carcass and ripped into it, tearing a piece the size of a horse from it. Dark blood sloshed everywhere as the huge dragon lifted his head and swallowed the mouthful whole. After three more such bites, Agarxus finally swung around and strode back to the waiting Desert Lord, informing, "He's your problem now."

Sure the little drake was dead, Shahly looked hard and was relieved to see Linnduron raise his head slightly, his wide eyes on the Landmaster.

"He'll hunt the border scrubland and the forest and plains just south of the Dark Mountains," the Landmaster added. "Nowhere else."

"That's part of *my* hunting range!" the black dragon complained.

His eyes narrowing, Agarxus growled, "Is that going to be a problem?"

Ralligor turned his eyes away and snarled, "No."

Shahly cringed as the Landmaster turned his attention to her again, and as he bent toward her with those massive jaws still dripping blood, she sank to the ground, laying her ears flat again as she stared back with horror-filled eyes. Blood stained his teeth and his breath smelled of the dead grawrdox and really stank.

His lips rolled back from his teeth and he warned, "Think hard before you challenge me again, grazer, and remember that the next time I see you, I may just kill you."

With her head planted against the ground, she nodded as best she could.

He sniffed her again and a growl rolled from him as he stood and leaned his head, observing, "You don't even know, do you?" He grunted again, almost a laugh, and turned away from her.

As he returned to his kill, Shahly slowly pushed herself back up, standing on wobbly legs as she watched this most powerful of dragons go about his grisly meal. She looked Vinton's way as he approached, but not at him. Something felt very amiss within her.

The bay unicorn nuzzled her ear and gently asked, "Are you all right, Love?"

She nodded, and when she tried to turn and step toward him her forelegs gave out and she stumbled to the ground. Quick to get her hooves under her again, she stood and assured, "I'm okay." She still would not look at her stallion or at anything specific as she turned and crept down the slope with unsteady steps. "Need water."

Vinton watched her for a moment, then turned his eyes up to the black dragon, who also watched her and looked really annoyed. "So, you still think this isn't your fault?"

Ralligor's eyes slid to the stallion and he grumbled, "I have to share my hunting range with that new drake she talked me into not driving away. How is that my fault?"

Vinton snorted. "I suppose nothing that happened to her was your fault."

The Desert Lord turned and followed his Landmaster. "Eat stink-weed and die. Agarxus, a word?"

Shahly heard them but really did not listen. Her legs were still shaking as she trekked to the creek. She had spent the entire spring and summer craving the excitement of the chase and had spent many an hour running from some angry predator she had antagonized. The big Landmaster was very different. He could have killed her easily, yet he was content to just frighten half of the life from her.

She strode up to the water's edge and took a few steps into the cool water of the lazy creek, then lowered her nose to it, closing her eyes as she took a long, slow drink. A moment later her legs were still shaking and her heart still raced. Raising her head, she swallowed her last mouthful and turned her eyes across the creek, past the thin line of trees and to the tall grass and bushes beyond. Her instincts finally seemed to be catching up to her again. Something over there was definitely amiss. Without moving, she panned her eyes back and forth, looking for any movement or something that looked like it did not belong.

A slight shuffle somewhere to her right drew her attention and her ear twitched that way first, then her head and eyes turned ever so slowly. She realized that the horrible shaking in her legs had finally stopped, but her heart still raced. Her eyes pierced the trees, searching for whatever was watching her. Reaching out with her essence, she finally contacted its mind, then another, and another. These were predators, simple minded and focused on their next meal—a unicorn!

Shahly knew that seeing them before they made their move on her would be important, but she felt from them that they were trying to stalk closer, to surround her and deny her a way to flee. Sweeping her essence behind, she felt two more behind her, silently closing the distance to her.

She focused on two trees on the other side of the creek, two trees that looked very much alike.

They were legs! Scaly and dark brown in color, they were a human's height tall, meeting a boxy, feather-covered body that was concealed in the foliage of the trees, but was clearly two or three times the mass of a large horse. The feathers on its belly were various shades of gray, meeting the tan and brown feathers of blunt wings that were folded tightly to its sides. It stood motionless, and as Shahly's eyes rose higher into the forest canopy, she could see its black head shrouded there in the leaves and branches. Its beak was very large, a triangular weapon larger than Shahly's whole head. It was black at the top, fading to yellow. Underneath, it was a dull red. The feathers of its throat formed a red stripe among the gray feathers there. Eyes that seemed too small for its head were trained on her in an unblinking, hungry stare.

She had encountered these big, predatory birds only once before and had Vinton and her father as well as another big stallion of the herd there to take care of them. Now, she was outnumbered, surrounded, and alone.

Shahly stared back for a moment. This one was waiting. The others were not and she could feel them slowly moving in on her and trying not to be noticed. In their primitive minds, they had a plan for her. She needed a plan for them.

They had her at a disadvantage and knew it. In the open, they were faster. At three heights tall and the weight of nearly two horses, they feared little. Working in groups like this, they were very successful at catching their prey. For birds, even these giant flightless birds, they were very intelligent, very ruthless and had few enemies.

And that would be her advantage, her *only* advantage.

The one she had in her gaze was waiting for her to bolt. He would drive her right to the others and screech horribly to them when he did. She needed him to screech a warning to them instead.

With the image of Agarxus still fresh in her mind, she bored into the primitive mind of the predator, her eyes narrowing as she passed that image to him.

Long black feathers on top of his head stood straight up, showing orange tips. His eyes widened. These birds were known to compete with dragons and would sometimes even attack them in force, but the dragon she showed him put pause and generous fear into him. One more suggestion, that this dragon was coming, pushed him over the edge and he backed away, raising his head as he swung his beak open and sounded a rippling, high pitched call.

A few others, seemingly all around her, responded.

When she heard them moving away to hide among the trees, Shahly turned and sprinted from the creek and she ran as hard as she could up the slope as she whinnied, "Ralligor!"

One of the birds, slightly smaller than the one across the creek, exploded from a grove of trees to one side of her. Another charged from the other side, angling to cut her off. She heard a splash behind her as several more ran across the creek in pursuit. Apparently her deception had already been forgotten.

"Ralligor!" she whinnied again as the birds drew closer.

The one to her left was almost upon her, its beak gaping to inflict the killing blow. The one to her right screeched as it also swung its beak open to take her.

Looking ahead, Shahly saw the grassy field, the dead grawrdox, but not the dragons! She gasped, knowing she was only a few strides away from death. Right before the predators were upon her, she locked her hooves and stopped, turning sharply to the one on her left. It was far more nimble than it looked and nearly matched her maneuver. The one on the right veered toward her and narrowly missed an anticipated collision with the first. The first one kicked at the unicorn, slamming a talon into her haunch. She stumbled from the blow and rolled to her side, now aware that four more were only a few paces away.

Shahly whinnied in panic as the second bird was upon her, then the bird screeched as Ralligor's jaws slammed shut around its body, his teeth plunging all the way in.

The other birds stopped and the one closest to Shahly backed away as its comrade was hoisted from the ground by the black dragon. With one of their flock in jeopardy, the other eight charged the dragon and attacked.

Ralligor swung his head around and slammed the mortally wounded bird into the one closest to Shahly, knocking him over, then he stepped over the unicorn and stood over her as he turned on the remaining seven and roared in nightmarish fashion through bared teeth. They responded with a screaming answer, the largest of them darting ahead of the rest to attack the dragon first. Spreading their blunt wings, they leapt at the Desert Lord and flapped hard to attack him high. Two of them charged on the ground to attack him low. Ralligor batted the largest away from him, but another clamped down on his wrist with its powerful beak. Another landed on the dragon's back and bit at the armored skin of his shoulder. Another went for the dragon's throat. Amazingly, they seemed to be overwhelming this powerful dragon.

As they swarmed on him, Linnduron flew in low and fast, kicking a bird off of Ralligor before he turned to land.

Agarxus swept in over the trees across the creek and slammed onto the ground nearby on all fours. One of the birds jumped from Ralligor to turn on him, but the Landmaster's teeth and tusks plunged into his body and his jaws crushed the smaller predator's body in one motion.

Ralligor spun around and the three remaining birds abandoned him. Now facing three dragons, one of them a giant among his kind, the survivors wisely retreated in all directions and were gone.

Linnduron would not allow his foe to escape and fought savagely against it. The bird seemed to forget about the two larger dragons for a moment and struck back. Its beak found the dragon's shoulder and ripped through his armor. The dragon responded with a savage bite at the base of the bird's neck and ripped at its breast with his hind claws. The struggle only grew more savage and blood spewed from them both.

Shahly finally stood as she watched the fray.

Ralligor took his Landmaster's side as he folded his arms, his eyes on the little dragon that was only slightly larger than the bird he fought.

Agarxus watched without expression, but when the small dragon finally vanquished his enemy, the Landmaster nodded, admitting, "He does have spirit."

"So he's not a total waste of effort," Ralligor observed. "I knew you'd like him."

"I didn't say I like him," Agarxus snarled.

Together, they turned and looked down at the little white unicorn, Agarxus also folding his arms as they just stared at her.

Vinton approached from between them, a look of patience lost in his eyes.

Her eyes darting to them in turn, she backed away and assured, "I didn't provoke them, I promise! They were down there and I didn't even know it!" When they just stared at her, she raised her head and whinnied, "I didn't! Really! I didn't even know they were there!"

The dragons looked to each other, then down to Vinton, who looked up at them and shook his head.

"Ralligor," she complained, "I'm serious! I didn't do anything wrong!" When they all looked back to her, she finished, "Okay, *this* time I didn't provoke them. I promise!"

Agarxus eyes slid to the Desert Lord and he observed, "You rushed right to its defense. One might get the impression you have some feeling for that little grazer."

Turning his eyes up to the Landmaster, Ralligor countered, "You also rushed to her defense."

The massive dragon grunted and turned away, striding back to the dead grawrdox as he corrected, "I dealt with lesser predators that have clearly been scavenging my kill."

Ralligor snarled, and growled a little, then looked down to Shahly as Linnduron limped up behind him. "Okay, little unicorn, do you think you can manage the rest of the day without getting yourself into some kind of trouble?"

She admitted in a frustrated sigh, "I don't know. I didn't mean for them to chase me, honest. I didn't even *want* to be chased today. They wanted to eat me."

Looking down to Vinton, the black dragon observed, "Even with four of us here she *still* managed to find something to chase her."

The stallion looked away and snorted. "I'm working on it."

"Work faster," Ralligor snarled.

Turning his eyes up to the Desert Lord, Linnduron anxiously asked, "Did I prove myself to the Landmaster? Was he pleased with me?"

Ralligor looked him up and down, seeing that he was bleeding from his shoulder, from behind one eye, and from a deep gash in his thigh. "It's difficult to tell which of you fared worse. These carcasses are yours. When you finish, fly to the Dark Mountains and find a fortress at the end of a box canyon. There are caves in the canyon wall you can lair in, but don't bother the humans of that castle."

The smaller dragon nodded to him, the turned back to the bird he had killed.

Looking to the stallion, the black dragon asked, "Can you manage to keep her out of trouble without me?"

"I'd *rather* keep her out of trouble without you," Vinton shot back. When the Desert Lord turned to leave, the bay unicorn added, "Give my best to Falloah, and tell her I'm sorry you were the best she could do."

Ralligor stopped and looked over his shoulder. "Shahly, are you going to be okay with this ass?"

Vinton snorted.

"Yes," she laughed in a whinny. "Thank you, Ralligor. I love you."

He simply nodded to her, then opened his wings and took to the sky.

"Must you say that to him?" Vinton grumbled.

She paced to her stallion and nuzzled him. "I love you even more, Vinton, with all of my heart." She turned her head slightly, closed her eyes and kissed him on the mouth.

His eyes widened. This was something he had not expected, nor ever experienced.

Shahly smiled, gazing up into her stallion's eyes.

"Why did you do that?" he asked.

"Kiss you?" She shrugged. "Just the moment, I guess." She paced past him, into the field where she veered wide around the Landmaster, and a slight smile curled her mouth as she said, "Sorry it bothered you."

He just watched her dumbly for a moment, then he cantered to her side. "I'm not saying it bothered me. You—you've just never done that before."

She glanced at him with that slight smile. Looking to the

Landmaster, she called, "Be well, Agarxus. I hope we can be friends someday."

He looked over his shoulder and responded with a perplexed look, dark blood dripping from his jaws, then he returned to his meal.

The two unicorns paced back into the forest, not really speaking. Once again Shahly had done something to surprise her stallion and his mind and heart raced.

"Now *you're* very quiet," she observed some time later.

Vinton stopped, and when Shahly turned to him he leaned his head over and kissed her mouth. They just stared at each other for a moment after, then Shahly slowly stepped toward him and gently touched her horn to his, pouring forth her love for him through her essence, and her spiral glowed emerald as she did. Vinton replied with his, a ruby glow enveloping his horn, then he slowly moved toward her, gently rubbing the side of his head to hers, then her neck, and she nuzzled him back.

CHAPTER 3

A morning attack was unexpected and the siege itself was brutally short.

Pinetop Castle was among the last of the timber fortresses left in the Abtont Forest. Not large nor wealthy, it was not as well defended as many of the bigger kingdoms in the area. It once sat atop a hill, overlooking a crossroads deep in the forest. The village outside was a place of peaceful trade and commerce.

Now, as the few hundred survivors were marched toward the North in chains, many glanced back at the four height tall fortress in the middle of the trees, a fortress that was now an inferno. Flames reached well over the tops of the ancient trees that surrounded the castle that were thankfully far enough away to not become food for this fire, so the forest itself was in no danger. The village outside of the castle was also in flames. Behind the prisoners and the army that marched them into captivity, those who did not survive the battle were consumed by the flames that erased the small kingdom forever.

Near the end of the procession, a girl of not quite eighteen seasons looked back yet again to see the highest tower of the wooden castle collapse into the hungry flames. She wore a grey hooded cloak, keeping her short black hair covered. This hair had once been very long and the envy of many a young maiden, but for reasons she never spoke of she had cut it just above her shoulders in the spring. It had grown over the season, brushing her shoulders when left uncovered. Her cloak was mostly closed, but for the chain that bound her wrists to the woman who marched in front of her by leather shackles.

This was not a girl who spent a great deal of time outside as her skin was rather pale. Full lips seemed rather plump for her thin face and tended to be slightly open in an involuntary pout. Thin eyebrows were held high as she watched the security of the castle she had called home consumed by the flames spawned by the invaders. She was a pretty girl, though average for the most part. She was not tall, nor very heavy. Womanhood had found her many seasons ago and she quickly learned that it was a useful tool to get what she needed when other means were not available. Still, she was a thin built girl and not as generously busted as many, though still quite shapely.

Tethered behind her was a young man who was a couple of seasons her junior, though one would never know it looking at him. He was a lad of truly massive proportions, a third of a height taller than an average man and three times the bulk. A large brow covered two small eyes that betrayed a stewing rage for his captors. He was simply dressed in brown trousers and a loosely woven white shirt with no sleeves and his long, very thick arms were bare. The brown wool jerkin he wore seemed too small for him and was open two hand lengths in front. It was torn in the back, succumbing to his large stature. His huge feet were covered by huge leather boots that were special made for him. They had to be.

Many of the armored soldiers who surrounded the prisoners had their eyes on the girl as they wondered what was beneath the cloak and hood she wore, but they kept a healthy distance, still fearing the massive boy behind her who snarled each time he saw them looking her way. Though he was tethered by the wrists to her chains by iron shackles made for a normal man's leg, they still knew fear of him.

The girl turned once again, looking to the castle that grew more and more distant behind them, then she turned her eyes up to the huge boy and whispered, "It's going to be okay, Jekkon. Just do as I say and everything will be all right."

He looked down at her. Seeing her and hearing her words seemed to calm him if only a little.

"Quiet there," one of the soldiers on horseback barked. "There'll be no talking in the line or I'll gut ya and leave ya here!" When Jekkon growled at him, he looked to the huge boy and grabbed the hilt of his sword, warning, "You want me to split ya like a fish, you little ogre?"

"He didn't mean anything," the girl assured. "He is just very protective of me."

"You've got no place to speak here, wench," the soldier snarled. "I'll gut ya both if I hear another word from anyone!"

"You don't touch her," Jekkon growled, his voice young but unnaturally deep.

Giant among his kind or not, this insubordination would not

be tolerated. The soldier jerked his sword from its place and turned his horse, shouting, "Stop the line!"

Other soldiers ahead of them stopped the procession of prisoners and looked back to the commotion behind them.

"Please, sir," she cried desperately. "He means no harm. I'll keep him under control. My word I will."

He didn't seem to listen and swung down from his horse, poising his sword before him as he approached them.

Jekkon growled at him, his eyes locked on the soldier who approached. His huge hands curled into tight fists as large as a normal man's head and his arms tensed, bulging in ominous fashion.

Backing toward the huge boy and pulling the woman in front of her back with her slightly, the girl raised her hands before her, clasping them together as she begged, "He'll not be any problem for you. I promise!"

Two others dismounted and approached.

The first ordered, "Cut these two loose. We'll leave 'em along the road."

In a panic, the girl turned and grasped the chain that tethered the huge boy's shackles. In an instant they began to burn with an unnatural yellow flame that did not singe his flesh but caused the iron shackles and chains to crumble to dust. In an instant he was free and she shouted to him, "Run! Get away from here!" Wheeling back around to face the guards, who had stopped when they saw him released by her, she raised her own chained and shackled hands. That same yellow glow overtook them, running quickly along the entire length of the chain that led along the line. It crumbled as Jekkon's had, freeing everyone on that side. "All of you run!" she screamed. She raised her hands above her, the yellow glow intensifying as she faced the guards, her fingers curling inward as she snarled, "We tried this your way. Now you've roused my anger." She half turned her head and hissed, "Jekkon, you need to go!"

He was confused and hesitant, clearly unwilling to leave the girl behind.

"Go on," she urged. "I'll catch up."

"Won't leave you," he insisted. "Stay and fight with you."

She noticed the guards regaining their bearing and their

courage and knew they were quickly running out of time. "Jekkon, you need to go. Please, just run away and find me later. I need you to do this!"

"Won't leave you," he repeated, despair clearly in his voice.

The guards, now joined by others, raised their weapons and advanced.

"Go, Jekkon," she ordered again, her fingers slowly curling inward. Yellow light lanced in disorganized, crooked lines toward their weapons, and as each sword, axe and spear was struck the metal glowed that bright and unnatural yellow and began to curl, shrieking as bending metal would do.

All of the guards and soldiers dropped their weapons and backed away.

Hoof beats from behind drew her attention and she spun around at the same time Jekkon did, unable to react in time but seeing the huge boy slam his fist into the rider's chest and brutally dismount him. Two other horsemen behind stopped their animals.

The girl waved her hand and the ground right in front of the horses exploded into a hurricane of dust and flying stones. The horses panicked and reared up, throwing their riders to the ground.

She turned back and quickly waved her hand again. A volley of arrows exploded into smoke and dust only a few paces away from her. Looking over her shoulder, she screamed, "Jekkon, please. Go. You have to go!"

He turned back to her, his thick brow arched and his eyes glossy with tears. He glanced at the advancing soldiers, then back down to her. The fleeing prisoners all around him escaped his notice as he was consumed by his conflict to do as he was told and stay and defend this girl.

"Go," she ordered again. "Run away and protect those I've freed. Please, Jekkon, protect them."

He glanced at the soldiers again, then turned and ran at a lumbering but quick pace into the forest.

She turned back to the issue at hand and quickly tried to reason a way out. Quickly lowering her hands, she slowly raised them again, ordering the forces beneath the ground to task.

As many more soldiers advanced on her this time, some of them pursuing the other prisoners, the ground began to tremble. Jagged columns of stone rose from the ground right in front of the guards and soldiers, each about two paces from the others. Spikes of darker stone lanced outward from each of the half dozen columns, ranging from a hand's length to an arms length. This stopped the army. The columns slowed as they reached two heights tall or so and finally stopped growing.

Strain showed itself on the girl's features. A drop of blood escaped from her nose, another from her eye. Gasping for breath, she finally dropped to her knees and caught herself on her palms. Her head hung limply for a long moment after. She was on the verge of passing out, but knew they would eventually figure out they could just go around, so she had to recover and recover quickly. Forcing her head up, she still breathed heavily through her mouth but saw the guards actually backing away from her barricade.

The enemy soldiers were all quiet as they stared at her and slowly half stepped away from the pillars of stone. Apparently just the threat of her power gave them pause, even the fifty or so that were gathered on the other side. This gave her strength time and motivation to return to her more quickly.

She reached to her face and wiped the blood from under her nose, then wiped it from her cheek with the back of the same hand. Slowly she stood, her eyes boring into the hesitant invaders. Her arms withdrew into the cloak she wore, then thrust outward to throw the cloak over her shoulders. She had forgotten about being roused from sleep with no time to dress and the thin white nightshirt she wore underneath was far from intimidating as it revealed much of her dainty shape and did not reach quite halfway down her thighs. That and tattered traveling boots which she had no time to lace were all she wore beneath her cloak. Still, these invading soldiers had seen her power and were hesitant to approach her.

Her eyes narrowed as she scanned their ranks. Once again she raised her hands before her, and when she did the spike bristling columns began to slowly rotate, turning faster and faster until the spikes were but a blur. Raising her chin, she challenged, "Which of you will be the first to have the flesh peeled from his bones today?" She scanned them again, allowing the yellow glow to overtake her eyes. This would intimidate them even more. "You've brought down my castle in fair battle and that is acceptable by the law of the land, but now you've roused my anger. It is time for you all to feel my wrath."

The columns suddenly stopped spinning. One by one they began to burst and crumble to the ground.

She ducked and shielded her head and face with her arms, then as the last one collapsed and she was pelted by small stones, she screamed and dropped to the ground. "Must have been too strong a spell," she murmured to herself. Hoof beats approached and she raised her head to see the soldiers parting and an elaborately dressed man riding through them. Nothing remained of the spiked columns but bare ground. She watched as the last fragments liquefied and were swallowed up by the earth beneath them, then she looked up at the man on horseback who stopped only a few paces away.

On horseback, he seemed huge, though in reality he was only of average height and build. His armor was shined to a mirror finish and was well adorned with gold. A long black cape hung from beneath his shoulder plates and was also adorned with gold and trimmed in purple and silver. The arming shirt and trousers he wore were red. Long black hair blew on the slight breeze and he had a hard look about him, though his features were actually quite pleasing to the eye of a woman, especially one just coming of age. A very ornate sword hung from his saddle and he crossed his hands on the saddle horn before him, the black steel gauntlets he wore shimmering with jewels.

He just stared at her for a long moment with very dark blue eyes and she stared back. Slowly, she pushed herself up and stood, facing him as fearlessly as she dared.

Raising his black eyebrows, he asked in the voice of a man in his thirties, "So, what is this that disrupts the procession?"

"We've a sorceress on our hands," a solder answered.

Tight lipped, the man on the horse nodded. "I see. She's a mighty one at that, so mighty as to free half my prisoners and keep so many men at bay." He nodded to her and commended, "Well done, sorceress. Well done."

She raised her chin. "You did well to take my kingdom. Do

you lead these men?" She was trying hard to sound as important and dignified as possible.

"I do," he confirmed. "*Your* kingdom. Did my men overlook one of the royal family?"

"Apparently," she confirmed. "They also granted no quarter. Your idea as well?"

He nodded. "It was. I didn't want to spend the next few days in a lengthy siege, nor do I wish to fight off vengeful soldiers for the next few seasons. May I ask this precious flower's name?"

She was careful in answering and took her time. "I... I am Princess Janees. May I ask this handsome gentleman conqueror's name?"

A slight smile curled his lips. "You may call me Lord Nemlivv of Ravenhold." He finished with a polite bow of his head.

She nodded back to him, stalling as much as possible. She needed more time to formulate some kind of plan of escape as well as grant more time for those she had freed to put some distance between them and his soldiers.

"I heard what you said about rousing your anger," Nemlivv said with an understanding tone, "and I apologize for that. I'll speak to the garrison captain about how he should treat prisoners. Now, will you be coming along with us the rest of the way quietly?"

She defiantly set her hands on her hips. "I don't think so. Release the remaining prisoners and leave at once and you will be allowed to go about your way."

He nodded. "I see. And I suppose you have a terrible wrath awaiting us should I not comply with such a demand?"

"Correct," Janees confirmed.

Nemlivv smiled slightly. "You don't look very old, Princess Janees, and I'm certain your father the king and mother the queen would never have allowed you to practice the art openly. In fact, I don't think you've had more than a few lessons, and those in secret. That would lead me to think you aren't quite as powerful as you would have me believe."

Her eyes narrowed and she tried with great success to mask the fear that crept along her every nerve. "I'm not asking much, Nemlivv of Ravenhold, and I have no intentions of revenge against you. We shall simply move on and put some distance between you and us."

"I'm certain you would," he agreed, "but you and your people are now part of the spoils of war."

Janees lowered her brow. "I do not believe in nor condone slavery."

"I, however, do. You and your people are now a commodity to that end."

Her hands clenched into fists, then flashed open as a yellow fire exploded from them. "I don't think so, Nemlivv of Ravenhold."

He rolled his eyes and loosed an impatient sigh. "Must we do this? I really have no wish to hurt you."

"Nor to be hurt, I'm sure," she snarled back. As before, her target was his sword but his hand was there first and her power slammed into a sudden red glow around his gauntlet, and she gasped and backed away a step.

He stared patiently back and raised his brow. "Two more, Princess of Pinetop Castle, and then you're mine."

This was a very confident man and now she knew him as a sorcerer. Still, it was time to end this once and for all. Holding one hand up, she made a fist with the other and slowly raised it toward the first. At the same time the ground near the sorcerer opened and a fist of stone reached up on a thick stone arm. She swung her fist and at the same time the stone fist swung toward the sorcerer, who casually waved his hand and responded with a bright flash of red light that shattered the stone fist. As it crumbled to dust and sand, pain Janees had never imagined crashed into her hand and she screamed, grasping her wrist as she sank to her knees. Her eyes were tightly closed for long seconds following as the pain slowly throbbed away and finally vanished.

Nemlivv shook his head. "As I said before, you aren't as well trained as you think. You have one shot left, sorceress. Try to make it worth my while."

His soldiers laughed.

She raised her head and looked up at him. Her confidence was draining away, but her anger was about to erupt. With power surging through her, she sprang to her feet and opened her arms, then shouted like a young woman possessed and thrust her hands at him. A white-hot ball of fire flashed from between her hands and yellow lightning lanced from it.

Nemlivv raised his gauntlet and easily caught the destructive spell, which exploded into fleeing orange sparks.

Janees was not done. She raised her hands above her head, summoning boulders from atop and beneath the ground to that height, and when she had a score or more at her command, she thrust her hands at him again, this time with a wild scream as everything she had left poured from her.

All of the boulders and ten times that number of smaller stones streaked toward the sorcerer, then slammed into some invisible wall and shattered like brittle pieces of dry clay.

As before, this time with blood pouring from her nose, she dropped to her knees and barely caught herself on her palms. Gasping for breath, she reached up to wipe the blood away, just staring at the ground as she struggled to regain her strength.

Long seconds passed.

Nemlivv cleared his throat and asked, "Are you done?"

Hesitantly, she nodded, closing her eyes as she gasped, "That's all I've got."

A moment passed.

"You should be standing for my response," the sorcerer informed.

Nodding again, Janees said, "Just give me a moment." She drew a knee to her, trying to plant her foot beneath her and stand.

"Come, sorceress," Nemlivv prodded. "I've things to do. Can't wait all day, now."

She shot him an irritated look, then forced herself to stand straight and tall, balling her hands into fists. Raising her chin defiantly to him, she glared back and challenged through clenched teeth, "Do your worst, Nemlivv of Ravenhold."

Even before he raised his hand, her eyes rolled back and she collapsed, dropping straight down to the earth she stood on.

He just stared down at her for a moment, then he turned and looked down at a soldier who strode toward him. "You see there, Captain? That is called giving it your all. You and your men would do good to take a lesson from this young woman."

The soldier nodded and said, "Yes, sir," then he looked up at the sorcerer. "We've run down many of the escapees but a number seem to have gotten away."

"The big fellow?" Nemlivv asked.

"Gone," the soldier confirmed.

"Very well," the sorcerer sighed. "We've still got quite a few, so let's get them collected and be on our way." He swung down from his horse and he and the captain strode to the unconscious girl. "She did give it her all, didn't she? Well, let's collect her and head north. I've got plans for this one."

***

Slowly, Janees' eyes opened and she blinked many times to clear her sight, a soft moan escaping her as she awoke. All she saw was red, and a moment later realized she was looking at the arming shirt of the sorcerer. Coming to her senses more, she found her head leaning against his chest. He was holding her almost tenderly to him. She was riding sidesaddle in front of him and was no longer wearing her cloak or her boots. Squeezing her eyes shut to clear them, she blinked a few more times and finally raised her head, looking around her and finally up into the eyes of the sorcerer himself.

No longer wearing his armor, he smiled back at her and greeted, "Well hello there. I was hoping you would awaken before we arrived."

She fearfully looked around her again, seeing that they were traveling down a canyon with high walls of grey and black stone. She also realized that her hands were bound tightly behind her and that her knees and ankles were also tightly bound. Some kind of cloth was rolled and had been forced into her mouth and was tied behind her head. She struggled feebly, feeling quickly that there was no escape for her.

"So how far did you get in your studies?" Nemlivv asked her. When he had her attention he continued, "Surely you learned enough to know that you can't wield your craft with your hands touching. Have you ever tried?"

Hesitantly, she nodded, her eyes locked on his.

"Then you know it's impossible, especially if they are bound together. If the skin of both of your hands, your wrists or your arms is touching, you are powerless." He smiled and reached up to stroke her cheek, smiling more as she shied away from him. "Not to worry. This will all be over soon. You do know that a duel between sorcerers can end only one way, don't you?"

Janees shook her head, feeling more and more afraid.

"One must die," he informed straightly. "That usually means whoever loses the duel must also lose her life. It is the way. That's why I was surprised when you challenged me the way you did. Your life belongs to me now. Every part of you is mine to do with as I will."

She turned her eyes ahead of them, a whimper escaping her as tears rolled from her eyes.

"A shame, too," he continued. "You are so young, so fresh, so lovely. A bit ordinary perhaps, but still a pity you must die so young. It's always a pity when a pretty little girl must die so long before her time."

Her brow lowered and she turned her eyes down. She had always hated to be called that and right now there was no point making a secret of it.

"Your death won't be wasted," he went on, "I can at least assure you that much."

At seventeen seasons old she was far from ready to die and wept still more.

He tenderly held her to him, patting her shoulder as he comforted, "Now, there there. Don't worry over meeting your end so soon. It will save you the horror of growing old and toothless someday. Just think of the suffering you'll be spared."

She tried to shout at him through her gag, but knew her words would be garbled beyond comprehension. Bowing her head, she resolved to cling to the last of her dignity.

"There it is," a soldier riding behind them announced.

As the horses stopped, Janees raised her head and looked over her shoulder, her eyes widening as she saw the emerald colored dragon lying on a stone outcropping beneath a cave halfway up the wall of the canyon. Cold breath sucked into her and remained there.

One of the soldiers raised a horn and blew a loud greeting.

The dragon's eyes flashed open and he slowly raised his head. As he saw the collection of humans who had approached, his dorsal scales went erect and he scrambled to all fours. The horn blew again and he leaned his head as if he understood. Opening his wings fully, the dragon leapt into the air and stroked them only once as he glided to the ground and gently landed right in front of them.

Unlike all of the other humans present, Nemlivv showed no fear of the dragon as he patted his horse's neck to reassure him, then kicked him a little closer.

The dragon raised himself up in a clear attempt to look as menacing as possible and a soft growl rolled from him, but he was not really showing his teeth. He seemed almost interested in entertaining an audience with the sorcerer. Something that was noticeable about him was the three fresh wounds, the worst of which being a gash on his thigh.

Janees found each breath coming with much effort. Just seeing the dragon made her feel like a beast of its size was sitting on her chest. This was the biggest dragon she had ever seen. Of course, this was the *only* dragon she had ever seen.

The dragon examined each of the humans in turn, folding his arms as he locked his attention on the sorcerer.

Raising his chin, Nemlivv greeted, "I had hoped the rumors that you had been seen here were true."

The dragon just stared at him.

"I am Nemlivv," the sorcerer continued, "the Lord of Ravenhold Castle. I've come with a proposition for you."

Raising his snout slightly, the dragon seemed to give the sorcerer his attention.

"I've been looking to ally myself with a wise and powerful dragon in this area, so I am ecstatic to see you have chosen a lair here."

Still the dragon did not respond, but he raised his eyebrow ever so slightly.

"I understand that your kind has distrust for men," Nemlivv went on, "so I've brought a tribute to demonstrate my good will to you."

"What kind of tribute?" the dragon finally asked.

"I figure that a dragon of your power and status would have little use for more gold, so I've brought something even more precious." Nemlivv pulled his arm from around Janees' shoulders and brutally pushed her off of his horse.

She barked a scream behind the gag as she fell and crumpled to the ground, unable to do anything to break her fall.

"As you can see," the sorcerer informed, "she is a virgin maiden of excellent stock, a princess and a sorceress on top of that. Just imagine her sweet flesh in your belly and her power coursing through you. You could potentially become even more powerful with her blood in you and her power at your disposal. I would even offer you my services as a mentor should you choose to develop that power even more."

The dragon's eyes shifted to the girl.

Seeing the dragon's attention on her once again, Janees froze where she was, her eyes almost bulging from her face as she whimpered and found herself trying hard not to be too noticeable, though she knew she was in his sights.

Retaining features of stone, the dragon turned his attention back on the sorcerer and growled, "What do you want for this tribute?"

"I could only ask for your attention and the honor of an audience with you, which you have graciously allowed. Even with this fine tribute I would still feel indebted to you just to be in your presence. I feel an alliance would be mutually beneficial. Surely even a dragon of your status might have enemies that a humble sorcerer might assist with."

Looking to the girl again, the dragon nodded and admitted, "I suppose you could be useful. Very well, Nemlivv of Ravenhold. I am called Linnduron. I will entertain such an alliance." He turned an ominous look on the sorcerer. "So long as I feel this alliance is somehow in my favor."

"I will be sure that it is," Nemlivv assured. He bowed to the dragon, prompting the men with him to do the same. "I shall not disturb you further today, but I will look forward to our next meeting."

The dragon nodded back and watched as the sorcerer and his party turned and rode out of sight, then he looked down to the girl who lay bound and helpless at his feet and leaned his head.

As the dragon reached for her, Janees lost her fight against the panic within her and it exploded from her. Screaming hysterically behind the gag, she struggled as hard as she could against her bonds, but to no avail. The dragon scooped her up with his hands and held her against his chest as he took flight. She made the mistake of looking down as the ground plunged away from her and lost her breath at the sight—and nearly her last meal. Tightly closing her eyes, she turned toward the dragon as best she could. Fears assaulted her, fears of being eaten, of being torn apart and dismembered alive, fears of the pain of being burned alive—fears of being dropped!

Finally overwhelmed, consciousness abandoned her yet again...

***

Once again she awoke in a strange place. The passing of wind was different, hotter and more humid. She blinked rapidly against the passing air and quickly realized the sensation in the pit of her stomach was different. Looking around her again, she realized they were almost on the ground and closed her eyes again as the dragon landed. Feeling him settle to the ground, she refused to open her eyes again, fearful of what the dragon had in store for her. Instead, she felt him put her down. This was curious and she felt compelled to look up at him.

He was looking down at her and backing away. To the horrified girl who had been sacrificed to a dragon, this could only mean that he meant to burn her alive. She cried out behind the gag again as he backed away more, but fell silent as he suddenly looked beyond and lowered his head. His jaws gaped and he trumpeted in a higher pitch than she was expecting.

Seconds later, he was answered with a deep roar that caused the ground to tremble.

Janees finally realized that the ground she was lying on smelled of sulfur and char. Looking around her, all of the land and ground for two hundred paces in any direction was burnt and flattened. Following the dragon's gaze, she saw a mountain rising some distance away and a huge cave opening into it. She gasped loudly as something truly massive and horrible emerged. She could not know that this was the largest and most powerful dragon in the world. She could only see the largest creature she had ever laid her eyes on.

He loped toward them on all fours, dark green and black scales glistening in the sunlight. She noticed his tusks most of all, and the other teeth he bared as he drew closer to the other dragon. That must be it. She had been sacrificed to the dragon by the sorcerer. Now, she was an offering to an even larger dragon.

Finding herself beyond fear at this point, she took the moment to study this massive dragon. He was looking upon the smaller dragon as a noble would look upon a commoner, with little more than annoyance and contempt. She could not call upon her power to defend herself, so she retreated into it to hear and understand the grunts and growls of the dragons. She had been shown this at an early age, but never actually expected to use it. She could hear the dragons differently now. She could understand them.

"Landmaster," the smaller dragon urged, "it's a tribute. I offer it to stay in your favor."

The huge dragon growled and looked down at her with a snarl and predator's eyes, then he looked back to the smaller dragon and scoffed, "I have no interest in a human and you are not in my favor. You'd best remember that."

"I will, Landmaster," the smaller dragon assured. "The human is yours. It's virgin with royal blood and sorcerer's gifts."

The massive dragon turned and strode back toward his cave. "I have no interest in it. Take it to Ralligor. Perhaps he will want it."

"I will, Landmaster."

Janees finally realized that the smaller dragon remained as low to the ground as he could while the Landmaster was present. She also realized that, in the last moments of her life, she was learning more about dragons than perhaps anyone else ever had.

Perhaps with good reason.

The smaller dragon growled and looked back down at her, then he snatched her from the ground and took to the sky again.

Janees whimpered as they went skyward again, then she distracted herself with the dragon himself. As she pressed her cheek against the hard scales of his breast, she realized they were not hard and cold like stone, rather they felt like velvet. He was also a warm creature, not at all like the cold reptile she had assumed he was. Pressing her ear to him, she could actually hear the muscles driving his wings, the squeak or creak of his joints within, and his powerful heartbeat. There was also the rumbling of a digesting meal within his belly.

Before she realized, the air was dry and hot and they were descending again, circling this time as he did. They glided down a box canyon and toward another cave. Even before they touched down she could smell the same sulfur and char as she smelled at the Landmaster's lair.

As before, he set her down and backed away, roaring as he had at the other dragon's lair, but this time she could make out the name "Ralligor."

A deep growl rolled from the cave and Janees found her nerves pulled taut all over again. Somewhere within the darkness she could hear an almost metallic drag and the thumps of heavy approaching footsteps. Retreating into her gift again, she listened for the dragons to speak to one another. This was a distraction she badly needed.

What emerged was a huge black beast, not quite the size of the last one, but still nearly twice the smaller green one's size.

She could actually read his features. He looked exasperated, and a little annoyed as he saw the smaller dragon.

"Oh," he growled, stopping just outside of his cave. "I'd hoped not to see you again so soon, Linnduron."

"I bring you a tribute," the smaller dragon offered.

"Tributes usually end up costing me," the black dragon snarled back, "much the way it cost me showing favor toward you in front of Agarxus."

The smaller dragon glanced down at her again. "I only want to be in your favor."

"It's really hard to hold you in my favor when I have to share my hunting range with you," the black dragon snarled. "Besides, I already have a human."

"Like this one?" Linnduron pressed. "This one's of royal blood and has sorcerer's gift. It's also virgin."

Ralligor looked down at her again, studying her for a second before saying, "Uh, huh. Sure she is. Linnduron, where did you get this girl?"

The smaller green dragon looked down at her again. "It was a tribute offered me by humans who came to my lair."

"And you're not sure what to do with her," the black dragon

finished. He looked away and growled a sigh, then shook his head and bade, "Wait here a moment." He turned and entered his cave again. From within a rummaging could be heard, the clank of metal and what sounded like dropping coins. There was a crash of metal and what sounded like a huge pile of coin and metal plate being dug through or piled. Such noise made one think the inside of the cave itself was being torn apart. A moment later the black dragon could be heard approaching in the darkness and there was a red glow within the cave that grew brighter from his eyes as he neared the entrance, a glow that disappeared as he emerged. In his hands was a round knight's shield of gold adorned with many jewels of many different sizes and colors. He threw the shield down in front of the smaller green dragon and insisted, "I'll trade you that for the girl. Consider it a start for your hoard. Now go annoy some other dragon."

Linnduron picked up the shield and carefully looked it over, then he turned his eyes to the black dragon and crooned to him before he turned and swept himself into the sky.

The black dragon watched him fly away, then he shook his head and mumbled, "All because Shahly has to befriend every wandering creature she comes across." He looked down to the bound girl, not studying her as much as he seemed to be wondering what to do with her.

Janees stared back, unable to do anything but wonder what was in store for her. This was clearly a creature of vast intellect and massive strength and her mind whirled as she scrambled to come up with some kind of plan to get free. The one thing at the forefront of her mind: Jekkon. She had to get free and find him. When the dragon leaned his head slightly and raised a brow, she struggled once more to free her hands, squirming and wrenching her shoulders back and forth. A whimper escaped her as her bindings began to wear her skin raw and it really hurt where it still rubbed on her.

The dragon growled again and shook his head, then he raised a hand and made a simple gesture.

In a second, the ropes that bound her so tightly were suddenly very brittle and crumbled from her. She pulled her very stiff arms from under her and rubbed her wrists, never taking her eyes from the dragon. Slowly, she sat up, the bindings crumbling away from her legs as she did. She reached up to remove the gag from her and it crumbled away as well, and she suddenly found herself turning her head to spit out a mouthful of dirt that had once been fabric. Spitting a few times more to clear the last of it, she slowly turned uneasy eyes up to the dragon.

He just stared back at her.

Fear gripped her and her mind scrambled anew. She knew from the scripts she had read on dragons that outwitting older and wiser dragons was next to impossible, but that they could sometimes be intimidated by the unknown. Perhaps that was the key, but she would have to show him nothing but respect.

Slowly, she pushed herself up and stood with her eyes fixed on his. She knew not to run and was too afraid to turn her back on him. Swallowing back her fear, she stood as straight and tall as she could, her palms facing the ground as she made her stand against him. Hesitantly, she asked, "Can you understand me? Can you speak?"

"I'm not an idiot," the dragon thundered in her language.

She raised her chin slightly and shook her head. "I would never think so. You've purchased me from that other dragon and I am grateful. He was led to believe that eating me would give him great power."

The dragon nodded. "He was also led to believe that you are a virgin."

Her lips tightened. "Great Dragon, I can see that you are too wise and experienced to believe that yourself and I am grateful for that."

"I'm sure you are."

"I must know, Great Dragon. What would you have of me?"

"Are you trying to stroke my ego for a reason?"

He was seeing right through her, and this made her uneasy. "I would prefer to be in your favor, not in your belly."

The dragon looked away and grumbled, "You and everyone else, lately."

"I would also prefer that you not try to attack me," she warned. "I am a s—sorceress of great skill. The smaller dragon was clearly too young to know the extent of my power and I have no wish to cause harm to such a magnificent creature as you."

A hesitant nod was his response.

"I must go," she continued, "and you must let me."

"And the gold I'm out?" he countered.

Janees raised her brow.

"I paid quite a heavy price for you," he informed, "and I've used up my all of my appetite for charity today. So, do you intend to pay me back or fight your way out of here?"

Her eyes narrowed and she clenched her hands into tight fists. She had but one more play to make, one that, according to the ancient scripts, was quite overwhelming to any dragon. "I humbly warn you, don't attack me. I only wish to go in peace."

"There's a classic response to that," the dragon said almost in a laugh, "but I'll spare us both." Unexpectedly, he stood to his massive five heights tall and walked toward her with long strides and heavy footfalls.

Frozen by terror, Janees kept her wide eyes on him as he strode around her. Ever so slowly, she turned to see him sit catlike between herself and escape.

"Okay, sorceress of unknown power. Let's see if you can use that great skill of yours to fight your way through me."

Nervously, she ran her thumbs over her fingertips, her eyes locked on his.

Long moments passed as she pondered her next move.

"Ah," the dragon observed. "I see your strategy now. Lull me off to sleep and then sever my head with that great, mysterious power of yours."

"I... I simply don't wish to harm you," she desperately countered.

"Perhaps I have no such qualms about harming you," he pointed out. "Perhaps in a moment I shall lose my patient and civilized tone and show you the fury that every human fears from dragons." He half opened his wings and warned, "Don't trifle with my patience, sorceress."

Janees nodded. "Then I'll do as I must. Just know I take no pleasure in this." She raised her hands, that yellow fire consuming them, then she turned her eyes to the rim of the canyon. Mustering all of the strength she dared, she summoned a boulder some three paces across from the top and watched it fall from fifteen heights above the dragon, guiding it toward his head.

He never took his eyes from her. Leaning his neck away from the boulder, he raised a hand and caught it in his palm, just holding it above him for a moment before he slammed it onto the ground.

Her mouth fell open and she took a couple of steps back. This dragon was far stronger than she had realized.

"I can see why you took no pleasure in that," he admitted.

"I—I've fought great duels before," she warned.

The dragon nodded and observed, "Doesn't look like you won the last one."

It was time for her endgame play. "I know your name, dragon."

"So do I," he countered dryly.

"Your name is Ralligor," she shouted. "Hear your name in my tongue with your ears and in your tongue from my mind to yours. Ralligor!"

He stared back at her and his wings folded slowly to his sides.

Her brow tensed, her eyes widening and glowing with that golden yellow fire. "Now, feel my power." She thrust her mind at him, her very essence. "Pain, Ralligor! Pain!"

Quite unexpectedly, he stood and grasped his chest, tightly closing his eyes and his jaws swung open to release a mighty, agonizing roar. He staggered backward, his tail thrashing. His wings opened and stroked back and forth as he roared again. A hand reached to his head, grasping it right behind his horns.

"Down!" she commanded, channeling her power as hard as she could. As she watched him slowly sink to his knees, she raised her hands to her ears as he roared even louder. "Down!" she commanded again, louder.

He growled, clearly resisting her, then he roared again. He released his chest and planted his hand on the ground as he fell forward, his eyes tightly closed. Shaking his head, his lips drew back from his teeth and his jaws clenched hard together.

As he roared again, she raised her hands, and gave him everything her mind had. She felt a trickle of blood from her nose and another from the corner of her eye as she clenched her own teeth together. "Lie down to your belly!" she shouted over him.

He suddenly opened his eyes and looked to her. "Sorry, but I didn't hear that last one. What was it you said?"

Janees gasped and took another step back. Sheepishly, she repeated, "Lie down to your belly."

The dragon roared again and collapsed, his bulk slamming into the ground with great force and shaking the ground all over the canyon. As a dust cloud rose around him, pebbles and sand dropped from the canyon walls all around.

For a moment, all was silent. As Janees watched him gasp for breath, her heart sank and fear began to push out confidence once again.

He opened an eye slightly and peered at her, then quickly closed it again.

She drew a breath, then released it slowly, turning her eyes down. The ancient scripts were wrong. Hearing her speak and think his name did not give her power over him, it amused him. He was just toying with her, and she knew he was laughing at her inside. When she looked toward him again and wiped the blood from her lips he had raised his head and was resting his jaw in his hand. The amusement in his eyes told everything.

The dragon raised his brow and asked, "So, do you have a sword or spear to ram into my soft underbelly, too?"

This was now the most humiliating moment of her life. She could only stare back at him, and feel like a fool.

"You have my grattitude for going easy on me," the dragon chided. "Another moment of *that* horror and I'm sure my tail would have fallen off."

Tight lipped and near tears, Janees looked away from him and said, "Please just eat me or burn me and get it over with."

He huffed a laugh. "Oh no, I think you're more entertaining to me alive. So tell me. How did you come to be in Linnduron's possession?"

"It doesn't matter," she admitted softly.

"Oh, come on," Ralligor pressured. "Amuse me more."

She glanced at him, then wiped blood and tears from her cheek. "You were right. I lost that last duel. Soldiers from

Ravenhold Castle attacked my home at Pinetop Castle and burned it down. Many of us were taken prisoner. I used my power to free many people, but their leader is a powerful sorcerer. We fought a sorcerer's duel and... and..." She sighed. "He beat me, then subdued me and took me to that dragon that brought me here. He wanted an alliance with him."

The black dragon raised his head. "With Linnduron? Whatever for?"

Janees shrugged. "I don't know. Please, I have to go and find my... my little brother, Jekkon. He cannot take care of himself." Turning desperate eyes to him, she pleaded, "Please, Great Dragon. Please let me go find him. I have to take care of him. He's out there frightened and all alone."

The dragon glanced up, then looked back to her and dryly said, "Let's assume for a moment that I give a— "

"Please!" she begged. "He's all I have left. Please! Please let me go and find him. I'll do anything!"

"So what exactly in it for me?" the dragon asked.

She glanced around, considering, then met his eyes again and replied, "I—I—I'm a princess. I can get you gold, tw—twice what you gave to the little dragon for me. Just let me find Jekkon and... and we'll bring you gold."

The dragon raised a brow. "It stands to reason that if Ravenhold sacked and burned your castle, they took your gold with them."

Janees looked to the canyon wall, quickly pondering, then, "There... there is a vault just down the hill from the castle, near a creek, a—a vault that no one knows about but the royal family." She turned her eyes back to him and promised, "Let—let—let me go back there and find Jekkon and we will... we will give you all of the gold in the vault. It will be ransom for me. I've read that dragons will ransom maidens."

"Just like you've read that knowing our names will enslave us to you and that we have soft underbellies." His brow arched. "One of us is *really* gullible."

"I... I promise!" she assured.

He casually turned his eyes to the boulder. A bright emerald glow slowly overtook them.

Janees also looked to the boulder, gasping as it lifted from the ground and moved ten paces closer to the mouth of the cave. As it settled back down, she turned her attention back to the dragon, shaking her head as she softly admitted, "I didn't know dragons could do that!"

"Most can't," he sighed. Looking back to her, he informed, "I'm what you might call a wizard's apprentice."

Her mouth fell open and her eyes flared. "You know magic?"

"Not on a first name basis, but I suppose you could say that I know magic."

She strode toward him a few steps and clasped her hands together, crying, "Teach me! Please, teach me!"

Ralligor drew his head back. "Teach you what?"

"Magic!" she answered desperately. "Please, I'm already your girl. I'll be the best apprentice I can to you. Please, teach me!"

"First," the dragon started, "I'm not looking for an apprentice. Second, as I told Linnduron, I already have a human. Third—"

"Please!" she begged, sinking to her knees and clasping her hands together. "I'll do whatever you want! I'll never leave your side! I'll clean your lair. I'll sing to you!"

"And your brother?"

She hesitated. Turning her eyes down, she considered for long seconds, then looked back to him and assured, "I'll go and find him and bring him here, then I'll be your very best pupil. I'll be loyal and attentive and I promise that Jekkon won't get in your way. Oh, please, Great Dragon. I am yours!"

"What about the gold in these secret vaults?" he questioned.

Janees found herself caught in a lie and her eyes betrayed this as she stared up at him. Slowly, she bowed her head and looked to the ground. "There are no vaults. There is no secret gold. I was desperate to find Jekkon and I would have told you anything for you to free me. Please, Great Dragon. Forgive me."

He grunted and looked away from her.

"I'll never lie to you again," she assured, "I promise!"

The dragon just stared at the canyon wall.

A moment passed and Janees desperately cried, "What must I do to prove myself to you? What must I do?"

"Not for me to say," was his answer. He finally turned his attention back to her and informed, "I can't teach you *magic*. I can really teach you nothing."

Janees felt herself beginning to cry and demanded, "Why?"

"You claim to be quite a skilled sorceress, don't you?"

"For my age," she added sheepishly.

"How long have you studied and who under?"

"Since I was eleven," she replied. "The, uh, King and Queen of Pinetop Castle, my... my parents, did not approve of m—my studies so... so I had to study in secret. I—I—I studied under any mage who came to the castle."

"Uh, huh," the dragon said dryly. "How many were experienced sorcerer *magisters?*"

Hesitantly, she shrugged.

"And," he continued, "I'll wager that you traded all kinds of favors for these lessons, didn't you?"

Her eyes betrayed shame as she looked away from him.

"You picked up a few tricks here and there, but that's all you learned: A few tricks."

Bowing her head again, she nodded, now feeling like that eleven season old child who was just beginning to realize her power, and knowing the wrath of the adults around her.

"You learned so much," he observed, "and yet you learned so little."

"I don't understand," she confessed, her eyes fixed on the ground before her.

"I didn't figure you would," he sighed, "nor will I teach you magic the way you want."

"Please," she begged, sobbing. "I am yours. I'll do anything."

He was quiet as he seemed to consider, and finally thundered, "Anything, huh?" He growled a sigh, then raised a finger to the canyon wall. A flash of emerald light lanced from the end of his claw and struck the wall, melting a deep hole that seemed to extend too far back to see. "Go in there."

She turned her eyes to the hole, her brow arching as her full lips parted a little more in fear.

"Go all the way through," he continued, "and don't even look back. When you emerge, you will find a cabin. Go inside and wait there."

She nervously looked up at him and asked, "How long should I wait?"

"Go," he snarled.

Janees got to her feet and fearfully faced the cave the dragon had made. It was an irregular opening about a height and a half tall. Hesitantly, she made her first few steps toward it, then strode cautiously on her way. She almost stopped at the mouth to look back at the dragon, but remembered his command not to do so and continued inside. But for the light that crept in from behind her, it was totally dark within. Extending her arms out in front of her to feel her way through, she trekked on with hesitant half steps.

CHAPTER 4

Evening was but a few hours away and two unicorns paced carelessly southwest on a human's road.

For most of the day, they had just enjoyed one another's company, but as they drew closer to a river they knew was there the stallion grew more and more uneasy. Something was on the wind and he raised his nose many times to test the scents that reached him.

Seeing him do this, the mare also tested the air, her nose wrinkling as she asked, "What smells so bad?"

"Humans have had a battle," the stallion answered. "Smells like they're burning the dead, and lots of them."

"Why would they do that?"

The stallion shrugged. "Not for me to say, really. Most of what they do is a mystery to me."

She whickered a laugh. "You need to just spend more time with them to understand them better."

"I'm sure I don't want to understand them," he grumbled.

"Why wouldn't they leave their dead to be reclaimed by the land?" she asked innocently. "Why use fire? It seems like they would want them to go back to the land."

He glanced at her. "Well, some humans seem to think that their dead should become smoke. Some think they should be buried to protect them from scavengers. Others entomb their dead in stone so that the bodies will last forever."

"Entomb?"

"That means they put the body in a place where it will be kept safe from predators and will dry out and otherwise not really decay."

"Eew!"

He whickered a laugh. "They want to keep it intact for later."

"Keep it intact for later? Why? What would they do with it?"

"Well, some humans think they will live again sometime after their deaths, and there are those who think that if their bodies do not decay then they can return and live again in the same bodies."

The mare paced in silence for long paces, her eyes showing

strain as she tried to comprehend this. "I don't understand. That doesn't make sense."

"I've been saying that about humans for a long, long time, Shahly."

"Yes you have," she agreed. "Some things about them make sense, though."

"Like?"

She thought hard again, her eyes narrowing somewhat. "Well, um..."

He turned his eyes to her and seemed to raise his brow.

Giving him but a glance, then finally answered, "They love."

Vinton smiled.

Shooting him another glance, she also smiled. "In that way they are much like us."

"I suppose they are," he said back. "So how else are they like us? You spent enough time among them to know."

"You spent some time with one, too," she countered.

"But not *as* one," he replied.

He got a sharp look from her. "Being a human was hard. I had to walk on two legs, learn to dress and how to use a fork and spoon and a hundred other things I don't care to think about. Did you know that they even dress to sleep?"

Vinton drew his head back. "They do?"

"Yes, they do. Ihzell made *me* do it, too. It wasn't comfortable but it was all very warm when the nights got cold. Did you know humans don't like to get wet? And yet they have little stone pools they call tubs that they sit in to bathe. The water is very warm and soothing and the shampoo smells like strawberries, but I could have gotten just as clean swimming in the river."

"The same river you almost drowned in?"

She snorted. "Yes, the same river I almost drowned in."

"You don't speak of your time as a human much anymore," he observed.

She looked away.

"Is it because of that prince?" he asked in a gentle tone.

"Yes," she admitted. "It's hard for me to think of him sometimes. My feelings still confuse me."

Vinton stopped.

Feeling she had hurt him, Shahly also stopped, and slowly looked back at him.

"You miss him, don't you?"

The young mare lowered her ears and loosed a hard breath, and nodded.

Looking aside, her stallion considered for a moment.

"Vinton," she started.

"No, Shahly," he interrupted. "We can't go on like this, not with you feeling the way you do about him."

She turned toward him, her eyes wide and betraying fear of his next words.

The stallion raised his head and informed, "You are going to have to go and see him."

She took a step back and gasped, "What?"

He slowly paced toward her. "You need to go see him. If you still have such feeling for him and if you miss him so, then it's time you paid him a visit."

"You... You *want* me to go and see him?"

"Of course I do. You have to face these feelings that confuse you."

Shahly looked off into the forest. "Vinton, what if those feelings try to take control of me the way they did before? I—I almost..." She closed her eyes, lowering her head. "Vinton, I'm so ashamed."

He paced all the way to her and tenderly nuzzled her. "All the more reason for you to see him. You have to face this."

"What if I want to stay?" she whispered.

"You won't," he assured. "You didn't before and you won't now."

She opened her eyes and let tears stream forth. "I don't know, Vinton. I'm afraid."

The stallion whickered a laugh. "You aren't afraid of forest cats or dragons but you're afraid of your own heart. You're afraid of the one thing in this world I adore the most."

"I don't want to betray you," she confessed.

"I'm not concerned at all," he assured. "When you fell in love with him you saw him with human eyes. I'm sure seeing him with unicorn eyes will be different."

"I still love him," she admitted softly.

"And I'll always love you," he countered.

Shahly closed her eyes and rubbed her cheek against his neck. "I will always love you, my stallion."

"I won't share you with a human," he suddenly said.

She whinnied a laugh. "He has a mate, already." Shahly jerked her head up and looked to him. "Audrell! We need to see Audrell, too! We should go right now!" She paced past him and headed north.

He turned and followed. "Right now? Why are you suddenly in such a hurry?"

"Because it really stinks here," she informed straightly.

Whickering a laugh, he was quick to catch up to her. "You seem just as anxious to see this Audrell as you do that prince."

"We got to be good friends," Shahly informed, "much the way you and Faelon did." She gave him a sidelong glance and a half smile. "You know, the princess you let ride on your back all that time."

"That was *your* idea, Shahly."

"You sure seemed to enjoy it."

He glanced back at her. "You aren't jealous of her, are you?"

"Of course not," the mare scoffed. "Besides, she's way too young for you."

"Yes," he agreed, "that's true. Much the way this little white mare in my herd is."

Shahly rolled her eyes.

This banter would continue for the next half hour or so as they journeyed north.

Without warning, Shahly stopped and jerked her head up, looking across the road and into the forest.

Vinton stopped beside her, noticing a faint emerald glow about her horn. This meant her essence was there and fully alert to something that he was not. He turned his attention to where hers was, he scanned the forest with his eyes first, then his essence. In a low voice he asked, "What is it?"

"Someone's in the forest," she replied, "someone who is very sad."

Reaching further into the forest with his essence, the stallion finally touched the mind of the creature Shahly had so easily found, and his heart jumped. "Shahly, uh..."

"Come on," she bade as she turned that way.

He leaped in front of her and made her stop, whinnying, "Whoa, there! What are you doing?"

"I'm going to see why he's so sad," she replied. Shaking her head, she trotted around him and continued on her way.

Vinton was quick to catch up. "Shahly, don't you know what— "

"He's sad," she interrupted. "It's not like he's a dangerous predator. I told you I would avoid them and I am."

"I didn't mean you should approach— "

"Vinton," she cut in again, "you also said that you would be at my side when I have to approach a poor creature that needs my help. You said *we* would help, remember?"

He stared at her for long strides, then quickened his pace to get ahead of her when the trail narrowed. "Just keep your distance and be ready to bolt should he turn aggressive."

"My strong, protective stallion," she said with a broad smile. "I am the luckiest unicorn in the whole world."

"As you've proven on many occasions," he grumbled.

They neared a clearing in the forest, one that was growing dark in the early evening sun and Vinton stopped, staring ahead of him with curious eyes. Shahly took his side and raised her head as she studied the massive form before her, then she leaned to her stallion and whispered, "He looks really upset."

"He also looks really hungry," Vinton countered. "Conceal yourself and let's approach without being seen."

"Right!" she agreed with her usual enthusiasm. As they slowly advanced, she whispered, "Vinton, why don't you want him to see us? He already saw us once."

The bay stopped, then looked to the white unicorn as she stopped beside him. He considered, then admitted, "Good point. And I think he ate already. Let's not startle him." He raised his head and crept forward.

In the center of the clearing, lying sprawled in the sunshine, the young green dragon seemed to be lost in his thoughts. When the unicorns were about thirty paces away, he finally noticed their approach and raised his head, turning his eyes to them.

"Hello again," Shahly greeted.

He grunted and laid his head back down.

"What's wrong?" she asked with a sympathetic voice. She got but a glance from the young dragon. Stopping only a few paces away from him, she leaned her head and said, "I thought you would be happy that you get to stay here."

"We'll see how long it lasts," he snarled. "I'm not exactly in the Landmaster's favor. His *subordinare* isn't happy about me being here, either." He looked to her. "And now I'm telling my problems to unicorns."

"Maybe we can help," she suggested.

"With the Landmaster?" He huffed a laugh. "You aren't exactly in his favor, either. I'm amazed that he didn't kill you."

Shahly half turned her head, her eyes narrowing. "Oh, that's not the first time I've tangled with him."

Vinton added, "But it was the last. What is it you want, Linnduron? You've established yourself here. Agarxus didn't kill you and Ralligor didn't either."

"Yet," the dragon interjected.

"Well," the stallion continued, "it's got to count for something. Ralligor stuck up for you. He won't do that for just anyone, especially to the Tyrant."

A long breath escaped the young dragon and he looked away again, finally conceding, "I suppose. Sometimes I wish I would never have come of age."

Vinton pointed out, "Well, of age you are and you should just make the best of it."

With a glance at him, the dragon snarled, "The wisdom of a grazer."

"I'm many times older than you," the bay unicorn pointed out. "I've had quite a bit of experience since coming of age myself."

"Like fighting for territory?" the dragon asked coldly.

"Vinton," Shahly cut in. "I need to go into the forest for a moment. I think there is someone who escaped the human battle there." She got an impatient look from her stallion and assured, "It isn't another dragon or anything of the like. I think it's a lost human child."

The stallion sighed and whickered, "Go on, then. Just don't stray too far and whinny if you get into trouble again."

She snorted. "I *won't* get into trouble again." She turned and trotted away, flicking her tail at her protective stallion as she did.

Vinton shook his head and looked back to the young dragon. "Take my advice, Linnduron. When you find a mate, make sure she's afraid of everything."

The dragon raised his brow.

CHAPTER 5

For many seasons, Jekkon had not been separated from Janees for very long. Even when he was there was someone to occupy his attention. Now, he found himself alone and lost. Janees was nowhere to be found. He could not even find his way back to the castle, not that there was anything to go back to there. He was not a lad of great wits. Formulating a plan to find her or even how and where to look was beyond his grasp. He sat on the thick trunk of a fallen tree, one that stubbornly continued to grow and sprout new leaves despite spending many seasons lying on the forest floor. Branches grew upward from its trunk but for a six pace long span near the upended roots. There he sat, waiting for his lost Janees to find him. After most of the day had passed, he wept, his child-like mind afraid and unsure. Lost and alone, he could do nothing else.

His face was pressed into his huge hands as he sobbed without the shame someone his age would feel. Within his mind, he was still very much a child, and this child longed for the one person who had always been there for him. He did not notice the approaching hoof beats until they were only a few paces away and he slowly turned tear-swollen eyes toward the sound. What he saw made him forget about his loneliness and despair for a moment.

The pony-sized white unicorn stopped, her sparkling blue eyes staring curiously at the huge boy as she leaned her head. Gold ribbons within the ivory of her horn seemed to give it a golden glow and cloven hooves of the same gold planted firmly in the earth beneath her, partly concealed in the short, well grazed grass and clover that grew there. Her snow white mane and tail glistened silver in the sunlight.

Like most humans, Jekkon had never seen a unicorn before and he stared dumbly at her. He knew something about this magical creature was different, but all he could muster to say was "Horsy." His voice was very deep, yet very child-like.

The unicorn's ears perked and she raised her head. Finally she asked in a gentle voice, "Don't you know what I am?"

"Horsy," he repeated.

She whickered a laugh. "No, I'm not a horsy."

His brow lowered and he seemed confused.

She took a step toward him. "I'm a unicorn. Some think we look like horses and I suppose to many we do."

He drew his head back.

"Are you lost?" she asked.

His jaw quivered as he was reminded and new tears streamed from his eyes. Slowly, he nodded. "Can't find Janees."

"Is Janees your mother?" the unicorn questioned.

He glanced away. "Janees… No, just Janees."

The unicorn nodded. "I see. There is a human castle that has burned some distance from here. Is that where you are from?"

He nodded.

"What happened?"

"Bad people came," he replied with clenched teeth. "They burned the castle and killed people. They killed my friends. They took people." He was silent for long seconds, tight lipped. "Janees wouldn't let me fight. She said I would get hurt."

Suddenly sensing his anger, the unicorn lowered her head and backed away.

He turned pitiful eyes on her and begged, "Don't go, horsy. Don't go."

She stopped. "You are very angry. I can understand, but I fear your anger."

"I won't be mad," he assured. "Need to find Janees."

"I understand," she said sympathetically, "but you must realize that my kind fears humans, especially big humans."

"Don't be afraid," he pled. "Not hurt you. Not hurt anyone. Janees says hurt people is bad."

"She sounds like a wise woman," the unicorn observed, slowly raising her head. "You don't know where she went?"

"Fought off the bad people," he answered. "I wanted to fight too. She told me to run away and protect the people she let go, so I did. Now I can't find her."

"Where was she when she told you to run away?"

"We were going with the bad people away from the castle. Janees wouldn't let me fight. We could have won if I fight."

"Or you could have been hurt," the unicorn countered. She looked away, considering what to do next. "I wandered about the burning castle and no one was there. You probably don't want to follow the bad people..."

"Did the bad people get Janees?" he asked softly

"I don't know," she replied. Turning her eyes back to him, she said, "I don't think you would do well in the forest by yourself."

"Stay with you," he announced.

Her ears drooped. "Um, that wouldn't be wise, either. You belong with your own kind."

"But I want to stay with you," he argued.

"I know you do, but I don't know how to take care of your kind. I don't even know that I could find you food."

"Janees makes good food," he informed.

Clearly this big, young human had a very short attention span. She considered a few seconds more, then offered, "I can show you the way to a human settlement, but I can't go there with you. I fear the humans and I don't wish to be seen by them."

"Why afraid?" Jekkon asked.

"I'm a unicorn," she replied. "Humans are strangely unpredictable and very few are of pure heart." She seemed to smile. "Like you are. I will help you find your way there, but then I will have to be on my way."

"Go and find Janees?" he asked eagerly.

"We will find her if we can. I'm sure the humans at the settlement can help you." She turned and paced toward the forest on the other side of the clearing, stopping halfway there to look back at the boy and asked, "Are you coming?"

He stood and lumbered toward her.

Once he was at her side, their trek began.

The unicorn soon learned that this large human had little to say. He absently watched the trail in front of them as he lumbered along beside her. Peering into his mind, she found his thoughts to be simple and guided by little more than what was right in front of him. His emotions appeared to be ruled by the moment and felt as volatile as she had ever experienced, much like a child of his kind, though he was almost twice the size of any adult she had ever seen. While she longed to help him find his way, she still feared his unstable emotions. She had to know more about him.

Looking up at him, she noticed the dark iron chain that hung around his neck, suspending a cobalt blue stone that looked way to heavy to be worn comfortably. Something about the stone felt unnatural, something more than the unshaped metal that composed it.

He glanced at her.

"Why do you have that around your neck?" she asked.

He reached up and possessively grasped the stone, glancing at her again.

She leaned her head. "Does it bother you to speak of? I don't mean to upset you."

Looking to her again, he stared back for long strides, then he turned his eyes down and admitted, "Horsy don't. Not upset. Janees says never take it off."

"Did she give it to you?"

Jekkon looked down at the stone. "No. Someone give me a long time ago. Never take it off until I know."

"Until you know what?"

"Don't know." He looked to her again, asking, "Do you know?"

She smiled. "No, I don't."

"How do I know when?"

"Your heart will tell you, Jekkon. Do you know what it does?"

He shook his head. "Not know. When to take it off will be important time. I won't need to be smart or seem like everyone else."

"Seem like everyone else? What do you mean?" When he glanced at her still again, she could tell that something was making him upset. Peering gently into his mind, she found a boy who had spent almost all of his life unable to fit in with his own kind. This was an issue of great sadness for him. Only one image in his mind was one that brought him comfort, the image of a girl. To help keep his anger in check, she subtly nudged his emotions that way. "Jekkon, you don't seem much different than any other humans I've seen. A little larger, perhaps, and you have a good heart, but I don't sense anything of you that is so different."

He stopped, watching as she stopped a couple of paces

beyond him and turned to face him. Frustration overtook him again and he extended his arms, demanding, "Look at me! Not like everyone else!"

Fearlessly, she approached a step and looked him up and down. "I don't know what all other humans look like. Is Janees like everyone else?"

Slowly, he lowered his arms. Just staring back for long seconds, he finally shook his head, admitting, "No. But... But Janees normal."

She leaned her head. "Why is she normal?"

Jekkon thought for a moment, and thought hard. He looked away and scratched his belly. Finally, he shrugged and admitted, "Don't know. Just normal and I'm not."

The unicorn raised her head. "You aren't normal because you are bigger than most? You aren't normal because you are, perhaps, stronger than others? Or maybe because you have such a pure and gentle heart?"

He just blinked and did not know what to say.

Her ears swiveled toward him.

Jekkon finally turned his eyes down and shrugged.

The unicorn whickered to him, then turned and continued on her way. "Well, then. It sounds like normal is not such a good thing after all."

He puzzled for a moment, then followed, trotting to catch up to her. "But not like everyone else. No one likes me."

She glanced at him. "That isn't true. Janees likes you."

"But no one else likes me."

"I do," she corrected.

That finally coaxed a smile from him.

"And I don't like many humans," the unicorn added.

"Do you like Janees?"

"I don't know Janees. You seem fond of her, though, so perhaps I would." Unexpectedly, she jerked her head up and stopped, her eyes locked forward.

Jekkon stopped beside her, looking curiously down at the unicorn.

"Don't speak," she ordered in a whisper. "Don't move. Don't make any sound."

He looked where she did but was unable to see anything past

a bend in the road. There was nothing to be seen beyond the trees except sunlight and what seemed to be a field of grass. He was not afraid, more curious. Fear for himself was not something that had ever concerned him. He knew this unicorn could more than tend herself in the forest, but she was suddenly very nervous about something.

Slowly, she lowered her head, still staring toward that field beyond the trees. Her eyes panned about and her ears swiveled to follow them. This happened for only half a moment before she whispered, "Wait here."

Jekkon watched her creep noiselessly toward that bend in the road and the grass-covered field beyond. She was not making the slightest sound and her movements were like water in a lazy creek. As she paced silently toward that grassy field beyond the trees, he kept his eyes on her, now feeling a little afraid for her, and felt more uneasy as she left the safety of the trees and shadows and waded into the tall grass just beyond. He dared to stride forward, remaining as quiet as he could, more for fear of a good scolding than the unknown terror that might be awaiting them.

He looked beyond her, squinting as he saw the figure that was seated in the middle of the field. It was a girl dressed in white with long brown hair. She wore a ring of flowers around her hair and just stared at the ground. This was a girl who was very sad. Her thoughts whirled around a sinister purpose, one which was burdened upon her not of her own choice, and of a betrayal she wished she did not have to be a part of. Jekkon could not sense this, but the unicorn in his company could, and she was both curious and wary.

Moving noiselessly toward the girl, the unicorn puzzled over why a human girl would be sitting alone in a field in the middle of the forest. Perhaps she was another who escaped the battle that destroyed the human settlement, another lost child of her kind. With her head low, she crept to within about five paces and paused, peering into the girl's mind with her own.

Slowly raising her head, the girl turned her eyes to the unicorn and whimpered, "Please. Not again. Please flee from here."

In an instant the unicorn saw horrid memories. This girl's

purpose was quite clear: She was bait! Ever so slowly, the unicorn lifted her head, her eyes panning about as she finally felt the presence of the other humans. Eleven in number, they were all around her, their thoughts focused on her. Her capture was in their minds, and she was not the first. They were experienced at this and she could see in their thoughts that the tools they used were very effective to that end. Now was the time to think about how to evade them.

Looking to her right, the unicorn saw three human men stand from their hiding places in the tall grass and behind a bush. As she looked left, four more emerged. They were all dressed in animal skin jerkins, dark, loose fitting shirts and tight trousers. All but one had hair on his face and all had long manes behind their heads. Belts of black or brown leather carried an assortment of things including swords and drinking bladders, and five had ropes in their hands and they appeared to be ready to toss the looped ends toward her. She could feel the presence of others behind her and heard at least three horses moving out of the forest. Why she had not sensed them before was something that both puzzled and frustrated her. Perhaps this is how they had captured unicorns before. Perhaps her distraction with the large boy was to blame.

Either way, it was time to make her move.

The humans on foot were only about fifteen paces away. Those on horseback were closer.

Unexpectedly, she wheeled around and reared up, tossing her head about as she whinnied like a unicorn possessed.

All three of the horses reared up and whinnied back, throwing their riders.

She bolted through them, not knowing about the rope rising from the deep grass until it entangled her forelegs. Falling hard, the unicorn rolled to her side in the grass and struggled to get her hooves under her and run the other way. They had clearly seen that trick before and were expecting her to do it.

Something cut the air as she got to her hooves and she ducked as the loop of a rope came at her and barely missed dropping over her head. With her footing solid again, she turned to flee another direction, but the rope that had tripped her was wrapped around her foreleg and she stumbled again.

As she tried to shake it loose, she dodged a second rope meant to snare her.

Backing away, she realized that the humans had closed the distance and were nearly upon her. She desperately tried to free her leg and finally thrust her horn at the stubborn rope, cutting it easily with a blue flash from her spiral. Finally free of it, she turned to flee—and a lasso finally dropped over her head! As it pulled taut, she whinnied and threw herself away from it. The man holding the other end was toppled, but several others soon joined his grasp and a tug-of-war ensued. The rope grew ever tighter and, near panic, she swept her horn toward it to cut it with her essence as she had done before. This one, however, was enchanted and pain ripped through her as something within the rope struck back at her, and it would not yield.

Another dropped over her head and pulled her from another direction, then another from behind.

"Careful!" one shouted. "Don't be injuring it."

"Keep that rope tight," another ordered. "Might have to tire this one out."

Looking to the girl, the unicorn whinnied desperately, begging for help, but the girl only watched from her perch in the middle of the field, and finally bowed her head in shame. Panic had the unicorn now and she bayed and struggled with everything she had, but the humans were overwhelming in the numbers they had. She was theirs now, and they all knew it.

She sounded another desperate whinny, hoping beyond hope that one of her kind would hear her cries for help and come to rescue her.

Her plea would not be answered by a unicorn.

Yelling like a madman, Jekkon burst from the trees and charged toward the unicorn hunters, the closest of whom turned toward him too late to respond to the giant boy whose wrath they were too late in avoiding. The first raised his arm but was crushed to the ground by the huge boy's fist. Not even braking stride, Jekkon brutally pushed the second to the ground and went after the man closest to his unicorn friend, who dropped his rope and fled.

By now, others had abandoned the ropes that held the unicorn and were turning to face the huge boy, drawing their weapons as they unsteadily backed away.

As her restraints were dropped, the unicorn turned and bolted toward the girl.

Jekkon stopped his charge and raised his arms as he yelled again, his voice more of a monster than a boy. Birds fled the trees all around as his voice carried through the field and forest.

Although they were all armed now, the site of this giant they were facing gave them all pause. He was a third taller than any of them and easily twice the girth. His arms were the size of some of their waists! Clearly, bulk was better than weapons and courage fled the field ahead of them. In a moment, they were gone.

Only one of them remained on the field. He was the first that Jekkon had encountered, and he was lying on the ground not moving.

Still growling with each breath, Jekkon looked around him, his eyes pausing on places where they had disappeared into the forest. With his brow still low over his eyes, he looked to the girl and the unicorn, who stood side by side staring at him with wide eyes and open mouths.

His eyes shifting to them in turn, his brow slowly lifted, then arched in the middle.

Unicorn and girl looked to each other.

Shame took the boy's features and his gaze sank to the ground. As the unicorn and girl looked on, his fierce rampage disintegrated into a regretful slouch and frown. His jaw quivered and he began to sob and whimpered, "I sorry. Didn't mean to. I sorry."

The unicorn hesitantly approached him, glancing at the unmoving man who lay crumpled on the ground. Peering into the boy's mind, she felt surges of shame and regret within him. Still, she would not quite go to within arm's reach. She stopped three paces away, still knowing fear of him as she offered, "It is okay, Jekkon. It is okay. You have my thanks for saving me from these men."

With slow, purposeful steps, the girl crept up behind the unicorn, not feeling the awe and avalanche of emotions she should have being this close to a unicorn, but instead feeling that awe and a little fear as she looked up to the huge boy who stood weeping before them. She stopped beside the unicorn, assuring him, "It is all right. Please don't cry. You didn't do anything wrong."

Jekkon's eyes slowly turned from the ground to the girl.

The unicorn could see there in his features that his rage had passed and her fear of him leaked away from her, and she dared another step toward him. "I've always known how to get away from humans who've hunted me, but these men seemed to know what I would do. I would be theirs if you had not come to rescue me."

"But you told me stay hidden," he reminded. "I sorry I didn't do what you said."

"I wanted you to stay hidden for your own protection," the unicorn informed. "You were right to come out and fight for me. You were very brave."

He lowered his eyes again.

Looking to the girl at her side, the unicorn asked, "How long have you been doing this?"

This time shame found the girl's eyes and she begged, "Forgive me. Please, I'm sorry. I really didn't want to."

"I know you didn't," the unicorn assured. "How did you come to be with them?"

"They conscribed me from my village," the girl replied. "They took me from my family and forced me to sit in this field every day."

"How many unicorns?" the unicorn asked, her demeanor less pleasant.

Looking away, the girl reluctantly answered, "Three."

Jekkon stomped forward. "Not take any more horsies!"

Gasping, the maiden backed away, her wide eyes locked on the huge boy.

"Jekkon!" the unicorn scolded, her eyes narrowing as he stopped in front of her. "She did not want to do what she did and she feels regret for it." Raising her head, the unicorn suggested, "Perhaps you should protect her as well."

He blinked, staring down at the unicorn, then asked, "Find Janees?"

Smiling, the unicorn shook her head and conceded, "Oh, come on." She turned, then paused and looked to the maiden.

"Will you come with us? Perhaps you know of a village nearby that has humans who will take care of you two."

The girl raised her hands to her chest, her breath fleeing from her. She looked up at the huge boy, then back to the unicorn and whimpered, "You would have me go with you? Even after...."

"Unless you prefer the company of the unicorn hunters," the unicorn countered.

Frantically shaking her head, the girl exclaimed, "No! No. I would be honored just walk the same path as you."

"I was hoping you would come," the unicorn said with a smile, and as she paced on she added, "Although I have no idea how I am to care for you two."

The maiden looked up at the huge boy, still knowing fear of him.

He smiled. "I'm Jekkon."

She forced a smile back. "I am called Dorell."

"You two coming?" the unicorn called back from many paces away.

They turned and hurried to catch up, Dorell stumbling a little as her bare foot found something sharp in her path.

"I think I can find my village," the maiden declared. "If we can get back to the road just to the north of here it should take us there."

"Then there is where we should go," the unicorn agreed. "I will stay with you until you know you can reach your village, but then I must be on my way."

"Won't you come with us?" the girl asked, sounding a little upset.

"My place is in the forest," the unicorn explained. "Yours is with your people. I shouldn't be seen by your people so I must disappear into the shadows."

"May I tell people I saw you?" Dorell asked hopefully.

The unicorn offered her a smile. "Of course, as long as you don't tell the hunters."

"I promise," the girl assured.

"I'm hungry," Jekkon complained.

Unicorn and maiden looked up at the huge boy and the unicorn suggested, "Perhaps we should find that village and get him something to eat—and very soon. Dorell, after we part ways, can you look after him and, perhaps, help him find his Janees?"

"My word," the girl assured. "I'll do whatever I can to help him."

The unicorn could sense that the girl would want to see her again and she gave her a coy, sideling look. "I'll be visiting from time to time to make sure you do."

A broad smile overpowered Dorell's lips.

Jekkon suddenly stopped.

Dorell and the unicorn stopped a few paces away and looked back at him.

"They won't like me there," he said with dread in his voice. "Nobody likes me."

"I like you," the unicorn corrected.

He looked to her, then to the girl.

She glanced at the unicorn, then her brow arched and she looked up at the boy. "Well, I guess I could get acquainted with you, then I would...."

His lips tightened until his mouth was barely a slit under his broad nose.

Dorell turned desperate eyes to the unicorn.

Shaking her head, the unicorn looked up at the boy and assured, "I think she will like you just fine once she knows more about you. You humans are strange about hiding what is in your hearts and even stranger at being able to find it in others. Come along, now. Let's find that village."

The trek resumed with one more, but this newest addition seemed reserved and lost in thought for the most part. An awkward silence followed them the rest of the way across the field and back into the shadows of the forest where they emerged onto a well traveled road a short time later. The unicorn would glance at them in turn, expecting one of them to ask about the other, but neither spoke. She loosed a deep breath, one that whickered there at the end, and she finally asked, "Aren't you two curious about one another?" Still they didn't answer.

Jekkon looked down to her and scratched his cheek. Dorell just glanced about.

Whickering a sigh, the unicorn shook her head again. In a

moment of inspiration, she finally asked, "What is this village like?"

The maiden was a moment in answering, but finally, sheepishly said, "It is a poor village. We farm the fields and raise a few animals, chicken and sheep and the like. We haven't much, just where we live and the few possessions of our homes."

Sensing the girl's shame about her lack of status, the unicorn simply nodded and observed, "You live closely with the land, much like I do." Slowly, she turned her eyes to the maiden.

Dorell smiled slightly, now feeling her place in life was not so shameful after all. "I'd never seen it that way, living as unicorns do." She offered the unicorn a shy glance. "Perhaps living among royalty is not such a pleasant life after all."

"Oh, why would it be?" the unicorn scoffed. "I've seen human highborns. They impress me far less than those of you who live closely with the land." She looked up at Jekkon and said, "Wouldn't you agree?"

He simply nodded.

Looking to the girl, the unicorn informed, "Jekkon has lived among royalty, but I think he prefers the forest over some castle."

Her eyes lighting up, Dorell also looked up to the huge boy and asked, "You lived among the nobles?"

He shrugged.

"What was it like?" she pressed. "Did you attend royal balls and banquets? Have you been to knightings and in the court of kings?"

Glancing at her, he nodded, then he sighed and informed, "Was boring. Had to get dressed up and bathe and look good for nobles. Had to be quiet and not say much."

"It sounds so glamorous," the maiden said dreamily. "I'll wager everything was just beautiful."

He shrugged again and mumbled, "Guess so."

Very little seemed to be of much interest to the huge boy, so the unicorn peered into his thoughts once again, looking for something that might nudge him out of this social cocoon he was wrapped in. There, she found that most primitive of male traits and needs, that one thing that was sure to rouse his simple and straying interest.

With a glance at the girl, the unicorn asked, "Have you ever seen someone who looks as strong as Jekkon?"

The maiden looked to him and shook her head. "No, I haven't. Even the blacksmith of our village doesn't look so strong.

A sidelong glance was the only response the boy would give, but he was clearly listening with some interest.

"I've never seen such a human," the unicorn went on. "I think he must be the strongest in the land."

"How strong are you?" Dorell asked.

Jekkon merely shrugged again.

She glanced around and pointed to a fallen tree at the edge of the forest, one that had much of it cut away by passersby looking for firewood or timber. It was easily seven paces long and thicker than a horse's body, and clearly very heavy. "Can you pick that up?"

He looked at it and shrugged again.

The unicorn stopped and scoffed, "Oh, come now. That is *far* too heavy for anyone to pick up, even someone as strong as Jekkon."

He stopped and looked down at the unicorn, a certain look of defiance in his eyes, then he looked to the log and grunted. Stomping toward it, he reached down and seized one end in his massive hands, growling as he tore it from its resting place on the side of the road. Walking his hands along the trunk, he raised it up on one end, then squatted and rammed his shoulder into it about the center. He wrapped his arms around it rocked it up on his shoulder, then he grunted again as he stood with the massive weight perched and balanced. Slowly turning, he offered the girl and unicorn a pleased smile that showed off many of his oversized teeth. This log must have been far heavier than any horse and he showed some strain in holding it, but he strode toward the girl an unicorn with it and held his head up, beaming with pride.

Dorell's eyes were very wide and she drawled, "Wow," as she stared up at him.

Also amazed, the unicorn smiled back at him and said, "I knew you were the strongest human in the land."

He nodded, then half turned and tossed the heavy log from

him where it slammed into the road with a mighty thump and rolled to the edge of the forest nearly where it had been.

The unicorn whickered to him and paced on, saying, "I don't see how anyone could help but like such a strong boy as you, especially one with such a sweet and gentle heart."

This is what the unicorn was looking for, and she could feel that the girl was seeing him with new eyes.

As the humans caught up to her, the unicorn glanced down at the maiden's feet, which she still walked rather gingerly on. "You don't seem to be well suited for a long journey. Just walking seems to hurt you."

"I don't have any shoes," Dorell pointed out grimly. "I guess they thought I wouldn't run away from them if I was barefoot."

"I suppose so," the unicorn agreed. She looked up to Jekkon and observed, "You don't seem to be having any trouble walking today."

He shrugged.

Many paces later, she was still staring up at him.

He glanced back.

"Does she look very heavy?" the unicorn asked.

Looking to the maiden, Jekkon shook his head.

More paces passed behind them.

The unicorn snorted. "Perhaps you should carry her."

Jekkon's eyes turned to the girl again. He finally took the hint and reached to her.

Dorell shrieked as the huge boy easily swept her from the ground and before she realized, she was cradled in his massive arms.

Perfect, the unicorn thought.

No longer distracted by her hurting feet, Dorell turned her attention once again to the unicorn and the three of them traveled in silence for a time. Once in a while the unicorn would look to the curious maiden with a pleasant, reassuring smile.

In short order the road crossed another, larger road, and the maiden directed them to the right.

"My village is not quite half a league from here," she reported. "I've been this way before. The grain fields should be just beyond those trees ahead."

"Then I should take my leave of you," the unicorn informed.

"Please don't go," the girl begged.

"I must," the unicorn explained. "I should not be seen by the rest of your village."

Dorell glanced up at Jekkon. "What should I tell the village?"

"Just be truthful," was the unicorn's answer. "Tell them he saved you from the unicorn hunters."

"What about you?" the girl asked. "What will you do?"

"There is no reason for you to worry over me. I shall watch over you for a time, to be sure you care for Jekkon." She winked at the girl.

With a nod, Dorell looked to the huge boy and wondered aloud, "How can I possibly explain him?"

"You will know what to do when the time comes." The unicorn stopped and looked up to them. "I shall bid you farewell. Be well, Dorell and Jekkon."

Turning toward her, Jekkon bade, "Bye horsy,"

The teary eyed maiden only managed a wave good-bye with her fingers before the unicorn turned and darted into the trees and disappeared. In seconds not even a sound of her remained, only the wind in the trees and the singing of birds. Now, tears flowed freely and she wept without shame or concern.

Jekkon looked down to her and held her a little tighter, assuring, "Horsy will come and visit soon. Don't cry."

She nodded, then smiled at him and slipped an arm around his thick neck. "Thank you. I'm glad you are here with me."

"Horsy wants us to stay together," the boy informed. "Said so. I stay with you until we find Janees."

"I'll help if I can," she assured.

They did not speak as he lumbered toward her village still carrying her. As the road snaked through grain fields, Dorell glanced about at the many peasants, half of them women, who were dotted about toiling with a variety of tasks, some of which included harvesting part of a field on one side. Ox-drawn carts sat idle as bundles of dried grain stalks were carried on the shoulders of a few women and young men were tossed on one of the three half full carts. A fourth was idle and unhooked from its ox team, leaning over at a sharp angle as a few men tended a wheel which lay on the ground beside it. It would seem that this part of the harvest had just begun, even though dark would be coming soon and the fields would have to be left.

Jekkon seemed to barely notice the activity around him and really did not acknowledge the looks from those who stopped what they were doing to stare. Dorell, on the other hand, nervously glanced about, unsure how her return with this giant boy would be received by her people. Her fears would be compounded as many in the fields slowly approached the road, all warily eyeing the boy who carried her.

One of the men at the damaged oxcart looked toward them, then alerted the others, pointing as he had their attention.

A score or so of people approached, many men at a slightly quicker pace than the women who neared with a mix of curiosity and fear. The men all paused to pick something up, some taking pitchforks, some taking squared cutting implements; a few of them carried sickles. It was clear that they were approaching with weapons, and Jekkon slowed his pace.

When Dorell felt as if he was going to put her down, she quickly ordered, "No, don't put me down." When he glanced at her, she could see a little fear in his eyes and assured, "No one will hurt you."

He glanced around at the approaching people again and stopped.

Unsure herself what they would do, she glanced around at them again, looking desperately for a familiar face. "Oh, I'm sure he's out here."

"Who?" the boy asked.

"My father. He works the fields and tends to the tools they use."

"That him?" the boy asked, raising his chin to a man with a pitchfork.

She shook her head as the closest of them neared to within about thirty paces. "No, he's taller with..." She pointed and declared, "There he is!" She waved and called, "Papa! Papa!"

A man with graying sandy blond hair and a white streaked beard stopped and raised his head, squinting as he looked sharp at her, then he called back, "Dorell!" as he quickened his pace and hurried ahead of the others. He was wearing what peasants wear, but his white wool trousers were stained almost completely brown and he wore no shirt, only a leather jerkin with many pockets that were laden with an assortment of tools. His arms were rather big and his dirty hands were rough and scarred. One was bandaged and the other carried a sickle.

Jekkon was even more uneasy as they drew closer and his brow was arched high over wide eyes that darted about at the men who approached him.

"It's okay," Dorell assured. "Put me down now." As he bent down slightly to set her gently to the road, she slid from his arms and turned to her father, running the few last paces to him and jumping into his arms.

They held each other tightly for a long moment as they had not seen each other for some time. Though her eyes were squeezed shut, a few tears escaped anyway as she buried her cheek in his jerkin.

He finally pushed her away a little and took her chin, raising her face to look down into her eyes. "I've missed you, little girl."

"I've missed you too, Papa." She saw his eyes shift to the huge boy behind them and guessed, "I suppose you are wondering about him."

He nodded.

"I have so much to tell you," she informed.

One of the larger men, a black haired, bearded fellow with similar wool trousers and no shirt, thrust his pitchfork toward Jekkon and shouted, "Go on, now. Away with you!"

Jekkon flinched and stepped back.

Dorell pulled away from her father and backed up toward the boy, spreading her arms as she informed, "He isn't going to hurt anyone. Just leave him alone."

"Step aside, Dorell," the man with the pitchfork ordered.

Many others approached, holding their weapons ready.

Looking back and up, Dorell saw the huge boy's face. His eyes were wide and glossy with tears and his lower lip quaked. He was so tall, so huge, and yet this was someone who looked very much like a young child who was about to cry. Though happy to finally be home, the maiden found her anger roused by her people and she turned scolding eyes back on them. "I said leave him alone!"

Her father took a couple of steps forward, reaching his hand to her as his eyes were locked on the huge boy. "Dorell, just give me your hand. Come now."

"No, Papa," she defiantly barked. "No one is going to hurt him."

"Now, Dorell!" her father ordered. "Now!"

"I won't," she cried. "I promised the unicorn I would take care of him and I will."

Everyone in the field froze. No one spoke.

Another man, one with long gray hair and a white beard approached her father and said, "She's been bewitched."

Nodding, Dorell's father agreed, "I see. Dorell, give me your hand and come to me now."

She glanced around at the people who now were crowding around them. "You don't believe me. Papa, the men who took me were hunting unicorns. It was a unicorn who brought Jekkon to save me from them. He freed me from them!"

Uncertainty rippled through the score of people who were gathered and their murmuring gave no comfort.

"Dorell," her father said in an understanding voice. "Just take my hand so I can take you home, and you can tell me all about it."

"I don't want anyone to hurt Jekkon," she whimpered.

The black haired man with the pitchfork shouted, "Then he should go back where he came from!"

All of the men raised their weapons and yelled in agreement.

"If he goes," Dorell cried, "I will go with him!"

A hush fell over them again.

The gray haired man leaned to her father and suggested, "So long as she is with him we'll never free her of him."

He nodded again, then he dropped the sickle and hesitantly stepped toward her. "It's okay, Dorell. We don't want to hurt him. I just want to take you home."

"I need to take care of him," she insisted. "I promised the unicorn I would."

Her father nodded to her and assured, "I know, Dorell. I know. Let's just go home and talk about it." He reached to her and bade, "Come along, now."

She hesitantly reached to him, a little suspicion in her voice as she insisted, "Promise me no one will hurt him."

He nodded, then abruptly seized her wrist and jerked her to

him, retreating with her into the crowd of villagers.

"No!" she screamed. "Please! I have to take care of him!"

Jekkon backed away as the men advanced on him. His eyes darted about to the weapons they carried and he whimpered.

Dorell's heart broke a little as she saw the first of the tears escape from his eyes. "Please," she implored. "Don't hurt him. Please."

Someone thrust a pitchfork at him.

He raised his hands before him and begged, "Don't!"

A sharp whinny behind him drew everyone's attention. When a hush fell over the crowd again and everyone froze, Dorell twisted away from her father and ran to the huge boy, grasping his hand with both of hers as he half turned to look behind him.

The unicorn paced casually to the boy's side, looking tenderly up at him. She leaned into his leg and brushed up against him almost as a cat would do, then she looked to Dorell, stopping before her.

"I'm sorry," the maiden whimpered.

"There is no fault here," the unicorn assured. "I was watching. Your kind fears what they do not understand."

"I tried to stop them," she said desperately, fearing the unicorn was angry.

"I know you did," the unicorn replied softly. "They will not embrace him as easily as you did, but perhaps I can help convince them." She winked, then turned toward the crowd of people who had quietly backed away a few steps. Rearing up, she kicked at the air and whinnied in spectacular form. None of those from Dorell's village had ever seen a unicorn before and they all just stared at her with wide, awestruck eyes.

The unicorn slammed her hooves onto the road, lowering her head as she kicked at the earth beneath her, then she raised her head and looked right to Dorell's father, ordering, "Summon him here." She seemed to know that none but Dorell herself would understand her.

Looking to the sandy haired man, the maiden beckoned him to her.

He hesitantly approached, his eyes still on the unicorn.

This time it was the daughter who reached out, and she took

his hand in hers, then turned and took Jekkon's hand, bringing them together. Her father was still afraid, but also felt trust now.

The huge boy gently took the man's hand in his and shook up and down, saying, "I'm Jekkon."

He nodded to the boy, then looked to the unicorn who backed away a few steps with his daughter.

Glancing at the crowd of peasants, the unicorn nodded and said, "I think they understand now."

The gray haired man stepped toward her, stopping just a few paces away before he announced, "This is a great omen!"

The unicorn rolled her eyes, then looked to Dorell. "I'll be going now. Just remember that I will be watching you and I may just visit when you don't expect me to."

"I will," the girl assured softly.

Nuzzling the girl, the unicorn whispered, "You have a good and pure heart. That is why the unicorn hunters chose you. That is why I did, too." She abruptly turned and galloped back down the road, whinnying back, "Tell them all I'll be watching!"

Dorell's eyes streamed tears and she smiled, covering her mouth as if she wanted no one else to see. When the unicorn disappeared into the forest, the maiden turned to her people, wiping the tears from her cheeks as she informed, "She'll be watching."

The gray haired man drew a breath, then nodded to her and offered, "Dorell, you have my humblest apology. You have been touched by a unicorn and we shall listen to you with trust from now on."

Turning her eyes from the gray haired man to her father, Dorell sheepishly asked, "We can take care of him, then?"

He slowly shook his head. "I'm not sure how."

The black haired fellow looked up at the boy and added, "How are we supposed to even feed him? We barely can feed what we have in the village."

Concerned mumbling rippled through the crowd.

Dorell glanced around, then took her father's hand from Jekkon and said, "He is very strong. He can help with harvest and all the many things the village needs."

Her father glanced at her. "I can see he's strong, but..."

Her eyes finding the damaged cart, the maiden bade, "Come

on!" as she started to run toward it, then she hopped on one foot, barking "Ow!" as she lifted the other and grasped it with her hand.

Jekkon strode toward her and scooped her from the ground as before.

"To the oxcart!" she announced, pointing toward it.

The crowd of people followed.

When they arrived, Dorell jumped out of the huge boy's arms, into the waiting bundles of grain, then turned over and grasped the cross-rail and looked up at him, ordering, "Pick up that side of the cart. Go on, show everyone how strong you are."

He looked down at the bare axle, one that was black with some kind of grease. Reaching to it, he grasped the axle where it was larger, inside of where the wheel would go on, and picked it up more than half a height from the ground, girl, grain and all.

Mumbling rippled through the crowd and many of the men nodded their approval.

"Come on," the black haired fellow ordered, dropping his pitchfork. "Let's get that wheel back on before the boy tires."

"It would've taken four of us to lift that cart half loaded," someone else observed.

Another added, "And time we don't have to unload and reload it."

As two men got the wheel back on and Dorell's father worked the keeper pin in place, the gray haired fellow strode up to Jekkon and patted his back, observing, "You're no monster. I'll bet you can be of great help with the harvest."

A woman in a dirty white dress and apron stepped forward and asked, "How will we feed him? We've barely enough to feed the village and Pinetop Castle hasn't yet come for their tribute."

Jekkon gently set the cart back down and informed, "Pinetop gone."

A collective gasp hushed the villagers.

A woman looked to one of the men near the cart and said, "The smoke you saw."

He nodded. "Aye, that would mean a battle."

"We've no protection now," someone declared. "Without Pinetop Caste's army we'll be open to attack by any wandering barbarians who come this way!"

The gray haired man countered, "We have him," pointing to Jekkon. "Their army only came to the village for food and our wares, often our women. I say good riddance."

"But how do we protect the village?" someone shouted. "One giant alone can't stand against a whole barbarian hoard or an invading army!"

The gray haired man raised his hands and ordered everyone to silence. Looking around, he declared, "The omen of the unicorn is clear. This boy has been brought to us by Addor's daughter to deliver us into freedom. The unicorn will not allow us to fall under another army's boots. We will convene the council in the morning to speak of our future." He looked to the huge boy and slapped his arm. "Maybe you'll stay on and help us with the harvest, eh?"

People crowded around him again, this time to welcome him.

And as he grinned at finally being accepted, Dorell grasped the cross-rail with both hands and laid her chin in her fingers, smiling up at the huge boy. Very quickly, and with the help of that magical unicorn, she had grown rather fond of him, herself.

CHAPTER 6

Janees found the cabin without any trouble. It was not very big, perhaps twelve paces across and eight or ten deep. The wall she was looking at had only a single shuttered window. The door, apparently, was on the other side. The tall stone chimney was cold and no smoke erupted from it. The cabin was located in a rather barren looking place that was surrounded by lush forest. Not much was growing here, only a little scrub and some odd grass. Looking around her, she had emerged seemingly out of thin air into the bright evening sunlight.

With a deep breath, she slowly approached, walking around to what appeared to be the front, and sure enough she found the big, wooden door. The timbers were gray and very thick, very heavy, and looked very old. This cabin had been here for many seasons. A large, neglected garden was only a few paces outside the door, one that looked to be as large as the floor of the cabin itself.

She drew another deep breath and reached for the iron ring that dangled from it, grasping it gingerly at first, then more firmly as she realized it offered much resistance. As she pulled, a mechanism clicked and she pushed the door open.

Ancient black iron hinges creaked loudly as she slowly opened it. There was light within and her nerves were pulled even tauter. She felt that once she was inside her life would change, and she feared change.

She peered inside, scanning what was within before she would commit herself to entering. On one side was a rather large fireplace. That whole part of the wall was stone and a long timber mantle, perhaps three paces long, hung above the fireplace that was perhaps two paces wide itself. Wood was stacked within with kindling beneath, ready to be lit. A large iron pot hung above it on an arm that could be turned to bring it out of the fire. A simple, old table sat in the middle of the room with a few books stacked on it and an oil lamp burning in the middle of it. The wall across from the door could barely be seen as it was shelves from floor to ceiling, shelves that bore a burden of hundreds of books. Janees' brow shot up as she saw them.

She loved to read and had taken to the written word in two languages very young. The other wall was where she found a simple cot with what appeared to be a feather pillow and a few blankets folded on it. A table beside it had more books on it and another lamp was burning to illuminate that end of the cabin. There, a window was closed and shuttered. The place smelled a little musty and did not appear to have been cleaned for some time.

"Hello?" she greeted. Stepping inside, she held her hands close to her, her full lips parted a little with uncertainty as her eyes darted about. "I'm here," she announced. "I was sent by that dragon in the desert."

No one was there to answer.

The door slammed behind her and she barked a scream as she wheeled around, her wide eyes finding it and locking on the top hinge which was a black, hammered piece of iron that spanned the width of the door and held the timbers together. Slowly, she reached for the ring and pulled it open again, propping it open with a stool that was near the door beneath a shelf full of what appeared to be supplies. Many clay jars were there as well as a few other cooking utensils. Shelves on both sides appeared to be loaded with ancient house wares and antiques.

Glancing around her again, she finally resigned herself to the fact that she was alone.

What to do now.

She turned to the cabin again, and first approached the cot, reaching to the shutters and unlatching them. She opened them and used the hooks that had kept them closed to keep them open with nails that protruded from the wall in the right place on either side. With more light within, she turned to the room and set her hands on her hips. A basin full of water and a full pitcher beside it was on the wall with the other supplies, and a crate full of rags was beneath it. It was time to start cleaning the place.

***

The dragon had not mentioned this part. Tending the things she needed to tend had always been part of her life, something she always had to do to get by. She never minded playing cook or hand maiden to whoever she had to. But this! This place was horrible! It did not look like it had been cleaned for many seasons, and that smell!

With windows open, including the one that had been hidden behind books on a shelf, and the door propped open, the smell was getting better. The wooden floor was nearly clean. She had ended up fashioning a broom out of some straw she had found outside, some twine she had found inside, and an old walking stick that was near the fireplace. Quite a bit of dust was taking to the air as she worked, but much of it fled out of the door as a breeze was blowing into both windows and out the door is where the sweepings went.

That was the last task, and once done she took her makeshift broom to the fireplace.

A couple of hours of cleaning this place had left her weary and she set the broom down in the corner and rubbed her brow with the back of her hand, then she turned to the door and barked a very loud scream.

The man who stood in the doorway consumed most of it. Dressed in black robes, black boots and a black hood, he was a menacing sight. The hood was over his head and she could not see his face above the nose, but what she could see of his mouth told her that this was a rough looking fellow with very dark skin, almost black itself.

Janees backed into the corner, her wide eyes on him as he reached to his head with one hand and slid the hood back. His movements were fluid and deliberate, much like those of a forest cat. His hands were huge. Dark eyes scrutinized her beneath a bushy brow and a bald head. She finally noticed the sack that was held in the grip of his other hand. At times like these she was always thankful to have Jekkon nearby. He always lent her that sense of security, almost invulnerability. Now, without him, she would face this big man alone.

He looked her up and down, then tossed the sack onto the table and folded his arms.

She swallowed hard, staring back at him with wide eyes. Finally mustering a little courage, she managed to say, "I—I was sent here."

He just stared at her, and his eyes narrowed slightly.

Janees drew a breath and continued, "I, uh… I encountered a dragon and he opened a void in the rock for—"

"I know why you are here," he finally said in a very deep, booming voice. "Do *you* know why you're here?"

Hearing his first words startled her and she found herself hesitant to answer, but nodded and replied, "I do. I—I—I was sent here to learn magic."

"Then you don't know why you're here," he countered.

"But... But he sent me here—"

"To learn magic?" he roared. "Did you come here to study the craft, to devote your life to what you claim you wish to learn? Or do you wish to indulge these little girl's fantasies of learning tricks to impress those of higher status than you?"

"I..." Janees found herself stammering and simply did not know what to say or do. This man was so intimidating, so overwhelming. It was almost like being back in the presence of that dragon again. Shamefully, she lowered her eyes and confessed, "I don't know how to answer you. I was sent here to learn."

He finally advanced into the cabin, his boots making such a horrible, hollow sound on the floor that she thought they would haunt her dreams for sure. He scrutinized her a moment more, then shook his head. "I don't think you are worthy. I don't think you wish to learn the craft and become part of the life that is the *sortiri.*"

"I cleaned your cabin," she informed, feeling herself about to cry.

"And you would like to be rewarded?" He huffed a laugh. Shaking his head, he turned toward the basin of water and finished, "I have no need of a house girl, but I suppose I can feed you before I send you on your way."

She turned her eyes to him and whimpered, "Send me away?"

"You have no wish to learn the craft. You simply want to learn parlor tricks to amuse those around you. You have no idea what the *sortiri* is or what it means to study it."

"Then teach me," she challenged. "If I'm so ignorant then—"

"Ignorant you are," he interrupted, "and ignorant you will stay." He reached his hands into the basin and lifted them out cupping water, which he splashed onto his face and head. He shook his head, then blotted his face on his baggy sleeve and turned to her. "Do you even know what you are asking me to do? Do you know what I will have to give up to teach you the craft?"

She was wringing her hands together without realizing, her brow arched in despair. "Please," she begged. "I've learned so much already. I... I've come so far."

He folded his arms again. "Have you, now? What have you learned? What forces do the *sortiri* control?" When she did not answer he continued, "Why this interest in the craft, anyway? Why do you think you can wield a sorcerer's power?"

"I already can," she informed. "Some consider me quite a powerful sorceress."

"The ignorant can be fooled into believing almost anything," he scoffed, turning away from her again. "You may stay here the night, then you will go home."

As he began removing his traveler's cloak, she looked away and said without realizing, "I have no home."

"You're young," he countered, "so you have time to find one,"

Turning her eyes down, Janees wiped a tear from her cheek and pitifully asked, "What must I do? How do I prove myself to you?"

"You can't." He hung the cloak on a hook near the basin and turned to face her. "You never answered me. Why do you want to learn the craft?"

She considered, then wiped her eyes and turned them to him, straightly answering, "I am a sorceress already. The gift is within me. It always has been. I just don't know how to use it."

He nodded, and seemed to be thinking over her words. "And how will you use this gift? What would you do with it?"

Again she hesitated to answer, but finally managed, "I... I will travel the land to help those in need. I can..." She stopped speaking when he laughed.

He seemed to enjoy himself for a moment, then he shook his head and observed, "You are nothing if not entertaining. Is that speech meant to convince me that you are worthy of the craft? You sound as if you are trying to convince your village to make them you their leader."

"I don't know how to answer you!" she cried. "Please, just tell me what to do!"

He just stared at her for long seconds, then he shook his head again. "Okay. Suppose I ask you something you should already know, since you are already a sorceress with this extraordinary gift within you. What is the first lesson a sorcerer should know?"

She blinked, then looked away as she pondered his question.

"It's easy," he informed in a loud voice. "You claim that you mean to take your knowledge throughout the land on a crusade of good, so what is this lesson? What should you learn before wielding the *sortiri?*"

"Um," she stammered again. "The lesson should... To wield the *sortiri*—"

"Answer in one word," he ordered.

She nodded and thought harder.

"Is it that hard?" he pressed. "Come now. Just answer."

Janees vented a breath and would not look at him, simply replying, "I don't know."

"What should every sorcerer know first?" he asked.

Again she struggled to find an answer.

"I see a storm raging between your ears," he observed, "but not much else." He growled a sigh and shook his head again, then took his cloak from the hook and turned toward the door. "You'll find rabbits in the sack and vegetables in the garden. I prefer them stewed. I may be back before nightfall and I may not. See to it dinner is ready by then."

As he left and slammed the door behind him, she glanced about in a search for cooking wares, then her eyes locked on the sack. Slowly, she approached and gingerly took the edge in both hands, hesitantly opening it. Peering inside, she grimaced and quickly closed it again. After a good shudder, she let go of the sack and turned to the shelves where the few knives and other cooking wares waited.

CHAPTER 7

Shahly galloped into the clearing, her flanks heaving as she gasped for breath from her long run. Glancing around, she called, "Vinton!" She looked to the grass before her where the dragon had been, seeing that it was crushed down where he had been lying, then she scanned the clearing for her stallion again. She had not realized she had been gone so long, but the sun was already low in the west.

The vast clearing in the forest, now shaded by the trees on the west side, was eerily quiet, but for awakening night creatures. Rabbits had returned to nibble on the greens, now that the dragon had left. Small predators were not quite so quick to return, fearing that the dragon would still be lingering about somewhere.

Something was amiss. Catching her breath, she calmed herself and her senses heightened. The slow summer breeze snaked through the trees and the grass in front of her undulated in gentle waves as it passed. The forest seemed a little *too* quiet.

Slightly turning her head, she warned, "Don't." As she looked behind her, she met her stallion's eyes. He was holding his head low and his bared teeth were dangerously close to her haunch. A bit of a smile touched her as she held him in her gaze. "I felt you coming up on me this time," she informed.

"I see that," he observed. Unexpectedly, he bit her anyway, then turned and ran.

She whinnied and jumped as she always did, then turned in pursuit.

They could not know how long their chase lasted, but they ended up near that creek where they had found the dead grawrdox, and as before, they veered wide around it on their way to the creek. The forest was almost entirely shadow now, but a unicorn can see well in dim light and they have senses most other creatures do not. Still, they are not at home in the dark and would only seek a drink before finding a safe place to bed down for the night.

On their way down the slope, Shahly paused at one of the bushes to nibble some of the berries from it, and Vinton joined her. This would not be a feast, only a snack and soon they were trotting to the water again, following the sound of the babbling water. They lowered their heads for a drink, exchanging frequent glances as they quenched a thirst born of a fast chase.

Vinton raised his head slightly and informed, "You bite harder than me."

She paused long enough to counter, "You have more to bite."

He whickered a laugh and looked back to the water.

"Where did you go for so long?" he asked.

"I found a lost human child," was her answer.

He raised his head, turning a probing look on her as he pressed, "And...."

Shahly also lifted her head to meet his gaze. "*And,* I helped him find his way back to his people. I couldn't just leave him there all alone."

The stallion just stared at her for long seconds, then heard himself ask, "So how many others saw you this time?"

"Just a few," she confessed, looking away from him. "Okay, much of their village saw me. I didn't want them to turn him away. He didn't seem like he could care for himself all alone."

He huffed a sigh and shook his head. "If you were any more caring I just wouldn't know what to do with you."

She smiled and lowered her head to the water, countering, "I'm sure you would figure something out."

Vinton just watched her drink for a moment, then he dipped his mouth into the water too.

Shahly raised her head again and glanced around her, suddenly feeling a little nervous as she remembered the huge hunting birds she had encountered that day. She could still smell what remained of the carcasses of those killed by the dragons, but she had seen others flee into the forest and feared that they may still be close by.

Vinton turned his eyes tenderly and protectively to her, assuring, "I'm certain they've gone, Love."

She nodded, and scanned the forest across the creek once more.

He butted her gently with his nose then he jerked his head up and looked behind him.

Shahly felt a slight tremor on the ground and heard the

distant thump of footfalls and also looked behind. Something was coming, something big! No, something massive!

Vinton turned slowly, noiselessly, and motioned for Shahly to take his side.

Her heart thundering, she glanced around at the cavernous shadows all around, expecting whatever it was to emerge at any moment in a full charge to attack them. She felt Vinton fold his essence around them both and was reassured by this, but still found herself gripped with fear and near panic, a feeling that part of her still craved.

It's okay, Love, he thought to her.

The footfalls were slow and very heavy. Whatever was coming was walking on two legs and Shahly feared one of the birds had returned. No. This was far bigger!

A dragon strode into view, and in the waning dusk light they could make out his massive form, his bull-like horns, and the tusks that were as long as Vinton's foreleg! The Tyrant himself was coming for a drink.

His tail was parallel to the ground and his back nearly was. He held his long, thick neck as he did his tail and walked with long strides, his feet slamming casually into the ground. He strode toward and to the other side of a small grove of trees about halfway up the slope and somehow looked even bigger as he passed them. Finally reaching the creek, he dropped to all fours at the water's edge where it was deeper and opened his jaws, scooping a horse's weight in water from the creek. As he lifted his head, his lower jaw sagged under the weight. Raising his snout, he swallowed it in one loud gulp.

He turned his eyes across the creek and they began to glow red as he tested the air in many loud sniffs, then he swung his huge head toward them, directing those red glowing eyes their way and illuminating the surrounding area.

Feeling that he knew they were there anyway, Shahly stepped from Vinton's protection and greeted, "Hi. It's just us."

Vinton withdrew his essence and took her side, wide eyes staring up at the massive dragon before them. Just his head was bigger than both of them combined!

The Landmaster stared them down for a long, terrifying moment, then he grunted and looked back to the water and took another drink.

"We'll go if we're disturbing you," she offered.

He swallowed a third mouthful of water, then he stood and turned toward them and back up the slope in one motion, circling around the close side of the grove of trees as he responded, "You would know if you were disturbing me."

They watched him stride slowly back up toward the clearing, and when he was out of eyeshot and they heard him crash onto the ground to go to sleep, they finally breathed the tension from them, lowering their heads in relief.

"I don't think the hunting birds will be back here tonight," the stallion said straightly.

"Do you think he would mind us sleeping nearby?" Shahly asked, staring up the slope.

Vinton glanced at her. "Well, he didn't seem to have a problem with us being here, so I suppose if we're quiet and out of his way… Honestly, I don't know."

"There is some thick grass in the trees over there," she observed, "and the forest is really dense there. I don't think we would be noticed by anything."

"Lead on," he whickered.

Noiselessly, they crept toward the trees that grew thick on the slope and found an opening between two large trunks that was just big enough to allow them to pass. The grass they found within had long, broad blades that were halfway up their legs and as wide as Vinton's hooves. Lying down in the middle of it, they pressed their bodies as closely together as they could, and as Shahly turned her head and lay completely to the grass, Vinton circled his head and neck around her, laying his cheek against hers.

Feeling safe with each other, they drifted quickly off to sleep.

***

Shahly could not know if this was real or a dream, she only knew that she was thirsty.

The short walk down to the creek seemed unusually long, and the heavy fog that surrounded her made the going that much more difficult. The fog was an eerie blue in the pre-dawn light and so dense that she stumbled a few times as she was unable to see well. This was a very thick fog, and an unusually cold one for summer.

Shahly finally stopped to get her bearings. Somewhere distant she could hear the water flowing over the rocks in the creek. Distant also was the wind in the trees, which she knew to be all around her. She proceeded slowly down the slope toward the creek, stepping carefully with all four hooves to keep from stumbling again. As the land beneath her began to flatten out somewhat, she expected to find damp earth or sand and rounded stones beneath her hooves, but instead found dry earth and flattened grass.

She stopped again, listening hard all around her. The coldness was beginning to penetrate her and the sounds she was expecting to hear were even more distant. She knew the creek should be right in front of her, that the wind in the trees should be all around her, yet it wasn't.

Lowering her head, she sniffed the ground. The scent of the creek was not anywhere. The scent of the forest was also gone. Fresh cut grass or hay was there instead—and the smell of horses!

She gasped as she raised her head, backing away. Her eyes darted about and her ears swiveled back and forth, seeking any sight or sound familiar to her. Within, her heart thundered so loud she could almost hear it. Still unable to see in the dense fog, she slowly turned and tried to make her way back to Vinton, then she stopped again. Something here was not right. Something here was unnatural. She had felt it a few months ago, when she was in the presence of the wizard that Ralligor called *Magister,* when they had traveled long distances by walking through the fog he had made.

Slowly, she raised her head. The fog was very cold, just as…

"Oh, no!" she breathed. Nothing around her felt familiar. Nothing was the same as it had been when she had risen to simply get a drink. The smell was even different.

She started forward again and in only a few steps ran nose-first into something which made a familiar wooden bump. Backing away a step and shaking her head, Shahly looked ahead of her, creeping a step closer and looking sharp through the fog.

"She's here now," a man's voice said from somewhere behind her.

Shahly raised her head, her eyes turning that way.

"That wasn't the ordeal I'd thought it to be," he continued. "I'm not even as tired as you said I would be."

An old woman beyond the fog replied, "You have grown very powerful very quickly. Just be warned that these creatures are not to be trifled with."

"Not to worry," he assured. "I know where I went wrong the last time."

The fog began to clear and Shahly dared to slowly turn her head.

"Don't underestimate their power," the old woman warned, "and don't assume that you can sway her so easily. She is a creature of the forest and should have been left there."

"Queen Hethan would disagree," the man countered.

Shahly gasped. Queen Hethan? The Queen of Red Stone Castle? She turned fully as she could make out a few figures standing there in the thinning fog a few paces away and she backed away from them.

"They brought their fate upon themselves," the old woman scoffed.

"Still," the man sighed, "I find it wise to be prepared as they are. You warn not to trifle with unicorns? Well, I find dragons to be a much greater threat than any unicorn."

"No dragon is of concern to a sorcerer of your skill and power," the old woman reminded. "In short order you will be the most powerful sorcerer in the land."

"With a unicorn as my prize," he added.

The old woman groaned. "This isn't about the bounty or power or dragons or anything of the like. You simply want a pet to show off."

"Perhaps I do," he confessed. "And perhaps I have one."

"No," Shahly breathed.

The fog thinned more and she could make out vertical iron bars that were mounted into timbers in the ceiling and into timbers on the short wall of the stall she faced. Instead of a wooden stall gate, she faced one made of the same iron that was more than a man's height tall. Straight ahead and beyond it and beyond the humans was a path between other stalls and the only door out of the stable. The other three walls of the stall she was in were of heavy wood from the earth floor and met the rafters of the roof above, far too high to jump over even if she had room to run. The stall she was in was only four paces in any direction and seemed to be in one corner of the structure. The earth beneath her hooves was covered with hay. This place reminded her of a place she had been before, a prison for unicorns at Red Stone Castle. As the fog thinned more and began to disappear, she could make out the humans who stood in front of her, one a tall man in a gold embroidered white shirt that was unlaced halfway down his chest and black riding trousers with similar gold embroidery that were very loose around his thighs. Black boots that covered his entire lower legs were also adorned with gold. His black hair was restrained behind his head and piercing dark blue eyes looked proudly on his captive in a stare that was a little frightening. He was not a big man, only one who fell about the same height and build that most other human males Shahly had encountered, but she could sense great power from him, a power something of the world all around that was concentrated within him. The old woman beside him was of a simple lot with long white hair and very ancient, haggard features. She wore a covering and heavy looking dress with a high collar and ornate gold and silver embroidery all over it. Dark blue in color, it made one feel that she was a woman of some importance. Shahly could sense in her a different power, one that seemed to have been formed of many things, many elements of the land and water, one born of stone and living things. It was confusing and a little frightening in itself.

Behind them stood guards or soldiers, three of them, all of whom also stared at her with fascination and awe.

The man with the black hair smiled. "She is beautiful, isn't she?"

"Aren't all unicorns?" the old woman countered.

"This one is much more than the last," he said almost dreamily. "She looks very young. Do you think she is fully grown?"

The old woman squinted at her, then replied, "Young she is, and mature as well. She's just small. Not very powerful, this one, and yet there is something about her that is. Can't quite put my finger on it."

"I don't think Queen Hethan needs to know about this one," the man informed. "No, she's staying with me." He raised his chin slightly with an inquisitive lifting of a brow. "Look at how she stares at us. Do you think she understands what we're saying?"

"I'm certain of it," the old woman confirmed. "The other one did, didn't it?"

"That he did. Do you suppose this one will speak to me?"

"It may, but will probably need coaxing like the last. We should leave her to get settled. She looks copious stressed and nervous." She turned to one of the guards and ordered, "Have the stable hands bring her food and water and leave her alone otherwise. She'll not be gawked at by the likes of commoners."

The guard nodded to her, then turned and hurried from the stable.

Shahly glanced around desperately. This stable was dark but for the lamps that had been brought by the humans. She did not want to be left alone in the dark. Yet somehow she knew that pleading with these humans for her freedom would be futile. They had her, and she could offer them nothing in exchange for her freedom.

The old woman squinted at her again, then nodded. "Not powerful at all, but still might be useful to us."

"What do you mean?" the man asked with a tone of suspicion.

"Our own talisman to turn on dragons," was the old woman's reply. "Powerful it is, but a strong dragon would shrug it off and level this castle anyway."

The man motioned to the unicorn with his chin. "How does that involve her?"

"The essence of the unicorn is how it involves her. The talisman at Red Stone Castle relies upon it."

"That also relies upon killing them for that essence."

"Aye, it does. But ours does not have to."

His eyes slid to the old woman. "I'm not sure I would want this unicorn used in some dangerous experiments to fight dragons. We should find a more powerful unicorn for that."

"You barely found this one," the old woman scoffed, "and you found the last by accident as well. They are far too elusive to just go into the forest and harvest as one would a deer or pig. We should use what we have."

He sighed. "I still don't like it."

"Oh, I'll not harm the beast. Just make certain you don't make the same mistakes that you did with that other one."

"I'll be careful. Let's allow her to get settled in."

Shahly could not know why she was there, how she was there, or even where there was, but as she watched the humans turn and file out, she felt a familiar loneliness within. They took with them the lamps and all of the light that was in the stable. Outside, there was not much light as the sun still had not risen fully, but what little light was out there was snuffed out as the door closed. She watched the door with desperate eyes for some time after the bolt slid into place. Just standing in the middle of this cage-like stall, her thoughts whirled quickly and in misdirected fashion. She could not bring order to them, and she did not know what to do.

An unknown time later she turned her eyes down. Her thoughts would not be silenced, nor would they find direction. She only wanted to get out of the stable and find her way back to Vinton. Slowly, Shahly laid down where she was, finding the hay beneath her very soft and inviting, no doubt how it was meant to be found. She was aware of her own breathing, quick and shallow. There was something to focus on. Closing her eyes, she made herself breathe deeply, slowly. She had seen Ralligor do this and it seemed to calm him. Perhaps what worked for a dragon wizard would also work for a captive unicorn.

Still upset and distraught, she felt tears roll from her eyes and felt her breath broken. This would not serve her and she knew it, but she could not stop this assault of self-pity, so she merely lived with it for a few moments.

In an instant she remembered many close calls with forest predators. One event involving giant ground birds was still quite fresh in her memory, as it had only happened the day before. Vinton was there, and Ralligor, and the massive dragon Agarxus. Today she had been caught, and not even in a reckless moment. How they had taken her was still a mystery. Point was they had taken her. At least they were not hungry forest predators that meant to eat her. She hoped.

Finally, some order was returning to her mind.

Her eyes flashed open as the bolt that locked the stable door was pulled back and the door swung open. She finally noticed, as more light swept in, that the stable had eight stalls, but only the one she occupied was built like a cage. The place was made of stone and old timbers with a dirt floor that had been raked and evened. No straw was in the other stalls, nor tack or anything that one would expect. The place was empty but for the stall walls and the enchanted iron bars around the one she was in.

As the humans had said, food was brought to her by other humans. Three of them sulked in, two female and a male who carried a rusty old oil lamp. They would not look at her. Shahly barely took notice of their appearance but they were not dressed as warriors or any humans she had encountered before. The fabric they wore looked old and dirty and as the wind swept into the dark stable she could smell that they did not bathe regularly. She watched their activities with half interest, standing and backing away as they approached the cage.

One caught her eye, the youngest of them. This was a female, a girl barely of age. All three wore hoods over their heads that seemed to be attached to the shirts they wore, but the girl brushed hers about half back to see where she was going. Dark brown eyes were on the burden she carried, a heavy looking bucket that sloshed with water inside.

They never looked up nor did they speak. The older ones set down the hay and wooden bucket of grain they carried, then turned and left, the man hanging the oil lamp he carried on a nearby hook as he walked by. The girl seemed nervous about being left alone, but continued with her duties nonetheless, silently pushing the fresh hay through the bars of the cage.

Now Shahly watched her with some interest, leaning her head as she peered gently into the girl's thoughts with her essence. What she found was not what she expected. Like most of her kind, she had a certain excitement about being so close to a unicorn, and yet she was very afraid. That is why she would not look Shahly's way and her every movement was made with apprehension. Shahly could not reason out why this girl would be afraid of a unicorn and for a moment she was distracted from her predicament by this odd reaction.

Daring to take a step forward, Shahly whickered to the girl, "Hello."

The girl hesitated and started to look up at her, then she hunched over and resumed pushing the last of the hay through the bars.

Taking another step forward, Shahly slowly lowered her nose to the hay the girl was offering and took a sniff. It smelled very sweet and inviting and much of it was topped with some kind of grain. As she sniffed, she felt the girl's heart jump, though she did not seem to react otherwise and simply continued with her labors. With a glance at the girl, the unicorn nibbled some of the hay, then offered, "Thank you."

Slowly drawing her hand back from the last of the hay she had pushed through, the girl almost glanced at her again. She was barely breathing and seemed very excited about a unicorn actually speaking to her, yet she was still very afraid.

"I am Shahly," the unicorn introduced. "What are you called?"

Shrugging her shoulders up, the girl was hesitant to answer, but finally whispered, "Ellyus."

"Why are you so afraid?" Shahly asked. "I won't hurt you."

Again the girl was hesitant to respond and still would not turn her eyes up, but whispered, "I am not to look at the unicorn."

The unicorn raised her head. "Why not?"

Quickly glancing back at the door to the stable, the girl replied again in a whisper, "No eyes of commoners should see the unicorn."

Shahly lowered her head closer and swiveled her ears forward as she whispered back, "Oh. I didn't know that." She glanced at the stable door and assured in a soft whicker, "I won't tell anybody."

Reluctance slowly lost to the girl's eagerness and she raised her eyes to meet the unicorn's, her brow lifting high as her lips parted in amazement. To her kind, she had ordinary features. Nothing about her would have really caught anyone's eyes. Her eyes were very dark brown, almost black. Her face was dirty and unwashed for some time. Unkempt brown hair framed her face and appeared to be very long beneath her hood. This was a girl who was innocent, unknown to her males and unknown to the evil thoughts Shahly had felt from her kind before. She only seemed to want to survive from day to day, and from the look of her she barely did as she was very thin and clearly did not eat well.

With a tilt of her head, Shahly whickered, "See? I'm not so difficult to look at."

A little smile curled the girl's mouth.

"I sure am thirsty," the unicorn informed.

They both heard some noise outside of the door and looked that way, then back to each other and Ellyus whispered, "They mustn't know that we spoke or that I saw you."

Shahly glanced at the door again and informed, "I'll take care of them."

The girl stood and backed away as the door to the stable opened.

The other two humans entered, keeping their eyes down as before. Shahly finally noticed that the woman walked with a limp and favored her left leg. She also seemed eager for contact or even sight of a unicorn, but fear kept her eyes down. The man seemed to have something about him that Shahly did not understand. He was more focused on the tasks ahead of him than he was on her and felt like someone who was impatient and had much on his mind that he had to do. To this end he had intent.

They reached the stall she was held in and she backed away as he pushed Ellyus aside and reached for the bucket of grain. As he picked it up and reached for the latch that held the gate shut, Shahly snorted and kicked at the ground before her. Despite the command to keep his eyes from her, he looked to her in bewilderment and backed away a step, then he backed away another step and held the bucket to the woman. This was a heavy burden that seemed to hurt her as she took the weight and again Shahly snorted and kicked the ground.

The man and woman looked to each other, then to the girl.

When handed the bucket of grain, Ellyus took it with both hands and hunched over a little, not daring to look at the unicorn again. She feared being punished for doing so.

This time, when the man reached for the latch to the gate, Shahly backed away, her eyes on the girl. Ever so slowly the man pulled the gate open, ready for any movement the unicorn might make. He opened it just enough for the girl to slip in with the bucket.

Shahly watched as Ellyus set the bucket down, then turned and reached for the bucket of water as the man handed it over to her. This was heavier and she strained under its weight, but took the burden with both hands and carried it a step further into the stall, setting it down closer to the unicorn than she had set the grain.

Taking a few hesitant steps forward, the unicorn whickered in thanks and lowered her mouth to the water, taking a long drink.

The girl was seized from behind and pulled from the stall and the door was quickly shut and latched.

Shahly raised her head from the bucket of water and watched the humans turn and head toward the door.

Last in line, the girl dared to look back at her, and smiled.

Shahly smiled back and once again watched the door for some time even after it closed. Loneliness crept back into her and she turned her eyes down again, then she took another drink from the bucket before she lay down in the hay to think. There had to be a way out of this. Perhaps the girl was the key to her freedom. Perhaps she could find a way to free them both.

CHAPTER 8

"Are you going to sleep until high sun?" the sorcerer shouted very close to her.

Janees shrieked and woke fully as she tumbled out of the chair and slammed onto the floor. Wide eyed, she looked up at him from her back, gasping for breath.

He folded his arms and looked down at her with nothing that resembled approval on his features. Shaking his head, he turned his eyes to the book that lay open on the table and seemed to read from it for a moment before looking back to her. "Is that what you did all night?"

She looked to the fireplace. No fire in it. The small cauldron she had cooked in still hung over the ashes there. Daring to look back up at him, she replied, "I... I made the stew as you instructed and cleaned up after I cooked. I pulled weeds from the garden... You didn't come back as you said you would, so— "

"I never said I *would* return," he interrupted, "I said I may return. You should listen more closely and pay better attention when someone is speaking to you." He glanced at the book again and demanded, "Why that one?"

She also glanced that way and timidly asked, "What?"

"The book," he stressed. "Why did you choose that one?"

"Um," she started hesitantly. "I... I saw it already on the table... It is a lesson that I started at Pinetop Castle that was incomplete and— "

"Don't tell me about what some hack has attempted to teach you. Frankly, I'm not impressed with what you claim to know or what power you claim you can wield."

"So my extensive studies at Pinetop Castle mean nothing?" she asked.

He raised his chin slightly. "Are you just going to lie there on the floor like that?"

"You didn't tell me to get up," she countered.

"Do I need to tell you to breathe or eat?" Shaking his head, the sorcerer turned and strode to the cold fireplace.

Janees got to her feet and watched him, laying a hand

gingerly on the table as he lifted the lid to the pot and peered inside. "It's probably cold by now," she informed.

"Had you stoked the fire it wouldn't be," was his response. He set the lid back in place and looked under the pot, then he turned and approached again.

Janees flinched as he slammed the book shut, but never took her eyes from his.

"See if you can build a new fire," he ordered, "and reheat the stew without burning it. I worked hard to catch those rabbits and I'll not have them wasted."

She nodded and hurried past him. Working with a crude little shovel, she scooped the ashes from it and carefully placed them into a metal bucket. She could feel his eyes on her as she worked and made her movements as fast and efficient as she could. Once she had cleared out the ashes, she picked up the bucket and turned to the sorcerer, asking, "Where should I go with this?"

He motioned with his head toward the door. "You'll find a pit near the garden." He watched as she hurried to the door and added, "Firewood's on the other side of the cabin. Bring in a few armloads."

She had to make many trips with heavy burdens of firewood until he was satisfied that they had enough for the day. After stacking a few logs in, she reached for the flints, but froze as he loudly cleared his throat, and she looked back at him.

The sorcerer shook his head and impatiently asked, "What are you doing?"

"You instructed me to build a fire," she replied.

He rolled his eyes and vented a deep breath. "So learned in the *sortiri* are you that you feel it is a waste of your efforts to use it to make fire."

Raising her chin, she just stared at him for long seconds, then she looked back to the fireplace, stood, and backed away from it. She held a hand toward the logs and ordered, "*Ignire.*" She shuddered a little as her power coursed through her and she felt it blast through her palm and into the fireplace. The logs exploded into flames which, for a second, engulfed the entire fireplace and rolled out toward the mantle. She shielded her face as she took a step back, and as the fire died down to consume only the logs, she folded her arms and turned back to the sorcerer, raising her chin as she gave him a proud, self-satisfied look.

He looked beyond her at the fire that raged beneath the pot, then looked back at her and said, "Perhaps next time you should only fire the wood. We wouldn't want you burning my whole cabin down."

As he turned to the table and picked the book up, her eyes narrowed slightly and her full lips grew tight in frustration.

He approached the shelves across the room and ran his finger along the bindings of some of the books, his eyes on them as he advised, "You shouldn't try to impress me. Nothing you can conjure or concoct will do so."

She watched him slip the book into its place, then she turned her eyes down as he looked to his left to select another one. She just stared at the floor as he flipped through the pages, her mind scrambling over how to convince him to teach her.

"I'm assuming you can read?" he suddenly asked.

"Yes," she simply answered.

"How many languages?" he asked.

She drew a breath and replied, "I was taught Common until I was eleven and spent the last few seasons learning *Latirus.*"

"That's good," he complimented. "Only a few of these are written in Common." He flipped through a few more pages and observed, "You seem to speak some *Latirus.*"

"*Ic specan Latirus mycel excellere,*" she informed.

He nodded, countering. "*Swa hit wyllan soemer.*" He turned to the table, still studying the pages, then he laid the book down where the other had been and looked to her. "Make sure that stew doesn't burn, and study from this page." He turned back to the shelves and walked to the right side.

She tensed a little, her eyes widening as she dared to ask, "Are you going to teach me?"

"If that stew burns you'll be on your way this morning," he countered.

Janees nodded and turned to her task. New excitement raced through her as she took a wooden spoon she had laid on the mantle the night before to stir the contents of the pot. Glancing behind her, she saw him take down another book, a rather thick one that was bound in wood with twine of some kind and he reached for a pen and inkwell on the top shelf. While she was curious about what he was doing, she knew she dare not ask. It was best to just go about her tasks.

***

A couple of hours later their morning meal was done, Janees had cleaned the bowls and spoons they had eaten from and now she sat with her cheek propped in her hand, studying the words of the book he had opened for her. Nearing the end of the book, she glanced at him every few moments as he sat writing in the old book he had been writing in since their meal.

She loosed a breath and turned the page.

The only other sounds that could be heard were his scribbling and the occasional crackling of the fireplace. The only light was from the oil lamp that burned in the middle of the table and from the one open window.

The room was growing hot and she wiped a few beads of sweat from her brow.

She looked to the fire as the last of the logs was burning down and just watched the flames dance for a time. When the sorcerer cleared his throat in a conspicuous, loud bid for her attention, she met his eyes with a glance before looking back to the words she read. This was something that had been taught to her by two others, written in Common and was, for lack of a better word, boring.

Another sigh escaped her as she struggled to keep her attention focused on the words she read, but it often strayed to other things, mostly Jekkon.

"Distraction will not serve you," the sorcerer suddenly informed.

Her eyes snapped to him again, then lowered to the book.

"What is so important?" he asked.

She was a moment in answering, but finally replied, "My—my brother Jekkon."

"The *sortiri* will demand your absolute focus and attention," the sorcerer told her.

Janees nodded, then loosed a breath, her eyes on the book before her but barely seeing it. "He cannot take care of himself. We were separated after the battle..." She sighed again and offered, "I'm sorry. I—I shouldn't burden you with this."

"No, you shouldn't," he agreed. "Also understand that such a burden will interfere with your studies. You should resolve such problems or put them behind you."

She nodded. When he turned his attention back to the pages he wrote on, she looked to him and asked, "How do I put my brother behind me?"

The sorcerer met her eyes. "How serious are you about studying the craft?"

"But he's my brother," she argued. "My kingdom was sacked and m—my family was killed but for him. I've lost everything and he's all I have left."

"You have your studies," he reminded.

"He needs me to take care of him," she insisted.

"You have a choice to make," he informed. "Choose wisely."

Janees abruptly stood and set her hands on her hips. "Why should I choose between studying the *sortiri* and caring for my brother? I can do both, and if you don't believe me then let's find him and I'll prove it to you!"

He raised a bushy eyebrow.

She lifted her chin. "I didn't want to do this, but I suppose I must. I am *Princess* Janees of Pinetop Castle. The Prince is out on his own and I insist that we go and find him. After that you will instruct me in the *sortiri* and be proud to have the privilege to teach a member of the royal family."

He just stared at her.

A long moment passed and she grew more tense and uneasy with every passing second. Glancing aside, she insisted, "We should leave while w—we still have plenty of daylight." When he still did not move or even blink, she added, "Your princess has spoken, sorcerer."

"We are a long way from Pinetop," he informed, "and I have no allegiance to that castle or its *princess*. If your brother is lost and cannot fend for himself then that's his problem." He stood, looming over her from across the table. "Bear this in mind before you speak again. As a princess you are nothing but a liability to me. You have no authority here or anywhere else, so choose what you will do with your life and choose wisely. Are you going to study the *sortiri* or do you mean to pursue the role of a princess of a beaten and forgotten kingdom?"

He really hadn't even raised his voice, and still he had humbled her like she had never been humbled before. Staring back into his commanding eyes, she was unaware that her mouth was hanging open. Slowly, she lowered her gaze and folded her hands before her, and tight lipped she softly offered, "Forgive me."

"Your answer?" he demanded.

She just stared at the book before her for long seconds, then timidly said, "I am your student if you would have me."

"That remains to be seen," he growled. "Sit down."

She complied, pulling the chair up to the table as she did.

"Close the book," he ordered.

She did.

The sorcerer sat down and folded his hands on the table. For some time he just stared at her as she stared at the book in front of her. Drawing a deep breath, he loosed it through his nose and asked, "What happened at Pinetop?"

Janees swallowed back against a dry throat and answered, "The castle was attacked yesterday morning. The invaders offered no quarter and killed all of the soldiers. They took captives of artisans and laborers and sacked the castle before they burned everything else." She closed her eyes. "The dead and dying were piled inside the palace before they fired it. There were people still alive in there when they burned it. I… I could hear some of their screams as…"

The sorcerer nodded. "I see. Are you thinking about cultivating your *facultas* to avenge them?"

Not looking at him, she simply shrugged.

"So why didn't you call upon this power you say you wield so well to defend the kingdom?"

Janees thought for a moment and chose her words carefully. "They were led by a sorcerer, one whose power and skill far exceed mine. We dueled…" She closed her eyes. "He beat me. He told me that when sorcerers duel, one must lose. One must die."

The sorcerer's eyes narrowed. "Well he sure didn't kill you."

Nodding, Janees admitted, "No, he didn't kill me. He had another fate in mind for me, something horrible." She turned his eyes to his. "He sacrificed me to a young dragon in exchange for that dragon's favor."

"Well, the dragon certainly didn't kill you, either."

Her lips tightened. "He traded me to another dragon, the very dragon who sent me here. He seemed to want the favor of the bigger dragon and thought giving me as a tribute would win him that."

"I see." The sorcerer looked past her, to the closed and bolted timber door. "So who was this bartering sorcerer who spared you to buy favors from a dragon?"

Janees absently ran her fingers along the spine of the book before her as she answered, "He called himself Lord Nemlivv." When the sorcerer groaned her eyes snapped to him and she noticed him direct his gaze and a scowl toward the ceiling. "You know this sorcerer?"

He hesitantly nodded. "I know him. He came to me many seasons ago and wanted to apprentice under me. Had his mother along. She did most of the talking for him."

Grimacing slightly, Janees observed, "That sounds awkward."

"To say the least," he confirmed. "He could not answer that first question, either. Do you remember that question?" His eyes narrowed and bored into her.

She looked down and nodded. "I remember."

"He couldn't answer," the sorcerer went on, "and now he uses his *facultas* in a quest for power. He doesn't understand what it is to master the craft, and he never will."

Janees vented a breath, still staring down at the book on the table. "I wish I had that answer. I don't want to end up like him."

"How do you want to end up?"

She shrugged. "I don't know, just not like him. He's cruel, and so conceited."

"And you still don't have an answer for me, do you?" He rested his chin in his palm and strummed the table with his other hand.

"One word for the first thing a sorcerer should learn," she said absently.

"One word," he confirmed. "What did you think of Nemlivv and his power? Could you feel how much stronger he was than you?"

Nodding, Janees shamefully admitted, "At the end I did. Nothing I did even came close to what he could do. He bound me and took me to the dragon as if I was just something else to trade."

"Humiliating, wasn't it?"

She nodded again.

"And still you don't know the answer."

Janees glanced at him and did not respond otherwise.

"Tell me your impressions of the dragon," the sorcerer ordered.

She thought in silence for a moment, remembering with fondness and dread. "The dragon I was given to by Nemlivv was a powerful beast and the biggest I had ever seen, and yet he cowed before the others."

"Others?" the sorcerer questioned. "I thought he took you right to..." He raised his chin, eying her suspiciously.

"He took me to a really big one first," she reported. "I mean big, as big as the mountain he lives in. He was not interested in me and told the smaller dragon to take me to the third dragon."

"What did he look like?" the sorcerer asked, an inquisitive tone in his voice.

"Huge," was the first thing that stumbled from her lips. "He was a dark green with scales like metal and blue wings. He had really long teeth that stuck out of the bottom of his mouth."

"Tusks," the sorcerer corrected. He leaned back in his chair, making it creak loudly in the quiet room and he just eyed her before he spoke again. "That dragon that had you took you right to the Tyrant. You saw him and lived to tell about it." He huffed a laugh and finished, "Not many have so you should consider yourself lucky."

A chill found her and she shuddered as she remembered hearing stories of a dragon that people called the Tyrant, horrible stories.

"And the other dragon?" the sorcerer pressed. "What are your thoughts on him?"

"The black beast," she confirmed. "I know his name. I'd read somewhere that one could use a dragon's name to control him."

The sorcerer smiled. "Found out different, did you?"

Janees looked aside, feeling a little embarrassed. "Yes. He laughed at me like you want to now."

"With good reason," the sorcerer chuckled.

She glanced at the ceiling. "I thought for sure he would kill me. I… I dueled him. No, I simply…" She loosed a breath and shook her head. "I thought I had learned enough to at least stand my ground, to at least earn his respect."

"Respect from a dragon," the sorcerer chided. "That, my dear, is an undertaking in itself. Power won't win his respect. Strength won't win his respect. There is much, much more you will need to learn."

"Do *you* have the respect of a dragon?" she asked before realizing, and she expected a scolding retort when she did realize.

"As much as a man could, I suppose," was simply his answer. "You must understand that we are little more than food to them, food that can reason and communicate. Try to outwit a dragon and you'll end up in his belly."

"I didn't outwit the dragon, and yet he didn't eat me."

Unexpectedly, the sorcerer smiled. "You amused him. He saw something of you that makes you worth more outside of his belly than within."

She shook her head. "But what could it be?"

"That is only for him to say. Did you learn from that experience?"

"I did," she assured.

"And yet you still cannot answer such a simple thing." He raised his brow and stood from the table. "It's best you think hard about that."

She watched him walk to the fire and pick a stick up, and watched more as he poked at the now smoldering log and ash within. Finally mustering her courage, she asked, "Will you be teaching me more about dragons?"

"I haven't decided to take you on as my apprentice," he answered flatly. "There's something you owe me before I'll even consider it."

She had been here before, and there was only one thing she had to give. Turning her eyes down, Janees drew a breath and slowly stood. He was a big man, very imposing, and she could only hope that he would be gentle with her. She slowly reached over her head, to her back, and seized the nightshirt that had been her only cover for two days. Ever so slowly, very reluctantly, she pulled it over her head and removed it from her. As he poked at the fire, she held the garment to her chest, just staring at the floor as she prepared to sell her dignity once more.

"I'm ready for you," she softly, sheepishly announced.

He nodded. "Glad to see you coming around." He leaned the stick against the stone of the fireplace and turned around, folding his arms as his eyes found her.

She could not look at him. Drawing another breath, a very deep one this time, she said in a tiny voice, "I'll do whatever you want."

The sorcerer looked her up and down, then he cleared his throat and rubbed this thick lips. "Um, what are you doing?"

She glanced about the planks of the floor before her. "I'll do whatever you wish, whatever I must to pay this debt to you. It's all I can offer. Please, just teach me."

He glanced around the room and was quiet for an awkward moment.

Janees managed to swallow back some fear as he finally strode toward her and she flinched as he jerked the nightshirt away and walked past. Closing her eyes as she stood naked in the middle of his cabin, she lowered her arms to her sides and clenched her hands into tight fists, all the while hoping for a gentle touch this time. And she trembled, right until she felt his cloak thrown over her shoulders. As he walked in front of her again, she looked down at the cloak that covered her now, then she turned a look of confusion to the sorcerer.

He folded his arms again and just loomed over her. He seemed to be rejecting her. In his hand was her nightshirt.

She felt tears welling up in her eyes and slowly shook her head, sobbing, "But it's all I can offer. It's all I have!"

"You were not sent here to be my whore," he scolded. "If that's all you are then take your shirt and get out."

"But I thought... I don't understand," she cried. "All of the others... I had to offer them something to teach me. Are you saying you won't teach me?"

"Do you think you owe me something tactile?" he asked with

a harsh voice.

"I don't know," she whimpered. "All of the others who trained me made me give myself to them, or they wanted gold or something." When he just raised a brow she looked away, glancing about. She grasped the cloak from within and pulled it closer to herself, her wide eyes still darting around the room, looking anywhere but at the sorcerer. Confusion and shame mixed within her.

He took a step toward her and held the nightshirt to her. When she gingerly took it from him, he informed, "You have two choices now: Put that on and leave here forever, or burn it." He turned and raised his hand to the fireplace and flames erupted from the ashes and coals. Looking back to her, the sorcerer ordered, "Return to your life as you knew it or burn that shirt and start over. Choose now."

She finally looked up at him, then walked past him and tossed it into the fire. As it exploded into flames, she shielded her eyes against the sudden heat and backed away. She heard him cross the room and stop, then he approached from behind and stopped beside her and also watched the flames, and in a moment all that she had was gone.

"Sorry to see it go?" he asked.

Ever so slowly, Janees shook her head, her eyes on the fire. Something suddenly felt different. She could not be sure, but something in her life had just been changed. Looking up at the sorcerer, she had no words for him, but she did have a new appreciation for him and now more than ever longed to be his student.

He simply watched as the fire burned down, then he raised his chin and said, "You'll prove yourself worthy if you wish to be my apprentice. You'll find that answer or you will be on your way." He finally looked down to her. "The price for my teachings is that answer, your undivided attention, and you following all of my commands."

She nodded and simply replied, "I understand."

"See that you do." He stared down at her for a long moment, then continued, "I'll teach you for a while, and give you time to prove that you are a worthy student. Don't expect this to last long. Give me that answer and your full attention and I may take you on permanently. Fail me and I'll send you back where you came from."

"Pinetop is gone," she reminded.

His eyes narrowed. "You came here from that dragon's lair."

A chill ran throughout her and she gulped an awkward breath.

He turned to the door and strode toward it, pausing to say, "I'll be back when I return. Finish what I told you to read and re-stoke the fire. The garden will also need to be tended to." He turned to the door, pulled it open and left.

Janees watched the door for some time after it closed. At long last, someone who actually cared to teach her. He had not taken advantage of her, and her attempt to give herself to him made her feel foolish and cheap. This embarrassment gripped her inside. What must he be thinking?

She finally turned away from the door and sat down in front of the book, daintily opening it to the last page she had been reading. Tears blurred her vision and she rested her forehead in her palms.

"Perhaps a whore is all I'll ever be," she whimpered.

CHAPTER 9

Agarxus turned his eyes skyward, his teeth bared as he squinted against the sunlight. His jaws swung open and fire exploded from between his teeth. He sidestepped and swung hard, his clawed hand slamming into the head of the dragon with the metallic green scales that descended upon him.

Batted from the sky, the green dragon hit the ground awkwardly and rolled to a stop, struggling to right himself before the Landmaster could attack again. The metallic green scales of his back and sides faded into dark green. The scales on his belly were glossy black as were the dorsal scales that stood erect as he found his footing and stood to face the dragon that was more than twice his size. About the height and build of the Desert Lord, this dragon faced the Landmaster with purpose. His dark blue horns curled downward and then back up, their points angling upward from his head. Baring his teeth as his green eyes bored into the massive dragon, he backed away, then opened his jaws and blasted the Landmaster with fire of his own.

The flames hit the massive dragon's chest and seemed to just shatter. Agarxus roared and fired back. His eyes panned to one side, then he fired the green dragon again and turned to meet the dark brown dragon that charged from his side.

Sweeping his wings forward, the brown dragon, slightly smaller than the green one, lifted himself from the ground and kicked with both feet, curling his claws at the huge dragon.

Agarxus responded in kind, stroking his wings and kicking toward the smaller dragon, but he sent one leg ahead of the other. His longer legs would prove to be an advantage as his foot slammed into the smaller dragon's belly and stopped him cold in mid-air, then he forced him downward and slammed him brutally onto the ground.

Swinging around, the Landmaster abandoned the stunned smaller dragon and turned to face the new threat that descended on him fast from behind.

Ralligor attacked his Landmaster head-on, roaring to announce his approach. As Agarxus raised his hand to counter-attack, the Desert Lord changed direction slightly and then arched his body over, kicking the massive dragon hard in the chest as he wrapped his arms around Agarxus' neck. Pulling one wing in, the black dragon pulled hard and twisted his body to take the Landmaster down.

Sidestepping to regain his balance, Agarxus twisted with the black dragon, spinning around him and eventually landing a blow with his fist to Ralligor's belly that loosened his grip. He spun once more as he seized the Desert Lord's neck, wrenching the black dragon from him and hurling him some distance away.

The brown dragon slammed his body hard into Agarxus' side, driving him sideways.

The Landmaster planted a foot hard onto the ground and brought his elbow down hard on the back of the brown dragon's shoulder.

Roaring, the brown dragon stumbled and dropped to his knees.

Attacking from the front, the green dragon rammed his horns into the Landmaster's throat, then he turned and clamped his jaws shut around the huge dragon's wrist. He underestimated the strength and resolve of the Landmaster and his eyes widened as his teeth failed to penetrate all the way and his head was twisted around as the huge dragon turned his arm and drew it to him.

Recovering from the blow to his shoulder, the brown dragon leapt to his feet and wrapped his arms as far around the Landmaster as he could, trying to drive him off balance as the green dragon struggled in the huge dragon's grip.

As they wrestled, Ralligor, lying crumpled on the dusty battlefield with his wings and limbs sprawled, growled as he slowly stirred and raised his head. The sounds of battle brought him to alert and he staggered to his feet, turning fully just as the brown dragon slammed back-first into him and knocked him backward.

As they rolled to the ground, the green dragon joined them, hitting the brown dragon's back tail first.

They lay in a moaning, growling heap for a moment and the green dragon slowly raised his head, blinking out some of the dust that had settled in his eyes.

Ralligor turned and looked as a shadow fell over them and raised his eyes to meet the Landmaster's. Ralligor snarled and pushed the smaller brown dragon from him, then slowly, stiffly rolled over and drew his wings in, slowly getting his feet under him.

The green dragon staggered to his feet and raised his snout as the massive dragon stared down at them. His eyes narrowing, the green dragon growled, "Have you had enough?"

Ralligor swung his fist and hit the green dragon in the side of the head, ordering, "Keep that snout of yours shut, idiot! *I've* had enough."

The green dragon turned and growled at him through bared teeth.

Agarxus shook his head, snarling as he observed, "You three are pathetic. Now get away from my lair until I summon you again."

They all three turned to walk away, and the Desert Lord looked back once more to ask, "Why can't you just go attack Mettegrawr when you want to fight?" When Agarxus' eyes narrowed, he turned back and opened his wings, sweeping himself into the air, the other two dragons following.

Some distance to the north, not far from the scarlet dragon's lair in a clearing in the forest near the river, the three descended and landed one by one in the center, the brown dragon stumbling as he touched down.

The green dragon dropped to all fours and rubbed his neck right behind his head, opening his jaw to stretch the muscles that had been pulled.

Still limping, the brown dragon reached for his shoulder, a soft growl escaping him as he closed his eyes and arched his neck and head backward.

Ralligor turned his head and spat blood into the trees. He rubbed his chest and extended and retracted one wing slowly to work the soreness out. He also growled, more from annoyance than his aching muscles.

The second oldest of the trio, the green drew a deep breath, then shook his head as he stared at the ground. "You know, we need to find another drake. I'm sure four of us would at least have a chance of getting him off his feet." His was a voice nearly as deep as the black dragon's, though it betrayed a dragon still in his the prime of his youth.

"We have a fourth drake," the Desert Lord informed, "but he's too young and far too small for this, and Agarxus is barely tolerating him as it is."

The brown continued to limp a wide circle around them, and he sighed. "At least he could take a little of the punishment from the rest of us." This was a voice of a dragon who had seen many more seasons than either of the other two, even though he was the smaller of the three.

"Agarxus didn't summon him," Ralligor informed, "and I don't think he had any intention of summoning him."

Finally standing, the green dragon stretched his back and said with a strained voice, "Well, the next time he decides to do this, I'm letting Mettegrawr know. He may just side with us and even things up."

"Bring in a rival Landmaster," Ralligor said absently. "Brilliant. Let Agarxus think that our loyalty is split and give him a reason to do some real damage." His eyes slid to the green. "There's not much going on above your neck, is there?"

"I don't hear you making any useful suggestions," the green dragon growled back.

"Nor useless ones," the Desert Lord retorted.

The brown just grunted at him, then shook his head. "I'm going south. We don't need the Landmaster catching us together like this. Good luck to you both figuring out how to deal with our next beating."

Ralligor and the green dragon watched him take to the sky, then they looked to each other and then into the forest.

"A lot of good that wizard training of yours did us," the green snarled.

"To provoke him more?" Ralligor growled back. "I don't think so."

"Hmm," rolled from the green's throat. "Not that strong with it, are you."

Ralligor shot him an irritated look. "Would you care to see *how* strong I am with it Drarrexok?"

The green dragon collapsed to his belly and slammed his head onto the ground. "Not today, Ralligor. Too tired."

The Desert Lord grunted, his eyes locked on the other dragon, then he followed suit and laid down, himself.

Drawing a deep breath, Drarrexok asked in a sigh, "How long will he let us recover before he summons us for that again?"

"Not long enough," Ralligor snarled.

They would not know how long they lay there resting, but the approaching wing beats of another dragon drew their attention skyward, and the green dragon sprang to his feet.

Sweeping her wings in air grabbing strokes, Falloah descended in her usual graceful form, extending her legs to touch down gently and almost noiselessly, then folding her wings to her. Her amber eyes found the black dragon's quickly and she leaned her head, observing, "How did your sparring with Agarxus go this time?"

He simply grunted and closed his eyes.

Sitting catlike, Drarrexok pushed his chest out and raised his head, his wings half open to add to his size as he reported, "Well hello there. I was hoping you would have the pleasure of seeing me today."

Her eyes shifted to him and she hissed through bared teeth.

"Sounds like the pleasure's all yours, Drarrexok," the black dragon observed.

"As you can see," the green dragon continued, "I'm ready for another go."

Falloah snarled back, "Then perhaps you should."

Looking to the Desert Lord, the green dragon said, "Feisty!"

Ralligor just laid there and grunted.

The scarlet dragon hissed at the green once more, then she turned her attention back to her mate and slowly approached, dropping to all fours as she cooed softly to him. When all she got was a grunt back, she leaned her head and asked, "Was the battle so fierce, *Unisponsus?*"

Drarrexok answered for him, "We showed him that we are not to be trifled with."

Huffing a rare laugh, the black dragon elaborated, "He demonstrated that while his head was between Agarxus foot and the ground." Finally opening his eyes, Ralligor stared off into the distance. "Sooner or later we're going to get that old drake down."

Falloah's brow arched. "Just don't get yourself killed doing it."

"Not to worry," the green dragon assured. "I'll have that old drake on the receiving end of my wrath in short order."

Rolling her eyes, the scarlet dragoness said, "Save your banter for those dragonesses in the East who think you are all of the drake that you do."

"You could also think that," Drarrexok informed, "if you ever gave me the chance to prove it."

The Desert Lord's eyes slowly closed and he warned, "Be very careful, there, Drarrexok."

Falloah hissed at the green dragon again, then turned and laid down beside her mate, her narrow eyes on the other dragon as she did so, but they slowly slid shut.

Drarrexok stared down at them for a time, then informed, "Well you two lead very boring lives, don't you?"

Their eyes flashed open and trained on him.

The green dragon looked away, admitting, "Yes, I heard about the incident with that so called dragon slayer early this summer. It's not like I haven't dealt with a great number of them, myself." He looked to the black dragon and added, "Had I but known sooner than I did I could probably have gotten her away from them long before you did."

Falloah met her mate's eyes and growled.

"I'm sure," Ralligor growled, closing his eyes again.

Hoof beats quickly approached and Vinton charged from the forest, lowering his haunches as he came to an abrupt stop only twenty or so paces from the black dragon.

Drarrexok stood and leveled his body to the ground, baring his teeth and growling as his wings shot out and his dorsal scales stood erect. His tail thrashing in a display of threat, he gaped his jaws and roared a challenge to this enemy of his kind.

Falloah sprang to her feet and turned, roaring in response and blasting the green dragon's head with a burst of fire.

Stumbling sideways, the green dragon shrieked and shook his head, closing his eyes against the flames, then he turned to the scarlet dragoness and bared his teeth, growling back at her.

Ralligor sluggishly raised his head and looked to the green, dryly ordering, "Just relax, Drarrexok. It's only a unicorn." He looked to the bay unicorn, then closed his eyes and laid his head back down, asking with an irritated tone, "What do you want, Plow Mule?"

"Shahly!" the unicorn whinnied, very out of breath.

Raising his head again, the Desert Lord looked back to the unicorn and roared, "What about Shahly?"

"She's gone!" Vinton shouted.

Drarrexok drew his head back, his eyes on the unicorn, then he looked to the black dragon and asked, "You lost another dragoness? How does this unicorn know?"

"Quiet!" Falloah snapped. She turned and strode over to the bay unicorn, dropping to all fours to bring her head down to him. "Vinton, what happened?"

Ralligor also stood and swung around growling through bared teeth, "What do you mean gone?"

Vinton's eyes were trained up on the black dragon's for long seconds, then they directed slowly downward, and he shook his head. "I awoke and found her gone. I followed her tracks and her scent toward the creek, as she awakens thirsty of late, but her trail just ended." He looked back up at the dragon. "It's as if she was lifted from the ground, yet nothing could have flown into the trees to get her and there were no other tracks. Her hoof prints just stopped."

Slowly raising his head, a low growl rumbled from the black dragon. His eyes were fixed on the unicorn's and a red glow began deep in the blackness of his pupils.

Falloah slowly turned to the Desert Lord, raising her head as she saw her mate's eyes. Her own widened a little.

"I couldn't find her anywhere," the stallion went on. "I... I didn't know what else to do or where to go."

Looking back to him, the dragoness assured, "You did the right thing finding us. We'll figure out what happened and find her."

"Where did she disappear?" the black dragon demanded.

"Near the creek where you fought the ground birds yesterday," Vinton answered straightly. "We slept in a grove of trees there last night. No one could even have known we were there."

"Show me," Ralligor ordered. He strode forward and opened

his wings, scooping the big stallion from the ground as he took to the air.

Vinton gulped a breath as the ground quickly fell beneath his hooves and he felt as if his stomach was left behind. "Uh..." he stammered, watching the trees below streak by and grow further below. He was firmly in the dragon's grip, but without the ground right under his hooves, he felt surges of panic shooting through him and he kicked his legs absently even as he fought to calm himself.

"Hold still," the dragon growled. "You aren't light and I'm having a difficult enough time holding onto you."

The stallion's eyes widened and he tore them from the treetops below and looked up at the dragon. "Difficult time holding onto me? How difficult?"

"Just quit fussing and hold still," Ralligor ordered.

"I wish you had warned me," the stallion whickered. "I didn't know I would be flying today."

"It's quicker than waiting for you to catch up," the Desert Lord informed.

"I suppose," Vinton stammered, his wide eyes turning back to the ground.

Ralligor glanced at him and snarled, "You aren't afraid of heights, are you?"

"I am now!" the stallion confirmed.

"Shahly's not afraid to fly with me," the dragon pointed out.

"Shahly's not afraid of anything!" the stallion countered.

Rolling his eyes, the black dragon growled, "Just hold still until we land." Stroking his wings for more speed, Ralligor climbed until the creek valley and dead grawrdox were in sight, then he pulled his wings back and descended quickly, taking a sharp angle toward the ground.

"Slow down!" the stallion shouted.

"I thought you wanted to be back on the ground," Ralligor snapped.

"I don't want to be *part* of the ground!" Vinton snapped back.

Sweeping his wings forward, the black dragon lowered his feet and hit the ground at a run. A few steps later he locked his legs and slid a few paces as he swept his wings forward once more and set the unicorn down in less than gentle fashion.

Vinton stumbled sideways and found his footing on wobbly legs. He was barely stable on the ground when he looked up at the black dragon who strode by with heavy steps, and he followed at a trotting pace, directing, "This way."

"I have her scent," the dragon informed. His eyes panned quickly from one side to the next, then fixed on a place about eight paces from the creek where the trees were denser. He squinted, looking sharp and found a few cloven hoof prints that could only have been left by a small unicorn. He dropped to all fours and lowered his nose, sniffing where the tracks ended. Beside them and circling were larger cloven tracks, obviously the stallion's. He looked up. As the unicorn had said, there was no way a flying predator could have swept in to snatch her from the ground, nor were there any other tracks. The faint scent of the ground birds was over a day old.

He raised his head as he looked down at the end of Shahly's path again, his eyes narrowing.

Vinton watched him, then impatiently prodded, "Well?"

Falloah landed some distance behind and as she folded her wings to her and strode to them, the metallic green dragon landed where she had been and followed her.

Ralligor's eyes began to glow red, then emerald. He leaned his head and lifted a hand, holding it over the end of the tracks as a green glow enveloped it as well.

Vinton looked to the dragon's hand, then behind him as the scarlet dragoness reached them.

"This is odd," the Desert Lord murmured as he held his hand over the ground.

"What is it?" the stallion eagerly pressed.

Drarrexok appeared on Ralligor's other side and watched with some curiosity.

Withdrawing his hand, the black dragon looked to the green and snarled, "What are you doing here?"

The green dragon shrugged and replied, "No big plans for the day."

"And the hoards of dragonesses you boast about?" Ralligor questioned.

"Won't they both miss you?" Falloah added.

He shrugged again and looked to the tracks. "They'll get

along for a while. What's so odd?"

Ralligor also turned his attention to the tracks. "She was taken by magic, but not a magic I'm very familiar with, not the *wizaridi.*"

"Oh, no," Vinton whickered. "Unicorn hunters."

"I don't think so," the black dragon corrected. "This was done with great care and concentration. It appears that they did not want her frightened or injured, and that would not be consistent with the hunters from Red Stone."

"Unicorn hunters?" the green dragon questioned.

"Long story," the black dragon replied. "I'll explain another time." He growled. "This is beyond my expertise. I need my *magister.*"

"I think he is still at Zondae Castle," Falloah informed. "Shall I go and get him?"

Ralligor closed his eyes and answered, "No." He was silent for a time, then he looked down at the stallion and asked, "You didn't wake when she got up?"

"No," he admitted, turning his eyes down. "Sometimes she will get up in the night or early morning for a drink or to find something to eat. She is always careful not to wake me when she does so."

"Hence," the black dragon added, "she tends to sleep until high sun from day to day."

"Much like her dragon friend," the dragoness interjected. "Will your *magister* be able to tell who took her and where?"

"I think so," Ralligor assured. "He was able to track where they had taken you, but this magic is different. It isn't the *wizaridi.*"

"The what?" Drarrexok asked. "Ralligor, you're mixing yourself up with humans and unicorns and now you're talking about different kinds of magic. Does Agarxus know about all of this or is he going to kill us all when he finds out?"

"Just don't worry over that now," the black dragon growled. "Can you sense her nearby, Plow Mule?"

Vinton snorted at him, then calmed himself with a breath and scanned the area with his essence, his horn glowing a faint crimson.

The green dragon looked to Falloah and asked, "His name is

Plow Mule?"

"Quiet," she snarled. "Ralligor, should we try to find her from the air?"

"We won't," the black dragon informed grimly. "I don't think she's within fifty leagues of here. Someone of power took her, and I don't think he would be inclined to stay in the middle of the forest with her. He's taken her to his own lair."

"Um," Drarrexok started, then he shook his head.

"Well," Vinton grumbled, "she's nowhere around here. I can't sense her anywhere. Ralligor, what are we going to do?"

The black dragon growled a sigh, his eyes still on the tracks. "I don't know yet. My *magister* should be here shortly. Perhaps he will be able— "

"What does shortly mean?" the stallion cried. "What if she's in danger? We can't wait for someone to— "

"Vinton!" Falloah cut in. "I know you are afraid for her. We all are, but we have to keep our wits about us."

The unicorn turned his eyes down and huffed a sigh. "Sorry."

She growled softly, then reached to him and gently stroked his back. "I understand, Vinton. Really I do. I cannot imagine being in your place."

"Ralligor can," the stallion mumbled.

"And in a way I find myself there again," the black dragon confirmed. That red glow overtook his eyes and he snarled, "Whoever has her will keep her safe or I swear the pain I deliver them will send shivers to those even in Hell!"

"Put thoughts of vengeance from you," a white haired human advised as he approached the dragon from behind.

The Desert Lord raised his head, but did not turn around.

Drarrexok wheeled around, his eyes quickly finding the approaching human who had long white hair and a long white beard, the one who wore the green robes of a wizard, the one who felt to be of great power. To this inexperienced dragon, a threat was approaching, just as the unicorn had been a threat. He bared his teeth, but did not get a growl out as his eyes slid to the dragoness, and found hers already on him and narrow with disapproval. Slowly, his lips slipped over his teeth and he took a step back.

Shooting the green dragon a short hiss, Falloah looked to the wizard and offered, "It's good to see you again. I only wish circumstances were better."

Nodding, the white haired human offered her a strained smile. "Always good to see you, Falloah, no matter the circumstances." He strode past the black dragon, right to the last of Shahly's hoof prints, and he knelt down, examining them closely. "Ralligor, thank you for calling me. I feel our little unicorn finds herself well over her head this time."

"When doesn't she?" the black dragon grumbled. "Can you tell where she was taken and by whom?"

"Patience," the wizard said as a teacher would to a student. Holding his hand over the area, he drew a breath and raised his head slightly, then shook his head. "*Sortiri.* This was a sorcerer of great strength and skill."

"Stronger than you?" the Desert Lord asked.

The wizard smiled and looked back to the big dragon. "Is the craft really about strength, mighty friend?"

"At times," the student replied, "but I understand what you are saying, *Magister.*"

Looking back to the ground, the wizard planted his hands on his thighs and stood, groaning as he did. "This sorcerer is a strong one, well taught and well skilled, but I get the impression he is relatively young, probably still in his prime." He turned and looked to the black dragon. "Ralligor, you've been through this before, and once again I urge patience. Act too quickly and you could bring your enemy's wrath down on her."

Ralligor growled and looked away. "You know where she is and you aren't going to tell me again."

"This time, no." The wizard kept his eyes on the dragon and raised his bushy eyebrows. "I cannot track the *sortiri* any more than you can. For that we need a sorcerer."

Nodding, the big dragon agreed, "I understand." He growled another sigh and informed, "I had a half-trained sorceress in my grasp yesterday. She said she had lost a duel with a sorcerer who had led an attack against a castle in the southwestern part of the forest yesterday." He looked back down to the wizard and leaned his head. "I see more than a coincidence here."

"Quite possibly," the white haired man confirmed. "It might be worth investigating. You don't think the unicorn hunters of

Red Stone Castle are involved, do you?"

"No, *Magister,*" the dragon replied, "not unless they've changed their tactics."

The wizard nodded. "Agreed. We'll not rule them out, though." He stared up at the dragon in silence for long seconds, then he turned his eyes to the stallion and strode to him. "Vinton, the tables seem to have turned on you."

The bay slowly swiveled his ears toward the white haired human and raised his head. "Tables have turned?"

"This spring we helped her seek your freedom," the wizard answered, "and now it seems that she finds herself in need of rescue."

Looking away, the stallion considered, then he closed his eyes and lowered his head. "I can't stand how I feel right now. Now I finally know what she endured when the humans had me. Surely if they went to this much trouble to take her then they are treating her well." He looked back to the wizard and insisted, "I have to do something. I have to go and try to rescue her."

"I'm not certain what you could do right now," the wizard informed.

"But you knew what Shahly could do," Vinton countered. He looked up to the dragon and said, "Make me human. I'll go in and get her when we know where she is."

Ralligor drew his head back. "Make you human? Do you know what you're asking me to do?"

"Yes," the stallion assured. He approached a few steps and pointed out, "Shahly was willing to endure that for me. I would gladly do the same for her."

"Circumstances were different," the black dragon informed. He looked to the wizard. "It may just be useful, though. He could find her in a human stronghold quite easily."

"We should keep it under consideration," the wizard agreed. "In the meantime, I think you know what we must do."

Ralligor looked aside and snarled, "Yes."

"Go on, mighty friend. Just get it over with." The wizard looked to the green dragon and raised his brow. "One more for the cause?"

Falloah looked to the green and lowered her brow. "I think he was just leaving."

"No," the black dragon countered. "He may be useful."

Drarrexok looked to the Desert Lord and said, "Well thanks for thinking that. What is it we're looking for, anyway?"

"My mate," Vinton grumbled. "You don't have to help us."

The green dragon looked to the stallion, then slid his eyes to Ralligor. "Uh, all this fuss for a unicorn?" When Falloah growled, he glanced at her, then raised his head and assured, "Any friend of Ralligor—human or unicorn—is well worth the time and trouble." He looked to Falloah and folded his arms. "And I'll be here to keep you safe as well."

She hissed at him through bared teeth, then looked to the black dragon and half opened her wings. "I'll go with you, *Unisponsus.*"

Ralligor and Falloah turned toward the South and opened their wings.

Patting the stallion's neck, the wizard asked, "How quickly could you get to Caipiervell from here?"

CHAPTER 10

Little ribbons of sunlight lanced into the stable from cracks and seams in the wall of the stable. Somewhere outside there was some activity, people talking, horses... Things Shahly had heard during her time at Red Stone Castle that spring. But for that light, the stable was a dark and still place. It smelled of horses and moldy stone. Somewhere, the wood that made up part of the stable was rotting. Mice rummaged around in the hay both inside and outside of her cage-like stall. Otherwise, there was nothing but boredom and the lingering fear of what the humans wanted from her.

Lying on her belly in the middle of her stall where a sunbeam shined through a gap in the shutters that kept her window dark, she stared at the hay in front of her and the mouse that darted about and nibbled at the seeds on the stalks of some of the hay she had been offered. Normally, she would not have given a tiny mouse a second thought, but at the moment there was simply nothing else to do. She tried not to think about why she was there or what the humans wanted her for. One of them she had encountered since her abduction was pure of heart, but only the one. Others were not and the man who claimed her as a pet seemed to have wicked intentions about him.

Her thoughts shifted to the outside. When Vinton had been taken, she did not know what to do and was given the way to rescue him by a kindly human and a chance encounter with a mortal enemy of the unicorns. She should have been killed that day. Ralligor had spared her and sent her to find her Vinton and his Falloah. That was a rough time, and her life had been changed forever. Now, enemies of the unicorns were her friends. Hopefully, Vinton would have thought to seek her dragon friend out for council, even though the two of them really did not get along well. To her, this was a mystery. She was sure that they would warm up to one another since they were both so dear to her, and yet they would do nothing but bicker. She also knew that the only thing that kept them from a fight to the death was her. Whickering softly, she wondered grimly how they would do in her absence.

Looking toward the wall near the cage-like door, she saw the bucket of grain and half empty bucket of water still sitting there. The grain was actually very good and the water had quenched her thirst nicely, but under the circumstances her appetite was not with her, though she could feel pangs of hunger beginning. Of late, hunger had been a problem and had been with her more and more.

The bolt of the stable door slid back and she slowly turned her eyes that way, squinting a little against the light that swept in. She hated the dark and seeing the light outside was something of a comfort. Some of the tenders from before entered, the girl with them. They did nothing but peer into her stall to make sure she still had water and grain in her buckets and then they left, but did not close the door. It opened wider and other humans entered, each carrying one end of a wooden chair with plush red cushions fastened to the seat and back. The wood was very dark, almost black and the velvet looking material was adorned with gold embroidery. They set the chair down, facing the door to her stall, then turned and left without looking at her.

Voices mumbled something outside, then someone else entered, the same man as before who had claimed her for his pet. She really did not want to see him, though she watched as he approached and sat down in the chair. There were two soldiers with him who stood on either side of the chair he sat in.

As he stared at her, Shahly looked away. The little mouse she had been watching had fled when the humans came in and a little sigh escaped her. Sure, he was just a little rodent, but he was company in the long hours that she had been left alone.

"Is everything to your liking?" the man asked, his voice slicing through the silence of the stable like a human's sword through water.

Shahly did not respond, nor did she even look toward him.

"I want you to be comfortable," he informed.

She laid her ears back and turned her head away a little more.

He was silent for a moment, then he said, "I was hoping we could eventually become friends. I want you to be happy here. I realize that you must still be uneasy about being taken from the forest like that, but believe me when I say that I did so as gently as I could. I really do want what is best for you."

She wanted to snap back at him, to let him know in no uncertain terms of her displeasure about being his prisoner, but she could not bring herself to give him the pleasure of hearing her. She needed to be certain that he knew she did not approve of him or his wants for her. For Shahly, this was very uncharacteristic as her heart had known only friends and no enemies, but for one.

He looked to the guards and ordered, "Leave us." He was quiet for a time as they turned and strode from the stable, and he was quiet longer even after the stable door closed. His attention was fully on the unicorn before him.

Shahly stared across the stall she was in. Her attention was not on anything specific, it was just not on the man whose eyes were on her. Perhaps if she refused to cooperate in any way he would grow bored or frustrated with her and let her go. It was worth a try.

"Can you even understand me?" he finally asked. When she still did not respond he nodded and assured, "Of course you can. You're just feeling timid in your new home."

Her eyes narrowed slightly. This was *not* her home, nor would it be.

He seemed to feel her frustration and could swear that he felt anger from her. Shifting in his chair, he rested his forearms on his knees and introduced, "I am Lord Nemlivv. Do you have a name?"

She did not move or respond.

"I sense some stubbornness in you," he observed. "Perhaps you don't know what I have saved you from." When she still did not respond, he elaborated. "There are those who would hunt your kind for their own needs. I would be one who does not want to see the world's unicorns hunted into oblivion. Until they can be stopped, I thought it best to preserve at least one of you and protect you from the hunters." He began to grind his teeth. "I would think that you would be grateful to me."

She snorted.

Nemlivv sighed and turned his eyes down. "Okay. Perhaps we should start over. Just so you know, remaining silent will only make your stay here less pleasant."

She still did not respond to him.

Nodding, the sorcerer conceded, "Very well. Perhaps you would prefer to remain here in the dark by yourself for a while longer." He stood and turned to leave.

Shahly finally raised her head and asked, "What is it you want of me?"

Nemlivv froze where he was and slowly looked back at her. He hesitated only a few seconds before turning back and approaching again. "Well, well. It would seem that you have a voice after all."

"I am not meant to be your pet," she informed with much venom in her words.

"If not," he countered, "then why are you here?"

"I won't be long," she warned.

He raised his brow and rested his arms on the stall gate. "Oh, really? Are you going to use your unicorn magic to free yourself, or manipulate me or someone else to get away? Are you going to storm the gate when the tenders come to care for you? Perhaps you will just disappear on me."

Shahly rolled her eyes. "You are such short sighted people."

"Then enlighten me," he challenged.

"What is it you want me for?" she asked coldly.

"There is a plan for everything," was his answer.

"So this plan is a secret?"

"To most."

"If I am a part of it, shouldn't I know something about it?"

He leaned his head. "Not necessarily."

She huffed a sigh and once again did not respond.

"I was really hoping we could be friends," he said softly.

Finally, she turned her head and looked at him. "I am your prisoner. You are no friend of mine so long as I am." She looked away from him again.

The sorcerer nodded. "I see. So we are to take the difficult path, are we?"

"That would be your choice," she countered.

He pushed off of the gate and backed away. "I'll leave you with your thoughts, then."

"Just so you will know," she said suddenly as he turned to leave.

Nemlivv turned back and trained his gaze on her one more time.

She met his eyes with hers and informed, "I'll not be swayed by cruelty. If you still intend to keep me here, just know that I am not responsible for what happens on the day I go free. Only you are." She looked away again.

Slowly raising his chin, the sorcerer felt a chill shoot through him, then he spun around and left.

Darkness enveloped the stable again and loneliness with it. She missed her Vinton and her home in the forest. Only two days before she had been banished from her herd. Now, she was a captive of a human she had never seen before and refused to get to know. For the moment, all that was left to do was lie in the hay and hope her Vinton would come for her soon. In that thought, she hoped also that there would be no bloodshed on the day she was finally rescued.

The morning she had spent in the stable already felt like half a lifetime and although boredom was taking her again, she refused to succumb to despair even as it wore her down little by little.

Light swept into the stable as someone else entered. Shahly tried to ignore the newcomer but she sensed something familiar about this one, something from the past, something that frightened her. Ever so slowly, she raised her eyes as the dainty footfalls drew closer. She could feel who was approaching her and her eyes widened as she recognized the mind and shattered psyche. Hesitantly, she turned and looked to the woman who approached and a little fear began to mix violently within her.

The woman was of average height for a female of her kind and well made, wearing a red dress of light material that had a very low neckline and was trimmed in black and gold. Her black hair flowed freely to her mid back. Her dark, almost black eyes were fixed on Shahly as the hint of a smile barely curled the corners of her mouth. Her face was all too familiar.

As the girl reached the stall and rested her arms on the gate, Shahly turned her attention away again, her mouth slightly open, her heart thundering and her breath entering her with some difficulty.

"Well, well," the girl said with a teasing voice. "What a small world we live in. When I'd heard of a white unicorn in Master Nemlivv's stable I just had to see for myself."

"Hello, Nillerra," Shahly greeted softly.

The girl's smile widened. "I'm touched that you remember me, Shahly."

"I remember you," the unicorn confirmed.

"Well, I certainly remember you, Shahly. You're the reason I'm not sitting on the throne of Red Stone Castle right now. You're the reason I'm nothing more than a miserable court wench right now. You're the reason Prince Arden has a price on my head instead of a gold ring on my finger!"

"I am not," Shahly denied.

"Of course you are. You were there to destroy me and humiliate me."

"That's silly, Nillerra.

Nillerra laughed, something evil in her voice. "You are slow witted, aren't you?"

Shahly shrugged. "I guess."

The black haired girl laughed again, softly. "Oh, if only you knew how many times I've dreamed of this moment."

Shahly turned her eyes down.

"Do you know what is sweeter than revenge, Shahly? Do you?"

No answer.

Nillerra leaned her face through the bars and hissed, "Nothing. Nothing at all. And I have the rest of your life to taste it."

Shahly's lips tightened as tears filled her eyes.

"Just think about it," Nillerra continued dreamily, looking toward the ceiling. "Day after day, month after month, season after season…" Her eyes slid back to the unicorn. "I'll visit you every day. I'll make sure you have plenty of food, plenty of water, and we'll have lots and lots of fun together every day. What more could you possibly want?"

"I want to go home," Shahly replied pitifully.

Nillerra bared her teeth and roared, "I don't give a damn what you want!"

Shahly cringed.

The black haired girl seemed to calm herself for a moment,

then she said in a cruel voice, "You are Master Nemlivv's pet now and you'd better just get used to it." She huffed a sigh and finished, "Of course, if you want your freedom that much, it wouldn't necessarily be beyond my control."

Shahly's ears perked and she turned her head slightly that way.

"I think I have enough influence to see to it," Nillerra continued as she looked toward an emerald ring on the middle finger of one hand. "I could probably have you out of here by tonight."

A long silence gripped the stable.

As Shahly realized what the black haired girl was doing, she lowered her eyes and observed, "But you won't."

Nillerra smiled and looked back to her. "Of course I won't. You know I can, but you know I won't. Absolutely delicious."

Shahly vented despair and frustration in a huff and demanded, "Why?"

"Because I want you to suffer!" the black haired girl hissed. "I want you to know that I can free you and choose not to. I want you to know you will be at my mercy for the rest of your life!"

Shahly closed her eyes as a tear rolled forth. "I don't understand why you hate me so."

"Sure you do. You want revenge on me. That's why you're here, isn't it? You're ready to stab me with that horn as soon as I turn my back."

"I have no interest in hurting you, Nillerra."

"Liar," the black haired girl snarled.

Shahly's eyes narrowed as she looked to her tormentor. "Do you remember when you took the form of that vulture thing this spring? Do you remember your fight with the dragon?"

Nillerra looked away and sneered, "What of it."

"You lost," the unicorn reminded. "He was going to kill you and I stopped him. Do you remember that?"

Silently, Nillerra just stared across the stable, her brow tense and her lips tight and shaking. Slowly, her eyes slid back to Shahly. "I believe it was the dragon that made me a woman again, not you. If he was going to kill me then he wouldn't have done that, would he? I think you were hoping he would kill me."

Shahly turned her eyes from Nillerra and shook her head. "I just don't understand you."

"I'm sure there is much you don't understand," Nillerra chided. "So why didn't he make you back into a woman?"

"I'm not human. I'm unicorn. This is who I really am."

"Oh, come now, Shahly. Why would a unicorn go to Red Stone to marry the Prince?"

"That's not why I was there."

"Then why were you there?"

"You would not understand."

"Sure I would. You were there to ruin me. That's all. And when I found you out you were turned into a unicorn to punish you for failing."

"You're being silly again."

"No I'm not," the black haired girl barked. A long silence, then, "Turn yourself back into a woman."

"I can't."

"Yes you can," Nillerra insisted. "Just do it. Make yourself into a woman." She half turned her head. "I'll let you go if you do."

Shahly closed her eyes, bowing her head as she said, "I really can't."

"So how did you do it before?"

"Someone helped me," the unicorn admitted.

Nillerra laughed. "Of course. I should have guessed that you couldn't do anything on your own. So who was it? A wizard?"

"Yes."

"Maybe I should have him brought here," the black haired girl suggested.

Shahly's eyes flashed open and she slowly raised her head.

"Yes, that sounds delightful, doesn't it?" Nillerra continued. "I'll have him brought here to Ravenhold, he will make you a woman again..." Her smile broadened. "It can be just like old times, Shahly, but there isn't anyone to protect you here. I will simply do to you what I want."

Shahly looked to the black haired girl with wide eyes. "I really don't think that bringing him here would be a wise idea."

"Why not? Do you think he is too powerful for even Nemlivv to handle?"

Shahly glanced aside and nodded.

"I don't believe you, Shahly. Now tell me where to find him."

Looking away again, the unicorn defiantly said, "Why should I? You'll just use him to make me suffer more."

Raising her chin, Nillerra warned, "Just try to imagine what you'll endure if I don't get what I want. Now tell me where he is."

Shahly pondered, then looked to the black haired girl, feeling desperate to regain her freedom. "If I tell you where he is, will you let me go?"

"No promises," Nillerra snarled.

"He is the one who sent me to Red Stone."

Nillerra's eyebrows popped up. "Oh, really?

Shahly turned her eyes down, staring at the hay in front of her. "He made me human. He sent me to the castle. I did not know about you before I got there. He sent me with specific things to do and I'm sorry that what I did hurt you, I really am, but your quarrel is with him, not me." She closed her eyes. "I just wanted my stallion back."

Nillerra was silent for a long time, then she finally said, "You know, that makes sense. I'll tell you what, Shahly. I will trade you for him."

Shahly looked to her.

"Just tell me where he is," the black haired girl continued, "and once I have him, you can go. Does that sound fair?"

"Do you promise?" Shahly asked hopefully.

Nodding, the black haired girl conceded, "Yes, Shahly. I promise. If he's who I really want then I will have no more need of you. Now where is he?"

Shahly just stared at her for a time, then she turned her eyes down and softly said, "He lives in the desert in a cave in the mountains."

"So I just go to the mountains in the desert, find a cave there and I find him?"

"It's at the end of a canyon of tan and red stone," the unicorn continued.

"And if I don't find him there?"

"He lives there. If you don't find him there it's because he's gone to find food or something."

"Well, you sound confident enough, but I can't help but feel you betrayed him a little too easily."

"What do you mean?"

"You know exactly what I mean, Shahly. You're sacrificing him to save your own miserable skin."

Looking away from the black haired girl, the unicorn corrected, "No, I'm really not."

Nillerra sighed. "Shahly, do you know what I am going to do to him?"

"There is nothing you can do to him, Nillerra, short of angering him."

The black haired girl raised her chin. "So you really think he is that powerful, too much for even Nemlivv to handle?"

"I told you before that he is." Even with the promise of freedom, Shahly's conscience would get the better of her. Turning her eyes down again, she felt shame for sending this hateful girl to her certain doom. Nillerra would no doubt take many others with her, and Ralligor would kill them all with ease. Shaking her head, a regretful unicorn implored, "Nillerra, you should not go to him. Just leave him alone there."

"Oh, I'm going, and just in case you aren't lying about how powerful he is I'll just have to prepare for him, won't I?"

Shahly turned her eyes to the black haired girl and shook her head. "Nothing you can do will prepare you. If you must go then I would suggest you just talk to him, be humble and try not to anger him. Tell him who you are and of your woes. Tell him you know me. Perhaps he will help you somehow."

"And now you are suddenly worrying over my well being." Nillerra shook her head. "You are truly a piece of work. Do you really think I'm going to walk into some ambush all by myself?"

"I'm not sure what ambush means," the unicorn admitted. "I only want to avoid anyone getting hurt or killed because of me."

Folding her arms, Nillerra sneered, "Even me?"

"Even you," Shahly confirmed softly.

The black haired girl's eyes narrowed slightly.

"You don't know anything about my kind, do you?" Shahly asked.

"I know enough about you," Nillerra snarled.

Shahly loosed a shallow sigh. "You know tragically little.

Didn't you ever dream about us when you were younger?"

Nillerra turned to leave. "Just keep your stupid little horn out of my dreams."

"What happened to make you so bitter?" Shahly called after her. Now she was succumbing to frustration despite fighting it back as best she could.

The black haired girl stopped and her hands clenched into tight fists.

"I'm not your enemy," the unicorn assured, "and yet you've always hated me, and I don't understand why!"

Slowly, Nillerra turned, her brow low over her eyes. "You want to understand why I hate you?" She took a few steps back toward the stall, her eyes boring into the unicorn. "There's nothing to understand," she hissed, then she shouted, "I hate you! I hate everything about you! I hate that people consider you so pure and innocent! I hate that you are too naïve to understand what a thorn in my side you are." She just stood there and glared through wide eyes, insane eyes, then she turned away and strode toward the door, "Just accept it. You are here for the rest of your life and I intend to make you suffer as much as I can." She paused at the door to look back one more time, spitefully saying through bared teeth, "And I guess since you'll be all alone in here you can *stay* a pure and pathetic little virgin for the rest of your days!"

As the door slammed and darkness returned to the stable, Shahly looked aside and said to herself, "Perhaps I shouldn't tell her that I'm not anymore."

CHAPTER 11

Dusk was not far off. The sun had found its way to the treetops west of the cabin and long shadows were cast from it.

Janees finished her labors in the garden and knew she would have to take more firewood into the cabin before the sorcerer returned. She knew his return would be awkward at best and dreaded it as much as she anticipated it.

Finishing all of the chores she could think of, she sat back down and put her eyes to the book, letting the cloak of his she still wore to open at the front to allow some cool air in. Summer days were hot and humid in this part of the forest and she longed for a good bath. The inside of the cloak had been soaked with perspiration a few times and was still damp. She had thought about taking it off completely, but did not want to be caught naked should the sorcerer return unexpectedly as he always did. Resting her cheek in her palm, she resumed reading, glancing at the fire from time to time to be sure it did not go out again.

Drawing a breath, she could not stop a yawn that forced its way from her within a half hour. She rubbed her eyes, then looked toward the fire again, gasping and nearly falling from her chair as she saw the sorcerer standing two paces away.

He was just staring at her with his arms folded.

She pulled the cloak closed and close to her.

In the sorcerer's hand was a bundle of red cloth, in his eye was something she had not seen there before, and she could not place it. Shame found her again and she turned her eyes away, then down.

An awkward silence filled the room for a moment.

He finally took a step forward and tossed the bundle on the table before her. When she only glanced at it, he informed, "It's better than what you came here in and will suit you better than my cloak does."

Janees nodded, still not looking at him.

Clearing his throat, the sorcerer turned to the book shelf and strode toward it with slow steps. "Get yourself changed. I need that cloak back so that I can wash it."

Glancing around, she slowly reached from within the cloak and took the bundle, but never really took her eyes from the floor.

Looking over the books for a time, the sorcerer did not turn back to her as he said, "Are you suddenly bashful? This afternoon you couldn't wait to get undressed."

She did not respond.

"Get changed," he ordered, "then we should talk."

Hesitantly, she opened the bundle and looked over the garments that unfolded. She glanced at the sorcerer who still had his back to her and slipped the cloak from around her shoulders. Dressing quickly, she noticed that the garments he had brought her were little more than a loosely fitting shirt that dropped to her knees and a cape of the same red material. The cuffs of the shirt seemed huge, so big that her head would probably fit within. The cape was light and breathed well, but she did not put it on right away, instead laying it on the table. Looking down to the long shirt, she smoothed it out over her belly before she began to lace it. The neckline to be laced was open just below her breastbone and that is where she started. She only tied three of the five laces, then ran her hand over her belly again. This did not satisfy her and she gathered some of the shirt at the sides and pulled it taut.

Pulling a book from the shelf, the sorcerer turned and looked her up and down, nodding as he observed, "It suits you well enough. Quit fussing over it so."

"Do you have a belt?" she asked without thinking. Slowly, she raised her eyes to him, her mouth hanging open slightly as she saw his less than pleased expression and one raised eyebrow. "I'm sorry. It's beautiful, thank you."

"Hmm," was his response. He tossed the book onto the table and slowly strode to her. "It's not meant to make you look alluring or the belle of the ball. It is meant to cover you and give you some semblance of dignity. I have some old boots in a trunk under the bed. They should fit you."

"Thank you," she offered again.

"Open that book," he commanded.

She moved the cape and the other book aside and pulled the new one to her, her eyes running over the complex designs of the ancient leather cover. When he loudly cleared his throat in that familiar disapproving manner, she looked up to him and asked, "Should I just open to— "

"Open the book," he ordered harshly. "The *sortiri* will guide you."

Without thinking, she opened it, nearly half way through.

"What does the page say?" the sorcerer asked.

Looking down to the words, her spine stiffened as she read, "*Appropia de draconus ve horrbillis vindicare, unis wilp escaeles ezt blaek ezt...*" Drawing a breath, she backed away from the book, her lips parted in fear.

Raising his brow, the sorcerer simply stared at her, and did not speak.

Janees turned wide eyes to him and gulped another breath.

Finally the sorcerer spoke. "The *sortiri* shares one of the elements with the dragon in an important way. Do you know the four elements?"

She hesitantly nodded, then looked away and recalled, "Um, fire, wind, water and earth." Looking back to him for his approval, she unconsciously wrung her hands together as she awaited his reply.

"And the *sortiri* is of which of those elements?" he asked.

Again her eyes darted about and the answer came quickly and very clearly. "Fire and earth."

"Dragons are of all of the elements," the sorcerer explained. "They are of the earth, they soar on the wind, the swim in and drink water, and their breath is fire. No other creature controls the four elements like they do."

Janees nodded and observed, "You know much about dragons."

"I've read what I need to know," he informed, "and observed more. You seem curious so I thought the time right to teach you something about their relationship with the *sortiri.*"

"I'm going to be your apprentice, then?" she asked anxiously.

"I didn't say that," the sorcerer growled back. "I'm going to teach you something about dragons and sorcery, that's all."

She looked down and nodded.

"Sit down," he ordered. As she complied, he took the other chair and sat in it slowly. As he did the chair creaked under his weight. Resting his elbows on the table, he folded his hands and rested his chin on his knuckles, his eyes trained on her.

She met his eyes only with a few glances and would not look at him otherwise. She knew what he wanted to talk about, and had dreaded it most of the day.

"There is something I need to know," he announced.

Her lips quivering slightly, she looked to the table and nodded.

"And you already know what," he continued.

She nodded again.

"Go ahead," the sorcerer prodded.

Janees was hesitant to answer and just stared at the table for long seconds. Finally, she sheepishly said, "I don't know what to say."

"How many?" he asked.

Again, she was reluctant to answer, but finally confessed, "Two."

He drew a breath and nodded. "I see. One thing will greatly inhibit your ability to learn the *sortiri.* One very important thing. Do you know what I'm talking about?"

She shook her head.

"Truth," he answered. "Truth will compel you to learn and distance from it will compel you to fail. Do you understand what I'm saying?"

Janees slowly nodded.

"Then how many?" he repeated.

She closed her eyes. "Four."

"Now we're getting somewhere," he said loudly. "Let's see if we can go forward from here, shall we?"

With a broken sigh, she whispered, "What do we go forward to?"

"Not *to* anything," he corrected. "We go forward. The craft is not about a destination it is about a great journey. If you wish to learn the *sortiri* then you will have to go with vigor and your absolute commitment."

"You haven't committed to me," she countered.

"And you'll let that little detail stop your desire to learn the craft?" he scoffed. "There is much more you have to worry over than if you'll be my apprentice tomorrow. Look what you were willing to do before."

Tears glossed her eyes and she looked away. "So a whore is all I am to you. That's all I've ever been to anyone."

"Is that a truth you've been hiding?"

"I guess so."

"So, did you aspire to be a whore, or was that something you did on the path to pursuing the craft?"

She finally looked to him and met his gaze.

"We've all done things we're not proud of," he informed, "and no I'll not tell you of my sorted past. Do you wish to pursue the craft?"

This time she eagerly nodded.

"Then I expect complete truth from you," he said straightly.

As he stood and walked to the fireplace, she puzzled over what had just happened. She looked back to the table and asked, "Are you ashamed of me?"

"You burned that past," the sorcerer reminded, picking his stick up to poke at the fire. "From here there is only now and what will be."

She watched him for some time, pondering his words. "I lied to you before," she heard herself say, and when she realized she had said it she found herself swallowing back the fear that surged forth.

An endless moment passed. Only the crackle of the fire and Janees' thundering heartbeat could be heard.

"Go on," he prodded.

"I'm not a princess," she confessed. "Jekkon and I were staying at the castle to seek shelter against the spring rains two seasons ago. I found a sorcerer there who was willing to teach me."

"For a price," he added for her.

"Yes," she confirmed softly. "He t—told me... He said I had to—"

"Truth," he reminded.

Turning her eyes down and nodding, she continued, "I told him I would give him whatever he wanted if only he would teach me."

"And he wanted a personal whore," the sorcerer guessed.

"I guess so," was her answer.

"Go on," he ordered.

"He ordered that I should lay with him at his command, that..." Tears began to stream from her eyes and she cried, "I didn't want to! I really didn't! He would not teach me if I didn't. I had to do as he said or he wouldn't teach me."

"And three others convinced you that was true." The sorcerer finally leaned the stick against the fireplace and turned around, seeing her hunch over and bury her face in her hands. As she wept, he asked her, "Did you know any better at the time?"

"I didn't!" she sobbed. "I swear I didn't! I just thought that I was supposed to!" She wept harder as emotions poured from her. Before she realized, another chair was set down beside hers and she felt his heavy arm around her shoulders. She allowed him to pull her to him, and as he squeezed her against him, she finally felt herself held by someone who did not make her feel cheap and dirty.

Patting her shoulder, he softly said, "Just let all of that out of you. Free those feelings you've kept penned up all this time."

She could not be sure how long she cried, but the storm of emotions that fled her finally weakened and her weeping slowly stopped. She blotted her eyes on her sleeves and finally raised her head, looking to the fire.

"How do you feel now?" he asked in a voice that was far too gentle to have come from him.

Janees could only shrug, but finally answered, "I feel tired, and a little ill."

He stood and walked to the book case, fetched a clean parchment and ink well and returned to the table, setting them down near her. "When you feel strong enough, I want you to write down the names of the sorcerers who took advantage of you. I would prefer them in the order of first to last."

She felt anxious and looked to the empty parchment, cringing as she saw it.

"How old were you when the first made you do that?" he demanded.

Hesitant to answer once again, she finally confessed, "I was eleven seasons old."

"Marrying age to some," he growled, "but far too young for the rest of us. You'll not lay with another man so long as you learn my teachings."

"Am I a disappointment?" she whimpered.

"Only if you fail me," was his answer. "Don't fail me and you won't disappoint me."

"Am I still not your apprentice?" she asked.

"You'll know if you are," he replied. "Put that out of your mind and put your studies into it." Now he was talking like the strong, short tempered sorcerer who she had first encountered. It was actually a little comforting. "Go fetch some water for the basin and add some to this stew."

She nodded and stood, pausing at the door to ask, "What should I call you?" She looked back at him hopefully.

He folded his arms. "My apprentice would address me as *Magister.* I suppose you can address me so for now."

A little smile curled Janees' lips.

He lowered his brow and barked, "Water!"

She jumped and rushed outside.

***

There were many more chores in store for her and she completed each with a new found enthusiasm and vigor. Sometime later she found herself back at that table with the *Scripti Draconus* open and her eyes following the Latirus words with such focus as she had never felt before. The sorcerer had gone outside and disappeared into the forest again. Where he always went was something of a mystery, but she knew she dare not ask.

She had left the door open for light and air and had also left the window open. A nice little breeze snaked its way through the cabin and was very comfortable and soothing considering how hot the cabin almost always was.

This time, she heard footfalls and would not be startled when he entered. As they drew close to the door, she looked over her shoulder to see him entering and met his eyes with a coy little smile.

"You've wasted all this time reading about dragons, haven't you?"

She nodded.

"Instead of learning the craft," he added.

She nodded again.

"Did you get everything done?"

Janees finally stood and faced him, answering, "Yes, *Magister.*"

He looked around the cabin as if seeking something out of place, then his eyes found her again and he ordered, "Close that book and open the one I told you to study this morning."

She nodded again and replied, "Yes, *Magister.*" Those words felt so good to say!

The sorcerer strode into the cabin and right to the fireplace. The fire was low and he growled as he saw this.

"I didn't want the stew to burn," she defended even before he spoke, "so I kept the fire low to just keep it warm."

"M-hmm," was his short reply. "Study."

She sat back down and read on, though her mind was on her teacher. Something was simmering in the back of her mind, something of her teacher and dragons. She had learned that powerful sorcerers could be shape shifters. Her thoughts shifted to the dragon. He was a mage. He was also very powerful and very sure of himself, much like…

Janees slowly raised her head and stared forward for a moment. Forcing her wits back to her, she slowly turned her eyes to the sorcerer, who sat in a chair near the fireplace and read from another book.

His cloak hung on the hook across the room. His deep brown skin was a little sweaty and shimmered in the firelight and lamplight.

She raised her chin slightly. The dragon was black!

The sorcerer's eyes slid to her.

Drawing a breath, Janees dared to ask, "You're him, aren't you?"

He raised his brow.

"The dragon," she went on. "You are the dragon!"

His brow arched.

Janees stood and faced him fully. "You knew you couldn't teach me as a dragon. You knew I belonged with my own kind. That's why you're gone so much. You can't keep this form for more than a few hours at a time. Why didn't I see this before?" She slowly shook her head and breathed, "This is amazing."

"It certainly is," he said. "Um, what gave this conspiracy

away?"

"Many things," she replied. "It wasn't easy. But everything just adds up, your treks into the forest, why you don't sleep here, even your build is more dragon than man!"

He raised his chin slightly.

"I mean that in the way of a compliment!" she added quickly. "No mere man can possibly have such a build as yours."

The sorcerer nodded. "Uh, thanks." His eyes suddenly darted to the still open door and he abruptly stood, his gaze on the outside. He strode to the door and tossed her the book he had been reading as he did.

Janees awkwardly caught the book and laid it on the table, then she looked to the departing sorcerer and followed him.

He was stopped just outside and was looking up toward the sky.

Looking where he did, Janees shrieked a gasp as the huge black dragon from the desert descended and landed hard just beyond the garden. A much smaller red dragon landed behind him.

The sorcerer advanced, shouting, "Don't trample my damn garden this time!"

Raising his head, the dragon snarled and informed, "My *Magister* wishes to see you on a matter of great importance."

Folding his arms, the sorcerer countered, "I'm a busy man, and if the matter is so important then it will await my convenience."

Growling, the dragon advanced a step and said through bared teeth, "It had better be convenient for you right now, sorcerer!"

"You won't sway me that way, Ralligor. You never have."

"I don't have the patience for your intolerable arrogance!" the dragon growled.

Janees gulped a breath and backed away.

"If your *Magister* considers audience with me so important then you'd best not rouse an irritation in me."

The dragon closed another four paces toward the sorcerer with a single step, lowering his huge head and bringing his nose less than two paces from the sorcerer's. "This is important, Rawl, so save your riddles and your foolishness for another time!"

"Did your *Magister* teach you nothing of patience?" the sorcerer asked with a raised brow. He seemed to almost be trying to provoke the dragon's anger.

Thunder escaped the dragon in the form of a growl and his lips drew further back from his sword sized teeth. "He's taught me plenty about patience. Apparently no one's taught you about the hazards of annoying an angry dragon."

Nodding, the sorcerer's eyes narrowed and he ordered, "Tell your *Magister* that I know where to find him and I will be there shortly after sunup tomorrow."

Drawing his head back, the dragon growled another deep growl, his narrow eyes locked on the sorcerer. "Time is not working in our favor."

"And yet your issue will wait until morning. Deliver my message."

Snarling, the dragon stared him down for a long, terrifying moment before he turned away. His eyes paused on the sorcerer's garden, and his throat began to swell as his jaws opened slightly.

"Do not put that thought to action!" Rawl warned.

Glancing at the sorcerer, the dragon opened his wings and lifted himself into the air, the scarlet dragon following.

Rawl sighed and shook his head as he turned back to the cabin, mumbling, "I don't know what that damn dragon has against my garden."

Janees watched as he walked past her, then she followed, wringing her hands together as she entered behind him. Stopping just inside the doorway, she watched him fetch his book and sit down in his chair near the fireplace. As he flipped through the pages to find his place, she could only stare and await the inevitable.

He finally turned his eyes to her and bade, "Well?"

She found herself looking to the floor again and confessed, "I feel like a… a fool."

"As well you should," he confirmed.

When she looked back to him, he was smiling—actually smiling—and she heard a chuckle escape him as he looked back to his book.

She stood there for an awkward moment and just stared into

the fireplace. Finally, she managed to say, "I meant what I said. You have an impressive build."

"Do you feel less foolish now?" he asked.

"No," she replied.

"Then sit down and learn something."

Reluctantly, she padded to her chair and turned the page on her own book, and for the next couple of hours would not be able to bring herself to look at the sorcerer.

CHAPTER 12

Not yet queen, but all of the responsibilities of the position were laid heavily on her dainty shoulders. And what a long day!

At sixteen seasons old, her eyes showed the strain of her position and the pressures of the day, and seemed to be a woman of twice her age.

She wore a formal gown, one that was light blue and embroidered in silver. Her gold and diamond tiara was set perfectly in place above her brow and her long black hair was worn up in the fashion of royalty. Diamond earrings dangled from her ears and white slippers covered her feet. The chair she sat on was the throne of Caipiervell Castle and had deep red cushions and a high back. The chair beside it was the same, but stood empty.

With her elbow on the cushioned arm of the chair and her chin resting in her palm, she looked into the depth of the twenty pace long royal hall of the castle as the end of Royal Court drew near. Her eyes were half closed and she felt weary much beyond her seasons.

A scribe stood beside the empty chair, a thin man dressed in a white shirt and red overcoat, black trousers and high black boots. He was an older fellow with graying dark brown hair that was growing thin over the top of his head.

Standing on her other side was a rather tall, rather muscular woman in light steel armor over a thin black halter top, white riding trousers and tall black boots. Ornate and well polished gauntlets were strapped to her forearms and a broadsword the length of her arm hung at her side in a leather and steel sheath that hung from her thick black leather belt. Long blond hair was restrained in a pony tail behind her head as her dark blue eyes watched the door on the other end of the room in an almost predatory stare. Flanking this door were two men. One was a guard from Caipiervell and the other a big warrior from Enulam. The blond woman's eyes shifted frequently to the man from Enulam, formerly a mortal enemy, but now an ally. His found her just as frequently.

The Princess sighed and asked in an exasperated voice, "How many more?"

"Just two," the scribe assured, checking his book. He looked to the door and announced in a loud voice, "Her Royal Highness Princess Faelon shall now entertain and audience with General Brodar of the Bludchon clan."

Faelon sat up straight in her throne and her back went rigid. She shot a look to the blond woman, hoping for some reassuring sign from her. This was the meeting she had been dreading for weeks.

The blond woman, a captain in the Zondaen army, slid her eyes to the girl and nodded once to her, then her eyes narrowed as the door opened.

Swallowing back as much fear as she could, the Princess' wide eyes were locked on the door as the Bludchon General strode in. He wore animal skins over his shoulders, and brown leather trousers. Heavy steel armor clanked as he walked, as did the long sword at his side. The armor itself was well polished, but that appeared to have been done recently. A gray shirt beneath the animal skin and steel was barely visible and looked like it had once been white. His long brown hair was not kept nor was his long beard which was streaked with silver. Dark, predatory eyes were locked on the girl who sat on the throne and he held his brow low over them.

Behind him strode in two men dressed very similarly in steel armor and animal skins, and each carried a sword and dagger.

Faelon stiffened more as she saw them and leaned slightly to the woman at her side, whispering, "Pa'lesh, I thought he was not supposed to have soldiers with him. I thought he was supposed to come in here alone and unarmed!"

The Field Captain raised her chin slightly and said in a low voice, "Ignore them. He's just trying to intimidate you."

"It's working," the Princess hissed.

"Just relax," the Zondaen advised. "Don't let him know you're afraid."

"What if— "

"Just let *me* handle '*what if*' and stick to your morals."

Faelon nodded, then raised her chin as the General stopped a few paces away.

Pa'lesh looked to the big Enulam man and motioned to the Bludchon emissary and his men slightly with her head.

The Enulam soldier nodded back, then leaned to the Caipiervell guard and whispered something to him. As the guard departed, the soldier slowly began to stride toward the Bludchon men from behind.

General Brodar folded his thick, arms and raised his head, staring across at the Princess with nothing less than contempt in his eyes. Custom dictated that he was to bow to her, but this was something that he was clearly not going to do.

Drawing a breath, Princess Faelon folded her hands in her lap and politely asked, "To what do we owe the pleasure of your visit, General Brodar?"

He huffed a laugh. "I'll not be so impressed by your court speak, little wench. You know why I'm here."

Her eyes narrowing, Captain Pa'lesh warned, "Think hard about how you address the crown of this castle, dog."

His gaze shifted to her for only a second, then bored into the girl before him once again. "These trade routes to the north we've been at odds over should be decided on, as well as the tributes this kingdom owes the Bludchon."

Faelon's lips tightened. "Tributes. You mean the gold you want in exchange for not attacking my people who mean to ride north to trade with the kingdoms there."

"That would be the gold," he confirmed.

She drew and then loosed a deep breath, averting her eyes from him in an effort to calm herself and maintain her bearing. She knew she dare not show weakness, not at all. This was one of those decisions that weighed itself so heavily on her. Looking back to him, she asked, "And how much gold are we speaking of?"

"One hundred," was his answer. "One hundred for this season, one hundred for last season, and you can advance me one hundred for the next." He smiled slightly, showing teeth that were yellow and brown. "Won't be looking good for you if I return without it, and I'm sure you're not so keen on war."

"No, I am not," she confirmed, "nor am I so keen on paying extortion."

He set his jaw and his features became less pleasant.

"Diplomacy escapes you. I would think that you'd want those roads kept safe for your people."

"From you?" she spat. "Be warned, General, not to underestimate me because of my youth. It is a strength I shall relish as long as I can. As far as paying you three-hundred gold just to use roads that my people built, I guess you know my answer to that. I'll not bankrupt my kingdom to appease you."

"How's your army fairing?" he asked in a sinister voice. "I'll bet they're not up to fighting when they don't have to, and I'll bet you have no allies to stand with you when they hear the Bludchon are coming for ya."

Fear was in control of the Princess and was there in her eyes as she looked up at her Zondaen bodyguard.

Pa'lesh half smiled, her gaze boring into the Bludchon General. "Be very careful of your threats there, General. Be very careful."

She got but another glance from him as he raised his chin and smiled at the girl again. "I know you're not one for fighting, so let's make this as painless as we can. Three hundred gold will keep those roads free of bandits and marauding barbarians for the next couple of seasons and you'll have no more worries from it."

"Until you come and demand more gold," the Princess pointed out. Nervously, she shook her head and informed, "I'll not pay extortion. I'll not subject my people—"

"Enough of this rabble!" he suddenly shouted, his hand finding his sword.

The two men behind him stepped around and also seized their weapons, one of them turning directly on the Zondaen.

She did not even flinch.

"You pay the gold," the General growled, "or you can be gutted here and now and we'll take what we want from you!"

The scribe backed away, hugging his book to his chest.

"You're forgetting three things," Captain Pa'lesh said.

He finally gave her his attention and demanded, "What is it from you, woman?"

She half smiled again. "You're forgetting the combined armies of Zondae, Caipiervell and Enulam who are already patrolling those roads. You're forgetting your manners in the presence of a couple of ladies."

"And?" he spat.

Her smile broadened a little. "You're forgetting the five soldiers behind you."

The Bludchons spun around, finding themselves facing two soldiers from Enulam, one from Zondae, and two from Caipiervell who had quietly approached and had not been noticed. Their weapons were already in their hands and ready.

General Brodar looked to each of the soldiers, then slowly withdrew his hand from his sword and just as slowly turned to face the Princess once again.

Pa'lesh folded her arms and asked, "Not feeling so cocky now, are you?"

When the General's eyes found the Princess instead of the Zondaen, his brow dropped low over them. "You think this changes anything? You'll be paying those tributes or your trade routes north of here will belong to us again."

"They never belonged to you," Faelon informed harshly. "Those roads were built by the people of Caipiervell and shall be used by the people of Caipiervell and those friendly to us."

"Things are different out there, little girl," the Bludchon General informed with a smile. "You want the slaughter of travelers there to start, then see to it I don't return with our gold or at all. That land and all in it belongs to us." He glanced at the Zondaen beside her. "You think your little solders can scare the likes of us? They'll be the first to die."

Diplomacy would clearly not work with this man and Pa'lesh seemed to know it. She stepped toward him, her boots making loud clops that reverberated throughout the cavernous room. She stopped right in front of him, and only at this time did he notice that she was just a little taller than him. Her eyes bored down to his and she was silent until his met hers. With a little snarl, she informed, "Hold your attack until you see me leading one of those patrols. I want to meet you on the battlefield personally."

He stared back at her for a moment, then he smiled. "So it's war you'll be wantin', is it? I'll be givin' ya war."

"Don't disappoint me, little man," she said in a voice that sounded almost as if it belonged in a bed chamber. "I want to deal with you myself. Bring all of your little soldiers you want, just make sure you are leading the way."

Still smiling, he nodded to her. "I'll see to it. Might just spare you for me tent that night."

She smiled back at him. "I would spare you for the same if you didn't smell so bad." She looked up from him and ordered, "See these dogs out and make sure they get on their way." Turning her eyes back to the General, she finished, "And make certain this one gets safely back to his people."

Faelon rubbed her eyes with a finger and thumb as the Bludchons were escorted out and she shook her head. "You know, just once I want one of those meetings with a hostile people to go well. Just once."

Pa'lesh took her side again and folded her hands before her, countering, "That one went pretty well, I thought."

"You challenged him to a fight," the Princess reminded.

The Field Captain glanced at her. "As I said, it went pretty well." When she got a familiar exasperated look, she added, "Oh, cheer up. We Zondaens have been looking for a reason to do battle with them for many seasons. They're raiders who have hit us more times than I can remember and Queen Le'errin is always looking for a reason to hit them back."

"Using *my* court chamber," Faelon observed.

Pa'lesh shrugged and said, "Well, whatever works."

The Princess shook her head and looked to her scribe. "We have to be done for the day. Please tell me that we're done for the day!"

He smiled and nodded to her, assuring, "Just one more, Highness. I promise." He looked down to his parchment and observed, "This one was added last moment and insisted he would be your most important visit of the day."

The doors opened before the scribe summoned anyone and a white haired fellow in the green robes of a wizard entered.

Hearing the tap of his walking stick, Faelon looked to the man who entered, beaming a big smile as she saw him approaching. Jumping from her throne, she ran toward him in her awkward dress and met him halfway, throwing her arms around him as soon as she reached him.

He smiled and dropped an arm around her shoulders,

greeting, "Well hello there, Princess Faelon."

"I'm so glad to see you!" she breathed. "You're the *only* one I've wanted to see today."

"That will change," he informed. "I'm not truly the one who has come to see you. Your business is with someone who is outside."

She pulled away and looked up at him with a little concern on her features.

"Not the dragon," he assured.

A smile overpowered her and she could not speak.

"You should probably change," the wizard said. "I'm sure you aren't comfortable and the air is a trite hot and close today."

She nodded, then buried her face in his chest again, squeezing him as hard as she could.

He patted her back, smiling tenderly down at her, then he looked beyond her greeted, "Pa'lesh. You are looking well."

Folding her arms, the Field Captain nodded to him and replied, "It's good to see you again, though the last time I did you had a dragon in tow."

"No dragons today," he laughed, "but our Princess has an important meeting."

Nodding, the Zondaen said, "I figured that when I saw you. You know, you can visit sometime just to visit."

"I was already planning to," he informed. "I left Zondae this morning intent on coming here, but circumstances changed my day."

"How are Chail and Le'ell?" the Field Captain asked.

"Joined at the hip and bickering every few moments," was his answer.

She nodded. "Good to see them back to normal." She looked to the Princess. "Okay, your Highness. Let's pry you away from our guest and get to your last meeting of the day."

Faelon nodded and turned her eyes up to the wizard's. "Will you be there?"

"Of course I will," he assured.

She smiled and hugged him tightly once more before spinning away to run back toward and around the thrones where another door waited.

Pa'lesh glanced at the wizard and groaned as she turned in

pursuit.

As best she could, Princess Faelon ran down the corridor that would take her toward a staircase and up to her room. Her formal gown was not well suited to this but she ran nonetheless, holding her skirts up with both hands as she did. The skirts rustled loudly as she ran and she seemed oblivious to everything around her until she heard her own name spoken and slowed down, looking back and forth until she saw a tall, brown haired young woman in a blue servant's dress striding toward her.

Leaning her head and with her brow high over her eyes, the tall girl asked, "Highness? Are you fleeing or pursuing?"

The Princess turned and took the girl's hands, smiling broadly as she squealed, "Darree, they're back! They're back!"

"Who is?" the tall girl asked.

"The unicorns!" Faelon's voice was a flurry of excitement that she could barely contain. "I've waited a month for them to come back and they're here!"

Darree's mouth fell open and she asked, "Can I come too?"

Drawing her head back, the Princess said with a matter-of-fact tone, "Well of course! I'll not be excluding my dearest friends. Oh, just bring apples! They love apples!"

The tall girl smiled and nodded. "I'll go get some. Do you think Miss Ordrene would mind?"

Faelon rolled her eyes and scoffed, "Oh, like I *care* if she minds. Just tell her it's an order from the crown and I'll have her slopping hogs if she doesn't like it."

They turned as they heard the clopping boots and looked up to the big Zondaen who approached with a cocked up eyebrow and tight lips. "While you two conspire you have someone outside awaiting an audience."

The girls looked to each other and Faelon ordered, "Catch me up as fast as you can!"

Nodding, the tall girl wheeled around and made a wide circle around the Field Captain.

Pa'lesh turned as the girl ran around her, then she looked back to Faelon and shook her head.

"What!" the girl barked.

"Nothing," the Zondaen replied. "Are you going to change or just stand there?"

"What should I wear?" the Princess asked, looking down and spreading her skirts with her hands.

"I really don't think they care," was Pa'lesh's answer. "Why don't we just go?"

Drawing a breath, Faelon reached to her hair and made sure it was in order, made sure her tiara was straight, then she looked once more to her bodyguard. "Okay, we must go calmly and with the dignity befitting a member of the royal family." She turned and began to walk down the corridor, turned left into another that would take her to the entry hall, then she suddenly began to run again.

Pa'lesh loosed a sigh and shook her head again. "Dignity befitting... Okay, little girl." She set off at a quick walk in pursuit.

Princess Faelon burst outside through the twin timber doors of the palace and ran as hard as she could across the Southern courtyard toward the gate in the castle wall. Somewhere in the field beyond was a creature of her dreams, one that had helped restore her to the throne. She could almost see him through the open gate. What she did not see were the many people who dodged out of her way, the soldiers who directed horses out of her path, and that little dip in the carefully manicured road that caused her to stumble and roll to a dusty stop in the road.

Slow to get her wits about her as she lay face down on the ground, she sluggishly pushed herself up and raised her head.

People gathered and someone took her arm, then someone else took her other arm.

"All right," a gruff voice commanded. "Back yourselves away and let her Highness breathe."

As she was helped up, she rubbed the dust from her eye and looked up to see a knight who had a firm grip on her arm. She smiled at him and offered, "Thanks," then she ran toward the gate again.

"Careful, Highness," the knight called after her.

Barely aware that half of her hair had fallen and her tiara was hanging off of the other side of her head, she stopped just outside of the gate and looked around, panning back and forth to find the unicorn friend she so missed. Dusting her dress off, she reached to her head and more or less put her tiara back in place, then she strode quickly into the field, wanting to call to the unicorn she hoped she would find but knowing not to.

There! He was only about thirty paces away and the wizard was standing there beside him. Quickening her pace off of the road and into the tall grains, she raised a hand toward them, toward friends she craved the company of, then fell forward again and disappeared into the tall grass. As she struggled to right herself again, someone grabbed the back of her dress and pulled her to her feet in one brutal jerk. Looking behind her, she saw her Zondaen bodyguard standing there with her arms crossed, and was once again shaking her head.

"I can see you're going to need a lesson in keeping your feet," Pa'lesh observed.

"Later," Faelon said quickly, turning to continue on her way.

"Slow down," the field captain ordered from behind.

Looking behind her, the Princess called back, "Do you know how long I've— " She fell forward and disappeared into the grass again.

This time Pa'lesh walked past her. "You're on your own now, speedy."

Faelon slowly raised her head but could see only the green stalks of the grains that grew knee deep in the field. She blew out a breath, then pulled her hands under her and pushed herself up once again, struggling to get her knees under her so that she could stand. Then, a shadow fell over her and she looked down as a big cloven hoof set down gently right in front of her. Turning her eyes up, she beamed a radiant, joyful smile as she was filled with all of the love and awe that she had felt the first time she had seen his kind. Ever so slowly, she stood and wrapped her arms around his neck, burying her cheek in his soft mane. "Vinton," she breathed. "I'm so happy to see you."

He did not answer, but he did nuzzle her as best he could.

Faelon could feel that something was amiss and pulled away from him, looking to him with a little concern. When he would not look toward her, she asked softly, "What's wrong? Aren't you happy to see me?"

"Of course I am," he replied, staring at the ground. "I only wish the circumstances were better."

She backed away a step and took his chin in her hand, gently turning his head toward her. "Tell me what's wrong. Please, I'll do whatever I can to help you."

He blinked, but tears still escaped his eyes. Whickering, he finally managed, "Someone has taken Shahly."

Gasping, the Princess shook her head, her mouth hanging open slightly as she turned her eyes to the approaching wizard. His expression was also of worry now.

"I shouldn't burden you with this," the stallion said humbly.

"You are no burden!" Faelon insisted. "Whoever has her shall deal with the whole of Caipiervell. I promise you that I shall do everything within my power to find and reclaim her. I promise, Vinton."

He nodded.

Pa'lesh walked around him and knelt down right in front of him, taking his jaw in her hands and almost forcing his eyes on hers. "Listen, my friend, and listen closely. We are going to find whoever has her. I'll dispatch runners to Zondae right away. Queen Le'errin will mobilize however many soldiers we need to find her."

"Ralligor is on his way there already," the wizard informed.

The Zondaen glanced at him and nodded, then she looked back to the unicorn's eyes and insisted, "You have me with you as well."

He looked away, tears streaming from his eyes. "All of this from humans." He looked down. "I don't know how I can ever repay such kindness."

"You paid in full months ago," Pa'lesh informed. "You didn't have to help us. You did so because you are of a kind heart."

Faelon also knelt down and stroked the side of his nose. "At last we can repay your kindness and show you how much you truly mean to us all."

He closed his eyes and nodded.

The wizard appeared beside him and patted his neck. "Vinton, you and Shahly have many friends about that you'd never even dreamed of. I'm proud to be among them, and more so to put my power to work in your service."

"I'm not used to all of this," the stallion admitted. He looked up and saw many people approaching, one a tall, thin girl in a blue dress like he had seen Faelon wear a month past. "Would your kind always have made such a fuss for a unicorn?"

"You know we would," the Princess assured. She looked behind her, her eyes finding her bewildered friend and she extended a hand to her. "Come on, Darree. He needs our help."

With her mouth hanging open, the tall girl knelt down behind the Princess and offered the unicorn one of the apples she had.

More from politeness than hunger, Vinton reached out with his neck and gently took a bite out of the apple.

Barely able to breathe, Daree smiled.

"We haven't much time," Faelon announced as she stood. She turned to a soldier who had approached and set her hands on her hips, ordering, "Assemble my advisors and send word to the Knight's Hall. There is much to do and we have little time." When he bowed and turned to hurry back to the palace, she looked to someone who was more common folk and ordered, "We'll need provisions for a long journey."

This simple man, a fellow in his late forties raised his chin and stood up straight as his eyes met hers, assuring, "I will see to it, your Highness." He bowed to her and turned to hurry about his task.

Looking back to Vinton, Faelon said softly, "I know you wish to resume your search for her. We'll not be far behind."

The stallion slowly raised his head and met her eyes. "Are you certain you should go about all of this?"

Gently taking his jaw in her hands, the Princess bent her head down and softly kissed him on the nose. Looking into his eyes, she said just above a whisper, "I am your humble servant, and you are my dearest friend. I am yours. All of Caipiervell is."

He just stared back into her eyes for a time, then he softly said to her, "I owe you for this."

She smiled a little and replied, "I hold no such debts over anyone."

He smiled a little back.

"Where should we meet you?" she asked.

He looked away and considered, then he answered, "I'm not sure. Perhaps somewhere near your castle, if that would not be too much of an intrusion. Would that be okay, or do you not want to be overrun by so many unexpected guests?"

"Not at all," she informed. "I haven't entertained anyone since

I took power and I've really been looking forward to it. I'll ready my army to march as quickly as possible and as soon as I hear from you."

"I'll return as soon as I can, as soon as I find her," he said.

"I hope you find her before then," she said softly, "just so that you won't be away from each other for too long."

"Thank you," he offered. Raising his head, the stallion turned to the wizard and said, "We should go."

Nodding, the wizard agreed, "Yes, Falloah and Ralligor will be waiting for us." He looked to the Princess and nodded once to her. "Thank you for your help, Princess Faelon." He nodded to Pa'lesh, then he turned and followed the unicorn toward the forest.

Faelon watched them disappear into the trees, then she raised her chin.

Pa'lesh took her side and folded her arms. "We have quite a busy day coming. A month ago we were here to rescue a dragon, then your whole kingdom, now we are going to mobilize three armies to search for a missing unicorn."

Looking up at her, the Princess raised her brow and asked, "A worthy endeavor?"

The Zondaen hesitantly nodded. "Considering the unicorn, yes, I think so."

Faelon turned and strode back toward the castle. "Come on, then, everyone. We have much to do."

CHAPTER 13

Deep in the bowels of Castle Zondae, a heavy timber door opened and a tall, auburn haired woman in a white swordsman's shirt, tight riding trousers and tall, black leather boots emerged and walked straight across the corridor, leaning her arm on the wall and her head against her arm. Her hair was restrained behind her and would not flow into her face as she bowed her head against her forearm and breathed a sigh. She was very young, only nineteen seasons, but felt the burden of a much older woman.

A huge man emerged behind her, dressed similarly but his shirt was light gray and was open down half his chest. Only twenty-two seasons old, he was a head height taller than her with thick arms, thick legs and a huge chest and back. His waist looked rather small and his belly was clearly lean and bulging with muscle. Long brown hair dropped to his shoulders. He gently grasped her shoulders and reminded, "We both saw this coming."

She sighed and nodded. "I just didn't expect it so soon. I don't get it. I thought they didn't trust each other."

He lowered his mouth close to her ear and whispered, "You should never underestimate them."

Pushing off of the wall, she turned and looked up, meeting his eyes with hers. He was very handsome and his eyes were usually calming to her, but in the moment she could not relax the turmoil within her. "It just isn't right, what they're doing."

"And what we're doing is?" he countered.

"That's different, Chail," she argued. "Our relationship is *supposed* to be wrong. Theirs is... It's wronger."

He smiled and slid his arms around her back. "They started that long before we were born, Le'ell. We'll just have to get used to it."

She twisted away from him, turning to walk down the lamp lit corridor. "No, I don't. And can you tell your father to keep his hands off of my mother when I'm about?"

He followed and replied, "I can tell him, but I doubt he'll listen."

Le'ell shuddered. "They're too old for that kind of behavior."

"I'm sure our children will one day say the same about us."

She stopped and wheeled around, surprise on her features as she looked up into his eyes again. "*Our* children?"

Stopping right in front of her, he found himself mentally disarmed and stammered, "Uh..." He could not take his wide eyes from hers.

She smiled slightly. "You've never said anything about children before. I rather like hearing you talk so."

As she turned and strode away from him, he just watched for a moment, then he trotted to her side and stammered, "Well... You know, in the event it happens... Um..."

He got a sidelong glance in response and she smiled a little bigger. "I didn't know you wanted to sire my children."

"Who else would I have do it?" he asked loudly. "It's not like I'd allow some other man to touch you."

She nodded. "I shudder to think about what you would do to anyone who did."

"You don't remember what I said about that this spring?"

Her smile slowly faded away and she turned her eyes down. She drew a breath and reluctantly shook her head.

"It will just take time," he assured.

"What if my memory of you never comes back?" she asked softly.

Chail took her arm and spun her around, grabbing both arms in his huge hands. When she finally looked up at him, he smiled at her and informed, "Then you'll have to just fall in love with me all over again."

Something in her eyes lightened and just the hint of a smile touched her face. "I'm afraid it's too late for that. It's happened already."

He slid his arms around her and crushed her to him. "Then I have you and I'm never letting go!" He squeezed harder and lifted her slightly from the floor.

"You've got me," she strained. "Can I breathe now?"

Chail considered, then observed, "If you pass out, you'll be easier to take advantage of. Hmm..."

"Let go!" she laughed. When he dropped her she stumbled and looked up at him with an annoyance in her voice as she cried, "Hey! I said *put* me down!"

His eyes were beyond her and narrow, his brow low over them.

Le'ell turned to see many Zondaen archers run across the corridor where it met another. They were heading out of the castle. As Chail and Le'ell ran toward them, more soldiers emerged, all heavily armed and some still pulling on armor. Grabbing one, Le'ell asked, "What's happening?"

The brown haired woman's eyes were wide and she raised her chin, answering in one word, "Dragon!"

Le'ell released her, ice creeping up her spine as her lips slowly parted. Somehow, she knew the dragon they were going out to meet.

Chail took her shoulders from behind, unable to speak as he stared at the departing soldiers.

She slowly shook her head, murmuring, "I was beginning to think this day would never come. I was hoping he had forgotten me."

Holding her tighter, Chail finally said, "Let's go and see what he wants."

"He wants me," she pointed out. "You don't have to go out there with me."

"And yet I will," he insisted, pushing her forward. When he released her and took her side, she reached to him and took his hand, holding it as tightly as she could. He squeezed back, careful not to hurt her, but letting her know that he was with her to the end.

As they got outside, they found the soldiers and archers taking their positions around the compound, finding cover behind wagons, the stables, and some of them kneeling out in the open to take aim at the battlement wall.

Perched on the wall was an enormous black dragon, and beside him was a smaller scarlet dragon. They glanced around at the activity below them, but did not seem to be ready to attack.

Chail raised his chin as he stared at the dragons. He had seen what the black one could do to an army. He had attacked that dragon himself with enchanted weapons and not even scratched his armor. All of the Zondaen soldiers and archers and the

Enulam soldiers with them stood no chance against that beast. Drawing a breath, he shouted, "Everyone out of the courtyard. Fall back into the palace. Now!"

The soldiers were hesitant at first, then they made their way to the various doors that would take them inside the protection of the palace walls. In a few moments the courtyard was clear. Even the horses were led to cover into the stables.

With no other activity outside, the dragons turned their eyes to the only two other creatures outside.

Holding Le'ell's hand tightly, Chail strode slowly out into the courtyard, his eyes on the dragons.

The black dragon grunted to the red, then he opened his wings and jumped from the wall, landing gently for his size fifty paces from them.

Stopping when the dragon left the wall, Chail and Le'ell simply stood there and stared up at him.

The dragon stood to his full five men's heights and folded his arms, his eyes boring into the humans before him. They shifted from Chail to Le'ell, and remained there.

Nervously yet bravely, she raised her chin, asking, "You've come for that debt I owe you, haven't you?"

The dragon nodded once.

Chail set his jaw, his eyes boring up into the dragon as he insisted, "We should negotiate this bargain of— "

"Negotiations have ended," the dragon boomed.

Clenching Le'ell's hand a little tighter, Chail growled, "Listen, dragon. I realize we made a bargain, but understand that I did not approve then and I don't approve now."

"I don't care if you approve or not," the dragon growled back. His eyes finally shifted to Chail and his brow lowered more. "I require the female."

Le'ell turned her head just a little. "You said before I am worth more to you alive than dead. Has that changed?"

"I did not come here for conversation!" the dragon roared. He took a step forward, his body leveling and he brought his head and his bared teeth down to them. "I have come for the woman." When the red dragon crooned, he half turned his head, then looked back to them and drew his head back, then standing fully, saying more calmly, "We have a bargain. I was good to my word and I expect you to be good to yours."

Glancing at her, Chail clenched his teeth and suggested, "Perhaps you could take another."

Le'ell's eyes darted to him and she hissed, "Chail! What are you doing?"

"Neither of us likes your sister, anyway," he pointed out.

Her brow arched and she looked away.

"That wasn't the bargain," the dragon corrected. "I haven't much time, so if you want your castle to remain standing and your people to live another day you will come with me peacefully."

Opening her wings, the red dragon leaped from the wall and glided to the black dragon, landing slightly behind him and trotting to his side as she quickly folded her wings to her. Only about two thirds his height standing, she turned her nose high to see him, showing off the ocher orange scales of her throat as she crooned at him again. Despite opening her jaws slightly, she really did not show much of her teeth. She seemed to be talking to him and she reached around with one hand and grasped his chest, slipping the other around his back.

The black dragon looked down to her, his lips sliding away from his sword sized teeth as he growled back. She was clinging to him and this seemed to annoy him. More than that, he seemed to be arguing a point.

She grunted, then a shrill trumpet sounded from her.

"They're talking," Le'ell realized aloud.

Looking away from the scarlet, the black dragon took a step away from her and twisted from her grip. He looked annoyed and was clearly making no secret of it.

The scarlet stood there and watched him stride a couple of steps away from her, then she leaned her head and crooned something to him.

He turned his back fully to her and grunted back, staring across the compound. He seemed angry, yet he would not direct that anger toward the red dragon.

Swinging her head and body around with a single step, the scarlet dragon lowered her body and her head toward the two amazed humans, her amber eyes finding them with a gentle gaze. "Forgive him," she said unexpectedly. "Troubled times are with us."

"I saw you before," Chail recalled, "at the confrontation at Aalekilk this spring."

Her eyes shifted to him and she seemed to smile. "You saw me before that, too, but there is no way you could have known me then." She glanced at the black dragon as he grunted, then she looked back to the humans. "This is not what you think. He is a proud dragon and what he wants from you is not a sacrifice of your life or your flesh in his belly."

Le'ell raised her brow and asked, "He doesn't want to eat me?"

Drawing her head back, the scarlet dragon snarled and declared, "Oh, heavens no! Your kind is simply not palatable! We need you in a different way." She glanced at the black dragon again, then sighed. "I'll be honest with you, and I shall appeal to you where he cannot. We could use your help."

Raising his chin, Chail's eyes narrowed and he straightly asked, "What will the price be this time?"

Her eyes snapped to him and she informed in a less pleasant tone, "I've come to ease this whole process. Don't make me step away and let you speak to him again." She leaned her head slightly and looked to Le'ell. "I see males of your kind are just as stubborn and confrontational as mine."

The Princess smiled ever so slightly and nodded.

Turning her eyes toward but not to the black dragon, the scarlet said a little more loudly, "Perhaps it is time for truth to prevail over the pride of both our mates."

The black dragon turned his head slightly and grunted, then he growled a sigh.

Standing, the scarlet turned and grunted to him, then crooned.

His chest swelled as he drew a breath, then it growled all the way out of him.

Le'ell pulled away from Chail and took a few hesitant steps toward the huge dragon, her eyes hopefully up on his. Her lips tightened and she lifted her head as if to help her voice carry. "If you need my help, great dragon, then I am yours."

He half turned his head and snarled, "*I* don't." When the scarlet barked a roar at him, he growled another sigh and lowered his head, staring at the ground for a time before he spoke again. When he did, his voice was softer. "You don't remember the man at your side, but I'm sure you remember an annoying little unicorn who approached you many times this spring."

Le'ell's eyes widened and she gasped, raising a hand to her mouth.

The scarlet dragon continued for him, "She is missing. Someone of power has taken her and we are looking for all who would lend their help to find her."

Turning her eyes to the scarlet dragon, Le'ell was unaware that her mouth was wide open. Her breath came hard and she slowly shook her head. Her gaze found the black dragon again and she declared, "I owe that little unicorn my life, and my dreams. If you mean to go and find her then I am yours, debt to you or not."

Ever so slowly, the black dragon turned and looked down to her. He did not speak. His eyes said it all for him.

Chail took her side and also looked up at the black dragon, raising his chin as he assured, "You have her, and you have me. We will mobilize the whole of the Enulam and Zondaen armies in your service."

Snarling, the black dragon asked, "And what interest is she to you, human?"

"Heart," was the Prince's answer, "the same as you."

Giving the big human a long stare, the black dragon nodded to him and conceded, "Fair enough." He turned his eyes away again and grudgingly said, "Any help you can provide in this matter will be appreciated, and if we can rescue her then your debt to me will be considered paid." He turned his bulk and opened his wings, sweeping them down as he leapt into the air and landed on the battlement wall. Half looking back, he let go a short roar.

Hearing this, the scarlet opened her wings and nodded to them, offering, "You have our thanks," before she turned and took to the sky behind the black dragon as he launched himself from the wall.

Watching the dragons fly away, Le'ell slowly shook her head and admitted, "I almost don't feel right about paying that debt this way."

"I'll sure take it," the Prince admitted. "Let's just hope what we face will be easier than what we did before."

She nodded in agreement, then turned and took his hand, pulling him along. "Come on. We've got to get going."

Following, he asked, "Going where?"

"Pinetop Castle," was her answer.

"And how do you know that's where we are supposed to go?"

She stopped and glanced about in front of her, then shook her head and replied, "I don't know how. I just know that's where we are to go."

His brow lowered and he glanced away. "Um, sure. Whatever you say."

"Don't argue with me about this!"

"I'm not arguing. I'm just not sure about how things are unfolding today."

"Sometimes you can't— " Le'ell stopped where she was and turned her eyes to the people who stormed out of the castle door twenty paces in front of them. "Here we go," she mumbled.

Chail nodded, assuring, "I'm here with you."

"As always you are," she confirmed softly, her eyes on the woman who approached, a woman who looked much like Le'ell, though age and bearing children had thickened her body slightly and her long auburn hair was streaked with silver. She carried a bow in her hand and a quiver dangled over her shoulder. The man with this tall woman towered over her, standing nearly as tall as Chail, whose chin came to the top of a normal man's head. As heavily made as the Prince, this man was showing the wear of twenty more seasons and was a little thicker around the middle and his face bore the burden of two decades of his station. A grey streaked beard hung from his jaws. He had his body armor pulled on over his swordsman's shirt, but it was not fastened. He also had his weapons belt thrown over his shoulder and had a double bladed axe in his hand.

Le'ell vented a breath as she and Chail stopped, allowing the approaching older man and woman to close the last few paces.

Before anyone spoke, the bearded man tossed the axe to Chail, who caught it easily. "Thought you might need that, but it looks like you've already scared him off."

Turning his eyes down to the axe, Chail shook his head and admitted, "Not exactly."

Le'ell's eyes were on the older woman's, on her mother's. "We have something we need to do. I already know what you're going to say—"

"Le'ell!" the woman interrupted, her brow lowering. She broke off as the bearded man grasped her shoulder and she turned her eyes to him. "Donwarr…"

"Errin, just hear her out," the older man advised.

Her lips drew tight and she vented a hard breath, then she folded her arms and said, "Very well, Little Dragon. I'm listening."

Subtly slipping her hand into Chail's, Le'ell raised her chin and informed, "I have a debt to that dragon to pay."

"Absolutely not!" Le'errin shouted.

"It isn't what you think," Chail assured. "He has no interest in eating her."

Setting her jaw, Le'errin shifted her eyes to the bearded man and snarled, "I'm already not liking the sound of this, Donwarr."

He nodded and looked to his son. "Chail, I've always trusted your judgment, but right now you seem to be pushing that limit."

"Again," Chail assured, "this is not what you think."

"He needs our help," Le'ell continued. "He saved our kingdoms, he brought down Aalekilk and now we are a united people with his help."

"This is the dragon you swore your life to?" Le'errin asked sharply.

"The same," Le'ell confirmed. "Ama, he seemed to know that he would someday need my help, and now he does." She turned her eyes down. "Do you remember when I told you about the unicorn?"

Raising her brow slightly, Le'errin replied, "I remember. I still don't know what to think about that encounter, but I remember."

"Someone has taken her," Le'ell went on. "He needs our help to find her."

Rubbing her eyes, Le'errin heaved a deep breath born of frustration and guessed, "And you feel the need to take the task upon yourself to find her."

"He asked for my help," the Princess pointed out.

Chail added, "You can't really say *no* to a dragon that size."

Donwarr nodded, raising his brow as he agreed, "No, I suppose you can't."

With her brow low over her wide eyes, the Queen straightly informed, "I do *not* want you putting yourself at risk again, Le'ell."

The Princess' eyes shifted down and she nodded, then they found her mother's again and she responded, "If you had seen her as I did, if you had spoken to her, if you owed her your life and your dreams as I do, you would not hesitate to put yourself at risk for her. Ama, please understand."

Queen Le'errin was quiet for a long moment, then she looked away and folded her arms. "I would ask that same understanding from you. Don't you know what losing you would do to me? Do you not yet realize what you mean to me?"

Seeing a tear roll down her mother's cheek, Le'ell's lips tightened and she closed the space between them with two strides and tightly embraced the Queen, tears fighting to emerge from her eyes too as she whispered, "I understand, Ama. I do." Feeling Le'errin's arms slide around her back, the Princess laid her head on her shoulder and assured, "Nothing will happen to me, Ama, I promise. I'll be okay. Please understand that I simply must do this."

Le'errin nodded. "I'm going to hold you to that promise, Little Dragon."

Pulling away slightly, Le'ell offered her mother a smile and informed, "I have a big dragon and a big Enulam prince looking out for me. They'll keep harm at bay."

Seeing the Queen's gaze find him, Chail nodded and assured, "You have that promise from me as well, Majesty."

"Still," King Donwarr cut in, "I think a detachment would tilt that scale in your favor."

Chail's eyes found him and he said, "We'll need to go light and fast, and I don't think we should attract too much attention. I would sure welcome a garrison or two a day behind us, though. Perhaps they could rendezvous with Captain Pa'lesh at Caipiervell."

The King nodded and turned to Le'errin. "How does that

sound to you?"

Reluctantly, with her eyes on her daughter, she also nodded, then she raised her chin and informed, "I'll be leading them myself. If you're going to risk your life for this unicorn then I want to see her."

Le'ell regarded her mother through narrow eyes. "That's not like you, Ama."

"I've never seen a unicorn," the Queen informed. "I think it's time to."

Nodding, the Princess confirmed, "Okay. In other words you still don't fully believe that I saw her."

Taking her daughter's hands, Le'errin assured, "Of course I do, Little Dragon." Her eyes strayed and she continued, "I just... I need to see her for myself. After what that wizard did to you..."

Raising her brow, Le'ell pressed, "Do you at least believe the part about the dragon?"

Nodding, the Queen conceded, "Yes, I do." She finally looked to her daughter again and informed, "I don't want you to go, not alone."

"I'll have Chail with me," Le'ell assured. "Nothing will happen to me."

"Like nothing happened to you before?"

Pulling away, the Princess turned toward the big Enulam Prince and just looked up at him, her eyes tense.

His eyes shifted to the Queen and he informed, "This is a rescue mission, Majesty. I don't foresee any confrontations with dragons or vampires this time."

"A rather irate dragon just left here," she reminded.

"We're going to help him," the Prince countered. "I think he will be on our side."

Le'errin's lips tightened until her mouth was a narrow slit. She turned her gaze down and nodded. "Donwarr, I suppose you see no problem with them going?"

"I see plenty of problem with it," the Enulam King observed, "but I see greater problems should they not go." When she turned her attention to him, he smiled and assured, "They'll be fine and we'll be a day behind them."

Nodding, Le'errin turned and strode toward the palace,

beckoning, "Chail, a word."

"Here we go," he mumbled as he followed her.

As she watched them enter the castle, Le'ell folded her arms, her eyes on the timber doors as people began to hesitantly emerge. "I'm nineteen seasons old. I'm a grown woman and warrior. When is she going to let me grow up?"

Donwarr laughed and took her under his arm, guiding her slowly toward the same door. "Never. You're the youngest child, you are her favorite and you'll always be her Little Dragon no matter how old you are."

"It isn't fair," she complained, leaning into him. "You see Chail as a man and you trust what he says and does. You don't treat him like a child."

"That doesn't mean I don't worry like a mother hen when he's out of eyeshot," the King informed.

Le'ell's eyes snapped up to his.

"You'll be a mother someday," Donwarr went on. "Only then will you understand, and only then will you appreciate what your dear mother has to endure with you."

She nodded and looked down again. "I suppose. Will you do something for me?"

"What is that?"

"Try not to grope my mother every time she's within arm's reach."

He laughed and shook his head, heartily informing, "No promises!"

CHAPTER 14

Night settled itself slowly in the forest. Long shadows grew longer and darkness began to overrun the meadow that was nestled in the trees. No wind or breeze blew and the forest seemed to be waiting. Many of the night creatures were also silent and none ventured into the meadow itself. Only one was there.

Lying in the grass, right out in the open, Vinton stared blankly down the slope that led to the creek, his eyes fixed on that spot where Shahly had disappeared. He felt sad, lonely, and a choking numbness consumed him. He knew he was not complete without her, and never would be. So many times had her adventurous ways raised his ire, so many times had she endured his scolding of something foolish she had done. Now, he would give anything to see her leap from a cliff into the river, or stare down a forest cat, or any of a hundred things she was known for.

Inside, he felt emptiness. Once held captive by humans once, he knew the feeling of being a prisoner. Now, he felt something that was even worse.

As darkness consumed the area and he could barely see anything, he finally felt the thumps on the ground that seemed to grow closer, then finally heard the crunching of grass and earth. He blinked and slowly raised his head, looking over his shoulder to see a huge, dark form approaching him. Uninterested, he laid his head back down and stared at the last spot where Shahly had been free.

Ralligor stopped a little behind him and also stared at that spot, then he seemed to fall forward and crashed to the ground on his belly beside the unicorn, crossing his arms before him. He drew a sigh and released it in a growl.

They stared in silence for a time as the darkness set in deeper.

Finally, the dragon spoke. "We should know where she is by tomorrow morning."

Vinton did not answer.

"Rawl is a sorcerer of great power and skill," Ralligor informed. "He'll be able to tell us exactly where she is and who has her."

"And then what?" the unicorn finally asked.

"We go and get her," was the dragon's answer.

"It'll be that easy, will it?"

Ralligor was a long time to answer, but finally admitted, "I don't expect it to be easy. This sorcerer who took her has some kind of plan for her and I don't think he will just let her go. He'll fight to keep her."

"You don't think he will hurt her, do you?"

The Desert Lord slowly lowered his head to the ground, a red glow beginning from deep in his eyes as his brow lowered between them as he snarled, "If he does I will show him pain he's never even imagined."

"I sure don't understand your need for revenge."

"That's why you should leave it to me."

They stared into the darkness for a time, the red glow in Ralligor's eyes slowly fading. In their thoughts were memories of Shahly and the many trials they had each endured with her. Vinton missed her laughter and her tender, adventurous presence. Though she irritated him often, Ralligor missed her the same way.

"Tell me something," the unicorn said.

"I'm listening," Ralligor replied.

"Why didn't you kill her this spring when you had her cornered near your lair? It would have been easy."

"I know," the dragon admitted.

"Then why did you just let her go?" Vinton pressed. "Why did you help her? Why do you remain friends with her even now?"

Ralligor's eyes darted about in the night, not focusing on anything.

Vinton raised his head, looking to the dragon as he awaited an answer.

The Desert Lord finally growled and admitted, "I don't know. She annoys the hell out of me. She's an enemy of my kind. She's brought nothing but trouble and misery to my life since the day she stumbled into my canyon." He would not look at the big bay unicorn as he puzzled over something so simple. "Why does *she* have to involve herself in matters that she should stay away from? She was at my side every moment she could be when the dragonslayer had Falloah. Her affection for me just doesn't make sense."

"Little about her does," the unicorn informed, "not to those who are blind to her heart and her giving and adventurous spirit."

Ralligor finally turned his eyes to the bay.

Vinton's attention drifted into the darkness. "There's that innocent presence about her, and that adventurous part of her that borders on madness."

"And brings insanity to those around her," the dragon growled.

Nodding, the unicorn admitted, "Very true. And yet the combination of everything that makes her draws us to her like bees to a flower." He looked back to the dragon. "She was an adventurous scamp long before she met you, and she'll be so the rest of her life."

Abruptly raising his head, Ralligor declared, "Ha! So her annoying insanity isn't my fault after all!"

"Oh, it is," Vinton countered. "She wasn't quite so reckless before you."

Ralligor raised a brow, then he laid his head back down.

"Do you know why you didn't kill her?" the unicorn questioned.

"Because I enjoy the pain of her constant annoyances. I also enjoy her awakening me at inconvenient times to assist in one of her damned crusades."

"Or," Vinton suggested, "you just couldn't see her as an enemy."

Looking back at him, the dragon growled, "What?"

"Do you kill just to kill? She told me what happened that day and how everything unfolded. When you two sparred, I don't think you had any intention of killing her."

"Perhaps I saw that she could be useful to me. Don't try to hang some emotional attachment around my neck, Plow Mule. She's an irritant and I should never have involved myself with her."

"And yet you did, and you are here now sick with worry for her."

Ralligor growled and looked away. "She still has my amulet."
"And your heart," Vinton added.
"You are every bit the irritant she is," the dragon snarled.
Laying his head back down, the unicorn pointed out, "And yet you tolerate us."
"Barely."
Another long silence passed between them, finally broken when the unicorn asked, "What do you suppose they want her for?"
Ralligor loosed a throaty breath and replied, "It could be any of a number of reasons. Could be vanity, just something to show off, it could be the mystical nature of your kind... I don't know for sure."
"Humans seek trophies all around them."
"That they do."
"If he can't be convinced to release her, do you think he would take me for her?"
"I wouldn't."
"I would glare at you but I don't know how well you can see in the dark."
"I see just fine in the dark, so glare away."
"Really. I can hardly see you right there."
"I'm told I am difficult to see in the dark."
"You're difficult to look at, anyway."
"Get fleas and die."
Vinton whickered a laugh.
Falloah landed in the darkness behind them and just stared at this odd sight for a moment, finally shaking her head as she admitted, "I half expected to see you two locked in combat."
"Later," they grumbled together.
She approached and sat down on Vinton's other side. Ever so slowly, ever so gently, her clawed hand stroked his back and she assured, "We'll find her, Vinton, and we'll get her back for you."
"You have my confidence," he softly whickered to her, "and my trust."
She looked to her huge mate, her brow arching as she observed, "This promises to be a long night, *Unisponsus.*"
"That it does," the black dragon agreed.
"She's so lonely," Vinton said softly. "I don't know where she

is, but her heart is so lonely. I've never felt such despair from her."

"Then give her your strength," the dragon ordered. "Can you feel her well enough to speak with her?"

"I think I could, if she was more experienced. Her essence isn't quite strong enough to understand what I would say."

"She'll understand well enough as she sleeps," the dragon informed.

His eyes shifting to the Desert Lord, Vinton asked, "You can sense her?"

"Barely," the dragon confirmed. "Her emotions cloud her and her guard is up. She can't sense us. When she sleeps, we may be able to find her twilight mind."

"She's very inexperienced, Ralligor."

"I'm not," the Desert Lord countered.

CHAPTER 15

Shahly glanced about, not knowing where she was. It seemed to be the forest, and yet it was surrounded by stone walls and iron bars. As she walked through the trees, something stopped her. Everywhere she went, she could not escape this place. She was lost, and could not find her way home, nor could she even stray far from where she was. Frustration mounted as she turned the other way.

Shrieking a gasp, she froze as she found herself facing the three huge timber doors of Red Stone Castle's arena. Slowly shaking her head, she backed away, her hoof finding the chain and ring that she had been tethered to.

"Well, well," Nillerra's voice teased from behind.

Shahly wheeled around, seeing the other side of the arena, and the black haired girl stalking toward her with a wicked smile.

"Welcome to the rest of your life," Nillerra greeted. "I have such plans for you."

"Please just let me go," Shahly whimpered as she backed away.

"You'll die first," the black haired girl hissed. She was only about five paces away when she stopped. "You have no friends here, Shahly, no one to protect you. You're at my mercy, and I wish to see you suffer."

As Shahly retreated, she was stopped and discovered that her leg was once again shackled to the chain and she could not move further.

"This is almost too easy," the black haired girl drawled, "but you know I'll enjoy it anyway. Oh, you might remember some old acquaintances."

Slowly raising her head, Shahly's eyes widened as the wicked guard appeared behind Nillerra. In the distance, the unicorn hunters rode into view. A forest cat also approached, and the ground birds that had almost killed her the day before. She tried to back away, kicking against the chain that held her, and she finally reared up in terror, kicking toward them as if to ward them off. The whinny she tried to cry came out as the scream of her human voice!

Nillerra shook her head and ordered, "Oh, none of that. If you won't behave you'll just have to be restrained."

Shahly came down and tried to back away again and reared up as the chain stopped her, and as the guard and hunters drew closer, three chains exploded from the ground and shackles reached for her, each clamping around a leg just above her hooves. Those around her forelegs jerked brutally backward, pulling her down where she slammed to the ground on her back. Breath exploded from her. As she struggled to regain it, she recognized the shrieks of her own human voice. Gasping, she held her hands over her, then looked toward her body, seeing her human form lying chained to the ground, naked and helpless. She slowly turned horror-filled eyes to Nillerra as the guard and hunters surrounded her, eying her with hungry, wicked intent.

The black haired girl grew in size and her form quickly shifted, sprouting feathers and wings. Standing four heights tall, the horrible vulture thing she was now stared down at her with horrible, solid black eyes, and she cackled a laugh. "We will have so much fun, Shahly. They have been waiting to have you for a long time, and when they are done, I get what's left." She raised her head and ordered, "Don't kill her, boys, but make her wish you had."

The guard was the first one to approach, unfastening his shirt as he stared down at her with sickening purpose.

Shahly screamed as he reached for her.

A blast of fire slammed into Nillerra's chest, knocking her backward and to the ground.

The men surrounding her backed away. Fire swept among them and flashes of green light lanced forth and killed many of them, and their burning bodies melted into the soil.

Nillerra was slow to rise, but she did stand, holding a hand-like wing over her burnt chest. Her eyes glowed white as she looked up.

A thumping on the ground approached from behind Shahly and she turned her head to see the black dragon striding toward her, his eyes glowing crimson. Afraid that he meant to harm her as well, she sobbed and begged, "Please, Ralligor. It's me. It's

Shahly! Please!"

"I know it's you," he snarled, his eyes still on the vulture beast that retreated as he approached. "Fight or flight, bird."

Wisely, Nillerra stroked her wings and fled, calling back, "This isn't over!"

The dragon stopped only a few paces away, finally looking down to Shahly. "Well, now. It seems you can't even stay out of trouble here in your own twilight mind." He reached to her and gently picked her up, the chains crumbling away as he did. He righted her and set her back down on all fours.

Shahly realized she was unicorn again and turned her eyes up to him, slowly backing away as she felt fear of him for only the second time since she had met him.

"Just relax, Shahly," he suggested. "This is supposed to be a safe place for you."

"What?" she whimpered.

"You're not accustomed to nightmares," he explained, "but it did help me find you."

"Nightmares?" she questioned. Her eyes darted about. Elements of the forest appeared around her. Trees were in the arena. Grass waved in a gentle breeze, grass that was not there a moment ago. She drew a breath and softly said, "I'm dreaming."

"If that's what you want to call it," the dragon countered. "I haven't got much time so we'll need to make this quick."

She stared blankly up at him for a moment, then shook her head and admitted, "I don't understand. You... You don't have time?"

"I can't explain now. Do you know where you are?"

She glanced about. "I'm in my dream."

"No, Shahly. I mean where were you taken?"

"Oh. Um, I don't know. I found myself in a stable. I just went down to get a drink and the mist came up and then I was in the stable."

"Okay, where is the stable?"

She turned her eyes down. "I'm sorry, Ralligor. I only know that it is a stable of some kind. That is really all I know."

"Do you know *who* has you?"

"That I know," she confirmed. "He calls himself Lord Nemlivv."

Ralligor looked away and growled, baring his teeth.
"Do you know him?" Shahly asked.
"I know of him," the dragon snarled. "He hasn't caused you harm, has he?"
"No, he hasn't hurt me. He has offered me food and water and we talked a couple of times, but he has left me alone for the most part."
Nodding, Ralligor said, "I suppose that's good for now. Are there any other problems where you are?"
She shrugged. "Just lonely and bored. I miss you and Vinton terribly and I really want to go outside. It isn't unpleasant here, it's just small."
He looked to her and vented a breath. Pity was in his eyes for the first time since she had known him.
Shahly blinked and raised her head. "Ralligor, will you be able to get me out of here soon?"
He was a long time in answering, but finally replied, "Help is coming, Shahly. Just be patient and don't do anything that might draw his wrath to you."
"I won't," she assured, turning her eyes down again. "Is Vinton okay?"
"As well as can be expected."
"Will you tell him I love him?"
"Of course I will."
"Tell him I'm very lonely here without him."
"I will."
"Nuzzle him for me?"
"Let's not push it."
She whickered a laugh and looked back up at him. "When will you be here? In the morning? I warned Nemlivv that he should let me go otherwise bad things could happen, but he didn't believe me."
Raising his head slightly, the dragon asked, "Does he know about me?"
"I don't think so. He hasn't said anything if he does."
"Don't tell him. That should be our secret."
"Okay. Will you be here soon?"
He looked away. "As soon as I can. I have to find you first."
"How will you do that?"

"It's nothing I should bore you with. Suffice to say come morning I'll know just where to find you."

"Just don't hurt too many people when you get here."

He growled. "There you go again. Someone has taken you captive, holds you against your will, and you are more concerned with me hurting someone than your own freedom." He huffed a breath and shook his head. "I suppose that's your nature."

"It is," she confirmed. "So, you won't be here in the morning?"

"Not at first light, no. As soon as I know where you are I'll make my way toward you." He tightly closed his eyes and raised a hand to his head, growling softly.

Shahly's ears swiveled forward and she asked, "Are you okay?"

"Doing this is a bit draining under the circumstances. I need to go."

Feeling herself near panic, Shahly mustered her courage and swallowed her fear back, looking down as she nodded. "I understand."

Looking back to her once more, the dragon warned, "If you think Nemlivv is going to hurt you at any point, just tell him he will answer to his greatest nightmare if he does."

"That's you," she said.

Nodding, he confirmed, "Yes, that's me. I need to go."

"Will you be able to come back before I wake up?"

"I'll try, Shahly." He turned and strode away from her, toward an opening in the trees.

"Ralligor!" she desperately called after him.

He stopped and looked over his shoulder.

She cantered forward a few steps. "I'll miss you. Please don't be too long."

Nodding once, he turned and continued on his way.

As he disappeared from sight, she suddenly felt very alone again, tears glossing her eyes as she said, "Don't be too long, Ralligor. I miss you." Turning her eyes down, she turned and wandered the other way.

Her dream was quiet the rest of the night. She was alone in the forest. Not even birds were singing in the trees. A bright light shined on her from somewhere ahead and she squinted as she looked up toward it, expecting to see the sun coming up.

Half opening her eyes, she got her wits about her as she realized the door to the stable was open and people were entering, and one felt frightening familiar. This would be the beginning of her second day as Nemlivv's captive, and hopefully her last. She could hear whispering, but could not make out what was said. As one approached and the others departed, Shahly slowly got to her hooves and approached the stall gate.

Nillerra's look was a smug one as she strolled toward the stall with her hands folded behind her. She was dressed in black boots and black riding trousers. Her shirt was white and full sleeved and seemed to fit her a little tight around her waist. It was also unfastened halfway down her chest. Her long black hair was restrained in a pony-tail behind her. Her dark eyes were locked on Shahly and her brow was held high over them. As she reached the stall, she raised her chin slightly, staring coldly at the unicorn before her for a long moment.

This felt awkward and Shahly turned her eyes away.

Finally, Nillerra spoke. "Well, today is the day, Shahly. I'm going to get your wizard and you may just go free."

"I wish you would not go," the unicorn said softly.

"Second thoughts?" the black haired girl chided. "It sounds like your conscience might be stinging you this morning. Wouldn't you rather go free today?"

"I would," Shahly admitted, "but not like this. I don't want anyone to get hurt because of me."

"Someone already has," Nillerra snarled. "Don't you remember what you did to me at Red Stone? Don't you remember hurting me then?"

A hard breath escaped Shahly and she looked back to the black haired girl. "You brought all of that on yourself, Nillerra. I no more hurt you—"

"Liar!" the black haired girl hissed.

"We've been over this," the unicorn countered. "I won't be blamed for what you did to yourself." Half turning away, Shahly felt frustration mounting within her, and her sense of compassion began to succumb to it for the first time. The silence between them did not last long when Shahly continued, "Fine. Go into the desert and face the wizard there. Bring more pain upon yourself and get someone else hurt or killed. You'll do what you'll do despite what I say. I don't see why I should even care anymore."

Shaking her head, Nillerra smiled and countered, "Do you really think I— "

"Just go," Shahly interrupted. "You have made up your mind so just go."

Taking a half step back, the surprise on the black haired girl's face lit up her wide eyes. She did not expect this unicorn to snap back at her so and just stared at her for long seconds. She glanced away as she observed, "So it looks like you've finally grown a spine."

"I've always had one," Shahly countered. "I choose not to be mean to those around me. If you really want the affections of those around you then perhaps you should try compassion and stop being so cruel."

"The way I am has always gotten me what I've wanted, Shahly."

Raising her eyes, the unicorn replied, "It didn't get you Prince Arden."

"Now who is being cruel?"

"I'm just being truthful."

"You aren't being truthful at all."

"I'm a unicorn. Truth is what we are."

"Sure it is." Nillerra folded her arms and looked aside. The silence thickened the tension between them. "Okay, Shahly. Tell me exactly what is waiting for me down that canyon. You'll tell me if you're so truthful."

"Or I could just let you find out for yourself."

"Tell me or I'll arrange for you not to be fed today."

"I'm leaving today, Nillerra."

The black haired girl's eyes snapped to the unicorn. "Are you, now?"

"You promised."

Nodding, Nillerra agreed, "Yes, I promised. But if this wizard is so powerful and I never come back then there will be no way I can convince Lord Nemlivv to release you."

Shahly sighed. "You should have already."

"Oh, no. Not until I have what I want."

"What exactly do you want?"

"I want to bring him here to face you. I want you to accuse him of ruining my life while he is standing right in front of you."

Her eyes widening, Shahly slowly raised her head.

"Once he admits it," the black haired girl went on, "then you can go."

"You won't bring him here," Shahly informed straightly, slowly turning her eyes to the arrogant young woman.

Raising her chin, Nillerra countered, "I've already made all kinds of preparations. Lord Nemlivv's strongest apprentice will be coming with me, as will fifty archers and fifty foot soldiers. If he's as wise as you claim then he'll surrender without putting up a fight."

"He won't surrender," the unicorn said with a stern voice, "and you won't beat him with an apprentice and a hundred soldiers. You will all die out there if you attack him."

Nillerra laughed under her breath. "That would sure make you happy, wouldn't it? I think you just don't want to face him."

"Think what you wish. Please just leave me alone now."

"I rather think I should stay and torment you a while longer."

Shahly's patience began to wear dangerously thin and she turned narrow eyes on the black haired girl. "I said leave me alone."

Nillerra snarled back, "I don't care what you said."

Turning fully, Shahly raised her head and an emerald glow enveloped her horn. "You are a pitiable, hateful girl, Nillerra. I do not want to see you again. Now go!"

"Or you'll what?" the black haired girl challenged.

Green flames overtook the unicorn's eyes and she unexpectedly lunged, slamming her head into the bars of the door and thrusting her horn through them and right at Nillerra's chest, and the point stopped only a hand width away.

With a sharp scream, Nillerra stumbled backward and fell, landing hard on her backside as her wide eyes were locked on the suddenly belligerent unicorn.

Shahly snorted with each breath, just glaring at the black haired girl with emerald glowing eyes that still seemed to burn. Slowly, she backed away, her lips peeling away from her teeth. "I said go, Nillerra. I won't tell you again."

Nillerra found herself trembling and knowing fear of her rival for the first time. Ever so slowly, she pushed herself up and managed to stand on wobbly legs. She backed toward the door, then turned and hurried out of the stable.

Shahly watched the door for long moments after, the glow about her horn and eyes fading to nothing. This was the first time her anger had seized control of her so, and so absolutely. Captivity was already taking its toll on her and she felt her wits slowly slipping away. She lay down to her belly in the hay and stared in disbelief at the door to the stable for a time.

"I wanted to kill her," she sobbed. "But I wish death on no one. How can this be?"

Vinton swept back into her mind. Surely he was coming for her. Soon, he and Ralligor would know where she was and rescue her.

"This won't do," she told herself aloud. "I won't become like Bexton. I won't." She closed her eyes again. "I'm so sorry, Precious One. I'm sorry. I won't become him. I won't become like him. I won't give in to all of this. They won't break me. We won't be here much longer, I promise. Ralligor and Vinton will come for us and we can go home." She heaved a breath and tried to stop crying. "I promise."

Darkness enveloped her again and she searched herself for strength, but it was not to be found. She would not know how much time it had been before the door to the stable opened again and she barely noticed the light foot falls that approached. Lost in her thoughts and despair, she did not move or even raise her eyes until she heard the latch on the stall gate and the subtle creak of the hinges.

The girl who entered got but a glance from the unicorn as she went about the task of checking the grain bucket and the water bucket. She kicked at the small pile of fresh hay that was left, then she was still for a time.

Shahly could feel the girl's eyes on her and she knew that the girl wanted to speak with her again, to just hear the words of a unicorn. Shahly wanted to be left alone, and yet this conflicted with a craving for company. Her eyes shifted that way slightly and she could see the girl's feet only a pace away.

Perhaps half a moment passed when the girl slowly turned to

leave.

Raising her head, the unicorn turned her full attention to the girl at last, asking of her, "Please don't go."

The girl hesitated, then slowly half turned. She was uneasy and glanced about.

Sensing this, Shahly turned her eyes down and continued, "I'm lonely in here. Can you stay for a while?"

"I shouldn't," the girl informed softly.

"Please," the unicorn implored. "I promise I won't be any trouble."

"You could never be trouble," the girl countered, her voice still soft like a gentle breeze. "I am not to look at you. I am not to speak to you."

"They'll punish you, won't they?"

Bowing her head slightly, the girl nodded.

"I don't want them to hurt you because of me," Shahly said softly.

"Thank you," the girl offered.

The stable door burst open and one of the guards stormed in, his eyes full of fury and his movements of brutal intent as he shouted, "What did I hear from you? You were told not to speak to the beast!" At a pace away he reached for the girl, who cringed at his approach as he clutched at her arm.

Shahly sprang to her hooves and whinnied sharply at him, laying her ears back as she did.

He stopped and backed away a step.

"Can you understand me?" the unicorn barked in a whinny.

He just blinked and backed up another step.

Rolling her eyes, Shahly grumbled, "I see you can't." She looked to the girl and whickered, "Tell him to bring Nemlivv here." Her eyes shifted back to the guard and she snarled, "Now!"

The girl timidly looked up at the guard and relayed the unicorn's message with hesitant words. "Um, she wants you to go and fetch Lord Nemlivv."

Raising his chin, the guard just stared back at the unicorn, not knowing that she already had his mind with hers as he nodded. "I'll be doing just that, then." He spoke no other words as he spun around and hurried about his task.

Slowly turning, the girl finally looked right at Shahly, and beamed a big smile.

With a smug little smile of her own, Shahly nodded to the girl and said straightly, "I guess they know who is in control of this stable now, don't they?"

"I guess they do," the girl replied. She glanced at the half empty grain bucket and asked, "Shall I fetch you more to eat?"

Shahly looked to the bucket herself. "No, thank you. The grain is very good but I just don't have much appetite right now."

"I understand," the girl said softly.

"Would you like some?" the unicorn offered.

Giggling, the girl shook her head. "No, thank you."

"It's really good," Shahly insisted.

The girl just shook her head again.

Squinting a little, the unicorn recalled, "Your name is Ellyus."

The girl's eyes snapped to her and she confirmed, "Yes, it is. You remember my name!"

"You only told me yesterday," Shahly reminded. "Am I the first unicorn you have ever seen?"

Ellyus shook her head. "No, Lord Nemlivv had another when I was just a little girl."

Slowly, the unicorn raised her nose. "He had another? What did he look like?"

"I was very young," the girl admitted, "but I remember he was very big, as big as a horse, and was a shiny black unicorn with a mane that was like strands of black glass."

Her eyes widening, Shahly took a few steps back, breathing, "Bexton."

"You know that unicorn?" Ellyus asked innocently.

Looking away, Shahly slowly nodded and confirmed, "I knew him."

"I heard he went insane," the girl reported. "One day he bolted through the gate while he was being given food and ran outside. The guards tried to stop him and he killed one and hurt another before he ran out of the gate."

Shahly closed her eyes and nodded.

"I'm sorry," the girl offered, seeing that this news bothered the little unicorn before her. "I shouldn't have said any of that."

"I asked you," Shahly reminded. "You did nothing wrong." Looking back to the girl, Shahly asked, "How long was he here?"

"I think about a month," Ellyus replied. "He was not happy to be here all that time."

"Any more than I am," Shahly mumbled. "I guess that gives me a month..." She would not continue with that line of thinking and instead looked to the girl and observed, "Are you sure you don't want any of that grain? You look hungry."

The girl nodded and assured, "I've had my meal today already."

Shahly's mouth went slightly ajar. She knew from her experience with humans that her kind ate two or three times a day. No wonder this girl was so thin! She looked away and nodded. Clearly others were deciding how often she got to eat and how much. It wasn't fair.

"Is there anything I might fetch you?" Ellyus asked.

Shahly's ears perked and her eyes shifted back to the girl. "Well, I really like apples. And pears. And berries, especially strawberries."

The girl took a step toward her and said in a low voice, "I'll see if I can snitch some for you."

Smiling, the unicorn assured, "Oh, you won't have to snitch anything. What does snitch mean, anyway?"

Ellyus giggled and answered, "I'll have to get them without anyone knowing."

"Oh. That could get you into trouble."

The girl shrugged.

A commotion outside drew their attention and Shahly raised her head, her eyes narrowing slightly as she observed, "Well, he didn't make us wait for him very long."

Slowly, the door to the stable opened and they could hear the sorcerer ordering someone about with an abrupt voice. The door opened fully and he finally strode in, two guards behind him.

"Make them wait outside," Shahly whinnied.

Nemlivv stopped, the guards stopping behind him. He gestured over his shoulder and they turned on their heels and hurried out.

"And leave the door open," she added.

He half turned and nodded to the guards as they left. As he approached the stall, his attention fell on the girl and he ordered, "Out."

She flinched and bowed her head, hunching over as she complied, but she stopped as the unicorn whickered at her.

"She stays here," Shahly sternly informed, her eyes narrow and locked on the sorcerer. She also held her head low and her ears were flattened against her head.

He nodded to her and conceded, "As you wish. I was told you wanted to see me."

Slowly, Shahly raised her head, her eyes locked on his. "I told you I would not look kindly on cruelty."

"Has someone been cruel to you?"

"Holding me here is cruel. How you treat the people here is cruel. You said you want us to be friends, and yet you do everything in your power to prevent it."

He folded his arms and vented a breath through his nose, bowing his head as he looked to the ground before him. "So, what you're telling me is if I release you right now then we can be the best of friends?"

"No, I am not."

"Then why would I release you?"

"Because it is the right thing to do."

"The right thing to do is what I wish to do. I wish to have a unicorn and I have one."

"You will never truly have a unicorn, Nemlivv."

His eyes lifted to her and he smiled slightly. "And yet you are here."

Shahly slowly blinked, turning her eyes away from him. "You just don't understand."

"What don't I understand?"

"We are not to be possessed by your kind. We are of the forest and that is where we belong. That's where I belong."

"You belong here, now."

"Freedom is coming for me," she informed coldly, "and your doom with it."

He smiled slightly. "My doom. What would you know about that?"

Turning away slightly, silence was her answer.

"I've brought down armies," he gloated. "Beasts of every description have trembled before my power and the armies I command."

"Not every beast is afraid of you," she countered.

"You clearly aren't," the sorcerer observed. When she did not respond, he raised his head and glanced at Ellyus. "I see you have a new friend."

"And so long as she is cared for you and I can speak to one another."

He nodded. "I see. So, I will arrange for her to be better cared for. What else do you need?"

Her gaze shifted back to him.

"Besides that," he added.

She stared at him for long seconds, then she glanced around her and suggested, "How about a larger room?"

Nemlivv smiled slightly and assured, "I'll see to it. And what do I get in exchange?"

"You get my company until I go free," was her answer.

"And you get this girl's good health."

Her eyes snapped back to him.

"Her life and comfort depend entirely on you now. I can leave this stall door open, but I can assure you that your little friend will not like the painful end of her life if you decide to leave."

Ellyus cringed.

Raising her head slightly, Shahly glanced at the girl, then looked to the ground before her and nodded.

"Your well meaning heart has acted against you," the sorcerer continued. "She is as mine as you are and her life is at my whim. It is best that you understand that."

Shahly looked to her and huffed a breath. "I understand," she finally, softly said.

"You can be very happy here," he tried to explain. "Just give me the chance to make you so. I will give you everything you need and want."

"Except my freedom," she snarled.

"The kingdom is your home now. I've given you the gift of my protection."

"And the curse of captivity," she added coldly.

He sighed and impatience was growing obvious. His gaze on the timbers above the stall, he asked with a harsh voice, "Would you rather find yourself fleeing from predators and hunters from day to day?"

"Yes," she answered straightly. When his eyes snapped to her, showing an aggravation that she had seen from Vinton and Ralligor many times, she added, "Really, I would." Looking away, she continued, "Maybe I like the chase, or something of the like. I suppose I don't truly understand, either, but..."

"Will you at least give life here a try?" he asked with exasperation in his voice.

"I won't be here that long," she said straightly. "You would be wise to just release me now."

He set his jaw and his eyes glanced over her, then narrowed. "What is that you are wearing?"

She raised her head slightly. "I'm not wearing anything."

"Around your neck," he specified.

The amulet!

Glancing about, Shahly stammered, "It's... This is a gift from a friend of mine."

"A gift?" he questioned, slowly raising his chin.

She looked away from him and would say no more.

Squinting slightly, he stepped toward her and looked closer.

Shahly backed away. She barely noticed the approach of someone else, and winced as she recognized the mind of the newcomer.

Nillerra took Nemlivv's side and folded her arms. "Good morning, my Lord. Has your unicorn learned to behave herself?"

"A gold chain," he murmered. "I'd never even heard of unicorns wearing gold before."

Nodding, the black haired girl informed, "I'd heard somewhere that unicorns... Oh, it's nothing."

He finally looked to her and ordered, "Go on."

"It's just a silly story," she said with a slight smile, her gaze still on the unicorn.

"Tell me anyway," he insisted.

Turning her eyes up to his, Nillerra raised her brow and said, "I would not want to bore you, my Lord, but if you think what I know would be useful to you then I will gladly tell you." She looked back to Shahly, something devious in her eyes. "There is a story about unicorns who barter their abilities to powerful men in exchange for favors. Sometimes they turn into people and wander among us."

His gaze shifting back to the unicorn, Nemlivv asked, "Is this true?"

Shahly would not look at him, nor would she answer. Nillerra was up to something. She could feel it.

"You look uncomfortable," the sorcerer observed.

"Oh, she is," the black haired girl confirmed. "She's done it before."

"It wasn't like that, Nillerra" Shahly defended.

Nemlivv's eyes narrowed and he slowly looked to the black haired girl again. "So you two know each other."

"Yes, my Lord, we do."

Shahly's eyes snapped to her and she whickered, "Nillerra, don't."

"She's the reason I was rejected by Prince Arden," the black haired girl went on. "This wizard sent her there to ruin our plans, which she did with horrible purpose."

Raising her head and stepping toward them, Shahly cried, "Nillerra, it wasn't like that at all! I've already told you—"

"Well, now," the sorcerer declared, folding his arms. "This seems a little convenient, doesn't it? Perhaps it seems a little *too* convenient. How did you manage to be where I found you?"

"We were just sleeping," she defended.

He drew a breath and nodded. "So I'm to believe this is all just a coincidence."

Shahly shrugged and looked away from him. "I don't know. I just want to go home."

"Why are you here?" he asked.

"You kidnapped me," was her answer.

"That amulet gives her dangerous powers," Nillerra warned. "It made her human and foiled our plans this spring."

"It isn't like that!" Shahly cried.

"Enough," Nemlivv sighed. "Shahly, I need to take that amulet."

She backed away, shaking her head. "No! It was a gift from

my closest friend!"

"A wizard," the black haired girl added.

"Is he a wizard?" Nemlivv asked straightly.

Shahly turned away. "I won't give it to you!"

"Oh, yes you will," Nillerra corrected.

Raising a hand to the black haired girl, Nemlivv's eyes shifted to her to silence her. "I believe you have a journey to take this morning, don't you?"

She looked away and smiled slightly. "Yes, my Lord, I believe I do."

His brow arched. "With a hundred men and my most gifted apprentice. Are you going to tell me about that part or is it still a surprise?"

"It's a surprise, my Lord."

"One that you will spoil right now," he informed. "It has to do with this unicorn, doesn't it?"

Turning her eyes down, Nillerra nodded and confirmed, "It does, my Lord. She told me where to find the wizard who gave her that amulet. I planned to present him to you as a gift."

"Perhaps," he sighed, then he smiled slightly. "If it's the old wizard I think it is then he will be a wonderful gift indeed. Go on, Nillerra. Go and fetch me this wizard. Just be careful about him and don't put yourself or my men at risk."

"I won't, my Lord." She leered at Shahly as she turned and strode out of the stable.

"Please don't go!" Shahly implored.

Nillerra ignored her and left the stable, and as she did the guards turned into the stable and approached, their eyes on the sorcerer.

Seeing them, Shahly backed away more, fear in her eyes as she shook her head. "Please, don't take my amulet. Please!" She was stopped by the wall across the stable.

Nemlivv strode right up to her and knelt down half a pace away, looking up at her with sympathetic eyes. "I only want to examine it. If it is an amulet of magic I have to make sure that it is not a threat to the people here." He motioned to the girl who still stood quietly just inside of the gate to the stable. "Shouldn't we make sure that Ellyus isn't harmed by it?"

"It won't harm anyone," Shahly assured.

"What does it do?" he asked.

She would not answer and looked away from him.

"Please tell me," he said in a gentle voice. "Is what Nillerra said true?"

Hesitantly, she nodded. "It is true."

"It makes you human?"

Turning her eyes down, Shahly nodded again.

"I'll wager you are a truly beautiful girl. Can it make you human now?"

She softly replied, "No."

"Why not?"

"I don't know. It just doesn't work anymore."

"I see." He raised his brow and dared to reach to her, scratching her gently under the jaw. "Then it can't be of much value. May I borrow it?"

"What do you mean?" she asked.

"That means I take it, I examine it, and then I bring it back to you."

She shot him a glance and did not respond otherwise.

"If not," he continued, "the guards will have to help me take it, and I don't want them to hurt you. I am going to take it one way or another. Please, just let me borrow it for a while on your own terms."

She stared at the hay on the ground and considered, then she closed her eyes and slowly lowered her head.

Slowly and gently, he took the chain with both hands and lifted it over her head and horn. As he held it before him. No longer around her neck, the sparkle of it and its glow slowly faded. He turned and held it to one of the guards, ordering, "Take this right to my study," and as the guard hurried about his task, the sorcerer looked back to her and assured, "Thank you. I'll have it back to you soon. Is there anything you want in the meantime?"

She nodded. "Can Ellyus stay with me for a while?"

"She has duties to attend," Nemlivv informed, "but I will send her right back here when she is finished."

Shahly's eyes found the sorcerer. "She should eat more than once a day."

"I'll see to it," he promised.

"And she should bring me apples."

Ellyus smiled ever so slightly.

Nodding, the sorcerer observed, "You are very fond of her. What if she becomes your personal servant?"

"I need no servant," Shahly informed coldly.

"Okay, your personal caretaker. I will see to it that she spends as much time here as you wish. She will bring you food and water and apples and whatever else you want. Would that be acceptable? I will arrange all of that for you."

Looking to the girl, Shahly replied, "If she wishes."

"I'm sure she does," he laughed. Standing, he stroked her mane and assured, "I will do everything I can to make you happy here, I promise."

"And my amulet?" the unicorn asked.

"I'll have it back to you in a day or two." He stroked her mane once more. "You are truly magnificent."

As he turned and left, Shahly shook her head, realizing that the lives of the people around that sorcerer meant little to him. She looked to the girl and said straightly, "When I get out of here, you are coming with me."

CHAPTER 16

The sun had been up for two hours and still no sorcerer.

As his wizard master sat on a large stone and watched, Ralligor paced angrily back and forth up the slope, just beyond the tree line. The dragon's brow was low over his eyes and every other breath that left him announced itself with a growl. Falloah sat catlike beside the wizard, also watching her huge mate with concern in her eyes. Drarrexok sat further down the slope, closer to the creek as he also watched the black dragon, and he wisely kept his distance.

Vinton did not watch him, nor did he have any interest in doing so. He laid on his belly near the spot where Shahly had disappeared, his head lying on the ground only a hand width or two away and right between his front hooves. This was his closest connection to her. He could almost still feel her there. Deep in thought, he was barely aware of those around him.

"Where the hell is he?" the black dragon roared.

"Patience, Ralligor," the wizard ordered. "You should sit and meditate for a time."

"I am meditating," he growled back. "I'm meditating on how much pain to deliver to this sorcerer who took her when I find him!"

"Vengeance, my student? That will not serve you right now."

"No," the dragon admitted, "it will serve me when I find this sorcerer."

"Patience is not his strongest attribute," Rawl called from across the clearing.

Ralligor stopped and bared his teeth, slowly turning his head toward the sorcerer.

Walking stick in hand and wearing his traveler's cloak, Rawl's eyes were locked on the dragon as he strode with long steps right toward him. Walking at a brisk pace a little behind him and to one side, Janees also carried a walking stick. A red cape covered her shoulders and back and the hood attached to it covered her head. Her eyes were locked on the dragon in a fearful stare.

With another growl, the black dragon turned fully toward

him, standing erect as he folded his thick arms and half opened his wings.

As he reached the dragon, the sorcerer swung his walking stick hard and struck the dragon's leg with a sharp crack, ordering, "One side, wizard's apprentice." Of course the dragon did not move and he walked around him anyway with Janees following.

Ralligor kept his attention on the sorcerer as he passed, following him with his eyes, then he turned fully and a low growl rolled from his throat.

The wizard picked up his own walking stick and stood, taking a few steps toward the approaching sorcerer with a blank expression.

A couple of paces away, the sorcerer's eyes narrowed.

Half a pace away, the men stopped and stared at each other. Rawl was the larger of the two, but size was of no consequence to the *facultas* they wielded. Each man released his walking stick and let them fall to the ground at the same time.

A hearty laugh erupted from the sorcerer and he threw his arms around the old wizard and pulled him into his chest. The wizard returned the big sorcerer's embrace with a broad smile.

"Leedon!" the sorcerer shouted. "Far too many seasons have passed since I last saw you, my old friend!"

"Far too many," the wizard confirmed. He pulled away to arm's length and smiled broadly. "I see time has been kind to you."

"And to you as well," Rawl countered.

"How are Rohsheen and the children?" Leedon asked.

Janees' mouth fell open and she stared at them with wide eyes.

"Rohsheen is as beautiful as the day we met and my boys are as strong as oxen, and my daughter as beautiful as her mother. What of your brood?"

The wizard turned his eyes away.

Drawing a breath, Rawl offered, "I'm sorry, old friend. I had forgotten."

Ralligor approached with heavy steps and growled, "Perhaps the small talk can wait for another time."

The sorcerer observed, "Still not a patient one, is he?"

"He's still a young dragon," Leedon defended.

"He's a hundred and forty seasons old!" Rawl countered.

Laughing, the wizard shook his head. "Barely of age for a dragon, my friend." He turned and looked to the spot that Vinton still stared at. "This is why I asked you here."

Slowly, Rawl raised his chin as his eyes found the unicorn. When the big bay finally lifted his head and looked to him, he could only breathe, "Magnificent."

"My thoughts the first time I saw his young mate," Leedon said, "and my thoughts of them still." He turned and led the way the ten paces or so down the slope. "His little mare is the very reason we are all here."

Vinton stood and faced the men as they reached him. His look was still blank and his ears drooped. He met the sorcerer's eyes only briefly, then he looked down, succumbing to the pain and loneliness that still consumed him.

"This is Vinton," the wizard introduced.

Janees also felt herself consumed by the presence of this magnificent unicorn, but something distracted her. This beast actually humbled the big man she wished to learn from. Not even the black dragon had been able to do that. She did not allow her attention to be consumed by this for very long. At her age, a unicorn was still the most magical sight her eyes could behold and they found the bay once again.

Rawl took the last hesitant steps toward the stallion, slowly raising his hand to touch him. He scratched the unicorn gently between the ears, careful to avoid contact with his horn as he did not know if such contact would be offensive to him. Nodding, the sorcerer declared, "I am in your service. Tell me what you need of me."

Vinton subtly bowed his head to the sorcerer, then he explained, "Someone of power has taken my mate, someone who uses the same magic that you do."

Staring back at the unicorn for long seconds, Rawl subtly raised his chin, then he turned his eyes to the wizard and raised a brow. "A sorcerer who would abduct a unicorn is not a man of great wisdom, and that is who we seek."

"We know who," Ralligor snarled. "You are here to tell us where."

"I see." The sorcerer looked back to the unicorn. "Show me where she last was."

Vinton turned to that place he had watched most of the day and night.

Seeing this, the sorcerer approached and knelt down, holding his palms over the ground and slowly moving them back and forth. After a moment of this, he barked, "Janees. Come here."

She hurried to him and knelt down beside him, her gaze on him as he awaited his command.

His eyes were on the ground and his hands continued to hover over one spot, turning tight circles, one in one direction and one in the other. He drew a breath and raised his head slightly, ordering, "Hold your hand over this spot."

As he withdrew, she hesitantly extended one hand, opening her palm over the last of Shahly's hoof prints.

"Do you feel it?" he questioned.

Janees did feel a sensation running from her palm all the way up her arm. Slowly, she nodded and replied, "It's cold, and it feels... It feels different."

"Almost as if from a different place," he continued. "What else do you feel?"

She squinted. "I feel power. It's like mine and yours, but..." She shook her head. "It isn't the same as ours."

"As I feel different from you and you from me," the sorcerer explained. "Each wielder of the *sortiri* has his own touch with it, like a face that differs from one person to the next. As we all look different, so our *facultas* is different."

Janees nodded.

"Now," he prodded, "follow the path."

She glanced at him. "The path?"

Ralligor looked aside and growled.

Gently stepping toward him, Falloah crooned softly.

In a low voice, the wizard Leedon urged, "Patience."

"This was a spell of gates," Rawl explained. "The gate was opened and then closed, but it will take many days to seal to the nothing it was."

"And still you took your time getting here," the black dragon snarled.

The wizard master cleared his throat, turning a disapproving look up to the dragon.

Extending her other hand over the hoof print, Janees asked, "How do I follow the path? How do I find the other side of it?"

"The same as you would any path," the sorcerer explained, "but not with the eyes in your head. Use the vision in your mind."

She nodded again and closed her eyes. As the effort began to drain her, her breath came shallower and shallower, quicker and quicker.

"Relax," the sorcerer urged. "Just follow the path with your mind."

With much effort, the student slowed her breath. "I see a castle. There are many horses about, many soldiers." She gasped loudly and sprang away, falling to her backside as her wide eyes were locked on that spot on the ground.

Rawl looked over his shoulder, his eyes narrow as he asked her, "What did you see?"

With her lips parted in fear, she answered, "The soldiers."

Ralligor reminded through bared, clenched teeth, "We're looking for a unicorn."

Ignoring him, the sorcerer demanded, "What of them?"

"Their markings and the banner they march under," she replied fearfully. "They are the soldiers who attacked Pinetop Castle!"

Leedon approached and knelt down beside the sorcerer, saying in a very low voice, "That doesn't sound good, my friend. Do you know where our unicorn is?"

Just barely, Rawl nodded, then finally looked back to that spot on the ground. "North. Castle Ravenhold." He motioned with his head toward the dragon and grimly finished, "He isn't going to like this."

"And still he must still know."

Glancing at the wizard, Rawl murmured, "Should we have that green dragon make ready to restrain him?"

The wizard shook his head. "No, for Drarrexok's sake we should not involve him, and trust that my apprentice can control his temper.

Leedon and Rawl stood and turned around as Ralligor approached with three long strides and an impatient glare. They did not shy away as the big dragon lowered his head to them and bared his teeth, knowing they dare not show him fear.

Janees also stood, but was content to cringe behind them.

"I believe we are here to find Shahly," the dragon growled, "and I don't think that involves teaching new tricks to your little apprentice."

Folding his arms, Rawl retorted, "All of life and every moment of it is meant to learn, wizard's apprentice. We have learned where your unicorn is, now it is time for you to learn to call upon your patience."

The dragon's brow lowered further over his eyes.

Taking a few steps toward his apprentice, the wizard reached up and placed a hand on the dragon's nose, pulling it down slowly as he met the dragon's eyes with his own. "Ralligor, she's been taken to Ravenhold Castle, north of the Dark Mountains."

Ever so slowly, the black dragon raised his head and stood, looking down at his wizard master with wide, furious eyes. He backed away a few steps, then turned and strode up the slope. Swinging his hand, he struck a tree that was twice his height tall and as thick as a horse's body. It snapped where he struck it and broke free of the ground, the two pieces folding over each other as they fell. He stopped near the top and roared, raising his arms and fire exploded from his gaping jaws, forming a boiling cloud of flames above him. The clouds overhead thickened and began to spit lightning in response to his anger and the wind kicked up and blew randomly in every direction, carrying with it leaves and dust and everything that it could make fly.

"Ralligor!" the wizard shouted. "Ralligor, calm yourself!"

The black dragon spun half around, his eyes burning red and his teeth were bared as he growled with each breath. His rage was just starting and everyone present knew it. His jaws gaped again and he loosed a burst of fire at a grove of trees, fire that was enveloped in swirling green lightning. As the grove was struck, the very ground exploded in a fury of flames and earth; stones and trees were blasted into the air.

Shielding his eyes against the ever increasing wind, the sorcerer yelled over it, "He'll destroy the whole forest if he doesn't get control of himself!"

Something primitive was in command of the dragon and he

was little more than an enraged predator as he turned back up the slope and roared again. As he gaped his jaws to loose another blast of fire, a sharp red light lanced forth and struck his back, exploding in a shower of red and green light. He stumbled and tried to turn just as another struck him and half enveloped him, and then another and he collapsed to all fours, weakened and barely holding himself up. His head sank nearly to the ground and his eyes were closed tightly against the pain that racked him. For a long moment he struggled to catch his breath, growling each time it left him, and he slowly sank to his knees as his body was shaken by tremors.

His horn still glowing crimson, Vinton paced up the slope toward the dragon and stopped about ten paces away, raising his head.

Ralligor opened his eyes and slowly turned his head, baring his teeth as his eyes found the bay unicorn.

Snorting his disapproval, Vinton barked a whinny at him and said, "If you mean to lose your temper and destroy half the forest then your help is not needed here and you should just leave!"

The black dragon pushed himself up and got his feet back under him, standing to his full five men's heights and half opening his wings.

Vinton's horn glowed brighter red and he trained it on the dragon's chest.

The sorcerer shouted, "Are you learning to calm yourself yet?"

Ralligor shot him and irritated look and roared, "Quiet, you!"

Vinton raised his head and informed with bared teeth, "Ralligor, one more burst from me and you'll not get up again until tomorrow!"

The Desert Lord's eyes glowed red as he fired back, "One burst from me and you won't get up at all!"

Falloah landed between them and extended her arms and wings toward the combatants. She looked to the dragon, to the unicorn, then roared through bared teeth, "Enough of this, both of you! While you are fighting with each other, Shahly is still in the hands of whoever has taken her. Now, both of you back away at once!"

Neither Vinton nor Ralligor would turn their wrath against

the scarlet dragon. Eyes resumed their normal color, the unicorn's horn ceased its glow and each took a few steps away from her.

Looking up at the black dragon with a low brow, Falloah said more calmly, "Ralligor, I know this news is not what we wanted to hear, but now is not the time to lose your temper. You have to calm down!" She looked to Vinton and turned fully, setting her hands on her hips.

The unicorn looked away from her. "I know, I know."

She half turned again and looked to them each in turn. "Like it or not, you two are her best chance for freedom, and like it or not you are stronger together and not trying to kill each other."

Rawl nudged Leedon with his elbow and pointed at the dragoness, suggesting, "Perhaps *she* should be your apprentice."

The wizard chuckled and reached his hand out, his walking stick flying to his palm, and he started the short walk up the slope.

Vinton looked back up at the dragon and asked, "What are you so upset about, anyway? We know where she is, so what is the problem?"

With a deep growl, Ralligor turned and walked away, up the slope.

"The where is the problem," Leedon informed as he approached.

Turning to meet him, the unicorn's ears swiveled toward the wizard and he raised his head, questioning, "What do you mean?"

Just a little out of breath when he reached the big bay, Leedon patted his neck, a solemn look on his face as he replied, "Ravenhold is north of the Dark Mountains."

"And?" the unicorn pressed.

Falloah explained, "It is in another Landmaster's territory. We can't go there."

"Why not?" Vinton cried. "What does that have to do anything?"

Drawing a patient breath, the dragoness answered, "That has everything to do with it. We cannot cross the dark mountains into another Landmaster's territory. That would provoke a battle with him and I don't think Agarxus would allow that."

The bay's eyes darted about, then turned back up to the dragoness. "Surely this other Landmaster would listen to reason and allow us to rescue Shahly. He would have to!"

Falloah shook her head. "No, Vinton, he wouldn't. Mettegrawr is not a dragon who worries over the needs of others."

"Then *I'll* go and reason with him!" the bay insisted.

Ralligor turned and strode back toward them, regarding the unicorn coldly as he asked, "Are you familiar with the word 'suicide' Plow Mule?"

As the dragon reached them, Vinton looked up to him and snorted. "I don't see anyone else doing anything! All you've done is stomp around and otherwise— "

"Territorial borders mean nothing to your kind," Ralligor interrupted, "so I can't expect you to fully understand the obstacle we have to overcome. Suffice to say, you would not wander into the ocean knowing you would drown."

With narrow eyes, the stallion growled with an impatient tone, "What does the ocean have to do with this other dragon?"

Falloah answered, "He will kill you as soon as he sees you, Vinton. He or his *subordinares* will attack any dragon who enters into his territory, and he will kill any unicorn he sees."

"Agarxus didn't," the unicorn argued.

"No, he didn't," the dragoness conceded, "but Agarxus is not Mettegrawr."

Vinton snorted and turned north, pacing away from them as he insisted, "I have to at least try."

"I see Shahly's recklessness has rubbed off on you," Ralligor observed.

The stallion stopped and looked over his shoulder, his eyes narrow and his teeth bared as he barked, "Come again?"

The Desert Lord turned fully toward him and folded his arms, raising his snout slightly as he regarded the unicorn with an icy glare. "She likes to take unnecessary risks as well. Of course, she's always had you and me to get her out of trouble when she does. So who is looking out for you, Plow Mule?"

Vinton glared back for a moment, then he lowered his eyes and turned his attention north again.

Leedon strode in his slow fashion to the stallion and patted his neck. "You'll not accomplish anything by getting yourself killed, my friend. Your absence will only make the world a darker place, and she will still be a prisoner of Ravenhold."

Drawing a deep breath, the bay closed his eyes and lowered his head. "I have to do something."

"I know," the wizard assured softly, "and we will."

"Perhaps her habits are rubbing off on me," Vinton whickered.

"Not a lapse of judgment as much as a desperate act of love," the wizard said straightly. "You would gladly lay down your life for her."

Vinton nodded.

Rawl strode up behind Leedon and patted his old friends shoulder. "Dragons are restricted by these borders and that old Landmaster will kill any unicorn who gets too close, but our kind can come and go as we please."

The wizard nodded and warned, "So long as our numbers are not too large. We must remember the others of our kind there."

The sorcerer nodded. "Agreed. We'll go ourselves."

"And take on his whole army?" Ralligor snarled.

"If need be," Rawl confirmed.

"We don't want to start a war," the wizard informed, "so we will have to be both diplomatic and strategic in this matter." Still looking at Vinton, he folded his arms and vented a breath through his nose. "It would help to have an ally in the Northlands to call upon."

Slowly, the stallion raised his head and turned his eyes to the wizard. "Perhaps we have one. I should leave immediately."

As he galloped away, Ralligor called after him, "Leave for where?"

"Red Stone Castle," the unicorn called back.

Shaking his head, the Desert Lord grumbled, "I guess he's forgotten what they do to unicorns at that castle. I'll fly that way in a couple of hours and get him out of trouble."

"I don't think you will have to," the wizard informed, smiling up at his student. "Don't underestimate that unicorn, mighty friend. He is far wiser than his young mate and I think he knows exactly what he is doing."

"Wiser than Shahly." Ralligor grunted and shook his head.

"That's really not much of a stretch, *Magister.*"

The wizard laughed. "Agreed, mighty friend." As he saw the dragon turn, he asked, "And where would you be off to?"

This time the dragon did not face him. He stared into the distance and squinted, growling softly before he replied, "Intruders are approaching my lair, probably another dragonslayer looking to make a name for himself. I should go and attend to him before he finds my hoard."

Nodding, Leedon said, "Again, I agree with you, mighty friend. But be swift. We shall await you at Caipiervell."

Ralligor nodded, then swept himself into the sky.

Looking to the dragoness, the wizard advised, "He will need all the help he can muster to keep that temper of his under control."

"I understand," Falloah confirmed. "Perhaps he will work out some of his aggression on that dragonslayer he sensed near his cave." She turned her eyes up and added, "I am going to go keep my eyes on him." With that, she turned and took flight after the black dragon.

Heavy footsteps seemed almost hesitant as they approached and the wizard and sorcerer turned to see the green dragon drawing closer, his eyes on the dragons who flew into the distance. As they disappeared behind the trees, the dragon turned his attention to the humans before him and drew his head back.

Rawl leaned heavily on his walking stick as he looked up at the dragon and asked, "So you'll be joining us as well?"

Drarrexok leaned his head slightly, then shrugged. "I don't have anything else to do today. Perhaps Ralligor can use my help, perhaps he doesn't want it." He turned his attention west where the black dragon had disappeared. "I haven't tangled with a dragonslayer for a few seasons, but I have no interest in getting in *his* way to face one."

"Perhaps you will meet us at Caipiervell," the wizard suggested.

"I hear their sheep are the best in the land," the sorcerer added.

His attention snapping back to the humans, Drarrexok opened his wings and announced, "I'll see you there."

As he took flight, the sorcerer and wizard enjoyed a hearty laugh, then Rawl noticed his young student creeping gingerly toward them, wringing her hands together as her eyes were locked on the departing dragon.

The sorcerer folded his arms and growled to her, "So you are determined that you should learn from me, are you?"

Still two paces away, she looked to him and froze, then timidly nodded.

Rawl met the wizard's eyes and nodded. "We'll be making the trek to Caipiervell on foot, old friend. I'll see you there in a day or so."

The men embraced once again, patting each other's backs, then the sorcerer turned northeast and beckoned, "Come along, Janees. Quit making me wait for you."

She darted back to where she had been and found her walking stick, then she hurried to his side, looking up at him with curious eyes as she asked, "How long have—"

"Does your question have something to do with the *sortiri?*" he suddenly barked.

Janees cringed, then turned her attention forward. For some reason she felt compelled to look behind her, back at the old wizard, and she drew a gasp as she found him gone and only a settling mist in his place.

"Still easily awed by the wonders of the craft, are you?" the sorcerer asked.

She hesitantly nodded. "Yes, *Magister.*"

"Hmph," he scoffed. "You'll go in wide eyed and ready to learn enough to perform tricks for royal courts."

Janees looked aside, trying to hide her annoyance as she assured, "I'll not be a disappointment to you, *Magister.*"

"Of course you won't," he growled back.

They walked on for an unknown time, finally leaving the dense forest and coming to a riverside where the water was shallow and swift. While the side they approached was mostly heaps of white washed stones of every size, the other was a sheer cliff of granite that held up layered white stone. Atop that were dense green things, trees and bushes that grew to the very edge of the seven height high cliff and ferns below them. In spots, water dribbled from holes and fractures in the cliff, some leaving long stains of rust while others left trails of white.

This is where the big sorcerer went. His walking stick seemed to be of little use to him as he barely used it for balance and instead negotiated the unsteady terrain of stones with purpose as he made his way toward the water. Janees kept pace as best she could, but good footing was not to be found here and she stumbled often.

The sorcerer's quick pace stopped quite suddenly and he turned his eyes down.

Janees managed to stop beside him and she looked where he did.

His gaze glanced about at the stones on front of him, then he reached down and picked one up that was covered in some caked-on white powder. Brushing it off to reveal the pink stone speckled with metallic flakes and black pocks, he asked her, "Do you know what this is called?"

She squinted at the stone he held and guessed, "Granite?"

He nodded and tossed the stone, half the size of his head, a hand's length into the air a couple of times. Leaning his head, he seemed to grip it tightly and Janees could feel a hum about him. She could feel energy being exerted. As he squeezed the stone, it actually gave as if it was made of sponge and a strange, golden metallic liquid seeped from its many pours. Holding his other hand beneath it, he allowed the gold liquid to drip into his hand and pool there. Looking closer, the girl's eyes widened as she realized that it *was* gold. She had seen gold melted many times and could feel the heat off of it even from a distance. This gold simply dripped as a liquid from the stone, but did not burn the sorcerer, nor did it even seem to be hot. Shaking her head slowly, she wondered how this could be.

"Very simple," he answered as if hearing her thoughts. "The metal in the stone is different from the stone. It is an element controlled by the *sortiri.*"

"It doesn't burn?" she asked in an astonished voice.

He smiled a rare smile, still staring at his hand where he collected the gold. "No, it doesn't burn." He seemed to wring the last of the gold from the granite, then he tossed the stone over his shoulder and clasped his hands together. A yellow light flashed from between his palms and fingers and in an instant he held a large gold coin in his palm. The image of a unicorn was struck into the center and the Latirus words *unire ta beon uno.* He looked to her, this time with a serious glare and a low brow. "I thought we could use some money." He made a fist and when he opened his hand again the large coin had become five smaller ones.

Janees raised her chin and slowly turned her eyes to his, unaware that her mouth hung open.

He looked down again, glancing about, then he reached around his back inside his cloak and shoved the coins into a sack there. Pointing at a stone half the size of the one he had squeezed the gold from, he ordered, "That one."

She looked and was quick to snatch the stone from its resting place, straining a little as it was heavier than it looked. Cradling it in both hands, she looked to the sorcerer for instructions.

"Can you feel what is within it?" he asked.

Fixing her gaze intently on the stone, she squinted a little and peered into it as best she knew how. Different elements felt different, but inexperience would be something for her to overcome here. Still, she had felt gold before and searched hard for the precious metal within the stone.

"Can you feel it?" he pressed.

She nodded, smiling slightly.

"Bring it to you," the sorcerer ordered. "Pull it from the stone as I did."

Calling upon her power, she felt it lance painfully through her as it always did and she shuddered ever so slightly as she unleashed the *sortiri* within her again. When the sorcerer cleared his throat, her concentration broke and she looked up at him.

He raised an eyebrow and asked in a growling voice, "What are you doing?"

"I..." she stammered.

"Is that how you call upon the *sortiri?* You allow it to tear recklessly through you?"

She felt a drop of blood escape from her nose and quickly wiped it away with her sleeve. "I was taught— "

"I can't believe I'm hearing this!" he shouted, his eyes turned upward. Looking to her again, the sorcerer shook his head. "What idiot taught you to do that? Don't answer. I don't really want to know." He sighed and shook his head.

She stared back at him timidly. "I don't draw it out from within me?"

"Is the *sortiri* a part of you?"

Janees nodded.

"Then don't disgorge it as you would from a sour stomach. Are you trying to kill yourself?"

Turning her eyes down, she shook her head.

He sighed in a growl and shook his head again. "Is your arm a part of you? Is your leg? Your eyes? Do you wretch and convulse as you use them?"

Slowly, she looked up at him. She heard his words, and more than that she felt them.

"How do you use your arm?" he went on.

Still holding the stone in one hand, she raised the other and looked it over, flexing her arm at the elbow, then her fingers. Feeling what happened within her arm and hand as she moved it, she concentrated harder to feel every muscle, every joint. A slight smile touched her full lips as the realization of what the sorcery master had told her finally shined in its full glory.

As the girl looked back up at him, he finally nodded and commended, "Good. Now, flex the *sortiri* as you would your arm. Use your *facultas* as you would any other part of you."

This was a life changing instant. She no longer felt the painful surge of power through her as she called upon her gift. Instead, she felt it envelope her. It surged through her again, but this time not as some kind of invader. Feeling deeper within her, she could feel it as she had the muscles in her arm, and control of this power suddenly made sense for the first time. That little smile broadened as she turned her gaze to the stone she still held and she held it up to belly level and concentrated hard on it. There. Every bit that made up this complex looking stone made itself known to her. Now, she only had to find the one and pull it out.

Rawl folded his arms as he saw her give a task her complete focus for the first time.

The stone burst into thousands of pieces and Janees barked a scream and stumbled backward, landing hard on her backside on the rounded river stones behind her.

With a hearty laugh, the sorcerer shook his head and stepped toward her, offering her his hand. "Little girl, I knew you would be an entertaining student!"

She took his hand and was pulled to her feet in an instant.

"Let's go," he ordered. "Find another chunk of granite and try it again as we walk."

CHAPTER 17

Nemlivv's study was not a huge room, but it was bigger than most. Many windows allowed in much light and oil lamps chased away any shadows. Shelves on one wall reached to the ceiling and were laden with books, human and animal skulls, flasks of different kinds and many gold and silver objects of countless designs. Another shelf held amulets and magic talismans of many kinds and colors. His desk faced one wall where he could look out of the two pace wide window into the forest. Parchments and books were scattered about and two oil lamps and a cantle offered more light. The stone walls that did not host shelves had ornate tapestries hanging from them. A simple bed was in one corner, to the left of the desk and was unmade. This seemed to be a room he spent much of his time in.

Today, he sat at his desk, staring down at the gold chain and amulet that lay on a blank parchment before him. He unconsciously rubbed his lips with two fingers, lost in thought as blank eyes were locked on the gold dragon's talon before him.

The only door in or out was on the far side of the room, behind him. It was a heavy timber door, clearly designed to keep intruders out, though he rarely had it bolted. Even as the hinges creaked as the door was slowly opened the sorcerer did not respond. He knew who was entering, and at this point a distraction was a welcome event.

Eying him from the doorway for a moment, the old woman's eyes narrowed as she hobbled into the room. Age had taken its toll on her body and the aches in her joints were with her with every movement and showed fully as she limped toward him.

Even as she stopped behind him and placed a hand on his shoulder, he just stared down at the amulet.

She finally broke the silence with, "How long will you sit there and stare at that thing? You've been up here for hours." When he did not answer she shook her head and asked, "What is it that intrigues you so about that? Where did it come from?"

"The unicorn," was Nemlivv's answer.

The old woman raised her chin, her eyes on the amulet. "Why would a unicorn have such a thing? Where did she get it?"

"A wizard," he replied. "A very powerful wizard."

"What wizard?" she questioned. "Would this be the one you sent Nillerra for?"

His eyes widened and he raised his head. "Oh, no."

"Well out with it, boy. What wizard?"

He turned his head and looked up at her. "We have a problem."

"You shouldn't allow a mere wizard to frighten you so," she scoffed. "Your power is equal to any wizard you would meet."

"Except one," he countered, looking back to the amulet. "I only have to figure out why the Desert Lord would give such an amulet to a unicorn."

"The Desert Lord?" she hissed. "Are you certain?"

He nodded. "This is him. It still channels his power, even though something is missing from it." He sighed and shook his head. "As I said already, we have a problem."

Her eyes shifted to him. "And still you don't want your unicorn hurt for my foolish experiments. Do you think your dragon killing talisman will even have a chance against him without the essence of a unicorn?"

He was a long time in answering, but finally, softly admitted, "I don't know."

"As I told you before, boy, a dragon with that kind of power would shrug it off and level this castle, and kill all in it. If he is allied with her somehow, we need her to ward him off or kill him." A slight smile touched her lips. "Perhaps we could even use her to collect that bounty that Red Stone has on the head of the Desert Lord. Either way, we dare not allow this opportunity to pass."

"Perhaps he didn't really give it to her," Nemlivv guessed. "Perhaps another wizard or someone else acquired it from him and gave it to her. Unicorn and dragon are enemies, so that must be it."

"I suppose we'll see when Nillerra returns, won't we? If she returns." The old woman turned and limped toward the door, pausing to add, "Don't allow yourself to be as naïve as your father. That will bring the whole kingdom down."

He nodded as she left the room and just stared down at the amulet for a time. Thoughts whirled in his mind. If this unicorn was somehow connected to the Desert Lord, a dragon feared by everyone who knew of him, then he knew his kingdom was in dire jeopardy. A sigh escaped him as he leaned back in his chair. This amulet was one of only a few pieces in his collection with such power, yet even with something missing it was the most powerful he had ever held.

Rubbing his weary eyes, Nemlivv slowly pushed away from his desk and finally stood. Answers were in order, and some of those answers had nothing to do with the danger this dragon posed to him and his kingdom. This amulet had made that little unicorn human, and a new curiosity about her stirred.

He left the study, descended the brightly lit stairway and strode into the main hall of the castle. Here, all of the adornments of royalty made one think that this was a kingdom of great wealth. Its whitewashed walls and marble floors were kept perfect. Many suits of armor lined the walls and the four ways in and out of this hall were each guarded by two that were plated with gold. This was a bright room, lit by five chandeliers made of gold and silver which held over a hundred candles each. Artwork and tapestries blurred by as he strode toward the castle's front timber doors which were also white and decorated with gold. He seemed not to notice the servants who stopped to bow to him, as if they were not even there.

He left the palace and strode into the courtyard outside. This place had many gardens and flowers bloomed in each one. All of them were square and walled with whitewashed stone and mortar and were about ten paces square with two pace wide stone walkways between them. Everything was kept in order, and as inside, he ignored the servants who bowed to him as he negotiated his way through the gardens and toward the stables that were fifty paces away toward the castle's defensive wall. The stone building closest to the castle was guarded by a score of his best men and all of them snapped to attention as he approached.

Nemlivv hesitated as he reached the stable. The door was open and blocked with a stone to keep it so. Raising his chin, his eyes narrowed as he strode toward it again, but he slowed his approach as he entered. He could hear the unicorn speaking from within, and once he was inside, approached as quietly as he could.

From the far end of the stable, he heard the unicorn speaking very clearly.

"It was quite a time," she went on. "I knew I had friends there, but Ralligor had told me to trust no one. Humans are very unpredictable, he said, and could turn on me." She sighed. "I know of at least four there who did not. You wouldn't remember Audrell, but she would become one of my closest friends. I still think about her, but I am a little afraid to go and visit."

Nemlivv drew close enough to see her. She was lying on the far side of the stable, facing the corner and chatting away. Glancing around her stall, he expected to see the little servant girl in there, but she was not. The unicorn was alone.

"We had some fun times," she continued. "I suppose my time there was not so horrible after all. I find myself thinking about some of the fun I had there." Her ears perked and swiveled back.

Feeling her essence sweep toward him, the sorcerer remained still and simply folded his hands before him.

Shahly turned her head slightly, making clear her intention to ignore him.

"I noticed the stable door open," he told her.

"I asked that it be left so that some sunlight could come in," she informed. "I won't tell you who because I don't want you to punish her."

"Ellyus," he confirmed.

She lowered her head a little.

"I won't punish her," he assured.

"You aren't afraid I will make it through these enchanted bars and escape?"

"No, I'm not."

"Because you have many of your soldiers outside waiting to kill me if I do?" she guessed.

He glanced aside. "Well, no. They are there to keep people out, not you in. I've promised a slow death to whoever would bring you harm."

"Very thoughtful of you," she snarled.

Nodding, he turned his eyes to the dirt floor before him, then he approached her stall. The door opened as he neared and closed after he entered. He dared to walk all the way across the stall toward her and he sat down near the wall, leaning back against it.

Shahly turned her head slightly away from him.

They were silent for a moment, and the sorcerer began to pick at the straw he sat on. Finally he asked, "Where did you say you got that amulet?"

She took a long time to answer, but finally replied, "A wizard."

"Which wizard?"

The unicorn tensed up a little. "Why do you wish to know?"

"For the safety of my kingdom, I need to know. Oh, and it is not polite to answer a question with a question."

"Sorry."

He nodded. Another moment of silence passed between them, broken when he prodded, "So, does this wizard have a name?"

"Yes," was her curt reply.

Raising his brow, he pressed, "May I know his name?"

She turned her head slightly toward him. "I think you already know."

"I have an idea," he confirmed, "but I need to know for sure."

Shahly lowered her eyes and did not respond.

Nodding, the sorcerer softly said, "Very well. So how do you know the Desert Lord?"

She considered, then finally looked to him. "Who?"

"The Desert Lord," he repeated.

Shahly just stared at him for a moment, then she turned her eyes down. The name was not one that was familiar to her, and yet she tried to recall who it was anyway.

"You are creatures of truth," he reminded.

"But not always great memory," she confessed, still struggling to put face to name.

"So, you've not encountered any large black dragons in your travels?" When her eyes snapped to him, she unwittingly told him everything he wanted to know. "So you have seen him."

Her eyes were a little wide as she just stared at him, then she looked toward the window and confirmed, "I've seen a black dragon, yes."

"You also said my doom would come for me should I not release you," Nemlivv went on. "Would that doom be in the form of a black dragon?" Her silence also betrayed her and he nodded again. "I'm sure you don't want anyone here to get hurt, especially your little friend Ellyus."

"No, I don't. That is why you should let me go."

"Does he know where you are?"

"By now he does. He is very powerful and very intelligent, much more than you."

"Aren't dragons and unicorns enemies?"

"Aren't unicorns and humans enemies?" she countered.

He smiled. "Well played. I can see your wit is a force to be reckoned with."

No one had ever said that to her before and she actually felt a little flattered. She shot him a glance, not wanting him to know how she felt and trying to look as irritated as she could.

"I'd always heard that the wisdom of unicorns has no equal," he went on. "Surely this dragon recognizes yours and yearns to be in your favor."

"No," she corrected, turning her eyes down again. "I'm pretty sure he does not care about that."

"So he's coming," the sorcerer observed. "What should we do about that?"

"There is only one thing you can do," she replied.

"I believe there are always options. Would you drive him away to save Ellyus?"

"I can't drive him away, and I don't think he will harm her. He will come for you."

A slight smile touched his mouth. "Then I suppose I should prepare for him."

"It will not matter," she informed straightly.

"I have allies not even he can match," the wizard informed.

"Must we talk about this?" she asked.

"No," he sighed. "What do you wish to discuss instead?"

She shrugged and looked down, admitting, "I don't know."

Nemlivv considered, then, "What do you look like as a woman?"

With another shrug, she replied, "A woman, I guess."

"I would wager that you are beautiful. I would love to see you as a woman."

She glanced at him. "You took my amulet, remember?"

"I remember. Perhaps I can fix it for you."

Turning her full attention to him, her ears perked and she asked, "You can fix it?"

"I think so," was his answer. "Was there something in the grip of that talon?"

She nodded. "It was a round green stone."

"An emerald?"

"I think so. Yes, an emerald. That sounds right."

"I'm certain I can find another to fit, and I have expert goldsmiths who can make it just as it was the first time you saw it."

She leaned her head a little. "You would do that for me?"

"Quite happily," he confirmed. "I would do much more than that for you."

Shahly looked away from him and nodded.

Silence gripped the stable again.

Absently, he brushed the straw aside to expose the bare ground beneath, then he began to smooth the dark soil there.

The unicorn turned her eyes slowly to what he was doing, more out of curiosity than interest.

With one finger, he drew an almost perfect circle in the dirt, then he made a few symbols in the middle of it. He knew the unicorn was watching, but he did not look that way and only continued what he was doing. Running his finger through the circle a few more times to deepen it, he whispered a few Latirus words, then waved his hand over his work. A yellow glow erupted from the circle and the symbols he had drawn within it. Some kind of thick liquid bubbled up from the ground in the small trench he had drawn to fill it, forming a golden ring there in the ground. In a moment, the liquid solidified into gold and he brushed some of the dirt away. Digging his fingers into one side, he carefully lifted out a perfect golden ring about the diameter of his head. There was a strange blue light in the middle of it, something unnatural.

Shahly drew her head back, now even more curious about it.

He turned his eyes to her and offered a little smile.

She glanced at him, but her attention was on the golden ring.

"It's a seeing ring," he explained. "By looking through it I can see things in different forms. I can even see clearly into the dark of night with it."

Her eyes shifted to his.

As he slowly raised the ring to his face level, he informed, "I don't need your amulet to see you as a woman."

A dense fog appeared within the ring, and slowly thinned. Shahly could only see him through it, but he saw her as he wished to, as many at Red Stone castle had that spring without realizing. There she was, a captivating, beautiful young woman lying on her belly before him. Propped up on her elbows, her long golden hair flowed all the way to her lower back and over her shoulders. Her shape was of such perfection that he could never have imagined and his breath hesitated within him. Though her skin was as pale as the peasants who served him, this girl was perfectly muscled and the curves of her body aroused everything within him that was man.

Finally, he turned his eyes to hers. They were still the deep brown pools of his unicorn captive, but they were human now, and beautiful in a different way. He had never seen an angel, but he was certain this is what they must look like. She was more lovely a woman than he had ever seen and something innocent about her gave him an unnatural longing.

Nemlivv finally realized that he was not breathing and forced a breath in, but could not take his gaze from hers, even as she raised her brow. He discovered also that he was not blinking and forced this too as his eyes began to feel dry.

"Um," she started hesitantly, "do you see what you expected to?"

Slowly and slightly, he nodded and confirmed, "Yes, and much more."

"You got kind of pale," she observed. "Am I that hard to see as a woman?"

"Far from it," he said just over a whisper, his eyes glancing over her again. "You are more magnificent a woman than I have ever seen." Through the seeing ring, he actually saw her blush as she looked away from him. "Has anyone ever told you how lovely you are?"

"My stallion has," she answered straightly.

He slowly lowered the seeing ring, seeing her as a unicorn again. The image of her as a woman was burned onto his mind and memory and would not fade even as he looked away from her. Laying the seeing ring back into its place on the ground, he watched absently as it melted back into the earth, then he blinked and mumbled, "I *must* repair that amulet." He drew a breath and got to his feet, standing on legs that shook a little. "I should go. I, uh... I have something to attend."

She looked over her shoulder at him and asked, "Can Ellyus come and see me?"

The sorcerer could not look at her, but he nodded in quick movements and assured, "I will personally see to it." He turned to leave and did not make two full steps before he stopped again, staring at the gate of the enchanted cage that held her captive. What she was to him was now dictated more by his heart than his desire to have a trophy, yet not entirely. Still, he wanted to do something to prove himself worthy. He wanted to do something for her. As he stared at the gate, he asked, "Would you promise me something, dear unicorn?"

"Depends on what," she countered.

He smiled a little. "Promise me that you will not try to leave, that you will stay of your own will just for today. Promise me that and the castle grounds are yours to wander." He finally turned to her, raising his brow hopefully. "I know unicorns are creatures of truth. If you make a promise, then you must keep it."

She stared back in disbelief and leaned her head slightly. "You want me to promise that I will not try to escape from you, but just for today?"

He nodded. "Just for today."

"That would be an awful risk for you to take," she pointed out.

"Not at all," he assured, "not with your word that you will stay."

"And I get to go outside?" she prodded.

"Escorted, of course," he added, "but outside nonetheless."

"Just for today?" the unicorn asked.

He nodded again. "I wish to show you my home."

Shahly looked away and considered hard. If Ralligor flew by and saw her in the open he would no doubt rescue her right then and there, and she would be forced to break her word unless he agreed to return her for the day and come back tomorrow. Or, perhaps someone would see her and tell him and they could come for her the following day. What if Vinton came for her? She could not just leave after... She closed her eyes and shook her head as her thoughts became dizzying.

Raising his brow, Nemlivv informed, "You don't have to if you don't wish."

She considered a moment longer, then she stood and turned around, looking to him with a little suspicion in her eyes, and finally she nodded. "Okay. I promise you that I will not leave today, but you must show me around yourself and Ellyus has to come with us." She raised her head and locked her eyes defiantly on his.

"Agreed," he said straightly. "I shall see too it personally. Everything should be ready within the hour."

This was the most excitement he had actually felt for some time and he spun around and hurried from the stall, from the stable, not realizing that he had left both doors wide open, not caring.

CHAPTER 18

Summer rains had kept the river full, though the water was not as cold as it had been during the spring thaw. On a hot day the water was quite refreshing to any who would seek refuge from the heat of day. Spanning the current was a timber bridge, one that had been there for some time and was well kept by those who used it. It was large enough to allow passage for horses and wagons and linked a well traveled road. On the north side was a collection of men who all wore the same red and black tunics over their armor, two of whom tended the horses near the river. Two others stood by the ornate carriage that was propelled by two large white horses. Deep cushions covered in red velvet covered a bench seat that was meant for royalty. All of the guards kept their eyes from the two people who stood on the bridge, but for the occasional glance that way to be sure all was well.

The two people on the bridge itself were dressed very casually. The man, who was only about twenty seasons old, only wore a white swordsman's shirt, red riding trousers and black boots. His shoulder length brown hair blew freely on the breeze and framed a face so handsome as to befit his title of Prince. A powerful jaw swept toward a solid chin. He was of average height and build and leaned his forearms on the railing of the bridge as he stared out over the water.

The young woman with him had barely been of age a few seasons and was well made and very appealing to the eyes of her kind. Still, she was of a simple bloodline and nothing about her really gave her much advantage to the eye over any other. Long blond hair was unrestrained and waved on the breeze. Full lips wore a slight smile as she leaned onto the railing beside the Prince, her dark blue eyes dancing as she looked out onto the water. Her dress was a thin yellow material with white lace on the cuffs and sweeping neckline. She purposefully displayed much of her chest, as the dress was unlaced at the neckline, but this was more for comfort against the heat than for the allure of the man beside her.

They stared out over the water for long moments, then the

Prince drew a breath and observed, "Well, we're out here yet again."

The young woman nodded, either ignoring or oblivious to his exasperation. "I love it here." She glanced up at him and smiled just a little more. "I loved this place from the moment I saw it, but now it seems perfect."

"How so?" he asked.

"You're here," was her answer.

Their eyes slowly drifted to each other's.

"Any regrets?" he asked.

She raised her brow and considered. "Well, let's see. I'm supposed to marry the Prince of Red Stone Castle this spring, I'll be a princess, my husband will be the most handsome man in the land, I'll live in a palace—"

"So no regrets," he interrupted.

She shrugged. "How can I have regrets in such a perfect life?"

"You never told me how badly I embarrassed you when I asked for your hand," he observed.

Smiling, she countered, "Embarrassed me? That was the most perfect moment of my life! The way you called out everyone in the village and then approached my father and asked for his blessing, the way you got down on one knee and took my hand..." She closed her eyes and rolled her head back. "Oh, it's still with me every moment!"

He reached up and gently stroked her golden hair. "With me as well. Of course, that night could have gone better."

She looked back to him and asked, "You would expect to bed me right after proposing? My father wouldn't hear of it!"

"That wasn't my intention," he defended, "nor was sleeping in the carriage that night."

"I come from a traditional family," she said straightly. Something serious took her features and she asked, "Arden, are you certain it is okay to have the ceremony in my village? I mean, her Majesty really doesn't mind, does she?"

"As long as she has her reception at the palace I think everything will be fine," he assured. "I did promised your mother a beautiful wedding and I can't think of one better than that river where you grew up."

Her hand slid across the railing to his as she just stared into his eyes for a time, then she smiled and bade, "Come on," as she turned and rushed to the other side of the bridge, pulling him along by the hand as she did.

As they got to the other side, he gripped her hand and stopped, bringing her to an abrupt stop as well as he ordered, "No water fight today."

She smiled big at him and innocently said, "I wouldn't. Let's just go a little closer."

He pulled hard and she stumbled into him. The hand he held was twisted behind her back and his other arm snared her tightly around the waist. "Oh, no. We're fine right here."

Giggling, she struggled to free herself, and when she could not twist free, she observed, "Captain Ocnarr was right about you, my Prince. You are a letch."

"And still good at it," he countered. When she struggled again, he spun with her and down they went!

She barked a scream and before she realized what had happened, she was lying on her back with him on top of her. His face was a finger length from hers and their eyes were locked on one another's once again.

He shook his head slightly and asked, "Why do I still feel like I have to steal every little kiss from you?"

"I think you prefer it that way," she teased.

They closed their eyes and, ever so gently, their lips met. They parted for a second, then he pressed his lips more firmly to hers, making no secret of the passion he had for her. She moaned softly, wanting to hold him, but one arm was pinned to her side and the other was pinned beneath her. No matter. She would make no secret of her passion for him, either.

They could not know how long they just laid there and kissed before he finally withdrew to see her eyes again, and he offered her a smile. "I rather do like stealing those kisses from you."

"Aye, that you do," she confirmed. "I rather like it, too. Prince Arden."

"Yes, Lady Audrell."

"My arm is going numb."

He laughed, and so did she.

Little could have distracted them, but when the Prince saw a shadow out of the corner of his eye, he found himself looking that way, then up. His eyes widened and his mouth fell open.

Seeing this, Audrell looked that way, gasping at what she saw.

Vinton stared back at them, looking more perplexed than curious.

Quickly but gently, the Prince got off of his fiancé and rose to his knees, awkwardly standing from there.

Audrell wrestled her arm from behind her and quickly went to stand herself, taking the Prince's hand as he offered it.

Side by side, they faced the big unicorn, clasping each other's hand as they stared wide eyed at him.

The girl was of little interest to Vinton and his attention was fully on the man at her side. Raising his head slightly, he asked, "Can you understand me?"

Hesitantly, Prince Arden nodded.

The stallion loosed a breath, then hesitantly informed, "I need your help."

Audrell glanced up at the Prince. "What would you have of us?"

Vinton finally seemed to notice her and his eyes turned that way. "She called you her closest friend here. She said you were kind to her when few others were."

Her eyes widening, Audrell breathed, "Shahly."

Arden's breath caught and he raised his chin, demanding, "What has happened?"

Again the stallion was hesitant to answer, but he finally looked away and replied, "Someone has taken her. I came here in the hope that you might be willing to help me get her back. I know you didn't part on the best of terms, but— "

"What can I do?" the Prince interrupted sternly. When the unicorn's eyes snapped to him, he nodded and confirmed, "We parted on better terms than any man could hope to have with a unicorn, and considering what my people have done to yours it is the very least I can do."

Vinton looked down and nodded.

Audrell squeezed her fiancé's hand a little and asked, "What may we do to help you? She's one of my closest friends and I still feel her in my heart, as I always will. Please let me… us help you. Please."

"I can't ask you to imperil yourselves," the stallion informed.

"And you haven't," Prince Arden countered. "We'll take on any risk of our own will. Do you know who has her?"

"Some sorcerer," the stallion replied. "He calls himself Lord Nemlivv."

"Of Ravenhold," the Prince mumbled.

Vinton's ears swiveled toward him. "You know this sorcerer?"

"I'm afraid so," Arden confessed. Turning his eyes down, he sighed and shook his head. "This will be a problem."

"Why?" Audrell demanded.

Hesitant to answer, the Prince finally explained, "Ravenhold is an ally of Red Stone and we dare not do anything that might compromise relations between us."

The stallion nodded and looked away. "I understand. Relations between the clans of your kind are delicate and complex and I would not have you jeopardize that or the hundreds of lives it would cost."

"I didn't say we can't help," Arden countered, "this will just make things more delicate than turning the brunt of our army on them, much more delicate."

Audrell considered, then suggested, "What if we don't need an army?"

The Prince's eyes shifted to her and he added, "We could just pay him a social visit."

Vinton looked to him and raised his head. "A what?"

Offering him a smile, Arden elaborated, "Just a visit. Ravenhold is only a day's ride from here, and Lord Nemlivv hasn't met my bride-to-be. Such an announcement wouldn't be unusual and should be made in person."

The unicorn's eyes snapped to Audrell.

She also smiled. "I once heard that if you see a unicorn then your first child will be a prince. Perhaps he would oblige a girl's story and let me see her."

"She must mean a great deal to you two," Vinton guessed.

Audrell stepped toward the stallion and knelt down before him, vulnerable eyes glossy with tears. "A lifelong dream of mine was to see a unicorn. Shahly gave me that and much more. She became my friend. That is far more than I could have ever prayed for. My life is hers—and yours should you need it."

"Mine as well," the Prince added.

Vinton's ears twitched toward the bridge and he looked that way.

Arden also looked and murmured, "Uh, oh."

Audrell stood and backed away from the unicorn, shaking her head as she whimpered, "Oh, no. Arden..."

Six guards approached, four of them on horseback and all of them with ropes or weapons in their hands.

"Tell them I'm a horse," Vinton whickered.

As the guards approached to within about ten paces, the leader among them insisted, "Not to worry, your Highness. We'll get him."

Prince Arden turned toward them and folded his arms. "Get him? Why would you want to get my horse?" In that moment he felt a wave pass through him and wash over the men. It felt like a wave of thought, almost like putting to motion an action, and yet it was not his own.

The men stopped and looked hard at the stallion, and the officer raised his head as his perplexed eyes studied the beast before him. "Huh. Could have sworn it was a unicorn. No worries, I suppose. Her Majesty will just have to find another. Sorry to have disturbed you, Highness."

"Quite all right," the Prince assured. "Just go about your duties and forget the matter." Again he felt that wave, but with it were the words, *Forget you saw the horse.*

The men turned and made their way back across the bridge.

"What just happened?" Audrell asked in a low, confused voice.

Arden turned and looked to the unicorn, nodding as he replied, "That was the true power of a unicorn."

Vinton's eyes narrowed. "Your people are still hunting us?"

"It would seem so," the Prince answered. "It would also seem that I still have a lot of work to do." He glanced away. "We may also use this to our advantage."

"I don't see how," the stallion grumbled.

"Just let me worry over that," the Prince ordered. "If we can get her out of there, where should we take her?"

"Find a road that goes south toward the Dark Mountains.

There should be a pass to get you back to the Southlands. Once there I think she will be safe."

"Unless Nemlivv catches up to us," the Prince added grimly.

"Just get her to the Southlands," the unicorn ordered, turning toward the forest and pacing away from them. "Nemlivv will be attended to."

"Don't underestimate him," the Prince called after him.

Vinton stopped and looked back. "Nemlivv has done the underestimating. He should pray that wisdom finds him before his fate does."

Those haunting words echoed in the Prince's mind as he watched the stallion disappear into the forest. Only when Audrell slipped her arms around him did he blink and look away from that last place he had seen the unicorn. As he met her eyes, he could only bring himself to say, "We need to go."

CHAPTER 19

Having seen nothing outside of the stable for so long, even a day, the prospect of actually going outside had Shahly's heart in a flutter as she heard activity outside of the door. Although the gate to her stall had been left open, she had not left it and instead remained within the only safety she had known in this place.

The latch on the stable door clicked and her ears perked. Her eyes were locked on the door as it opened in anticipation of seeing Ellyus come through, but her ears drooped in disappointment when it was the black haired girl who entered instead.

Dirty and tattered and still wearing the same riding attire she had been that morning, Nillerra strode in slowly, holding her head with a slight lean, her gaze locked on the unicorn before her. Exhaustion was there, and defeat. Still, they were a little wild with that familiar madness and she slowly shook her head as she drew closer.

Shahly's eyes narrowed ever so slightly as she reminded, "I told you not to go."

"That was all a trick," the black haired girl insisted. "You knew I would go with more determination the more you begged me not to. You were trying to kill me like you did before!"

"We both know that isn't true," Shahly defended, raising her head as this tormentor grew closer.

Stopping only three paces away, Nillerra shook her head again, recalling, "He killed almost all of those soldiers. A hundred men, Shahly. That's how many people died because of you. Are you happy with yourself now?"

Looking away from her, the unicorn countered, "No one had to die. You led them there, not me."

"You didn't even warn me," the black haired girl hissed.

"It wouldn't have made any difference. You would have called me a liar and gone anyway. Just go away now."

"That beast almost killed me," Nillerra went on, bordering on rage. "I..." Breathing came hard for her as she looked away, horror in her eyes as she recalled what had happened.

"Did you recognize him?" Shahly asked.

Nillerra considered, then her eyes grew wider as she looked back to the unicorn, meeting her gaze. Pointing a shaking finger, she accused, "You're in league with him, aren't you? You're in league with that beast!"

"I'm not sure what that means," Shahly admitted, "but he is my friend, and he is none too happy about my being held captive here. That is why you should have let me go when you could have."

Snarling, Nillerra hissed, "When Lord Nemlivv finds out about this— "

"He already knows," the unicorn informed straightly.

The black haired girl's eyes widened a little more and she raised her chin slightly.

"He's showing me around the castle today," Shahly continued. "In fact, he should be here any moment. Perhaps you would like to explain what happened out there when he arrives, or would he punish you for it?"

Nillerra clearly felt cornered and just stared back at the unicorn in disbelief, slowly shaking her head. In an instant she seemed to get her wits about her and her lips drew back from her teeth. "You are going to pay for this. You *won't* take Nemlivv from me like you did Arden. I'll kill you first!"

Leaning her head slightly, Shahly asked, "Now how would Lord Nemlivv feel about that?" She was unaware that she was feeling more and more comfortable under the sorcerer's protection. For the first time she felt like she had the advantage with Nillerra, and she liked it.

Glaring at the white unicorn, Nillerra backed away a step.

Shahly advanced, her eyes narrowing. "I think you like being cruel to others. I think you get pleasure from watching others suffer. In fact, I know you do."

Slowly, the black haired girl backed away.

Raising her head high, Shahly looked into Nillerra's eyes and guessed, "I think you are far more afraid than you want others to think. Outside of Nemlivv's protection and his favor you know there is much for you to be afraid of."

Nillerra could feel Shahly's mind peering into hers and she turned away, raising her hands toward the unicorn as she snapped, "Stop it! Don't use your tricks on me!"

"What are you so afraid of?" Shahly pressed, taking another step forward. "Is it something you did? Are you ashamed of something? Why must others pay for your deeds, Nillerra? You know it isn't right, so why do you— "

"Stop!" the black haired girl screamed as the unicorn's essence drew closer to something within her. She turned to escape and ran right into Nemlivv as he approached. She looked up at him as he took her shoulders, her eyes wide and spilling tears as she begged, "Please, make her stop!"

He looked to the unicorn, appearing a little surprised.

Nillerra looked over her shoulder, wild eyes boring into the unicorn as she hissed, "She's mad, my Lord. You have to get rid of her. She'll bring— "

"Enough!" he ordered. Shaking the black haired girl, he drew her attention back to him and held her gaze with his. "What happened out there? Where are the men you took with you? And my apprentice. What happened to him?"

Her eyes fixed on the sorcerer's, Nillerra shook her head and whimpered, "It was a trap, my Lord. She led us right into the jaws of a horrible beast."

"A dragon," he confirmed. "You had already arrived there when I found this out. What of my men?"

"They fought bravely," she sobbed.

His lips tightening, he nodded and drew a breath, then ordered, "To your chamber. Get washed and rest for a while, and stay there until I come for you."

"I will," she whispered to him. Laying her head on his chest, she wept and offered, "I'm so sorry, my Lord. I wanted to bring him to you as a gift."

He stroked her hair and assured, "I know, my pet. I know."

"I'm sorry," she offered again.

Nemlivv pushed her away slightly and said, "We will discuss it later. Go on and do as I command."

Turning her eyes down, the black haired girl sobbed, "Am I in trouble?"

"No, pet. Just go on, now. Things will be fine."

As Nillerra slipped from the stable, Nemlivv turned his attention to the unicorn, folding his arms as he looked upon her with blank eyes.

Shahly stared back, then finally said, "I thought I was the pet."

A smile cracked his stone like features and he chuckled. "Oh, I have many pets. Would you care to walk about the palace grounds with me now?"

She glanced around him and observed, "I don't see Ellyus."

"I sent for her," the sorcerer assured. "She should be on her way."

Nodding, Shahly turned her eyes to the brightness outside. She had not seen sunlight for just over a day, but it felt like much longer and an eagerness grew restless within her. "I suppose we can wait for her outside."

"You do remember your promise," Nemlivv said in a near warning tone.

"I remember," she replied softly. With a deep breath, she paced toward him, past him and into the bright light. Looking up at the clouds, she squinted against the sunlight she had not seen for some time. The sky looked different somehow and the air was different in odor. It was also a little thinner. These were little nuances that humans would not detect, but a unicorn would feel them in an instant. The stone that the palace and the wall were built of was darker than even Red Stone Castle, a very dark gray.

She only paced out a few steps before she stopped and had a good look around, first looking to the wall that surrounded her. Her eyes followed it, glancing about at the thin towers that rose from the ground and seemed to anchor it, the battlements at the top with timber structures that she could not know were catapults, and the many soldiers who stood at the ready up there. As her eyes swept across to the palace, she noticed first what a dark and imposing structure is was. Sheer walls rose from the ground three times Ralligor's standing height and were built between thick towers of that dark stone. High, thin windows were square at the bottom and arched at the top. It was twice as wide as it was tall, a mountainous assembly of stone that looked as if it was meant to dominate all of the land around it.

She caught something sweet on the air and her gaze swept down the wall, locking wide on the many flower gardens that surrounded the castle. They seemed out of place, and yet they were a beautiful sight here, arranged in ornate blocks of stone surrounded patches that were a little higher than the rest of the ground.

"Do you like the flowers?" the sorcerer asked.

Smiling slightly, Shahly nodded and confirmed, "I like all flowers." She looked to the sorcerer and added, "Except there's one in the desert that smells like something died and it is a really awful shade of blue. I don't like that one so much."

"I'll be sure not to plant any of those," he assured. "Would you like to walk among the flower beds first?"

She glanced around at them again and replied, "We should wait for Ellyus."

Looking almost anxiously at the palace door, his lips tightened and his eyes grew tense. This was clearly not a man who was accustomed to waiting for others and his annoyance was all too clear.

Almost as if he had summoned her, she came running out of the palace, holding her skirt up as she did. Reaching them out of breath, she dropped to her knees and gulped a few more breaths of air as she trained her eyes on the sorcerer's boots, finally gasping, "I beg forgiveness, my Lord."

"I told you when to be here," he said harshly as he folded his arms. "Why are you just now arriving in my presence?"

She took another couple of breaths and replied, "Master Attuane ordered that I should attend to some things in the kitchen when I went for Shahly's apples. I tried to explain, but he would not allow me to speak and made me attend to those things. It took longer than I thought and I beg forgiveness."

"It wasn't your fault," the unicorn assured, pacing toward her.

Seeing this, the sorcerer nodded and ordered, "On your feet, now. I'll attend to Master Attuane shortly. Did you remember..." He looked to the unicorn with a raised brow. "Shahly?"

She returned his look and countered, "Did you think I wouldn't have a name?"

He glanced away as Ellyus slowly got to her feet. "I suppose I hadn't thought about it since you did not tell me the first time I asked."

Shahly nodded. "And you meant to give me a name of your

own, something human sounding like Snow or something."

Nemlivv shrugged.

Rolling her eyes, Shahly paced toward the flower beds, saying in an exasperated tone, "Come on. Let's explore the kingdom."

Ellyus gasped, staring straight ahead with horror filled eyes as she recalled aloud, "I forgot to bring the apples!"

Shahly stopped and looked back at her, assuring, "I'm sure there will still be some later, so you shouldn't worry over it."

"I'm sorry," the girl offered sheepishly.

Smiling a little, the unicorn countered, "You shouldn't be. Now we can go into the castle and get them together."

As she watched this magical creature wander about her way, the girl could not help but smile and tears welled up in her eyes. When she heard the sorcerer sigh, she shot him a glance, surprised to see him smiling a little, too, as he watched her wander away from them.

They could not know of her true intentions. Shahly had never been one to plan ahead or really to plan anything, but she looked around the castle with purpose. This was a study for more of a reason than finding out about Nemlivv's home. She would do her best to memorize everything she could, every detail that might be needed by those who meant to rescue her. If Ralligor did not appear today, then perhaps he would come to her dream again tonight, and this time she would know what he needed her to know.

Hearing the sorcerer and girl catch up to her, she glanced back at them in turn and observed, "The flowers are very pretty."

"Much work went into rebuilding the castle itself," Nemlivv informed. "It was in dismal condition when we came here."

Still looking about as she paced on her way, Shahly asked, "If it was so bad, then why did you come here?"

"The walls and foundations were still very solid," he replied. "It seemed that we could repair what was here much faster and easier than building a new one."

"Why not just live with the land?" she questioned.

"The people around here needed protection," was his answer.

"From other humans?" she snarled. "You people need to learn to live together without fighting so much, that way the land could remain as it should be."

He nodded. "Sadly, that just isn't the reality. We are a warring people."

"Some more than others," she mumbled.

Their trek would take them all the way around the palace. Nemlivv seemed eager to tell her all about his home and told her every detail he could recall about it.

They circled all the way around the palace and Shahly memorized as much as she could, every detail she thought would stay in her memory. This place was one that was well suited to defending itself against human armies and it was an imposing sight to say the least, but she could imagine Ralligor almost easily laying waste to the whole thing. This was not something she truly wanted, and yet the thought would not leave her.

A couple of hours passed and they looked over every part of the broad space between the palace and the wall that defended it. A shallow creek ran through what looked like the north side of the compound and smelled dirty of washing and human waste. While she wanted a drink, she did not want any of *that* water.

Arriving back at the gardens near the stable, Shahly noticed Ellyus blotting the sweat from her brow yet again and realized that the day was hot and the sun very intense. With a deep breath and a sharp snort, she said aloud to no one special, "I could use a swim and a long drink."

"I know where there is a swimming hole," the girl barked before realizing. When she finally did realize, she slowly turned fearful eyes up to the sorcerer's.

Raising his chin, Nemlivv folded his arms and gave the unicorn a commanding stare.
"Do you take me for a fool?"

"No," Shahly replied, "but it's hot and I want to swim."

"And then what?" he continued. "You disappear from sight and you are gone just like that." His displeased gaze turned to the girl, and she cringed under his attention.

With narrow eyes, Shahly turned and paced between the sorcerer and the girl, giving him a sharp look of her own as she spat, "Do not turn your anger on her and do not stand there and question my honesty. I made a promise to you this morning, do you remember?"

"I remember," he confirmed. "I trust you do?"

Ellyus backed away as the unicorn turned fully on her master.

Raising her head and bringing her nose very close to his, Shahly bared her teeth and narrowed her eyes further, snarling, "Just what are you saying, sorcerer? Did you forget that I am unicorn? Do you confuse me with a deceitful creature like you are?"

His eyes shifted away from her. "You want me to just trust you?"

Shahly snorted into his face, then paced around him and said, "I'll be in the stable."

Nemlivv looked to the girl, who again cringed under his attention, then he turned his eyes to the ground. With a deep breath, he conceded, "I want a squad of guards to go with you."

Stopping, the white unicorn stared ahead of her for a second before snapping, "No."

"Why not?" he demanded.

"Ellyus wants to swim, too," she answered. "She will have to do so without her clothing and your guards should not see her like that. It isn't proper."

"How about just I go?"

"You're still male, Nemlivv, and it still wouldn't be proper."

He turned fully to her and asked, "What would a unicorn know about what is proper?"

"If Ellyus and I can go swimming then I'll tell you."

"I do wish to speak with you," he informed harshly.

"After we swim," she countered. Slowly, she turned her head to look back at him.

He considered again, his eyes on hers, then he looked away. "I don't think it would be a wise idea."

"Like questioning the honesty of a unicorn," she observed.

Nemlivv's eyes snapped back to her and he smiled a little. "We still need to talk."

"We'll talk as long as you like," Shahly informed, "*after* I swim."

Raising his brow, he nodded slightly and summoned, "Ellyus."

She hurried to him and dropped to her knees.

Looking down on the girl, he ordered, "Have her back in a couple of hours."

Ellyus smiled up at him and offered, "Thank you, my Lord!" In one motion, she spun around and leaped to her feet, darting to the unicorn as she squealed, "We can go!"

Shahly offered the sorcerer a warm look and a nod, then she turned with the girl and they paced toward the open gate. "I don't think he is so bad," the unicorn observed. "I just need to work with him more."

"So you are staying?" the girl asked anxiously.

"For a while, anyway," Shahly replied. "I have my word to keep, after all." She looked to Ellyus and bumped her with her shoulder. "And I have you to look after."

CHAPTER 20

Difficult tasks were nothing new to the Desert Lord. Dragonslayers, intruding dragons, the learning of the *wizaridi*... All of that might seem overwhelming to anyone, even a *subordinare* dragon. Many times he had faced death at the hands of some enemy. Many times, he had been tested by overwhelming adversity, but to a dragon in his prime, especially one of Ralligor's size and strength, all of those tests were just another day, just one more adversity to overcome and then boast about later.

Less than one hundred fifty seasons old, the black dragon had faced down many enemies, many seemingly insurmountable tests. But one thing still proved to be the most difficult of all: His friendship with a unicorn.

Soaring on a high wind, his wings were full with that wind, his arms pulled to him, and his eyes locked forward in a stare that squinted against the passing air. His thoughts were heavy and bothersome, as was the next task that awaited him.

The scarlet dragon stroked her wings a few times, meeting his pace easily, but careful to remain just a little behind his wingtips. Air currents could disrupt flight and this was the best way to avoid them. She could not see how the air swirled coming off of his wingtips as there was little moisture in the air to condense, but she knew it was there as dragons have a sense for these things. This was not something done consciously, as her thoughts were fully occupied with her big mate, and her eyes were locked on him.

Shifting her tail slightly toward him, she turned slightly and gracefully, then stroked her wings again to bring herself above him.

Finally, she observed, "You are very quiet, *Unisponsus.*"

He turned his head slightly and glanced at her, then his attention was drawn forward again.

"They couldn't have been dragonslayers," she went on. "I've seen many humans who considered themselves so and not one among them had power even close to any of those. I can see them wanting to build a reputation by attacking you, but that wasn't even a fight. Even that wizard they had didn't have anything to challenge you with."

"He wasn't fully trained," the black dragon finally said.

"Yes," Falloah agreed, "much like you."

He glanced at her again and added, "He wasn't a wizard, either. He was a sorcerer."

They flew in silence for a time, but the scarlet dragon's mind whirled about as she searched for some way to distract her huge mate from his troubles.

"I suppose allowing me to join the fray would have been asking too much," she said sharply, yet with a tone of amusement to her voice.

"Yes," was his simple reply.

She sighed and growled as she looked away. Looking back to him, she offered, "I can speak to Agarxus for you."

"No," he snarled. "This is my problem and I'll— "

"There you go again!" she cried. "Ralligor, you aren't the Landmaster nor are you are alone in this matter! Don't you think that I might want her freed just as much as you?"

A soft growl rolled from the black dragon as he turned his eyes aside.

Falloah continued, "It isn't my place to question you and I don't mean to challenge you, but I so want to be at your side and you never let me! Why can't you accept the help of those all around you?"

Once again, he was quiet for a time, and finally he admitted, "Plow Mule is right."

Falloah leaned her head. "What do you mean?"

"She's the way she is because of me," he explained. "She has no fear of dragons. She craves the chase of predators. She befriends every wandering creature she runs across." He growled and shook his head. "I used her this spring. I used her to get you out of that castle and destroy the Talisman. She was a tool, nothing more. I saw an opportunity and I took it. That was all."

"And we are all grateful that you did," Falloah pointed out.

"Unicorns should fear me," he snarled. "They used to, and now one comes into the desert looking to me for safety and advice. I was once one of the most feared dragons in the land."

"And now you are the most respected dragon in the land," she countered. "Humans and unicorns alike would rally to you for whatever you need them for. Fear won't make them do that."

"They rally to Shahly," the black dragon pointed out.

"And but for you," she countered, "they would never have even known her. The land owes you a growing debt, just as I do. Do you think I have forgotten how you saved my life when Terrathgrawr meant to kill me?"

"Agarxus actually defeated him," Ralligor pointed out.

"Yes, he did," Falloah agreed. "Agarxus was and is more than a match for him. You were not. You had no way to win, and yet you attacked him anyway with such ferocity that I had never before seen. You got him off of me. You saved my life that day."

He glanced back at her again. "Do you have regrets about that day?"

She took a while to answer, but finally admitted, "Yes. There were those hours that you tried to catch my eye, and I scoffed."

Ralligor's brow arched and he snarled slightly as he remembered all he had done to try and impress her, the foolish acts of an adolescent dragon.

Falloah growled a sigh, looking aside as she continued, "You had my attention, you cocky drake, and I regret not having told you sooner. I regret the waste of those precious first hours."

He glanced up at her. "You've harbored that for over forty seasons?"

"Every moment," she confessed softly.

Ralligor turned his eyes forward and down. A moment later he raised his head and informed, "I'm glad you didn't make it too easy. I like a challenge."

She cooed at him.

"There's his lair," the black dragon informed.

"I'll be behind you the whole time, *Unisponsus*," she assured.

"No," he corrected. "I would have you at my side."

She turned slightly and flew beside him and just behind his wingtip. "Then I'll be at your side, *Unisponsus*, even when danger beckons."

"When danger beckons," he corrected, "then you'll be behind me."

She rolled her eyes and growled.

They descended sharply at first, flying in echelon all the way down where they stroked their wings forward to reduce their speed. The cleared area around Agarxus' lair, half a league in any direction, was one well suited to giving a very big dragon room to land, and these two smaller dragons swept in toward the cave at the other end with much room to spare. Stroking their wings forward again, their legs descended and feet found the earth beneath them in a manner so as not to land in a hard challenge. Dropping from the sky and slamming into the ground as Ralligor often did was a sign of strength and authority, of superiority over his enemies. Today, his Landmaster would not be impressed by this and he knew it, so the softer the landing the better.

Trotting off the last of their speed, they folded their wings and strode toward the cave opening, stopping about fifty paces away, side by side. Now was the time for Ralligor to announce his arrival as he had done many times before. Today, he looked to his smaller mate and she to him. Turning back toward the cave, they announced their arrival in concert and as one.

No answer came from the cave.

Ralligor drew his head back. Glancing at Falloah, he announced his presence again, and she joined him.

A moment passed.

"Is he in there?" she asked.

Testing the air, Ralligor confirmed, "His scent sure is strong." He tested the air again, then his eyes widened and he murmured, "Oh, no."

A growl finally erupted from the cave, a deep growl from a huge, angry dragon.

Falloah also tested the air, and took a step back. "He has company in there, doesn't he?"

"He does," the black dragon confirmed grimly, "and she's in season."

A heavy thumping on the ground announced the approach of the Landmaster from within the cave, and judging from the weight of the steps he was not happy.

Taking another step back, Falloah assured, "I'll be right behind you, *Unisponsus.*"

He reached back and seized the back of her neck, pulling her two steps forward. "At my side, remember?"

Agarxus emerged from his cave on all fours and stood as soon as he was clear of the entrance, his eyes narrow and his brow low over them as he stormed to his subordinate dragons with heavy steps. He growled with each breath as he approached and stopped his advance only about ten paces away, looming over the Desert Lord and demonstrating both his power and his displeasure at being disturbed.

Ralligor simply stared up at him as Falloah raised her snout submissively and cooed.

The scarlet dragon did not get even a glace as the huge Landmaster folded his thick arms and growled, "Well?"

Ralligor drew a breath. "I would ask something of you."

"Right now?" Agarxus snarled.

"It's a matter of great importance to me," the black dragon.

Agarxus turned and strode back toward his cave. "But not to me, I think. Be on your way, Ralligor, and don't disturb me again."

The Desert Lord's eyes narrowed and began to glow red, and he announced, "Then I'll face down Mettegrawr on my own."

The Landmaster stopped, his fingers curling inward. Slowly, he turned and trained his attention on his *subordinare*, growling, "What?"

"I have business in the Northlands," Ralligor informed, "and I'm certain Mettegrawr will not approve of my being there."

"Another of your schemes, Ralligor?" Agarxus shook his head and approached a step. "Or are you just determined to tangle with him again? Don't you remember the last time?"

"I remember," the Desert Lord assured, "and this matter has nothing to do with him."

"Nor did the last," the Landmaster reminded. "Tell me of this business of yours."

Venting another breath, Ralligor set his jaw and answered, "A little white unicorn challenged you twice this season, and twice you allowed her to just be on her way."

"Your pet," Agarxus snarled.

"Yes, my pet," the Desert Lord confirmed. He lowered his eyes before he continued. "Someone has taken her, and I have tracked her to a castle in the Northlands."

The Landmaster turned his gaze to Falloah, and to her surprise his expression was not as hard as it had been. Finally, he asked, "What is it doing in the Northlands?"

Falloah answered, "She was taken in the night. Agarxus, I know she is only a unicorn, but she means a great deal to us. She was at the center of getting me away from Red... from the dragonslayer. We don't wish to disturb you with this matter, we only wish— "

He barked a roar at her and silenced her, then looked to the Desert Lord. "This little grazer means that much to you? So much that you are willing to raise Mettegrawr's ire with you again?"

Ralligor met his Landmaster's gaze with eyes that glowed red. "She means that much to me."

Looking away, Agarxus growled and shook his head. "There was a time when you would have just killed it and that would have been that."

"There was a time you would have done the same," the black dragon countered.

The Landmaster huffed a rare laugh and looked back to his *subordinare.* "Perhaps so. I won't forbid you to go, Ralligor, but I have an accord with Mettegrawr. I have given my word that the land north of the Dark Mountains is no longer in my interest."

"And you have no interest fighting him again," the black dragon finished.

"I never said that," Agarxus corrected, "nor will I violate our agreement because of a unicorn. Know that I will not support you in this matter, and I'll not challenge Mettegrawr because of a unicorn."

Ralligor nodded, then turned to leave, making it only a few steps before he looked over his shoulder. "How long until Trostan sends the next crop of dragonslayers your way?"

Raising his snout slightly, the Landmaster replied, "Twelve days, I think. What of it?"

The Desert Lord shrugged. "Nothing. I'm sure they'll defeat your boredom the way they always do."

Agarxus' eyes narrowed as he watched his lieutenant stride toward the tree line.

Falloah looked past the Landmaster as she saw movement

within his cave.

Peering out from the darkness, a pair of eyes glistened in the dim light that penetrated the cave, the same light that barely illuminated dark blue scales that betrayed the curving features of a female.

Seeing the scarlet dragon's attention directed behind him, the Landmaster half turned his head and roared through bared teeth.

The blue dragon within his cave quickly retreated into the darkness.

Falloah leaned her head and looked up at the huge dragon. "I would ask you something, Agarxus."

He regarded the scarlet dragoness almost cruelly.

Choosing her next words carefully, she hesitated before asking, "You can have any dragoness in the land. Seasons ago you could have had me, but you never have."

"You belong to Ralligor," he informed coldly. "Why is that not clear to you?"

"It is," she confirmed, cringing a little. "But you are Landmaster. Am I not yours first?"

"You are," Agarxus replied. "Why do you need to know these things?"

Turning her eyes down, she answered timidly, "It isn't vanity and— "

"You are Ralligor's," the Landmaster said flatly. "He chose you forty seasons ago and you chose him."

"And you'll not try to take me from him as Terrathgrawr did?"

"I'm not Terrathgrawr. Ralligor is loyal to me. He always has been. I would not consider violating that loyalty."

She raised her eyes to his again.

"Loyalty works two ways, Falloah," the Landmaster explained. "Ralligor is a strong dragon, the strongest of my *subordinares,* and I am stronger with his loyalty."

"It's more than that," she said softly.

The Landmaster raised a brow slightly.

"Ralligor means more to you than that," she went on. "You tolerate him more than you do any other dragon."

Agarxus' gaze shifted slowly to the black dragon, who stood

at the edge of the tree line waiting less than patiently for his mate to catch up to him. "He is an open wound, one that festers and annoys me every time he is within smelling distance." He looked down to Falloah again and folded his arms. "He never swore loyalty to me. When he approached that first day he had barely come of age." The big dragon shook his head. "He was smaller than you are now, and overflowing with confidence and fire. He didn't challenge me, nor did he cower when I showed him my strength. All others before and since have trembled in my presence."

"You would kill any drake that does not show you such respect," she pointed out.

A very rare smile curled his scaly lips, just slightly. "Respect was always there, dragoness. He made his loyalty known the first time he made eye contact, and he has never wavered." He looked toward the black dragon again and snarled slightly. "Honestly, I'm not certain why I tolerate him the way I do."

Falloah smiled a little herself. "He is to you what Shahly is to him."

The big dragon's eyes snapped to her.

"His unicorn," she explained.

"The very unicorn he means to risk his life to rescue from the Northlands." Agarxus nodded. "I see a fire in that one, too. Clearly that is Ralligor's doing somehow. They are not that different, I think."

"She annoys him," Falloah informed with amusement in her voice, "just like he annoys you. He loves her, Landmaster. He doesn't know why, but he does, and so do I. I wish to go with him to rescue her."

The big dragon's eyes rolled up and he growled a sigh. "One dragon is a challenge, Falloah. More than one is an invasion, and I don't think raising Mettegrawr's ire is a wise thing for you two to do."

"We can have Drarrexok along," she added, "with your permission."

Agarxus growled again and shook his head, his eyes still on the clouds above.

"It seems foolish to do all of this for a unicorn, doesn't it?" she asked softly.

"It does," he confirmed.

She nodded. "It also seems foolish to wait for dragonslayers to come and try to kill you every month or so."

He trained his eyes on her again, his brow low over them.

Falloah cringed and looked down, taking a step back as she added, "It does to me. I don't have your strength to deal with them."

"It breaks up my boredom," he snarled.

She nodded again. "I understand. With Shahly around us we're never bored, so I suppose Ralligor and I never have to find such things to amuse us."

"Are you finished?" the huge dragon growled.

"Forgive me," she offered. "I have— "

"Yes you have," he snarled.

Slowly, Falloah turned her eyes up to his, and raised her snout submissively. "I'm sorry that there are no challenges left for you, Landmaster. I would help if I could."

His eyes narrowed and for a long moment he just stared down at her, and every second made her more nervous. Finally, he said, "I will not forbid you to go, Falloah, nor will I forbid Drarrexok. This is Ralligor's problem and he will attend to it." A soft coo came forth from his cave and he looked over his shoulder and roared, "I'm coming!"

Falloah cringed again.

He growled another sigh and looked down to her. "When do you expect to cross the border?"

"A couple of days, I think," she replied. "I will send you word when we are going."

"See that you do."

"I've disturbed you long enough, Landmaster."

He turned and strode back to his cave, growling back, "Yes you have."

As he entered his cave, Ralligor strode up behind Falloah and grunted at her. Once he had her attention, he asked with a less than patient voice, "Are you just looking to annoy him further?"

"No, *Unisponsus,*" she assured, staring into the cave. Finally turning her eyes up to his, she urged, "We should go. Your little unicorn awaits."

CHAPTER 21

They would not know it yet, but the longest part of the journey was behind them. They had ridden hard, stopping only a few hours to rest, and already taut nerves would be tested, as would the patience of one of them.

Prince Chail knew they would have to travel light, so he wore no armor, only a well tended white swordsman's shirt and gray riding trousers. His black boots were as polished as could be hastily done, as was the thick leather belt he wore, the same belt with four pouches hanging from it as well as his dagger. Today, he carried no sword, but his double bladed axe hung on the saddle behind him, right in front of the polished brown saddle bags on his horse's flanks. Strain was in his eyes and his jaw was set in a tense clench as he stared forward.

Dressed more for comfort than battle, Princess Le'ell wore a laced up leather jerkin of brown suede that conformed tightly to her body and riding trousers that had been cut off high and near her hips. Of course her riding boots of dark brown leather were well polished and contrasted the bare skin of her legs and reached nearly to her knees. Her belt only had two pouches, but also had her ornate dagger hanging on the right, her scimitar on the left. Her long hair was restrained behind her in a single pony tail that swayed back and forth as she rode. Her features betrayed less tension and more aggravation as she glanced at the Prince often.

Almost half an hour had passed with nothing said between them, only glances from Princess Le'ell.

She finally broke the silence with, "We only had to stop in that last village for an hour or so."

He rolled his eyes and growled a sigh.

"If we had stopped there for directions," she went on, "we wouldn't be lost right now."

"We aren't lost," he grumbled.

"Do you know where we are?" she snapped.

"I know where we're going."

"You said that yesterday."

"And it holds true today."

"I don't think you know where you're going."

His eyes slid to her. "The map showed that we stay on this road through two villages and all the way to Pinetop."

"You haven't looked at the map since yesterday," she pointed out, "and we've already passed through two villages."

"One was a village in another territory. We should be coming up on the second village any time."

"Yes, the second of the three villages that are supposed to be just two."

"I already told you— "

"Are you certain this is even the right road?"

"Yes, I'm certain it's the right road. Would you quit badgering?"

"I'm just saying— "

"You're nagging, Le'ell."

"I don't nag!"

"Next time I'm bringing your sister."

Her eyes flared and she turned that fury on him. "How dare you!"

"Little Dragon suits you," he observed. "You have the mouth of one."

Le'ell bared her teeth and she began, "Look, you oversized..." She stopped when he raised his chin, his eyes locked on something. Looking that way, she saw the forest road open a little as the trees suddenly gave way to a grassy field, one active with simply dressed people who worked to harvest the grains of the field. She straightened up on her horse and gave him a sidelong glance, assuring, "This isn't over."

"Is it ever?" he growled back.

As they rode out of the forest, activity in the field stopped as people noticed them. These simple peasants could tell they were being approached by warriors but they could not tell if these two people were simply passing through or if they were preceding an invading hoard. With uncertainty among them, many of the larger men turned toward the approaching pair, brandishing the implements of the harvest as weapons should they be needed.

Glancing about nervously, Le'ell murmured, "I don't think we are exactly welcome here."

Chail subtly nodded and asked, "Would you like to ask them

for directions?"

"No, Chail, I wouldn't. What do we do if they attack us?"

"Unlace your jerkin," was his reply.

She rode the next few strides in shocked silence, then her eyes slid to him and she stammered, "Uh... What?"

He explained, "While they are awed at the sight of you we can easily make our escape." He raised his brow and looked to her.

Rolling her eyes, she was all too aware that she was blushing and smiled ever so slightly.

As the peasants, a score or more in number, gathered in the road ahead of them, Chail nodded and advised, "Let me do the talking, and be ready to unlace that jerkin."

"I'll take care of another plan should we need one," Le'ell informed.

They stopped their horses and the Prince raised his chin slightly, taking on the manner of his station as he asked with authority in his voice, "Which of you is the leader here?"

A man with a wooden pitchfork stepped forward, holding his weapon ready as he countered, "I would ask who wishes to know."

Chail stared at him for a long moment before answering, "I am Prince Chail of Enulam. And you would be?"

"What is your business here?" the man asked sharply.

The Prince's brow lowered slightly as he replied, "My business is with Pinetop Castle. I have identified myself and would thank you to do the same."

The men from the fields began to surround them and Le'ell glanced about with a growing anxiousness within her.

"Others had business with the castle," the man informed harshly. "They came to take the castle and enslave us all. Perhaps you are among them."

Chail smiled slightly. "Why, exactly, would Enulam have such interest in a little kingdom like Pinetop?"

"Conquest," the man spat back.

"If that were true," the Prince went on, "I think there would be more than just the two of us. Do you mean to stop an invading army with pitchforks and a couple of dozen men?"

"Wait," Le'ell chimed in. "Others came this way? Do you mean invaders?"

His eyes shifted to her and he did not answer.

Chail's eyes narrowed. "Someone has marched on the castle already?" He looked to Le'ell and observed, "That would explain why they are so hostile."

"Just go back the way you came," the man shouted.

"As I said," the Prince informed harshly, "we have business here. Move aside or I shall move you."

Another man, a gruff, bearded fellow with a scythe stepped forward and growled, "You'll be on your way or you'll face twenty of us. Think you're ready for that, Prince of Enulam?"

Chail reached behind him and took his axe from its place there, bringing it across his lap as he conceded, "Well, if that's the way you want it. Le'ell, your bow. It looks like we're…"

"Jekkon!" the leader of them shouted as they all backed away a few steps.

Le'ell saw him first and gasped as he lumbered toward them from a cart in the center of the field. Her eyes widened as he drew closer and she stammered, "Um… Uh, Chail. Chail!"

"Just get your bow," the Prince snarled, positioning his axe in his hands for battle. "I've been civil as long as I intend to be."

The peasants divided and allowed Jekkon to stride right up to Le'ell's horse and he stopped only two paces from her, looking her in the eye with his brow held low and a challenge on his features.

Le'ell did not notice that his lower lip poked toward her like an angry child's would. No, she only saw the largest man she had ever seen in her life. She was on horseback, and he was looking right across to her. Swallowing hard, she raised her brow and tried to speak again, only managing, "Chail, um…"

He finally looked her way, his own eyes widening a little as he saw the huge boy who stared down his Princess. He pursed his lips and nodded, complimenting, "Well played." He looked back down to the peasants and raised his brow. "Okay, so I may not be through being civil."

The leader's eyes narrowed and he informed, "I am. Be on your way."

Chail raised his chin down the road ahead of him. "That is our way. Can you give us the road so that we may proceed?"

The man with the scythe corrected, "Your way is the way you

came."

Tearing her eyes from Jekkon, Le'ell assured, "We are not invaders. We are here on a mission of rescue."

"No one here needs to be rescued," the leader informed coldly.

The huge boy advanced another step on Le'ell.

She glanced at him, nervously and slightly shrugging her shoulders up.

"Look," Chail explained, "we can turn around today, but we'll only return with a garrison tomorrow, and twenty of you with this little fellow beside us will simply be swept aside. So, today, we can avoid any misunderstandings or bloodshed by you simply giving us the road so that we can be on our way peacefully."

"You admit there are more behind you," the leader observed.

Jekkon snarled a little and growled, "Not want you here."

Le'ell glanced at him again, then she scanned the peasants and asked under her breath, "Unlace?"

He looked to her and smiled. "I'll tell you what, friend. I will allow my woman to explain why you should allow us to pass."

"Chail!" she hissed.

"Go ahead," he prodded calmly.

She swallowed hard again, feeling everyone's eyes on her, then she murmured to the Prince, "I am going to get you for this."

"I'll add it to the list," he responded in a low voice.

Her lips tightened and she looked to the huge boy again. Finally turning her eyes down, she started, "We were sent this way to… to rescue…" She vented a hard breath. "We've come to rescue a unicorn."

Soft gasps among the peasants were followed by an ominous hush.

Le'ell turned her gaze to the leader and assured, "I'm not mad, I swear. We were sent this way with many others to find her."

"Horsy?" Jekkon asked, now with a little distress in his voice.

An older fellow with a white beard came forward, dropping his scythe as he stared up at her with wide eyes. "Someone has taken the unicorn?"

She looked to him and nodded.

The older man took the leader's shoulder and whispered something to him.

Nodding, the leader looked back to Le'ell and folded his arms. "And who sent you to rescue this unicorn?"

She glanced at Chail, still nervous about answering. "Um... I—We were sent by the Desert Lord." She cringed as the crowd responded with tense whispers again. Not everyone knew of the Desert Lord, but those who did passed this on to the ignorant around them. "Chail," she warned through clenched teeth.

Others had begun to leave the fields around them and gather around. There were women among them now and in that few moments their numbers doubled. An ox-drawn cart approached, full of bound stalks of grain and more peasants. One walked beside the ox and six more walked around the cart itself.

A wave of dizziness slammed into the Princess and she shook her head. Something had awakened within her, something not of her. Things around her looked different, somehow much sharper and clearer than they should, and she found herself hearing nuances around her she had been deaf to before.

The leader among them leaned on his pitchfork and almost smiled. "So. A dragon, the Desert Lord himself, has sent you to rescue a unicorn, a beast that is his sworn enemy."

Raising his brow, the Prince asked, "Does it sound so odd?" He looked aside. "Yes, it's odd." He turned his gaze back to the man and assured, "Believe me, it's no more odd to you than it is to me. This young woman beside me belongs to him and is under his command. She acts according to his wishes, and I remain at her side to see to it she is not impeded."

Nodding, the leader pursed his lips and considered, then he smiled. "So, just to be sure that I have your story right, the Desert Lord sent you here to rescue an enemy of his kind that you think you will find at the castle, and yet you have a garrison of soldiers a day behind you. I think, perhaps, you are here to see how easily you could conquer this land."

The Prince shrugged. "Very well. There are only two of us, one from Enulam and one clearly from Zondae, and we mean to take on your armies and your hoards of heavily armed peasants, lay waste to your land, burn your homes and plunder all of your riches."

"And the garrison behind you?" the leader asked, still smiling.

"I want all of the glory for myself," Chail countered, also smiling. "Now, be a good chap and surrender peacefully so that we can avoid any bloody confrontations and I don't have to share the spoils with my army."

The men in the crowd laughed.

The Prince dismounted, axe in hand, and strode across the three paces to the leader, making his size and build clear to the man before him. "Look, what she told you about the dragon is all too true. If you don't believe her, then you can wait for him to arrive tomorrow and he can explain it to you himself."

That hush swept the crowd again and the leader raised his chin slightly, trying not to demonstrate how nervous those words had made him. Finally, his eyes narrowed. "I can only assume that is another lie. I do not believe you are a prince from Enulam, I do not believe she is from Zondae, I do not believe you have soldiers behind you and I certainly don't believe that the Desert Lord is your ally."

"He isn't," the Prince assured, "but you would be a fool to believe the rest is not true."

"Zondae and Enulam are sworn enemies," the older man pointed out, "as are unicorns and dragons."

Suddenly feeling very light headed and near fainting, Le'ell raised a hand to her head. She blinked, trying to clear her blurring, weakening vision, then she rubbed her eyes. She felt as if she was not watching with her own eyes nor listening with her own ears. Breathing a little harder and deeper as she grew more and more weary, she scanned them once more, but again not of her own will.

"Things change," Chail informed. "We would be glad to wait for him with you."

"I think you will," the leader agreed.

"But not as your prisoners," the Prince informed harshly.

The man with the scythe stepped forward, brandishing his implement in a threatening manner as he countered, "That's not up to you, barbarian, and— "

"Chail!" Le'ell shouted.

He spun around just in time to see her head roll back.

As she fell from her horse, Jekkon stepped forward and caught her, cradling her in his huge arms as he looked down at her with confused eyes.

The Prince rushed to her, pushing past the horses to reach her. He dropped his axe and raised a hand to her throat, demanding, "What happened?"

With a shrug, the huge boy knelt down with her and replied, "Went to sleep."

Chail took her head in his hand and rolled her face toward him. She was limp and seemed to be barely breathing.

The peasants gathered around and someone asked, "Is she all right?"

A woman struggled through the men and knelt down beside the Prince, taking the Princess' hand. "The girl did not seem sick a moment ago."

Looking desperately around him, Chail's mind scrambled, and finally he looked over his shoulder to the peasant's leader and demanded, "Did someone do something to her? We came here in peace!"

Screams erupted from the peasants and many fled, dropping their weapons as they headed toward the trees and the safety of the forest.

The Prince saw movement above the forest behind him and stood, spinning around at the same time. A few of the men, including the leader and the older fellow, faced that way as their eyes were also directed skyward.

Ralligor swept in right over the treetops and quickly lowered his legs, slamming his feet into the ground and trotting to a stop as he stroked his wings forward. Falloah landed beside and behind him in the same manner.

Chail looked over his shoulder at the unconscious princess, still cradled in the arms of the huge boy who stood as the dragons approached.

Ralligor stopped only ten paces away, then folded his arms as he regarded the Prince with a shaking head and a growl. "It seemed easy enough. Go to Pinetop Castle and wait. Yet I had a feeling you would find a way to muck it up."

Chail shrugged. "Well, we're here."

"Pinetop is two leagues away," the dragon snarled. He

looked down at the leader of the peasants and his eyes narrowed. "Do you believe him now, human?"

Swallowing hard, the leader nodded, his wide eyes locked on the dragon's.

The Prince looked over his shoulder at his unconscious Princess again. "Something has happened to her. I need—"

"She'll be fine," Ralligor assured. "She just needs to sleep for a while." His gaze shifted to Jekkon and he raised a brow, then he strode toward the huge boy, the other humans present fleeing from his path, as did the horses. Bending down for a closer look, the dragon brought his nose only an arm's length from the boy and he sniffed, then his eyes glowed emerald as he examined him more closely.

Jekkon stared back at him and did not react otherwise.

The Desert Lord growled softly and he leaned his head, observing, "You aren't afraid of me, are you?"

Sticking his lower lip out slightly, the boy shook his head.

Ralligor stood erect, staring down at the huge boy before him as he growled again. He murmured, "Interesting," as if to himself.

Jekkon just stared up at him and blinked.

The dragon squinted slightly. "All humans know fear of my kind by instinct, but you don't." His eyes shifted back to the Prince and he informed, "You will take him with you. Head north in the morning."

"North toward where?" Chail asked.

His eyes narrowing, the Desert Lord repeated, "North."

Chail nodded and agreed, "North. I understand."

"I doubt it," Ralligor grumbled. He looked to the leader of the villagers and ordered, "Make certain they are made comfortable tonight. The girl will need to sleep and they will need to eat in the morning, then they will be on their way."

Wide eyed, the leader nodded.

"There will be more behind them," the dragon added. "Be certain you are ready for them as well. Inform them that I will send instructions for them at my convenience and to wait here. Can you remember that?"

Nodding again, the leader assured, "I will."

"See that you do," Ralligor snarled. Looking back to the

Prince, he asked, "Do you think you can do the rest on your own now?"

Chail nodded and confirmed, "I shall do my best."

The dragon turned his eyes up and growled a sigh. "Of course you will." He turned his head and grunted something to Falloah, then opened his wings and swept himself into the air.

The scarlet dragoness watched him take off, then she looked down to the Prince and assured, "Ralligor watched and listened through her, but she is not strong in the inner senses and was exhausted quickly from it. She will be fine in a few hours. She only needs to sleep."

"What are we heading for?" Chail asked straightly.

Falloah looked away and shook her head. "I am hoping for an easy rescue, but I doubt it will happen that way." She turned her eyes back to him and warned, "Stay on your guard, Prince of Enulam. Much may rest on you and your mate." She glanced at Jekkon. "And much may rest on him as well." She looked skyward as the circling black dragon roared down to her, then she opened her wings and bade, "Farewell," as she swept herself skyward.

Everyone watched them fly out of sight, then Chail turned to the huge boy and looked over his Princess again, then up to this gigantic young man who held her and took his shoulder. "If we manage to get out of this, there is someone at Enulam I simply *must* introduce you to."

Jekkon leaned his head, then shrugged and nodded.

***

Ever so slowly, Le'ell opened her eyes, blinking sluggishly to clear her vision. She quietly drew a breath and rocked her head to the left on the stiff pillow she lay on. She was covered to the shoulders with what felt like a wool blanket, one that was soft and warm. As senses grudgingly returned, she found herself in a simple hut, one with few furnishings, two windows and one timber door. Nothing but a simple clay vase full of flowers decorated the place and all that hung on the walls was shelves laden with clay jars, simple tools and folded material that could have been blankets or clothing. All of the colors were drab, white, grey or brown, much like the clothing on the peasants had been wearing. This was a very simple life she was unaccustomed to and would give little thought as she awoke fully, hearing the voices of men somewhere in the hut.

Rolling her eyes across the room, she found her prince with the village leader and one of the older fellows they had encountered earlier sitting around the one small table. In the middle of the table was a large clay flask and each man held a different kind of mug in his grip, one of clay, one of tin and one that appeared to be made of wood. She could not hear what they were saying, but then she did not find herself especially interested, either.

With Chail's back to her, she knew he would not even notice that she was awake, but the older fellow peered around him and raised his chin to her, summoning the Prince's attention to her.

Mugs in hand, the three men stood and slowly approached her, the Prince kneeling down beside her.

Le'ell almost always awoke a little cranky, but the smiled at him and whispered, "I dreamed about her."

He smiled back. "That means she must be well."

The older fellow took a sip from his mug and offered her a nod. "You had us worried, lass. Didn't know what that beast had done to ye."

Her eyes turned to him and she countered, "I didn't know what you would do to us."

"Must say I'm sorry 'bout that," the village leader offered. "Times being what they are we couldn't well say who is friend or foe."

With a little effort, Le'ell sat up and swung her legs to the floor, pulling the blanket from her and laying it gingerly beside her as she looked to the Prince's mug and gently took it from him. Turning her eyes to his, she asked, "What happens now?"

"We find the missing unicorn," was his straight answer.

She nodded. "It'll be that easy, huh?" Absently taking a drink, she grimaced and squinted her eyes shut as she exclaimed, "For Goddess sake! What the hell is that?"

The three men laughed softly and the older fellow answered, "Some of the local made ale. Not for a woman or a weak stomach, but good for a restless mind."

Her eyes watering a little, she looked down into the mug, glanced at Chail, and dared to try another sip.

"We can leave first thing in the morning," the Prince informed. "It's a couple of hours until sundown, so no use leaving now. The village has kindly offered to put us up for the night."

Staring down into the mug, she just nodded.

"Offered," the village leader grumbled. "That dragon had a bit to do with it."

"Either way," Chail started.

A girl entered and hurried to the older fellow, her eyes on Le'ell. Long brown hair was restrained with a white ribbon behind her head.

The older fellow regarded her with a slight smile and bade, "What are you doing in here, Dorell?"

She glanced up at him, then her gaze shifted from Le'ell to Chail and back many times before she answered. "I was told Jekkon is to go with them to find the unicorn. I should also go."

Roughing the girl's hair, the older man asked, "Should you, now? Does your father know of this decision of yours?"

She turned her eyes down and shook her head, finally arguing, "I told the unicorn I would look after him. I promised. I have to go with him."

Chail raised his brow. "Take care of him? He faced down one of the biggest dragons in the world and he needs a caretaker?"

"The boy isn't of great wits," the village leader informed. "We've taken him on by word of the unicorn." He smiled a little. "And I think she has a softness for him."

"I have to go with him," she insisted, her eyes finding the Princess again.

Chail stood to his towering height and faced the girl, folding his arms as he shook his head. "No. This is going to be way too dangerous."

Looking up at him, tears glossed her eyes and she insisted again, "But I have to go with him! I told the unicorn I would stay with him and I have to!"

"I understand," the Prince countered, "but we'll need to travel hard and fast. He'll slow us up enough and I can't even guarantee his safety or ours. I'll not put you at risk, too. Just go home."

Shaking her head, the girl backed away and cried, "I won't!

They saved me from the unicorn hunters and I promised her I would look after him!"

"Dorell!" the village leader scoffed, turning on her as well. "Go on home. Don't you make me fetch your father to get you."

Le'ell finally turned her eyes from the mug.

Tears filled the girl's eyes as she faced off with the three large men in the room who meant to drive her out. With her mouth quivering, she folded her arms and harshly informed, "I'll not break my word to her. You can't make me!"

The village leader seized one of her arms and looked up at the Prince. "Sorry about this. Children here are usually much less trouble. I'll just get her home."

"Let go of her," Le'ell ordered casually.

The stunned man looked to her as she stood, then complied.

Handing the mug off to Chail, she walked right up to the girl and folded her arms, looking the girl up and down, then she nodded slightly and observed, "You have a little Zondaen spirit in you, don't you?" She motioned to the men with her head. "You don't have to listen to them. They only want what's best for you. They only want to keep you safe from all of the horrors beyond the land you know."

"I've seen many of them," the girl informed sheepishly.

Le'ell raised her brow and nodded again, then looked left, then right, then she knelt down and took the girl's shoulder, looking into her eyes. "Go tell your mother I want to have a word with her."

Nodding eagerly, the girl spun and hurried from the hut.

The Princess glanced at the men in turn and asked, "Now what was so hard about that?"

The older fellow informed, "She'll be back here shortly with her mother."

"Exactly," Le'ell confirmed. "I don't want to take the girl anywhere without her mother knowing."

"Um," the Prince started.

Le'ell turned on him in an instant, her narrow eyes finding his a she snarled, "Yes?"

"She isn't going," Chail said straightly.

Raising her brow, the Princess nodded and countered, "So what are you going to do when that horse-sized boy gets cranky or when he simply goes berserk looking for someone familiar to him? What do you plan to do, Chail?"

The men in the room exchanged looks and the village leader observed, "She does bring a good point."

Pursing his lips, Chail nodded and agreed, "That she does. I suppose the girl will be coming with us after all. I'm sure Le'ell can arrange it, and I'm sure she won't mind having the girl on her horse."

"Oh," the Princess snarled, "now you're asking for it.

CHAPTER 22

Darkness would settle soon and Nemlivv sat atop his horse at the castle's main gate, his eyes panning back and forth. Dressed in his black riding gear and light armor, his face showed strain as he peered hard into the dimming light of dusk. Behind him were forty or more soldiers and two other sorcerers, a young man and a young woman who were his surviving apprentices.

The old woman strode up beside him, also scanning the forest outside as she informed, "I told you she would trick you. I told you."

"Not now," he snarled, his brow lowering over his eyes.

"You'd better hope she's stopped to rest somewhere," the old woman went on. "You've had contact with her, so finding her again should be simple enough."

He nodded. "Unicorns are creatures of their word. I'm confident she'll return before sundown."

"Sundown is moments away," the old woman pointed out.

Venting a sigh, Nemlivv's frustration began to surface and he clenched his jaw.

A couple of long, silent moments passed.

The sorcerer half turned his head and ordered, "Go patrol the perimeter of the castle, and keep your eyes open for her."

Slowly, the soldiers filed out and turned in two different directions.

Another few moments passed.

The old woman shook her head. "Perhaps you should go yourself."

Nemlivv grunted back.

Silently, Shahly crept up from behind him and to the other side of his horse, holding her head low as she also scanned the forest outside. She glanced up at the sorcerer, then looked out into the forest again, her horn glowing slightly emerald as she swept the area with her essence.

The old woman's eyes narrowed and she observed, "I sense nothing out there, Nemlivv."

"Nor do I," he admitted grimly.

Shahly squinted and laid her ears back, informing in a low

voice, "All I sense are some deer and your soldiers and horses, and some rabbits."

Slowly, Nemlivv turned his attention down to the unicorn.

The old woman took a few steps forward and peered around the horse, under its head.

Looking up at the sorcerer, Shahly softly asked, "What is it you are afraid is out there?"

"Where did you come from?" Nemlivv asked.

She blinked, and replied, "The forest, remember?"

He closed his eyes and shook his head. "No, where did you come from just now?"

"I was in the stable," she answered in her matter-of-fact tone. "The water was a little cold and we got tired quickly, so we returned a few hours ago and took a nap." She looked behind her, toward the stable. "Ellyus is still asleep and I didn't want to wake her." Looking back up at the sorcerer, she asked, "What is it you're looking for out there?"

The old woman grumbled something and shook her head as she turned and walked back to the palace.

Shahly's eyes narrowed and she spat, "Wait a moment! You were looking for me, weren't you?"

He looked back out the gate and stammered, "Um..."

With a snort, the unicorn turned back toward the stable and flicked her tail at the sorcerer as she paced that way. "Well. I can see you still have a lot to learn about my kind, don't you? I'll be in the stable."

Nemlivv watched her walk casually toward the stable, then he turned his attention forward again, venting a quick breath from him through his nose. He shook his head, feeling something inside of him he was not used to. He had enjoyed almost absolute power over nearly everyone around him most of his life. Now, he had been put in his place by a unicorn he'd meant to keep as a pet.

Pursing his lips, he grudgingly turned his horse and followed the unicorn. As he reached the stable, he stopped his horse and swung down, handing the reins to a nearby handler who had rushed to him. Otherwise ignoring the man, he strode into the stable and found the unicorn standing just outside of her stall and looking inside, and he just stared at her for a long moment before he approached. "Shahly, I— "

"Shh!" she snapped at him. With another look into her stall, she silently turned and paced toward him, butting him in the chest with her nose and pushing him backward.

He almost stumbled at first, but finally turned and left the stable at her urging.

Once outside, the unicorn glanced behind her again and looked back to him, saying in a low voice, "I don't want to wake her yet. I thought you were going to take better care of her!"

"I have ordered that she— "

"Did it happen?"

He glanced away. "I would think so. I did command that— "

"You have much to learn, sorcerer, much to learn. You say you want to befriend a unicorn, and yet you mistreat those around you. Why must everyone around you be afraid? Why must they grovel or fear punishment?"

Nemlivv struggled for an answer, finally shaking his head and saying, "That's just how it's always been."

Shahly's eyes narrowed. "And you have no power to change what has always been?" She nudged him aside and paced toward his well kept gardens. "Look around you. Did this place always look so, or did you use that power you have to change it?"

He followed. "You don't understand. Managing the people under me and growing flowers are two different matters all together."

"Are they?" she prodded. "If you are cruel to a flower and deprive it of water and sun, do you think it will bloom for you out of fear?"

"People are different from flowers. They require a firm hand. And, yes, it helps that they fear me."

"Why?"

"It just does. It..." He struggled for an answer, and soon found that he had none.

Shahly stopped and turned toward him. "You don't believe this now, sorcerer, but in time you will release me on your own. I just hope it is before he gets here. And believe me, there is nothing you can do to make *him* fear you."

Staring back dumbly, Nemlivv found himself humbled a little

more. The last unicorn he had captured had not, could not, but this one seemed to wield a power over him that he knew quickly he must curb, though that influence only seemed to be getting stronger. "Perhaps I will in time. Perhaps I will find a way to defeat your dragon friend whether he fears me or not."

She sighed, lingering patience in her eyes. "Someone once told me that tyrants always fall and fall very hard. Today you are a tyrant, and tomorrow will be looking for that tyrant."

"You're supposed to be my captive," he informed, "my pet."

"I may be your captive, but I'll never be your pet. No unicorn can be."

"I'm sure those of seasons past once thought that way of horses."

"We aren't horses," the unicorn pointed out, "though we look somewhat alike." She looked toward the open gate as soldiers slowly returned from their patrol just outside. "I have to go free soon. In your heart you know I do."

"I know no such thing," he corrected.

She nodded slightly. "I see. Very well, sorcerer." She turned and paced back toward the stable. "I wish you luck tomorrow, when my promise to you is at an end."

His eyes followed her all the way into the stable. Turmoil was within him, and he felt his power over her slipping away. He rubbed his mouth, then he turned his eyes down and strode toward the palace.

"My Lord!" a young woman called from somewhere behind him.

His steps hesitated, but he did not waver from where he was going. Someone ran to catch up to him and finally was at his side, and he turned his eyes to see her.

She was a tall woman, almost as tall as he was. A long, hooded cape of black silk covered her, though the hood was down and her long black hair was unrestrained behind her. She turned green eyes to him, eyes that were bright and young, mesmerizing and almost unnaturally beautiful. Her face was very pleasing to the eye, though she had very strong features and a heavy jaw for a woman. The open cape caught the passing air as she walked to show her generous and powerful build beneath, covered only by a red undershirt that had no sleeves and fit her tightly and descended not quite halfway down her thighs. Shiny black boots reached nearly to her knees and were heavy against the ground, betraying the muscular weight of her body.

Almost anxiously, she asked, "Did it finally return on its own?"

He nodded, turning his eyes forward as he confirmed, "Yes, *she* did."

"Quite well," the tall girl said almost happily. She strode with him silently even after they entered the palace and the clopping of her boots seemed to drown out his own. Finally, she spoke again. "So, Turlok did not return with Nillerra?"

"No," was his curt answer.

"A shame," she observed wistfully.

"You don't really think so," he informed.

"He was your most powerful and gifted apprentice," she pointed out, "more so than Shenton and I."

"Barely more than you," Nemlivv said flatly, "and it is clear you will lose no sleep over his death."

"You know me better than I know myself, my Lord."

"Just tell me what you want to."

She turned her eyes down. "I think my Lord already knows."

"You aren't ready for the power you want," the sorcerer pointed out.

Her lips tightened and she nodded. "What am I to do, then? Please guide me."

He vented a breath and stopped, raising his chin as he considered. Perhaps it was something the unicorn had done or seen. Perhaps it was something else. He had known this young woman at his side for almost ten seasons, taught her the *sortiri* all that time, but now he seemed to see her with new eyes. She was hungry for power, not for the sake of the *sortiri* itself, but for her own gain, and she was willing to do anything to get it. Even as she stopped a couple of paces beyond him and spun around, allowing her cape to open fully and expose the curves of her body beneath, and even as her eyes met his with a subtle yearning and her pouty lips parted almost sensually, he finally saw through her, and finally saw what he had been in seasons past. She would say or do anything to advance to a position of power.

He looked past her, down the corridor for a moment, then continued on his way without answering.

She took his side again, glancing at him but once before starting, "*Magister* – "

He raised a hand and silenced her. He did not need a reason, only her silence, and she complied without question.

This was a much larger castle on the inside than one would think and his destination seemed leagues away down corridors and up flights of stairs, but his thoughts passed the time and he was to the door he wished to enter in short order.

Turning the handle and pushing the door open in one motion; he strode into the lavishly decorated bed chamber, one he had spent many nights in. The bed was huge and canopied and made of glossy black wood that was meticulously carved and ornate. The bed coverings were red satin of some kind and it was perfectly made, but for the edge Nillerra sat on. Dressers and other furnishings and the tapestries on the walls were a blur to him as his attention was consumed by the young woman in front of him, and he stopped three paces away and folded his arms.

The sorceress apprentice was careful to stop a pace behind him and to his side, also folding her arms, but something cruel was in her eyes as she stared almost unblinking at Nillerra.

Slow to stand, the black haired girl barely noticed the tall young woman at the sorcerer's side. Her eyes were locked on his, and filled with fear. Unconsciously, she was wringing her hands together, expecting his worst wrath. His expressions were impossible to read and fed her fear more with each second. Now she was more of an anxious child awaiting the wrath of a scolding parent as was evident by tight lips and a quivering jaw.

Venting a breath through his nose, he turned his eyes down and pursed his lips slightly, then, as he stared at the marble tiles beneath him, he said, "Okay. Now you will tell me how all of that transpired, and how a hundred of my men and my most gifted apprentice happened to be killed today."

Answering almost as a child would, Nillerra drew in as much air as she could and finally replied, "She tricked me, my Lord. She told me – "

"You were tricked by a unicorn," the sorcerer interrupted. "You are telling me that as intelligent and strong willed as you are that she convinced you to go attack a dragon of that size and power with only a hundred men and a sorcerer's apprentice. Nillerra, why would you think that I would have a difficult time believing that?"

"She didn't tell me he was a dragon," the black haired girl defended. "She led me to believe that I would be going after— "

"A wizard," he finished for her. "She just omitted the dragon part. I understand that part. You had no idea that it might be a dragon and not a wizard living in a cave in the desert."

Nillerra turned her eyes down and admitted, "No, my Lord. I am not as wise as you."

"That was never in doubt," Nemlivv's apprentice chimed in.

Once again he raised a hand to silence the arrogant young woman, but this time he half turned his head and showed displeasure in his eyes as they found her. "Deshett, your silence is called for at this time, and you will be so."

She gave him a glance and a humble nod, then turned her eyes back on the black haired girl.

He looked back to her as well and raised his chin. "Nillerra, I've pondered what to do about this. You do understand that I can't let it go unanswered."

Nodding, the black haired girl softly confirmed, "I understand, my Lord."

"So, now is when you would start begging for forgiveness, leniency, mercy..." He raised his brow. "Go on. What would you like to tell me?"

Nillerra turned her eyes down, looking to her hands which she was still wringing together nervously. At this point, the many parts of her fractured personality backed away and nothing vied for control of her. This had been a gift and curse since childhood, the many people within her, but they were strangely silent now. Taking a long moment to answer, she chose her words carefully, tactfully, and finally looked back to him. "I wanted to bring you a gift. I wanted to finally give you something worthy, as you have given me so much here. I misjudged what I should have done and it has instead cost you in men for your army and your most gifted apprentice." Her gaze slowly descended, fixing on her hands again. "I don't deserve your leniency, or your mercy. I beg you, do with me as your wisdom tells you."

Nodding slightly, the sorcerer observed, "Well played."

"My Lord," Deshett hesitantly, softly said.

Slowly and ominously, his attention returned to her.

"Forgive my speaking without your command," she went on, "but you have much more important matters awaiting you. I would attend to this for you if you think I'm worthy and ready to assist you in such things."

Nillerra's eyes widened with fear, but she did not dare to turn them toward the sorcerer or his apprentice.

Regarding the apprentice coldly for a long moment, he set his jaw and assured, "I will consider it, Deshett. Be warned that this girl still has her place here and I'll not want her scarred or otherwise badly harmed, or such a fate may just befall you."

She offered a nod and assured, "I will remember, my Lord, should you find me worthy in this matter."

"See that you do," he snarled, looking back to the black haired girl. "Now, dear Nillerra. You will tell me exactly how you managed to become associated with this unicorn, and tell me everything."

Her lips tightening, Nillerra sheepishly turned her eyes to the sorcerer. Fear was still there, but what no one could see was the grasp she had on yet another opportunity.

CHAPTER 23

Janees sat up and screamed, not realizing she had been asleep, nor realizing she was awake. Her eyes, still wide with terror, stared into the blackness beyond the firelight and she breathed in quick shrieks as her wits slowly returned to her. Clutching the sorcerer's cloak tightly to her, she found herself shivering, but not from the cool night, nor was the sweat that beaded her from the heat of the fire.

Finally, she blinked, the memory of the horrible dream still fresh with her. Breathing slowed and she dared to turn her head and look toward the fire, only three paces away, her eyes finding the sorcerer.

Rawl stared back, his brow raised and slightly arched. He was sitting on a boulder near the fire pit he had created by manipulating the stone from the very ground. A stick was still in his hand, one that he had been absently poking at the fire with.

She finally managed to make her breath catch up to her and turned her eyes forward and down. From within the cloak she was wrapped in, she pulled it closer to her, then finally realized she had not had it when she had gone to sleep. Her eyes glanced over it, then she bowed her head and softly offered, "Thank you."

"You looked cold," he grumbled, looking back to the fire. "I don't need you getting sick on me during this journey." He poked the fire for a moment before he spoke again. "What did you dream?"

Janees pondered her words, her eyes darting about in front of her.

"Our dreams tell us what we have forgotten," he informed, "or what we try to forget."

Closing her eyes, she shook her head and tried not to let the horrible dream bring her to weeping, and tried unsuccessfully.

"What did you remember," he prodded.

She shook her head and cried, "I really didn't want to! They wouldn't teach me if I didn't!" She drew her knees to her and wept, holding tightly onto her legs as if to ball herself up in the smallest form she could.

As the girl cried harder, the sorcerer stared into the fire and shook his head, growling a sigh. He let her cry for a while, then he looked to her and ordered, "Janees, come here."

Her whole body quaking with sobs, she slowly stood and pulled the cape from her, watching the ground as she turned and took the few steps toward the sorcerer.

He extended his hand over the ground beside him and another boulder pushed its way up through the soil and leaf litter, the pine needles and grass and rose to about a comfortable height to sit on. As she stopped beside it, still staring down, he ordered, "Sit down, girl."

Janees complied as one would expect, and worked hard to compose herself. Even before he could say anything else, she shook her head and insisted, "I really didn't want to. I didn't. They— "

"I know," he interrupted. Venting another sigh, he said in a more soothing voice, "Janees, I won't make you relive that time by telling me about it now, nor will I forget what has been done to you."

"It was by my own choice," she admitted, looking into the fire. "They didn't make me, but they would not teach me if I didn't. I did it to myself."

"Did you, now?" he countered. "What was it you wanted?"

Slow to answer, she finally, softly replied, "I wanted to learn the *sortiri.*" Tears streamed forth again as she recalled, "It was so horrible! I was just a little girl and they made me... They did awful things to me!"

"In time," the sorcerer assured, "those things may not seem so awful." When she turned a look of bewilderment to him, he smiled and finished, "Not with the right young man. You weren't ready when that happened to you. Don't let what they did deprive you of the experience when you are ready."

Her lips tightened and she nodded, feeling a little reassured by his words. Finally, she softly offered, "Thank you, *Magister.*"

"For what?" he growled.

"For not taking advantage of me," she replied sheepishly. "For teaching me what you have. For not making me feel cheap and dirty."

He sighed and nodded, and absently poked at the fire.

A silence between them followed as they watched the flames and listened to the fire's crackle, the breeze in the treetops and the activities of the night creatures all around.

"There's more on your mind than that, isn't there?" he asked.

She slowly turned her eyes to his, and almost reluctantly nodded.

"This Jekkon you told me about?" he added.

She nodded again.

"Use the *sortiri,*" he commanded.

Her mouth fell open a little.

"Look into the fire," he instructed, pointing toward it. As she did, he went on, "Fire is one of the elements of the *sortiri*. The *facultas* within you is part of that. Fire can be many things, especially as it relates to the *sortiri.* One thing you will learn is how to see through it." He gestured toward the fire again. "Go on. Take the boy from your mind and put him into the gateway that is the fire. Look for him there."

She had never done anything like this and was not sure where to even start, but she found herself guided by the sorcerer's words and concentrated on seeing Jekkon in the flames. A disturbing thought coaxed her attention back to the sorcerer and she asked in a nervous voice, "This won't burn him, will it?" His impatient stare told her all she needed to know and she looked back to the fire.

As instructed, she took Jekkon's image from her mind and tried to see him in the fire. The flames changed. As her eyes widened, they took shape, becoming what she saw in her mind, and Jekkon took shape right in the middle. In a moment, she did not see the flames, though they were still there. She only saw the huge boy, and a smile touched her lips. She had not seen him for some days and had expected him to be sad and lonely and despaired, but he was smiling. The fire formed more around him and she could see he was surrounded by people. They were sitting outside, near a fire. There appeared to be some kind of feast going on. A large, muscular man was with him, and tall woman beside him. Others were there and they seemed to be celebrating, or just having a good time.

Then she saw the girl.

This slight girl sat close to Jekkon, much the way Janees always had. While she openly spoke and laughed with the others present, she was clearly protective of the huge boy beside her.

Janees' heart sank a little and the smile faded from her.

"At your skill level," the sorcerer explained, "you can only see the present. Seeing into the past or future requires a concentration you aren't even close to yet."

She nodded absently.

"Something's bothering you," he observed.

She continued to just stare into the fire and nodded again.

"A touch of jealousy?" He guessed.

Janees considered for long seconds, just staring at Jekkon among this new group of people, and she finally answered only with a shrug.

"He seems to be taken care of," Rawl observed. "It looks like you can give the *sortiri* your full concentration now."

Her lips tightened and she could feel new tears coming into her eyes.

Raising his chin, the sorcerer asked, "So what's wrong with you? You should be happy that he is being cared for."

"I guess so," she conceded.

"Out with it," he demanded.

She drew a breath, and shook her head again. "I guess I didn't think I would be replaced so easily. He just found someone else to care for him."

"You should be glad he did," Rawl pointed out. "Now you don't have to worry over him. He looks like he's being well tended so now you can attend to your studies."

Looking away, Janees nodded yet again.

He sighed. "Janees, I know you are fond of the boy, but at some point you'll have to let him go. The life you wish to pursue will leave no time for him."

"Do you think he's forgotten me?" she asked softly.

"Not for me to say," the sorcerer replied. "The important thing is that you remember him. He's your brother, did you say?"

She turned her gaze from him and admitted, "Well, what I told you wasn't exactly true."

"I figured it wasn't," he informed. "Little that you told me at first was. So how did you come across him?"

Janees was a little amazed that he was actually interested and looked back to him. "Well, a really old woman approached me with him when I was nine. He was already way taller than me, but he seemed younger. She put my hand in his and told him that I would care for him from then on, then she looked at me and said that a great destiny awaited us both. She made me promise that I would care for him until the time." Janees thought for a moment, then looked to the fire and shook her head. "She knew I had the *sortiri* in me even then and told me I should do everything I could to make the gift grow, that both our lives depended upon it."

"Huh," the sorcerer said absently and under his breath.

Janees watched Jekkon in the fire and continued, "He had that stone around his neck and she told me he must never remove it for any reason and that there would be horrible consequences if he did before the time, then she left me alone with him."

The sorcerer nodded, his eyes still trained on her. "I see. So what did your parents say about this new mouth to feed?"

She turned her eyes away again, mostly to hide the shame there as she replied, "I never knew my father. My mother told me before she died that he was a soldier who would visit her from time to time, and one night when they were together they made me. She died some months before Jekkon was given to me. She had been sick all winter and was finally taken in the spring." She closed her eyes, fighting tears as she remembered. "I went to her and tried to wake her, but she would not wake up. She was cold and pale." Shaking her head, she looked away, into the darkness. "I was alone then and just struggled to survive from day to day. Then the old woman came and left Jekkon with me."

"And you set about doing what you thought you needed to do to learn the craft," the sorcerer finished.

She nodded and absently answered, "Yes, *Magister.*"

"Is that why you are so determined to learn?" he questioned.

Janees nodded again and replied, "She made me promise. I had to take care of Jekkon and learn about the power within me. She kept muttering about my destiny intertwined with his and I don't even remember what all she told me, but she made me promise. I was just a little girl."

"And ill prepared to attend yourself, much less a young giant with a grand appetite."

"And does still," she finished for him. Shaking her head, she asked as if to herself, "Why would she do that? Why would she leave him with a little girl like that?"

"You were carefully selected," Rawl informed straightly. "She did not randomly find some girl to leave the boy with, she had a purpose. I think you will know about that in short order."

Turning her eyes to him, Janees said straightly, "I'm just a girl who wants to learn the *sortiri.* There really isn't anything special about me."

"Well," Rawl started in a sigh, "the old woman thought there was, and so did that dragon who sent you to me."

"Do you?" she asked hopefully.

He put his arm around her and pulled her to him, pushing her head to his shoulder as he ordered, "Get some sleep, girl. We've a long day ahead of us tomorrow."

"Yes, *Magister,*" she complied, closing her weary eyes.

CHAPTER 24

Nillerra did not like for her thoughts to be interrupted, especially with so much to plan, so when that knock came at her door, she shouted, "Just go away!" Most often, whoever was there would, and she expected them to this time. Undressed for bed and wearing only a black satin robe, she sat at her dresser slowly brushing her long black hair and brooding over the day's events. She did not want company of any kind, and was sure that Nemlivv was too distracted by other matters to visit her tonight.

Still, the door opened and she stood and wheeled around, ready to deliver her wrath to whoever dared to defy her order to leave and was entering anyway. Then she saw who it was and her lips parted slightly as her eyes widened in a fearful stare.

Deshett slowly, quietly closed the door behind her, never taking her gaze from Nillerra's. Dressed as she had been earlier that evening, she was an ominous figure, and though very appealing to the eye of any man who happened her way, to Nillerra, she was a frightening and deadly sight.

Turning back to her mirror, Nillerra slowly began to brush her hair again with a shaking hand and demanded, "What do you want?"

The sorceress' walk was a smooth and sultry one as she slowly approached, her eyes glancing about as she informed, "Master Nemlivv thinks that you and I should spend some time together. I'm rather enchanted with the idea, myself."

"I am not," Nillerra snarled.

Smiling slightly, Deshett stopped right behind her and gingerly placed her hands on Nillerra's shoulders. "Oh, but I am. You still have to answer for that little mistake you made earlier today, and I get to be the one to punish you."

A heavy, fearful sigh was the only response Nillerra would give. Slowly, she set the brush back down and lowered her eyes, now more fearful than ever of what the sorcerer's apprentice wanted. "You also should remember that Lord Nemlivv said not to hurt me."

"Injure you," Deshett corrected. "I can hurt you all I like, but

I'm not to leave marks."

Tightly closing her eyes, Nillerra suggested, "Perhaps we can make a deal."

"What can you offer me that I don't already have?" the sorceress asked, almost laughing.

A change took place in Nillerra's thoughts, her very mind and personality. She raised her head and turned around, looking up into the apprentice's eyes as she folded her arms. "I know what you really want."

"Do you, now?"

"Yes, I do. That's really why you're here. That's really why you offered to attend to me so that Lord Nemlivv wouldn't have to bother. Now let's put aside all of the nonsense you've been throwing about and get to business."

The sorceress also folded her arms. "Okay, I'm listening. Tell me what you want."

"Oh, I have many wants," was Nillerra's answer. She smiled slightly, then pushed past the sorcerer's apprentice and strode slowly, absently toward the center of the room. "First and foremost, I want revenge. I want to get at that little fiend who is masquerading as a unicorn down in Lord Nemlivv's stable right now." She turned her narrow eyes to one side. "You know, it's only a matter of time before she does to you what she did to me."

"And what is that?" Deshett asked in an unbelieving tone.

"Haven't you noticed how much time he spends with her?" Nillerra asked straightly. "Have you had any actual time with him since she arrived here?"

The sorceress raised her chin slightly. Something about what this young woman was saying was actually making sense.

Half turning, Nillerra raised her chin and continued, "You have, haven't you? For the last couple of days you've had quite a difficult time just getting his attention for more than a passing moment. And what about your lessons?"

Deshett looked away, her lips tightening slightly.

That's just what Nillerra was looking for, and she leaned her head slightly. "Don't look for his teachings and don't look for him in your bed any time soon. He will become more and more consumed with her, and sooner or later she will become a woman again and you and I will be outside of that wall for good."

Looking back to Nillerra, the apprentice glared at her with scrutinizing eyes for a moment, then, "Do you think me so naïve? I know exactly what you're doing, and I have every intention of carrying out your punishment."

A slight, wicked smile curled Nillerra's mouth. "Oh, now we both know you want more from me than just that. Why settle for the spanking that you want to give me when you can have so much more?"

With the raising of an eyebrow, Deshett admitted, "Okay, you have my attention. What is it you want?"

"Same as you," Nillerra replied sweetly. "I want to hurt her. I want to destroy her. I want to see her in such pain that Lord Nemlivv will either get rid of her or put her out of her and our misery for good."

Nodding slightly, the apprentice admitted, "I do like what you are saying."

"You like hurting people, don't you?" Nillerra asked suddenly, and when Deshett smiled, she smiled back. "Well, now is your chance, isn't it?"

Her eyes narrowing slightly, Deshett observed, "I don't think Master Nemlivv would approve of us taking such liberties with his pet."

"Hence," Nillerra said straightly, "he doesn't need to know. We can have all kinds of fun with her and see to it he suspects not a thing, and you can cause her pain to your sick, demented delight."

"Two where I once had one," the sorceress observed. "I'm still going to want something directly from you." She liked the uneasiness that put in Nillerra's eyes and she closed the distance between them with two steps. As she reached for the sash to Nillerra's robe, she smiled ever so slightly as the black haired girl tensed up and winced. "Now, now," the sorceress comforted, her eyes on the sash that she slowly pulled from its place around Nillerra's waist. "I'll be gentle your first time." With the sash dangling from her hand, she slowly reached toward the black haired girl's throat with both hands, hesitated, and slid her fingers into the robe, brushing it away from her shoulders.

Nillerra did not dare move and kept her arms at her sides,

allowing her robe to slide from her and to the floor. Breathing was difficult. She was not sure what to do or what would happen to her. Despite trying to suppress it, she felt herself growing more and more afraid, and knew the sorceress drew great pleasure from this.

Deshett took a step back and ran her eyes up and down the black haired girl's body, raising her brow as she observed, "Well, now. I can see what Master Nemlivv likes about you now. No wonder you are his favorite whore." Meeting Nillerra's gaze, her eyes seemed to turn to steel as she raised a hand to the black haired girl's throat and pushed her backward.

Grasping the sorceress' arm, Nillerra retreated as much as she could, finally stopped by one of the posts of her bed.

Backing up a step, Deshett looked to her other hand, at the sash she still held. It began to move on its own, rising up like a serpent would. "This is nice," Deshett observed. "Only the best for Master Nemlivv's favorite little toy, huh?" She finally released Nillerra's throat and held the sash toward her. "If I help you, I have you. Do we have a bargain?"

Nillerra's eyes were locked on the sash as it reminded her of a serpent, something she feared, but an opportunity was here, one that she could not afford to let go. Her eyes widened more and more as it snaked its way to her arm and gently wrapped around her wrist, then continued on behind her, around the bedpost.

"I'm waiting for my answer," the sorceress pressed.

Forcing herself to look into the apprentice's eyes, she also forced her eyes to narrow with some authority and demanded, "What do you mean by that? What do you mean you have me?"

"Simple," Deshett replied, smiling slightly as she ever so gently took Nillerra's arms and pushed them to her sides and back a little. "It means I do as I wish to you when I wish to do it. It means you are mine as much as you are Master Nemlivv's"

The black haired girl raised her chin slightly. "Don't you think Lord Nemlivv would disapprove of sharing me with you?"

"Hence, he doesn't need to know," the sorceress drawled seductively.

Nillerra felt the sash begin to slowly wind around her other wrist with soft, gentle movements. It slid across her skin almost sensually, almost as if it did not want to frighten her, but it did.

"Your word you will help me?" Nillerra asked straightly.

Deshett drew in close to her, whispering in her ear, "You have my word, pet."

Staring with fearful eyes across the room, Nillerra drew a breath, and finally barked, "Done!"

The sorceress smiled slightly more and took the black haired girl's jaw in her hand, moving her face toward her own forcefully, yet somehow gently. "Then we'll properly seal our bargain, and you are mine. She leaned her head slightly and touched her lips to Nillerra's gently at first, then with a growing, almost animalistic passion.

Terrified, the black haired girl whimpered, and tried to shrink away, feeling the sash grow tighter around her wrists and drawing them together. She knew quickly that she would have to cooperate, and even as the sash forced her wrists together behind her and wrapped around them both tighter and tighter, she returned the sorceress' kiss as best she dared.

Deshett finally drew back and offered a possessive smile.

"What are you going to do to me?" Nillerra asked in a shaking voice.

Dragging her fingers across the black haired girl's cheek, she replied, "Anything I want, pet, and everything I want. I'm going to teach you that pain and pleasure are one. And when I'm through with you we can attend to the unicorn. I already know just how to hurt her, and hurt her badly."

CHAPTER 25

Shahly's thoughts were not on her freedom, but on that amulet Nemlivv had taken from her.

Hence, in the middle of the forest somewhere, she sat on a fallen log in human form. She was wearing that first dress that Ihzell had made her. It wasn't comfortable, but she really did not mind. She *was* a little disturbed at being stuck in human form again.

Deep in thought, she barely noticed her surroundings, how the wind whispered through the trees yet was still all around her, how the sky was dark, yet it was daytime, how that familiar stream behind her was no longer running, rather the water inside was still. This was a wide open field with ankle deep grass that all seemed dead at the time.

She pondered for a while how to get her amulet back. While unicorns care nothing of possessions, this was one given her by a dear friend, and being without it left her feeling like something was missing. Her brown human eyes seemed blank and blinked periodically and automatically as she stared off into the distance, not really seeing or noticing anything.

And all was quiet, until a shadow fell over her.

Half turning her head, her eyes panned that way and she greeted, "Hello, Ralligor."

The black dragon folded his arms and observed, "Well this is a slight improvement over last time, but I notice you are human again."

She nodded absently. "He took my amulet." Turning her eyes down as the dragon growled, she continued, "He said he only wants to look at it, then he'll give it back to me. He promised."

"And you just gave it over?" he asked harshly.

Her gaze went forward again and she defended, "He didn't want to hurt me taking it, and I didn't want him to."

"So he knows about me by now," the dragon guessed.

She bowed her head a little and nodded, softly offering, "I'm sorry."

He strode around her and sat catlike at her side, staring off into the distance where her attention had been. "Don't fret over it."

"You told me to keep you a secret from him," she reminded.

"He figured it out on his own," Ralligor pointed out, "as he should have. And he would have figured it out sooner or later."

"Now he'll prepare for you."

"Let him."

Shahly turned her eyes up to him. "Please don't let him hurt you."

Slowly, his attention shifted to her. "Was that a joke of some kind?"

She smiled a little. "You know how I worry over you."

He raised a brow.

Her look growing a little more somber, she asked, "You won't be coming for me soon, will you?"

With a long stare, he finally admitted, "Not soon, not in the next couple of days, but I am coming, and there will be many more with me."

Her brow lifted slightly.

"You've made more friends around the land than you knew about," he explained. "I went to call in some old debts to free you, but... They all seem to be determined to free you regardless. You have an importance to them I hadn't realized."

Looking away, Shahly's human features showed bewilderment.

"You have a way of growing on people," he went on. "You're an annoying little pest most of the time—"

"Hey!" she barked, shooting him a sharp look.

A rare smile curled his mouth.

She smiled back a little. "When will you come for me?"

"I'm formulating a plan," he assured. "There are complications, but nothing you should be concerned with. I wish I could come for you sooner, but circumstances being what they are we simply have to wait for everything to come together."

"It's okay," she said in a reassuring tone. "There is something here I want to do before you come for me."

Turning his eyes up, he drew a calming breath and asked through clenched teeth, "What now?"

"I think I can get through to him," she replied.

"Another crusade," he grumbled.

"Yes," she admitted, looking down at her dress as she smoothed it over her belly. "If I can touch his heart then I am sure he will let me go and we can save everyone all the trouble of coming for me."

"Do you *ever* just think of yourself?" he growled.

"No," was her direct answer, still slowly running her hand over the course outer material of the dress she wore.

His brow arched slightly as he stared down at her. "Strange little unicorn."

A little smile brightened her face and she looked back up at him and said, "I am still closer to you than anyone but Falloah. We both know it."

His eyes narrowed and he ordered, "Tell no one."

She giggled and assured, "I won't. I promise."

Looking away from her, he almost reluctantly asked, "How are you fairing in there?"

"It isn't so bad," she replied. "I have plenty to eat and drink, I got to walk the gardens today, got to go swimming, I've even made a friend here."

He huffed a rare laugh, still not looking toward her. "You have a gift for doing that wherever you go."

"It's not so difficult, really. Ralligor, have you ever had an enemy?"

Slowly, his gaze returned to her. "Have *I* ever had an enemy? Are you trying to be funny again?"

"Just wondering."

"I have many enemies, Shahly."

She nodded and turned her eyes down, still absently running her hand over her belly.

He stood and strode in front of her, his brow lowering as he growled, "Having enemies is not in your nature, little unicorn."

"I know," she admitted softly. "It just sort of happened."

"Do you think this enemy will hurt you?"

"She would if she was given the opportunity."

He growled. "Then I may have to expedite things."

"Nemlivv protects me," she informed, "so it's okay. He thinks I am his pet."

"Really," the dragon said in a challenging tone. "According to Agarxus, you're *my* pet."

She smiled just a little, still staring down at her hand as it slowly moved up and down against her dress. "I'd rather be your pet." Drawing a breath, she hesitantly asked, "How is Vinton?"

"He is proving that he can be as big a thorn in my side as you," the dragon answered straightly. When she looked up at him with uncharacteristically hollow eyes, he continued, "Of course he's worried over you, but we're keeping him occupied and in company." He turned his attention away, then looked back to her and finished, "For some reason he thinks you are worth unleashing on the world again."

"And you don't?"

Looking away, he growled a sigh and snarled. "I've gotten used to having you about, I suppose."

"I've gotten used to you, too," she admitted softly. "I don't see how we could ever be enemies, no matter what other unicorns say."

Ralligor nodded. "And that's what makes you strange." He blinked hard and shook his head. "I need to go. Just remember what we've talked about and don't do anything foolish."

"I won't," Shahly complied.

CHAPTER 26

Nothing would happen for a couple of days.

Shahly found herself settling into something of a routine. Visits from Ellyus were what she looked forward to the most, and yet she found herself enjoying the time she spent with Nemlivv more and more. She felt as if she was getting through to him, and she felt his heart opening, very slowly, but opening nonetheless.

Those who would go to a unicorn's rescue quietly made their way north and in short order were finding those passes that would take them north of the Dark Mountains, and into the territory of Mettegrawr himself. Armies would stop short of the mountains and camp as they awaited other armies. Only a few would cross the mountains in three small groups, one of them half a day behind the rest. Two were meant to rendezvous north of the second highest peak, right on the other side of the mountain from Aalekilk Castle. They did not know about the third group, one from a castle they did not know to expect help from.

The Prince of Enulam, with a young girl, a giant boy, and the Princess of rival kingdom Zondae decided to stop in a wooded part of the pass two leagues south of Aalekilk. Their small group was able to travel fast and he felt as if he was making good time.

It seemed that the only flat ground was fifty paces away from the only water source, and while Dorell and Jekkon set up the camp and Prince Chail went to collect firewood, it fell to Le'ell of Zondae to take water bladders to the creek at the base of one of the mountains where they could all hear a waterfall.

The going was treacherous. Dense trees, thorny vines and slick ground made the trek to find water a difficult one and her mood darkened a little more with each slip and stumble. Mumbling away her irritation, her verbal wrath found its target in Prince Chail, as it usually did. Riding boots were not well suited for such a hike down an incline of rock and loose soil, but she had small trees and thorny vines to grab onto and soon found her hand pricked and bleeding by one long and sharp vine.

"As soon as he falls asleep," she plotted with angry intent as she negotiated her way along the narrow trail, "these water bladders are going right up his nose."

Ahead was a tangle of vines that were a strange mix of ivory white and gray within what appeared to be cracked bark of brown. Beyond the thorny bushes and small trees, these vines were a tangled forest right between her and the small waterfall. They were either growing from the dark gray stone or attached to it, she could not tell, nor did she really care. With six water bladders hanging over her shoulders and snagging on everything that could catch them, she struggled her way past the trees and bushes and toward the little vine forest, pausing to free one from a branch that had snared it, and pausing again to free another. Her aggravation grew, but she was finally clear of the densest part, only to slip on the wet stone, grabbing at one of the vines as her feet skipped down the smooth slope toward the water that was still nine paces away. The vine pulled free of where it had been anchored above and she landed hard on her backside, sliding another pace or so on her behind.

She stared blankly at the pool that had been formed over many thousands of seasons by the water that cascaded from a crack in the cliff on the other side of it with an almost deafening roar. More of those vines were coming out of the cliff. What she failed to notice was that none of the vines had branches or leaves, and she did not look up at all. Annoyance had a firm grip on her and she vented a hard breath, a little snarl on her mouth as she went to stand.

As she tried to release the vine she still held, she found she could not, and looked to it with a low brow. Her grip had squeezed some kind of white goo from it, a thick, pasty stuff that grew sticky as it tasted air.

"This is just perfect," she grumbled as she drew her dagger. Sawing the blade back and forth, she realized that it was fibrous and did not cut easily, and as sharp as her dagger was it was making little headway through. As she worked on the stubborn, sticky vine, it released fully from above and two heights of it fell over her free arm, her already snared arm, and over her legs, more of that sticky ooze seeping from the cracks between the brown bark.

Her eyes darting over it, she set her jaw and huffed a hard breath in frustration.

Le'ell tried to pull her once free arm loose. The thick glue or sap held firm and did not give easily, but she finally wrenched her arm free only to have the vine snap back and snare her other arm even more.

This was becoming a mess and she growled and planted her palm at her side, turning halfway to struggle to her feet. Almost there, she slipped again and spun all the way over and fell again, belly down this time. As she pushed herself back up, she realized that the vine had completely wrapped around her legs and tightly bound them together, and the more she struggled to free herself, the more of that ooze leaked from the vines. Looking back to her legs, she knew trying to struggle free would be useless, so she turned herself back over and sat up to try and free her other hand again.

Hooking the vine with her dagger, she pulled back and finally freed her hand of it, finding her dagger now stuck, but her hand no longer. Carefully, and with two fingers, she reached to the vine that was wrapped hopelessly around her legs and tried to pull it from her, finding little success here as it was both wound tightly around her and stuck to her. She drew her knees to her and tried to cut it with the dagger again, then gasped loudly as she slid another pace down the slope toward the water, and instinctively reached for whatever would stop her descent. More vine tore loose and she looked up in time to see it coming, crossing her arms before her and turning her face away.

It draped over her arms and more of that ooze snared her. When she tried to deflect it away, she found her arms and wrists tangled in fine, sticky fibers and hopelessly bound together.

She tried unsuccessfully to pull her arms apart before she laid her head back and stared straight up to allow some of the frustration to subside. She had not felt fear until that moment, until she saw skeletal and some mummified remains ensnared in the tangle of vines way above her. There were also what appeared to be cocoons of some kind and her breath caught as one appeared to be in a human shape. Her eyes darted from one wrapped up bundle of bones to the next, one cocooned mummy to the next. The vines grew in more of a tangle above her, yet...

Le'ell's eyes widened. They weren't vines at all. This was a web! Lifting her head, she looked down at herself, struggling just a little to test the many strands that had her hopelessly bound. Her dagger was still in her hand and she positioned it to try and cut her way through the webbing that bound her arms together. This was difficult as every movement seemed to tangle her a little more and she finally realized that the web that had fallen on her last was still connected up there somewhere in the denser webbing above her.

"Oh, goddess," she whimpered. The web still would not cut easily. Every strand and fiber she cut laid over onto her skin and glue itself to her as it oozed with even more of that pasty, sticky white stuff. Her heart thundering, she looked back up the slope and shouted, "Chail!" No answer. She shouted to him louder, "Chail, I need you down here!"

Finally realizing that she could probably not be heard over the waterfall, she set her heels as firmly as she could and tried to push herself back up, making little progress, but progress nonetheless.

Movement over her caught her eye and she froze. Whatever was up there was huge, big enough to cause movement to many of the strands at once, and when she saw the long, spider-like legs ten heights above her and just inside a white tunnel of silk in the cliff, she suppressed a scream and instead clenched her teeth together.

Far above, in a cave that was fully lined with bright white silk, four long, dark gray legs reached out over a man's height and each took a different strand of the web with the many claws on the ends of them that made up its feet—and one of those strands led right to Le'ell!

She was frozen in terror at this point, too afraid to move or even make a sound. Her chest heaved with deep, shaking breaths as she stared above her with wide, terror filled eyes. Help was only fifty paces away, if only it could reach her in time.

For long moments nothing happened. The horror above her was still, was waiting. It knew she was there. It had already sensed her. Now it was only a matter of time before it came out to get her.

Movement on the ground drew her attention and her eyes shifted that way. What she saw only three or four paces away appeared to be a child, one only eight or nine seasons old. She could not tell if it was a boy or a girl, but it had long black hair, bushy black eyebrows and eyes that seemed too large for its face, eyes that were deep black within the white pools and locked wide on her. It was not dressed and its skin appeared to be almost a blue-gray. She could not look away from this strange looking child, but finally managed to glance at the enormous spider above her.

"Can you help me?" she finally whispered.

The child leaned its head a little. On all fours, it crept toward her, never taking its eyes from her.

Le'ell looked once more to the giant spider above her, then whispered to the child, "Please help me. Go up the hill and get the man I'm with. He's a big fellow you can't miss. Please hurry!"

The child blinked and looked to her hands, to the dagger she held. With quick movements, it scrambled the rest of the way to her and plucked the dagger from her grip, retreating back a pace just as quickly with its gaze on the prize it held.

Shaking her head, Le'ell begged, "No, don't try to cut the web. It will feel what you're doing and end up getting us both!" Movement behind the child drew her attention and her breath caught as an identical child appeared, then another. Three more appeared. All of them had their eyes fixed on her.

Le'ell's gaze shifted from one to the next. Their presence made her feel even more trapped. She could sense that something about them was terribly amiss. The way they looked at her was not even curiosity, it was almost… almost hunger.

The closest of them dropped her dagger and cautiously approached again, its eyes on her. It leaned its head again as it looked her over, and others approached behind it.

When the closest reached for one of the strands that tethered her to the huge spider above, she frantically shook her head and begged, "No, please! It will… Please don't touch that!"

It ignored her and grabbed the web anyway, violently tugging against it, then it reached up and grasped it with another hand, then another!

Le'ell shrieked a breath as it began to climb up the web and she noticed it did not have legs, it had eight arms! The web did not stick to it. As it ascended, she saw that its back was covered with long, course hair that was glossy black. Its eight arms were evenly distributed along its otherwise normal looking body. "Oh, Goddess," she whimpered. Looking around her, she saw others moving in on her from all around, and a few were climbing up and down in the web. The one climbing right above her stopped only three heights up and violently shook the strand again.

When the spider began to slowly emerge from its nest, panic took Le'ell and she struggled with all of her strength as she screamed, "Chail! Chail!"

Ever so slowly, more legs emerged, growing darker toward its body, and each foot seized another strand of the web and relentlessly worked its way down right toward her. Its body was black and bright white could be seen in the joints of its legs and where it met its body. The legs had rows of spikes on them that faded from black to red toward the points. Three similar rows of spikes ran over its head and abdomen and a bulbous face showed two huge, black eyes surrounded by six smaller eyes on the sides. All of the eyes reflected what was around them, and as it drew closer, four, three heights above her, Le'ell could see her inverted reflection in the largest two, a reflection that showed her hopelessly ensnared in this horror's web. Long red fangs, half the length of her forearms, took turns working back and forth as it neared. Drawing closer, Le'ell realized that its body was easily the size of a horse.

The gray, eight armed child leapt from the strand it climbed and to another out of the path of the enormous spider, stopping to look back as it neared.

A height above her, the spider stopped. For a long moment it did not move.

Girl and spider held each other in their gazes.

One of the other children climbed up the web and to the spider, crawling over the spider on its way toward the nest.

Two smaller legs flanked its fangs. No, not legs. They were more arms. All spiders have them in addition to their eight legs, but these were more the form of human arms and ended in human-like hands, though they were armored and jointed like the spider's legs. As it descended a little more toward her, it reached to her with these glossy gray and black striped arms. Its forearms bore a single row of red spikes, ranging from half a finger length to a hand length and back to finger length near its elbow.

Le'ell tried to shrink away and tears emerged from her eyes as the fangs of the spider opened again.

With seemingly gentle movements, the spider stroked the girl's cheek with the back of its black clawed hand, then it took her jaw and turned her head. It seemed to examine her, and turned her head the other way, and she closed her eyes.

"Well now," it said in many raspy voices, some very deep, some higher. "We've a beauty of a girl this time."

Le'ell did not expect it to speak and her eyes snapped back to it.

Its other hand ran along her upper arm, almost sensually. "Very nice. Haven't seen one like this for a long time."

The voices of the spider almost eased her fears, but fed them at the same time. Her mind scrambling, she knew she had to make herself more than food to it. She had to try and reason with it. Her breath caught again as one of its legs reached behind its abdomen and returned pulling a strand of bright white silk.

"Please don't," she finally whimpered.

It ignored her and took the silk in one of its hands, and began to wind it around her wrists and forearms.

"Please stop," she implored as it bound her further. She tried to struggle, but one of its forelegs released the web and slid around her back, lifting her from the ground and toward it. Panic began to erupt from her as she felt it begin to wrap more silk around her legs. As it pushed her forearms against her body and began to wrap them tightly to her, she struggled against it, knowing in her heart that it was useless to resist. This creature was hundreds of times stronger than her, and she had no hope of escaping the silk that already held her tight and helpless. "Please stop," she repeated. "You don't want to eat me."

"Don't I?" it finally answered as it continued to slowly bind her in its silk.

Its reply told her that it could be reasoned with and she made the only play she could. "Don't you think I'm beautiful?" When it hesitated, she continued, "It would be a shame to kill me, wouldn't it? Can't I serve you better alive?"

"Perhaps," it said absently as it resumed its work to bind her. "The children are hungry. I am hungry."

"I'll bring you food," she assured frantically.

"You already have," was its reply. "You fear me, don't you? All of your kind fears us. I like how your fear makes you taste, and so will the children."

A new silk emerged, one that was like soft wool but so much stronger. It began to wrap her legs in this and Le'ell knew she was about to be cocooned like the others. Her own fear of spiders began to burst forth and she screamed, "Stop! Please stop! Please let me go!" She tried desperately to kick her legs free even as she was bound tighter and tighter.

"Yes," it drawled. "Struggle and surrender to your fear of me."

"You can't do this!" she screamed.

"But I can, and I am." It hesitated once again and moved its body to focus on her eyes, pulling her a little closer as its hands took her face and forced her to look at it. "Who did you call to before? How many more are with you?"

Her breath caught again, this time not out of fear for herself, but for those with her.

The spider retreated up the web for two more heights, carrying her with it, then it stopped again and ordered, "Call out again. Bring me who is with you."

Tears streamed from her eyes even more as she stared back at the spider, and she defiantly whimpered, "No."

"I'll spare you," it assured. "I'll not kill and eat you if you bring me something else. I'll keep you for my brood. I'll keep you bound and safe if you bring me those with you."

Le'ell sobbed and turned her eyes away. "I won't."

"Your death will hurt," the spider informed. "I have many venoms to use. One will kill quickly, one will paralyze. Another will make your innards liquid for me to drink."

Le'ell closed her eyes, sickened and horrified at the thought.

"Want to be eaten alive?" it asked.

Her jaw trembling, the Princess shook her head.

"Bring them to me," it ordered. "Summon the one you called Chail and I'll eat him instead. Summon all with you." It's grip on her face tightened and it forced her eyes back to it. "I'll wrap you so tightly you can barely breathe, then I'll paralyze you and make your body liquid a little at a time before the children and I eat you over many days, and you will be alive and awake through it all. Do you prefer that?"

"Please no," she sobbed.

"Bring me the others," it ordered.

"I can't," she cried. "I won't!"

"Princess Le'ell," Dorell summoned from somewhere on the other side of the trees.

Even as the Princess gasped and tried to look that way, the spider clamped a hand over her mouth, then pulled some of the silk up and wrapped it around her mouth and head many times to silence her.

"Well," it whispered. "I suppose I do not need you to summon them at all, do I?"

"Princess Le'ell," Dorell called again, closer.

She could hear the girl making her way through the trees and brush and tried to scream a warning to her from behind the silk gag, but could barely make enough sound to hear herself over the waterfall.

The spider moved to one side slightly, toward two nearby vertical strands of the web, then it bound her ankles to one and quickly formed something of a hammock to the other, wrapping her snugly in it and cocooning her only up to her waist. Her upper body and face were left exposed but her legs, her wrists and upper arms were bound tightly to her, and as the silk dried, it only grew tighter. The spider turned her about half way, making certain that she could be seen from the ground, then it drew close to her again and whispered, "I'll surely keep you for later, anyway. The children and I will eat those with you, then you will carry my next brood." With a gentle stroke of her cheek, it turned and disappeared above her to wait.

Le'ell struggled more to free herself. It was hopeless. Seeing movement at the edge of the trees and brush, she frantically shook her head and screamed behind the silk gag, knowing she had to warn the girl away, knowing there was no way she could.

CHAPTER 27

Of course the going was very difficult and Dorell was, for once, thankful for her small frame and stature. The village had supplied her with a small swordsman's shirt, left over from a visitor from the late Pinetop Castle, that had once been yellow but was now faded to an ivory white. It was way too big for her and she wore it like a dress with a thick belt around her waist and an undergarment beneath it. It was a thin material, but was still unlaced almost fully. The baggy sleeves, tied off as tightly as she could get them around her wrists, were proving to be something of a liability as she negotiated what appeared to be an obscure path through these dense trees and bushes. Her eyes darted around, searching for the Princess of Zondae. It seemed an easy enough task, but she was sure her voice would not carry far over the roar of the waterfall somewhere down that little, slippery hill she negotiated.

Holding onto a small tree, she paused to get her bearings, her eyes dancing about as she tried to pierce the thick foliage in search of her traveling companion, but to no avail. Huffing an impatient sigh, she called, "Princess Le'ell!" once more before shaking her head and moving on. Ahead of her, the vines and bushes and trees seemed to open up and she could actually see beyond them, to a cliff of dark gray stone, water cascading from it to a small pool below. Surely this is where the Princess was. Between her and the pool were numerous strange vines with some kind of brown bark that revealed ivory white and gray fibers within the numerous cracks of the bark itself, and she paused right at the edge of the tree line. The boots she wore were too big for her and not well suited for a hike down slippery rock so, holding onto a small tree for support, she lifted her foot and pulled one off, then the other. The stone was damp beneath her feet, but barefoot she had a better chance of staying upright.

Slowly, she negotiated her way down the slope, toward the tangle of odd, finger thick vines, gingerly grasping the first for support as her eyes were on the sloping ground before her. She was a sure footed girl and intended to stay so. Only four or five paces down the slope, she grabbed a thicker vine and suddenly stopped as she felt something sticky, and she turned her eyes to it. With some effort, she pulled her hand free and looked down at the sticky goo that she had squeezed from it. Her brow low, she realized that sap was not white, no sap she had ever seen, anyway.

Ever so slowly, she scanned the area before her again. Something felt wrong. There was a strange familiarity here. She retreated a step as she took in what was now all around her, and struggled to remember.

Some months ago, while she was bait for unicorns sitting in the middle of a field with nothing else to do, she had watched a little drama unfold beneath a nearby log. A beetle had stumbled into a trap. A spider of some kind had attached its web from the bottom of the log to the ground and… She remembered the beetle becoming ensnared, and when it tired, the spider came for it.

Surely not she assured herself.

A vine in front of her jerked suddenly and her eyes snapped to it. Slowly following it up with her gaze, she sucked a shrieking breath through her mouth, her eyes widening as she found the half cocooned Princess bound in a tangle of web above her. Staring back with horror in her eyes, Le'ell was trying to scream to her from behind the silk that sealed her mouth, and she was motioning with her head the other way.

Paralyzed by fear, the girl could not understand her. Her eyes locked on the bound princess, Dorell slowly began to back away. Movement higher and a glint of red caught her eye and she paused, seeing the horse sized giant spider two paces above the Princess and waiting. Absently, she reached to her side and grasped one of the vines, one of the strands of web for balance. Her grip was tight this time and more of that thick, sticky paste oozed forth and had her stuck to the strand of web before she realized. When she did, her eyes darted to it and she whimpered as she realized that she was caught, and horrible images of the spider coming down to get her flashed through her mind. She had sympathized with the beetle that had been caught. Now, she found herself in its place.

In a panic, she tried to pull her hand free, grasping the strand with her other to yank it free, too late realizing that both hands were now snared. She screamed and tried to back away, slipping on the damp stone and falling to her backside. When she did, the strand broke free from where it had been and fell toward her. As Le'ell had done, she tried to shield herself with her arms, and as before, the web had her forearms snared before she could realize what had happened, but when she did, and when she saw her arms tangled in the sticky thread of web that had fallen on her, a scream exploded from her and she struggled to turn and run back up the hill. Quickly on her feet, she continued to try and pull her arms free as she stumbled toward the trees and brush, but the other end of the strand dragging behind her snared on something and half turned her by the arms. Screaming again, she pulled back hard against it, and finally turned her head and cried, "Prince Chail!" as loudly as her young voice could. "Prince Chail, please! It's going to kill us! Prince Chail!" Breathing in shrieks, she screamed, "Jekkon!"

Something three quarters her sized slammed into her and knocked her down, then another jumped on her. Struggling against them, she kicked at the spider's human-like offspring as they fought to restrain her. They were incredibly strong for their size and four of their eight hands grasped at her. The first of them took her wrists and with quick motions began to wind more silk around them. The second wrapped two of its arms around her legs and quickly bound her knees. A third appeared and went for her as she struggled, grasping her ankles. Still screaming, the girl was overwhelmed and quickly subdued, bound tightly in the silk in only a moment. A fourth appeared and looked right down at her, its odd, big eyes locked on hers as it was only an arm's length away.

Dorell was still and quiet for long seconds as it stared down at her and she whimpered, "Please," and as it opened its mouth much wider than it looked like it should be able to and as horizontal fangs emerged, she screamed anew and struggled with everything she had left as it bent toward her.

From behind it, Prince Chail's axe split it from head to chest and it went down, it's green, purple and red inner body parts spilling out as it collapsed.

The others looked up at him and two quickly scrambled away. The third turned to retreat and screeched as the axe was buried in its back.

A crashing from overhead and violent jerking of the web all around drew their attention and they looked to see the giant spider charging toward them with amazing speed.

Chail set his axe in both hands, his brow low over his eyes as he shouted through bared teeth, "Come on and get it!"

The spider leaped from the web and the Prince darted aside as it crashed onto the ground only a pace from the terrified girl.

Swinging his whole body around, Chail brought the axe down against the spider with killing force, but the blade barely penetrated the spider's armor carapace. Responding with the shrieks of a dozen voices, the spider struck back, its foreleg striking the Prince's side and knocking him to the ground. Turning quickly, it tried to pounce on the fallen human and found the axe striking it again, right between the third and forth leg where it was vulnerable. This time a little of its clear blood, mixed with a milky orange stuff spurted forth and it retreated a few steps down the slope.

Chail scrambled to his feet and set his axe in his hands again, his wide eyes locked on his far larger enemy.

Both charged, the spider shrieking and the Prince yelling. When they came together the Prince's blade struck the spider's back hard and it stumbled, reaching toward him with its arms and thrusting its fangs toward the big human. A foreleg from the spider's left side swung around Chail and he was quick to back off a step and respond with his axe. This time the blade struck true and lopped the leg off.

Screeching with all dozen voices as more of its clear and orange blood spurted forth, the spider retreated again.

One of the gray-blue children landed on the Prince's back, all eight arms and hands clutching at him. When it found its hold, its mouth gaped and its fangs came out, and sank deep into the Prince's shoulder.

Yelling in pain, Chail swung the axe over his shoulder and cleaved the spider child's head all the way to his neck, but he knew the bite had already done its damage.

Seeing this, Dorell screamed, "Jekkon! Jekkon!" as she watched the Prince stagger backward and fling the dead thing from him.

This distraction was all the giant spider needed and it charged forward. Chail responded with his axe, striking carapace again, but it was too late. The spider's arms and forelegs grasped him and the Prince cried out in agony as the fangs plunged into his already bitten shoulder and chest, and lethal venom was pumped into him.

Chail fell quickly.

Two heights above, Le'ell screamed behind the gag of silk, her wide eyes dropping tears as she saw her prince fall.

"No!" Dorell cried, tears flowing from her eyes as well.

"Oh, he's not dead," the spider informed, drawing silk from the back of his abdomen. "Not yet, anyway. The venom will kill him slowly, as slowly as he deserves for killing my children.

Trees and vines were swept aside with one stroke of Jekkon's thick arm and the angry, giant boy charged forth. Before the spider could respond, Jekkon's huge fist slammed onto its back, its body slamming hard onto the stone below. Jekkon yelled and seized two of the spider's legs, hurling it into the bigger trees to one side. As the spider crumpled to the ground again, the giant boy lumbered toward it, grabbed two legs again and flung it hard down the slope and into its own web trap where it ripped most of them down as it rolled all the way down and into the pond.

For the first time since being attacked, Dorell finally felt the balance shift and she struggled with new vigor to free herself, still to no avail.

Hearing her girlish grunts, Jekkon looked that way and strode toward her, pausing at the Prince. He knelt down and placed a hand on Chail's chest, staring down at him for long seconds before he stood and approached Dorell again.

As he knelt down beside her, she looked up at him and said, "We need to find something to cut the web with. Prince Chail should still have his dagger on his belt."

Instead, he grasped the web that bound her knees and strained against it for a second or two before it pulled apart.

"Careful," she urged as he reached for her bound arms. "You don't want to break me." She offered him a little smile and a wink.

He smiled back at her and, as gently as he could, began to

snap the strands one by one.

Le'ell watched as the girl was freed, then her eyes shifted to the spider as it staggered from the pond on its remaining seven legs and paused to pull some of the web from it. When it turned its attention back up the slope, it looked angry and the Princess tried to scream down to them, to warn them, but she could not be heard over the waterfall.

With amazing speed for its size, the spider sprinted up the hill and jumped when it was four paces away, landing squarely on the boy and sinking its fangs into his neck and shoulder.

Jekkon screamed in an unusually high pitch for him and sprang up, staggering backward as the spider pumped lethal doses of venom into him. He fell and landed right on his back, right on top of the spider.

Pushing the giant boy off of him, the spider righted himself and backed away, his full attention on his enemy.

Slow to get to his feet, Jekkon grasped his neck where he had been bitten, his mouth gaped open and he loudly cried as an injured child would. The chain around his neck had been broken and the weight of the stone pulled it from him, and the boy's necklace hit the ground and bounced once before rolling a few paces down the hill. Sinking to his knees, Jekkon held on to his bitten neck and fell forward, holding himself up with his palm planted firmly against the ground.

Le'ell and Dorell could only feel pity for him, and Dorell cried for him a little, too.

As the boy cried, the spider limped back a few more steps and pointed a human-like finger at him, coldly informing, "*That* venom will kill you quickly, and I'll dine on you first."

Tightly closed eyes flashed open and his brow lowered over them. He no longer seemed upset, rather he looked more and more angry. He turned his eyes down to the broken chain and stone that had formerly been around his neck, then his gaze shifted back to the spider. His lips curled back from his teeth and he slowly stood, his whole body shaking.

The spider backed away a little more.

His breath coming deeper and growling back out of him, Jekkon slowly reached over his head, grasping his shirt and tunic and pulling them off. No one had noticed before that he suddenly seemed larger, and how his body was covered with short, course hair that was light brown. His whole body seemed to breath in, but not out, and arms and legs swelled to even greater proportions. The wound from the spider bite was still there, still bled, but it grew smaller against his expanding body.

Dorell's mouth slowly gaped open as her eyes followed the progression of what was happening to the boy, and high above, Le'ell's eyes widened further.

Cracking and stretching sounds came from the boy's body, and in a moment it was over. His forehead was lower, his arms were four times thicker, and he was two and a half men's heights tall! His hair covered form was all mountain ogre, and a thick brow was held low over small eyes, yet his face was still recognizable as Jekkon.

The spider backed away a few more steps, looking up at the ogre before it as it mumbled, "Oh, my." As Jekkon advanced on him, the spider turned and ran toward the water, then leapt over it and scrambled as fast as it could up the cliff side.

Walking with quick and heavy steps, Jekkon tore through the web in his path and roared a mighty yell as he sent his fist toward the retreating spider, barely missing and instead slamming it into the gray stone of the cliff, which shattered into hundreds of dark, cascading flakes where he struck it. Turning his eyes up, he watched with bared teeth as the spider reached the cave and slipped quickly into it.

Le'ell struggled and tried to scream down to him, and he heard her and turned that way. Fear was in her eyes, fear of him, and he saw it right away.

But Dorell saw through this and called to the boy, "Jekkon, get her down from there before it comes back out!"

He looked back to the girl and nodded, then reached to Le'ell and grasped her as gently as he could, pulling her free of the web and pressing her bound body to his chest as he turned back up the slope.

Dorell struggled free of the last of the web holding her and scrambled to Prince Chail. He was lying on his back with his face turned away from her. He barely breathed and the wounds from the spider's fangs bled slowly with a little milky white liquid seeping out with his blood.

Jekkon gently laid the Princess beside her stricken Prince, then he turned his eyes to Dorell, seeking further instruction.

Le'ell struggled to free herself, her gaze locked on her unmoving Chail. "Get me out of this," she ordered from behind her silken gag.

"Lost my chain and stone," Jekkon complained. He was still crouched down beside the Princess and his voice deeper and more fitting the monster he was now.

Taking the Prince's dagger, Dorell reached for the web that still tightly wrapped the Princess, pulling if from her mouth as she assured, "We'll find it, Jekkon, right after we get her free." Her eyes darted around. "Will you keep the spiders away while I free her?"

He looked to her and nodded, then stood to his full two and a half heights and folded his thick arms, scanning the area around them for any danger that might approach.

Le'ell's jaw trembled as she stared at the unmoving Prince and she assured, "You just hang on, Chail. Just hang on." She looked to Dorell and suddenly snapped, "Can you hurry that along?"

CHAPTER 28

Evening was coming, and still no Ellyus.

Locked back in the stable after a visit from Nemlivv, Shahly stared blankly across the stall she was in. Her thoughts really went nowhere, but hovered around running free once again.

All of the shutters about the windows of the stable were open and sunlight poured into those that faced the West, bathing much of the inside of the stable in a warm, golden orange glow. A steady breeze also blew through the stable, bringing with it the sweet aromas of the flower beds outside.

Shahly barely took notice. Ellyus had never been this late before. In fact, she had not seen the girl since that morning and could not avoid feeling that something was amiss. Shaking her head, she asked aloud, "Where could she be, Precious One?"

When the stable door latch clicked and the hinges creaked, Shahly's ears perked and she raised her head and looked that way, her eyes a little wide with anticipation.

She did not see the girl enter. Instead, Nillerra strode in.

Dressed in a long skirt of red silk and a white shirt with a red vest that was trimmed in black lace, the black haired girl's steps were slow and a little long. Her hands were folded behind her and her eyes were locked on the path she walked between the stalls. There was something smug about her. Her hair was unrestrained this day and dropped long down her back.

Watching silently as the black haired girl strode to her, Shahly remained expressionless, but when Nillerra's gaze shifted to her, the unicorn's eyes narrowed slightly and she demanded, "What are you doing here, Nillerra?"

Nillerra shrugged. "Just wanted to say good evening and see how you're faring."

"You know I don't believe that," Shahly informed straightly. "I told you I don't want to see you again."

Nodding slightly, the black haired girl informed, "I know, I just don't care."

Shahly looked across the stable and ordered, "Then go."

"As you wish," Nillerra conceded as she half turned. "I suppose you are waiting for your little friend."

"Yes I am."

With another slight nod, the black haired girl confirmed, "I see. You know, things can happen. Little peasants like her have few people looking out for them. In fact, if something happens to one of them, no one really notices. There are hundreds to take their place."

Something quaked in the pit of Shahly's stomach and she slowly turned her attention back to the black haired girl.

Nillerra's eyes slid to her. "I thought I would see her here personally." She snapped her fingers, then turned fully to the unicorn and folded her hands behind her again.

Two guards entered the stable carrying what appeared to be a rolled up carpet. They each had an end of it and it sagged in the middle, but not under its own weight.

"I thought she could use a few comforts in here as well," Nillerra went on. "You don't seem to get that others around you might not enjoy life in a stable as much as you do."

Shahly backed away as the guards entered her stall, then she looked back to Nillerra and spat, "Since when are you worried over the needs of others?"

"I've had some time to think about it," Nillerra sighed. "I suppose I have been a little insensitive to those around me." Her features hardened and she regarded Shahly almost as a predator would. "In fact, I found someone here who is in need of a unicorn's power to heal. You'll help her, won't you?" She raised her chin to the guards.

They each grabbed the edge of the rug and allowed it to unroll, and Ellyus' broken and bloody body rolled from it to the center of the stall.

Wide eyed, Shahly gasped loudly and backed away, her gaze fixed on the tortured form of her little friend.

Shaking her head, Nillerra said with a sympathetic tone, "You really should have watched over her more carefully. Just look what has happened to her."

"Nillerra," Shahly breathed. "What have you done?"

"Me?" Nillerra gasped, placing a hand on her chest as her brow shot up. "How could you even think that?"

Slowly shaking her head, Shahly repeated, "What have you done?"

"I found her like this and brought her to you. If you don't believe me then perhaps you'd like to peer into my memory and see for yourself." She leaned her head and turned an artificial look of pity on the girl, one laced with deceit. "You can help her, can't you?"

Her breath coming labored, the horrified unicorn looked to the black haired girl with wide eyes.

"You helped Audrell," the black haired girl reminded. "I'm sure you can do something for poor Ellyus. I'd better leave you to your work. Oh, and I'll see to it you aren't disturbed tonight. We wouldn't want you distracted with such an important task ahead of you." She motioned with her head for the guards to leave ahead of her, then turned and followed, looking over her shoulder with a little smile as she sweetly bade, "Good night, Shahly, and pleasant dreams."

Shahly watched her until the stable door closed. One by one, the shutters were also closed and sunlight was banished from the stable. Shaking her head slowly, she whimpered, "No," as she was enveloped in darkness. The scent of Ellyus' blood grew stronger and stronger in the still air of the stable and Shahly looked to her, approaching hesitantly as her horn began to glow emerald. She could feel what remained of the girl's essence and the pain and the anguish and terror of her last conscious moments. Her life force was very weak and almost gone. Her injuries were grave and terrible, very numerous and of all kinds that could have been done to her.

A young and inexperienced unicorn would work through the night to save the girl. Knowledge and strength of essence were not on her side, but sheer determination was. She worked to exhaustion, and after that, worked more, unwilling to give up or succumb to fatigue. She used her own life force to strengthen the girl, doing this seemingly every few moments as she poured every bit of what she had into healing her many injuries.

Ellyus died a few hours before sunup.

***

Morning brought no comfort. Shahly had not slept and she lay in the straw beside her little friend's body. Her head laid over Ellyus as if to protect her from the night itself and even the coming of day. The girl's skin was cold and the color had drained from her. Many of her wounds and injuries were still unattended, not that it mattered now. At least her suffering was over. At least she had passed on to something better than the life she had. At least she finally got her dream of being touched by a unicorn.

There were few things Shahly had to look forward to here at the castle. One was seeing Ellyus come to visit her. Another was the nightly and reassuring visits she would get from Ralligor in her dreams. Having not slept, she did not see Ralligor, and Ellyus would no longer come to give her grain and company. Her heart felt so heavy it was more of a burden to her than something that was the warmth of her spirit. Captivity slowly closed its crushing grip around her again and she found herself lost in grief and despair, drowning in it.

At some point in the morning the stable door opened and light swept in, but she did not react to it at all. She barely noticed.

Carrying a basket and dressed casually in light boots, black riding trousers and a white shirt that was open down his chest, Nemlivv seemed to be full of joy. He had a smile on his face and a little bounce in his steps as he strode toward the stall Shahly was in and greeted, "Good morning, my little unicorn. I trust you slept well?" He paused and looked around him. "Why are all of the shutters closed? I know I told them to keep them open for you." He sighed and shook his head. "I'll attend to it myself, I suppose. Are we awake yet?" He finally reached her stall and stopped at the gate. The basket he held hit the ground at his feet and apples rolled out of it as it turned over.

Shahly just stared across the stall with blank and hollow eyes.

Nemlivv raised his hand and all of the shutters opened at one time, and as light poured in he sucked a breath and took a step back. Slowly shaking his head, his wide eyes were locked on the broken girl before him and the unicorn who still seemed to want to protect her.

When he slowly approached and knelt down, Shahly jerked her head up and glared at him with tear filled eyes as she whinnied, "Stay away from her!"

He flinched, looking a little bewildered at her, then he turned his eyes back to the girl and softly asked, "What happened here?"

"You are horrible people!" Shahly barked. "You are all horrible! She was innocent and never hurt anyone!" She stood and backed away. "Look at her, Sorcerer. Look at her! Do you see what your order has brought? Do you see what keeping me here has brought? You are all horrible!"

He slowly drew in a breath as he stared down at the girl, then his gaze shifted to the unicorn and he demanded through tight lips, "Who did this?"

Shahly looked away from him.

Nemlivv stood and closed the distance between them with two strides. He gently took her jaw as he knelt down before her and turned her face toward him, demanding again, "Shahly, who did this?"

She would not look at him as her eyes dropped tears, but she finally answered, "You already know."

He set his jaw and nodded, then he released her and turned back to the broken girl, and sat down beside her. Shaking his head, he mumbled something, and slowly stroked the girl's hair.

Shahly approached from behind him, looking down on the girl herself. "And now you'll seek avenge. You'll taint her spirit and her memory to get even."

"A fair punishment will be handed down," he assured.

"Why?" the unicorn demanded.

"To see to it this doesn't happen again," was his answer. He half turned and raised a hand to Shahly's cheek, stroking it ever so gently as he offered, "I'm very sorry, Shahly. I should have seen this coming. I should have done something to protect her."

Shahly turned away from him and looked out the window, confirming, "Yes, you should have."

He nodded and looked back to the girl. After a moment to collect his thoughts, he said, "I'll see to it she is buried with honor and given—"

"No," Shahly interrupted. "Give her to the forest. Let her lie as a passed unicorn would, and let her go back to the land. She loved my kind and I loved her. She should be honored so."

"I'll personally see to it," he assured. "I'll take her myself. Do you want to come?"

Shahly lowered her head and closed her eyes, shaking her head as she softly replied, "No."

"Very well," he said just as softly.

Two guards entered the stable, apparently summoned by his thoughts and he looked up at them and ordered, "Take this little girl's body to my carriage, and be gentle with her. Have a detachment ready to ride within the hour." He glanced down. "And have fresh cut flowers ready, as many as the carriage will hold."

They bowed to him and one gently picked up her body, cradling her in his arms as he turned to leave.

Nemlivv turned his eyes to the blood stained rug that lay crumpled in the corner of the stable and he snarled, "And have that removed and burned, and let everyone in the castle know in no uncertain terms that if I come here and see these shutters sealed again I will unleash a fiery hell on whoever is responsible."

The other guard nodded and collected the rug, hurrying out of the stable with it.

Nemlivv, stood and approached Shahly. For a moment, he just stroked her mane, then he slipped his arms around her neck and embraced her as tightly as he dared, offering in a whisper, "I am sorry. I am truly sorry for this."

She nodded, then, "Do you remember yesterday when you said something funny and she laughed until she almost cried and started coughing?"

"I remember."

"She wasn't just one of your pets then, was she? She was truly starting to see who you really are. And I think she was starting to like you more than she feared you. Now, because of me, she's dead."

Nemlivv stepped back and took her jaw again, turning her head toward him, and this time her eyes found his. "Shahly, this didn't happen because of you. This was not your fault! Not even remotely was this your fault!"

"Then why?" she asked pitifully.

He could not answer. Slowly, he turned away from her, and fled the stable.

CHAPTER 29

Prince Chail had always been an early riser, but today he did not awaken with the sun. In a strange forest in a half pitched camp, all four were claimed by an unnatural sleep. Le'ell lay beside her prince, intent on watching over him the whole night and unaware that all of them had fallen asleep about the same time. Dorell had been doing her best to attend the camp, not wanting to disturb the Princess as she had been very short of temper since their encounter with the spider. No fire had been build. She had found Jekkon's chain and repaired it as best she could, and once he wore it again he slowly transformed back into the giant boy he had been, and he slept soundly on his back with little Dorell curled up beside him, beneath his thick arm.

Le'ell had known even as Chail's injuries were treated and he was laid beneath the blankets that he would probably not live through the night. The spider's bite was too fierce to allow anyone to live through it, even the big Enulam Prince. Sure, Jekkon had survived easily, but his kind, his true kind, was known to be immune to almost everything. Even the surprise of what he was could not distract her from what had happened. Everything had been moved to the back of her mind but the Prince who lay dying at her side.

The unnatural sleep that had claimed them all shortly after sundown found them sleeping soundly as the sun illuminated the countryside all around and their dreams had been pushed far beyond the events that had unfolded the day before.

As the light alerted her to the coming of day, Le'ell squinted against it and laid her arm over the Prince, snuggling into the warmth of his body as she reluctantly became aware of what was around her.

Ever so slowly and gently, he stroked her hair and she stirred at his touch, her eyes blinking open. Raising her head, she looked to him and met his eyes, still squinting against the morning sunlight. He was smiling at her, a strained and weary smile.

"Chail," she breathed, throwing herself over him and embracing him as tightly as she could.

His arm wrapped around her and he strongly returned her embrace.

Le'ell knew she was dreaming, she had to be, but she did not want to awaken and find him dead. She would hold on to this moment as long as she could. Still, she wept for him.

"Don't cry, Princess," he whispered to her.

"I'm not crying," she sobbed, hugging him tighter.

"No, really," he said softly. "Don't cry. I'm going to be fine."

She nodded and wept on. When she heard the deep growl her entire body went rigid and her head snapped up. The first thing she saw was the huge, black clawed hand only paces away on the other side of the prince and she sprang up with a loud scream, backing away as her wide eyes found the black dragon staring down at her.

Alerted by the scream, Dorell also jumped up and backed away. Jekkon slowly sat up and turned toward him, groggily rubbing the sleep from his eyes as he looked up at the dragon.

Ralligor stared back and raised his brow, observing, "You flatter me."

Le'ell took a moment to catch her breath, and swallowed hard as she stared up at the black dragon.

Chail sat up and worked his shoulder a few times, then pulled the blanket from him and glanced around for his shirt. The holes left by the spider bites were gone, as if he had never been bitten.

"As I figured," the black dragon boomed, "you two can't stay out of trouble any better than that unicorn we're looking for."

"Doing our best," the Prince assured as he pulled his shirt on. He looked up to the dragon and stood, folding his arms. "You have my thanks, Desert Lord. I find myself indebted to you once again."

Ralligor nodded and looked to Jekkon. "Well, now. It seems your secret's out. See to it you don't lose that stone again until it's time."

"Spider broke the chain," the ogre boy said. "Also bit me."

"You'll live," the black dragon informed dryly, "unless Agarxus sees you in your true form. He has no love of ogres, believe me. Just keep that stone around your neck."

Jekkon nodded.

Looking back to Chail as Le'ell took his side and slipped her arm around him, Ralligor asked, "Do you idiots know where Ravenhold Castle is?"

"I believe so," the Prince assured. "Enulam has tangled with them a few— "

The dragon interrupted, "Do you think you can get there without any more intervention on my part, or should I hold your little hand the rest of the way?"

Chail raised his brow and observed, "You sound annoyed. We'll make it, assuming we have no more run-ins with oversized spiders."

"The web is usually the first indication that there is one in the area." His eyes shifted to Le'ell. "And being a little aware of your surroundings might help as well."

The Princess looked away and nodded.

Chail rubbed his chest and shoulder where he had been bitten and offered, "Thank you again."

Ralligor turned and strode away, opening his wings as he corrected, "You have someone else to thank for that."

As the dragon lifted himself into the air, the Prince's eyes narrowed slightly, then he heard the footfalls behind him and wheeled around.

Vinton was smiling at him. "While I hate to admit this, he's right. You do need to be more careful." His eyes shifted to Le'ell. "Especially with her at your side."

Chail smiled back at him and rubbed his shoulder. "You have my thanks yet again, my friend."

"Same shoulder, too," the unicorn pointed out.

Dorell gasped loudly and slapped her hands over her mouth as she turned and saw the big bay unicorn.

Jekkon, who had been watching the dragon fly away, looked down at her, then to the unicorn and pointed at him, declaring, "Nother horsey!"

Hesitantly, the girl padded to him, her eyes fixed on him. As she neared, she ever so slowly reached out her hands to touch him, then stopped only a pace away and drew her hands into her chest. Her wide eyes were fixed on him and began to tear up. When the big unicorn looked right at her, she drew in a deep, shaking breath and a tear finally escaped and rolled down her cheek.

Vinton looked to the Prince and guessed, "With you?"

Chail nodded, a little smile on his face as he confirmed, "The Desert Lord insisted we bring the boy, and he is really attached to this one."

"Just standing around again," a woman observed from the edge of the forest behind the unicorn.

Everyone turned to see Pa'lesh riding from the trees where the unicorn had emerged. She was dressed for battle in light armor, her sword at her side and her bow hanging from her saddlebag behind her. Riding beside her was the crowned Princess of Caipiervell, dressed in red riding trousers, high, shiny black boots to her knees and a white shirt with puffy sleeves. She wore no jewelry, but she did have a big smile as her eyes found the unicorn.

Behind them were three more soldiers, also in light armor. Two of them were from Enulam, and the third from Zondae.

Pa'lesh stopped her horse and swung down, her hand casually resting on her sword as she strode to the unicorn and patted his neck on the way by him, and she smiled slightly as he whickered in response.

Princess Faelon tried to quickly dismount in the same way and stumbled to her backside when she did, but was quick to scramble to her feet and sprint to the unicorn, throwing her arms around his neck as she buried the side of her face in his mane.

He looked back and greeted, "You've been wanting to do that since we broke camp, haven't you?"

With her face still buried in his mane, the Princess nodded.

Folding her arms as she stopped before the Prince, Pa'lesh nodded to him and informed, "We heard about what happened. I just wish I had gotten here a day sooner." She glanced at Le'ell. "I can see another round of survival training is in order for someone."

Le'ell set her jaw and pulled away from the Prince, and walked the other direction.

"I can't really fault her," Chail said straightly. "Giant spiders are not exactly the kind of thing one looks for in the forest."

"Awareness of her surroundings is," the field captain corrected. "We should be off quickly. I have a garrison camped about a league behind us." Her eyes caught the huge boy standing behind Dorell, and she raised a chin to him. "Some relation of that Gartner fellow?"

Chail shrugged.

Dorell took those last hesitant steps toward the unicorn and slowly dared to raise her hand to touch him. His mane was as soft as she had imagined and a smile touched her lips. At the same time, she felt a little jealousy of this other girl who was clinging to him and obviously knew him.

Faelon looked over her shoulder, then turned fully and set her hands on her hips, looking the peasant girl up and down. She pursed her lips and shook her head.

Dorell could see that this other girl came from royalty and quickly turned her eyes away and back to the unicorn. She knew her station was low but still did not like others looking down on her.

"May I be so bold?" Faelon asked, then she took one of Dorell's sleeves and spat, "What the hell is this?"

Her lips tightening, Dorell turned her eyes down.

The Princess shook her head and informed, "Won't do. Just won't do." She took the girl's hand and pulled her toward her horse, informing, "Come on. You're about my size and I have a few outfits you would like."

Dorell shot a bewildered look back to the Prince, and he just smiled and shrugged.

Pa'lesh motioned to the departing girls with her head and informed, "Little Miss *Travels Light* brought four packed saddlebags of clothing with her. Your little girl's in good hands. Chail, we need to talk." She strode past him. "Let's break down this pitiful excuse for a camp while we do."

He rolled his eyes and turned to follow.

Vinton looked up to the huge boy, who smiled and said, "I'm Jekkon."

The bay unicorn nodded to him.

***

In short order the camp was broken down and the riders rode in pairs toward the rescue of a little white unicorn. Near the head of the procession, two Zondaen women were in yet another heated argument, and most of the rest of them were silent and trying not to listen.

Le'ell angrily swung her arm around and pointed behind them, shouting, "It's right back there only half a league behind us! Why don't you ride back to it and see how well *you* would fair against it!"

Through clenched teeth, Pa'lesh ordered, "I'm telling you for the last time to watch your tone with me! Next time I'm knocking you off of that horse!"

"Try it then! And quit questioning my abilities!"

"Your so-called abilities have nearly gotten you killed yet again. Perhaps you would like to bury that pride in yourself that you haven't quite earned and listen to someone else for once before you end up on a funeral pyre!"

"Maybe you should listen yourself and you would know what is really going on around you!"

Riding right behind them, Chail looked to the unicorn beside him and smiled, saying, "It's so nice for her to yell at someone else for a change."

Both Zondaens swung around and shouted in one voice, "Quiet!"

Unicorn and Prince flinched as they did, then looked silently to each other.

As the argument before them continued, Chail looked to the unicorn to continue their own conversation. "So, you're saying that she was once a woman?"

"For a few days," Vinton explained. "The amulet you may have seen her wearing the last time you saw her gave her the ability to do so. She endured that to rescue me from Red Stone Castle this spring." His eyes turned toward the road before him. "I only wish it was that easy for me to do."

"Was her experience as a woman so horrible? You sound as if it was something she painfully endured."

"She never said it was unpleasant, but that time haunts her still. I think some of that experience lingers within her and dulls her judgment." Vinton shook his head. "She was always adventurous, perhaps even a little mischievous, but now she's just reckless. She's become a maniac, and it's all that damn dragon's fault!"

Chail considered, then raised his head as he stared ahead into the distance. "You said before that you wished he could make you human to go rescue her. Do you think he would be willing to do that?"

"That is not *fair*!" Le'ell shouted. "You should realize that I'm still a Princess of that kingdom and you should conduct yourself toward me accordingly!"

Prince and unicorn exchanged looks yet again, and shook their heads.

Pa'lesh growled back, "My conduct toward you is appropriate when dealing with such a flighty, spoiled brat as yourself. Perhaps you should think about your own conduct for once."

Chail rolled his eyes. "It never ends. So, do you think he would?"

"I think so," the unicorn confirmed, "if for no other reason then just to torment me." He looked up to the Prince. "You seem to have a plan to that end."

Giving him a sidelong glance, Chail confirmed, "I do. I'm thinking perhaps it's time that Nemlivv of Ravenhold got a visit from a few emissaries who would like to establish a lasting peace with him."

"And then you steal the little unicorn who he wishes to keep as his pet," Vinton finished. "You aren't afraid that this could cause war between you again?"

"Not worried," the Prince confirmed. "We defeated them handily before and I don't think he will want war with us again over a unicorn. Besides, I think we can get her out of there without raising suspicions about ourselves, especially if we can pin the crime on the emissary of the castle of Rhine Keep."

"Never heard of them," the unicorn informed. Then he glanced about and added, "I also don't see their emissary here."

Slowly turning his eyes down to the unicorn, Prince Chail corrected, "He's here. I'm looking at him right now."

Vinton raised his head as he looked back. "You're just making this up as you go, aren't you?"

"As always," the Prince confirmed.

Le'ell shot Pa'lesh an angry glare and informed, "In my mother's favor or not, you'd best remember your place, Captain."

"My place is keeping you in line," Pa'lesh countered, "on your mother's orders. Perhaps you should remember *your* place and realize that you are not in line for the throne the way you think you should be."

Tight lipped, the Princess looked forward again.

"And you'd better start thinking about the duties you owe Zondae," the Field Captain continued.

Her eyes sliding to Pa'lesh, Le'ell warned, "Bitch, you are out of line, and I'm one word away from putting my fist to your jaw and you back in your place where you belong."

The Field Captain's brow tensed and she challenged, "Consider the word spoken, you spoiled little brat!"

Snorting, Vinton's eyes narrowed and he growled, "I've heard enough of this nonsense." He quickened his pace and strode between the arguing women, their horses separating as he came up abreast of them. Looking to Pa'lesh first, his expression was one rarely seen in unicorns, and she knew right away he was annoyed and angry. Pa'lesh was not one to be easily humbled, but this unicorn had done so with only a look. When she looked away from him, he turned his attention to the Princess.

Also humbled and feeling more like a child of six than the nineteen season old warrior she was, a little pout took her mouth and she looked forward again, accusing, "She started it."

Vinton whickered and subtly motioned behind him with his head, and she slowed her horse to come abreast of Prince Chail.

Behind the commotion and completely ignoring it, two girls of about the same age engaged in conversation that was befitting of them. Now dressed in a white riding shirt, light blue trousers and a pair of the Princess' walking boots, Dorell forgot completely that she was a peasant. Faelon was easy to talk to and did not seem to be a Princess at all.

"It was horrible," the Princess complained. "I know I have to conduct myself like a proper lady when dignitaries visit the castle, but it was so boring. I mean awful!"

"Especially with boys about who can't even look at you," Dorell agreed.

"And those were my thoughts." She glanced around and spoke more softly. "I slipped away and went to the servant's quarters. I have friends there who know how to have a good time."

Dorell's brow shot up and she barked, "What? You would

rather spend time with commoners than royalty?"

Nodding, Faelon confirmed, "Oh, so easily. They know how to have fun. We went outside, at the back of the castle, and brought with us some of the castle workers who know how to play music. I had some food and wine brought out and we had a little party of our own."

"Didn't they miss you at the banquet?"

Smiling, the Princess leaned toward her companion and said in a low voice, "I had someone say that I felt ill and had to retire for the evening."

Both girls giggled.

"What about *your* conquests?" Faelon asked.

Dorell rolled her eyes. "Not much conquest to be had in my village."

"That's sad," the Princess said sympathetically. "Oh, I know. I'll annex your village and have some boys taken there!"

Giggling again, Dorell said flatly, "They'd better be cute."

Looking ahead, Faelon raised her chin and announced, "I only allow cute boys at my castle. Others must live elsewhere."

Dorell laughed again, then a moment of silence passed between them. Finally she said, "It must be so nice to be a Princess."

Faelon shrugged. "To be honest, I'd rather be doing something else most of the time. Being a Princess and running a whole kingdom is a lot more work than one would think. I often don't have time to do much else. If not for my friends there, the other girls about my age, I mean, I simply couldn't stand it." Her eyes slid to the other girl and a little smile curled her mouth. "You should come to Caipiervell."

Dorell considered, then her mouth tightened and she shook her head. "I have responsibilities to my village and I'm sure my parents wouldn't allow it."

"Maybe just to visit for a while," Faelon suggested. "Oh, please? I would so love to have you there."

Finally turning her eyes to the Princess, Dorell regarded her with blank features, then shrugged slightly.

"You'd feel out of place, wouldn't you?" Faelon guessed.

Dorell nodded.

Looking forward again, the Princess informed, "I used to

when I would go to the laundry rooms behind the kitchen, but they sure took me in and made me feel at home."

Her eyes snapping to the other girl, Dorell raised her brow and asked in an astonished tone, "You help with the laundry?"

"I have friends there," Faelon sighed. "Darree showed me how to do pretty much anything, and while we're hanging stuff to dry or folding is a great time to catch up on all the gossip."

Dorell smiled. "That sounds lovely."

Faelon's eyes slid to her again and she informed, "Lots of cute boys in that part of the castle."

Dorell's eyes panned toward the Princess. "Cute boys? Perhaps I can spare a few days for a visit."

They giggled again, unaware that the soldiers behind them were groaning, and shaking their heads.

Having put three more leagues behind them, Chail had managed to formulate a plan, and after telling his Princess about it, he waited eagerly for a response.

She was quiet for a while, then finally looked to him. "Let me get this straight. We should just march through their gates as visiting dignitaries from three different kingdoms." She blinked. "Chail, we've all been in battle with them recently."

"At some point we'll have to bury our hostilities," he pointed out.

She raised her brow. "Do you think they'll feel the same?"

"Considering how badly we beat them that last time I don't see them refusing talks of peace." He turned his eyes to the unicorn in thought. "It's all coming to bear on me."

"What is?"

"When you were being held by Poskleer this summer… I felt exactly what he does now. I sure hope he's holding together inside better than I did." When he looked back at her, he found he had her full attention, and her lips were parted ever so slightly.

"You've never spoken of that before," she said softly.

He nodded and looked forward again.

She smiled and observed, "You're always trying to show that armored exterior of yours, but it's good to see something soft in that big heart inside of you from time to time."

The corners of his mouth curled up slightly and his eyes slid to her.

Galloping hooves drew the attention of all and everyone turned to see what was charging them. All of the soldiers had weapons in their hands, and two of the Zondaens had bows ready to shoot.

"It's all right," Vinton assured as he turned and paced toward the charging hoof beats.

Another unicorn burst from the forest, a much smaller unicorn than the bay, a very young cream white mare with snow white mane and tail. Silver ribbons glittered from the spirals of her horn and her green eyes were locked on the bay unicorn as she galloped right toward him.

As the younger unicorn, just slightly larger than a pony, brought herself to an abrupt and awkward stop, Vinton drew his head back, watching her gasp for breath for a moment before he greeted, "Relshee?"

The smaller unicorn started drawing deeper and deeper breaths, and finally gasped, "Vinton." Her eyes darted around from human to human, but she did not seem unnerved by their presence. Her breath finally caught up and she closed her eyes as she drew one more deep breath. "I've been running since yesterday," she strained to say, looking to the stallion. "I didn't realize you had already gotten so far."

"Well, you found me," he observed. "Why were you looking for me?"

"Shahly," she replied.

Vinton's ears perked and he drew his head back. "What of her?"

"When the elder's banished her, they divided the herd. Many of us left the herd to find her, and then we heard of her abduction by humans. There are others coming. Do you know where she is?"

Looking away, the stallion replied, "We know where she is." His eyes shifted back to her and narrowed as he asked, "What others?"

The younger unicorn smiled. "As I said, not all of the herd agreed with her being banished in her greatest time of need."

The old silver unicorn with the white mane and beard emerged from the forest, his gaze locked on the big bay. With him came a sizeable tan unicorn with a black mane and a white beard. Vinton knew well these two, but was unsure what to feel seeing them here. They took the sides of the little cream white unicorn, both looking to the big bay with a new purpose to them.

Vinton looked to them in turn, then his gaze settled on the tan unicorn and he raised his head slightly. "Dosslar. A change of heart?"

"My heart never changed," the old unicorn informed, "but my judgment has. I can see with clear eyes now, and see well enough to know that the elders were wrong. We should have listened to you, Vinton, and I will always regret not coming to my daughter's defense when I should have."

"You had the whole herd to think about," the bay reminded.

Dosslar countered, "What kind of herd banishes a young unicorn like that? We should have just kept better watch on her." He turned his eyes down and added, "Or listened to her."

Vinton touched the tan unicorn's horn with his own and smiled at him. "Wisdom comes in time, my friend."

"If a little late," the tan sighed. "I shall always celebrate that day you chose her, Vinton. Of all the stallions in the forest, she could not have chosen better."

The old stallions did not notice that Dorell had dismounted and quietly approached, but the young mare had.

To a girl her age, unicorns were magical and of dreams. Though she had been in Vinton's company for many hours, he was a big and imposing presence and not like the carefree, innocent creature of her imagination, but Relshee was.

Dorell had stopped a few paces away and Relshee approached the girl with curious eyes, leaning her head a little as she examined her to measure against her learning. Ever so slowly, Dorell reached to the unicorn to gently stroke her mane, and as the girl began to softly weep, Relshee drew her head back slightly and observed, "Humans don't seem dangerous at all. Why would we be afraid of them?"

The silver paced to her and motioned toward Chail and the other warriors, answering, "We are supposed to fear humans like those, but I've seen that many are as harmless as this one."

Faelon approached behind Dorell, her eyes shifting from one

unicorn to the next, and as Vinton turned to her a big smile found her lips and she hurried to him.

The big stallion informed, "These are others from my herd."

She took Vinton's side and nodded to Dosslar, greeting, "It is an honor to meet you."

He nodded back. "You must be Faelon. Vinton has spoken of you before. You have my thanks as well for your invitation to graze the fields about your castle."

"I wish you would come," she said with pleading words. "You are all welcome there."

The old unicorn glanced at Vinton as the silver took his side. "You know, we really should."

"Been there," the silver informed straightly.

"Before we make any long term plans," Vinton interrupted, "we should think about getting Shahly back."

Relshee turned and looked to the old stallions, asking with a little concern, "What if the herd will not let her back?"

The old silver raised his head, his eyes narrow as he replied, "Then we'll start our own herd."

CHAPTER 30

Nemlivv had attended many funerals in his thirty seasons. It was just the way of things. He had never wept, he had just been respectful and then departed. The dead were gone and their problems were over. Today, that had changed. He had personally carried Ellyus' body from his carriage and left her in a clearing deep in the forest a couple of leagues from the castle. There were flowers about and rays of sunlight lancing through the trees. The location was perfect, as if the Creators had put it there right out of the unicorn's mind. All of the flowers that had been taken with her were left around her body. He had laid her among them as gently as he could, as if he wanted her final rest to be the most comfortable she had ever had.

Leaving the girl's final resting site, he had sought the solitude of his carriage, closed the curtains, and wept for her. The unicorn's words were fresh in his mind, and he knew that his heart was broken a little for a peasant girl who should not have mattered to him.

Arriving back at the castle, he still mourned a little, but now anger began to replace sorrow. Even before the carriage stopped, he threw the door open and leapt out, trotting to a walk as he stormed toward the palace and up the stairs.

Finally arriving at Nillerra's door, he kicked it open and strode to her as she rose from her vanity and turned to greet him. His hand was a blur as he struck her hard with the back of it across her cheek. He just watched as she was spun around and crumpled to the floor. He had always been in full control of his thoughts, his emotions, of everything around him. Now, as he watched Nillerra slowly turn toward him with her hand over her cheek and her lip bleeding, he knew that control was escaping him, and he didn't care.

Nillerra was too shocked to speak and just stared helplessly up at him.

His lips curled back and he shouted, "What did you think you were doing?"

The black haired girl drew her shoulders up, her eyes glossing with tears as she whimpered, "I don't understand, my

Lord."

His rage took control again and he reached to her, brutally grabbing her arm and jerking her hard from the floor. When she stood before him he grabbed the other arm and backed her against her vanity. "You know damn well what I mean! Don't try to act innocent and ignorant with me! I will have the flesh torn from your bones piece by piece! Now tell me why you did such a thing to that girl!"

She whimpered back, "But I didn't! I found her like that and too—"

"Don't lie to me!" he yelled.

"I'm not! I swear!"

He slapped his hand into her forehead and pushed her head back as he forced his will into her mind, her memories. His eyes narrowed as he found the memory of her finding the girl, of having the guards roll her up in a rug and take her to the unicorn.

"You had some knowledge of this," he hissed. "Tell me about this plot you're concocting or I'll burn you alive right here and now." He withdrew his hand and it burst into flames. "You'll burn for five days before you die and I'll see to it you don't even sleep while it's happening."

Looking with horror-filled eyes at the sorcerer's burning hand, she frantically shook her head and begged, "Please, my Lord, please! I... I only had your wishes in my thoughts, I swear! Please!"

The flames burned out and his hand lanced toward her throat and slammed into it, arching her backward against the vanity. She did not dare to resist him even as he squeezed off her airway, and her wide eyes dropped tears as they were locked on his.

For long seconds he slowly strangled her, then he spun around and hurled her to the floor, watching as she controlled her fall as best she could. Shaking his head, he growled, "You always claim to be serving me, no matter what it is you're doing. You are a lying, treacherous bitch, Nillerra. Now explain why I shouldn't have you slowly killed."

Her thoughts scrambled, but she finally looked up at him with very sheepish eyes. "The girl was a distraction to your unicorn. With her gone the unicorn can turn only to you for comfort. I thought you were going to rid yourself of her in time anyway, so when I found her..." She shook her head. "I took the opportunity to give her cause to turn to you. That is really all I wanted, really. My Lord, you must believe me."

"Why should I?" he snarled as he turned to leave.

"Go to her then," she said suddenly as he reached the door, and when he hesitated she continued. "You will see, my Lord. Just give her the chance to seek comfort in you and she will do it."

Still facing the door, Nemlivv observed, "Your history with this unicorn tells me that you don't have her interests in your heart."

"And she knows that," the black haired girl confirmed. "I'll be the villain for you."

He half turned his head. "Self sacrifice is not something you do, Nillerra."

"It is the best way I have to serve you."

Forcing a hard breath from him, he took the door handle and pulled the door open, ordering as he left, "Stay in here until I give you permission to leave."

He bounded back down the stairs, only to be intercepted by a guard who spun around and met his pace.

"What is it?" the sorcerer growled.

"A runner from Red Stone Castle has arrived," the guard reported.

Nemlivv stopped, his eyes now hollow and blank.

The guard stopped a few steps down and turned to him, continuing, "He brought word that Prince Arden is coming to introduce you to his wife to be, said something about letting her see the unicorn."

"Prince Arden, huh?" Turning his eyes away, the sorcerer mumbled, "How did they know about the unicorn?" He looked back to the guard and ordered, "Have the reserves quietly called up and double the guards at the gate and around the stables. Have my apprentices meet me in my study within the hour." Orders given, he hurried past the guard and outside of the castle, past the flower gardens and to the stable.

The old woman met him half way there and stopped him.

With her were two older men, warlocks from the look of them, each with wooden boxes that had brass handles.

She regarded him with narrow eyes and placed her ancient hand on his chest. "You're letting her snare your heart, boy. You'd best think hard before you let her in deeper or you could doom this castle."

He looked away, knowing the old woman was right, just not wanting to admit it.

"Follow my plan and my lead," she ordered, "and she will stay on her own."

His eyes snapped to her and he raised his chin. "You can make that happen?"

She smiled a wicked smile. "You know I can, and no magic will be called upon. This one is young and simple of mind, and we can outwit her as we would a child."

Nemlivv's heart conflicted with him, but he nodded, complying with the old woman's words as he always did. "Very well. What did you have in mind?"

"The tenders will bring her out in short order to release her," the old woman informed, "and you will know what to do as I speak. She has spoken of another unicorn that has her heart, and he is the key to keeping her here." She turned and looked to the stable, forty paces away, as the unicorn was led by a guard outside. "Just follow what I say and she'll stay of her own accord."

He looked to his little unicorn as she followed the guard toward the castle's southern gate, and his eyes widened as he saw a little line of blood running from her haunch. "What did you do to her," he breathed.

She turned and walked toward the unicorn, replying, "I've used her to save this kingdom, something you should already have started." She waved her hand and the two warlocks strode quickly toward the palace. "You'd best harden your feelings about her, boy. She'll bring your death if you don't. Now come on, and follow my words."

Shahly was stopped at the gate, but looked outside with wanting eyes, just staring toward the forest outside as Nemlivv and the old witch reached her. Slowly, her ear swiveled toward him and she asked, "You are really letting me go?"

His eyes turned to the old woman.

"Off with you," the old woman confirmed. "Your essence is not strong enough for what we need. Now go."

Shahly glanced back at them, then looked out toward the forest and hesitantly paced toward it.

Looking up at the sorcerer, the old woman asked, "The other unicorn, the big bay you saw yesterday is still close by. Watching the castle, I think."

With wide eyes, Shahly stopped and her mouth fell open.

"We should be able to take him easily," the witch continued. "As soon as we're rid of this one you should go to the stable and start the spell."

"Um..." he stammered. "I should meditate first, collect my thoughts and strength. If this other one is as powerful as you say then snaring him will be an unholy task in itself."

Shahly looked fearfully over her shoulder at them.

The old woman turned toward the stable and bade Nemlivv to follow. "I'll help what I can, but he is a beast of immense strength. Copious difficult to catch, I think, but he'll be what we need. Lots of experience in that one, I feel, and the strongest essence I've ever encountered in a unicorn."

Shahly turned and followed them, trotting to catch up as she protested, "You can't just go after another unicorn. Please, just let me go and leave my kind alone."

Glancing over her shoulder, the witch scoffed, "We'll do as we do. No be off before Lord Nemlivv changes his mind."

Shaking her head, the little unicorn followed them and protested, "Please, just leave them in the forest as you should have left me. We are not for your kind to possess."

"We have need of him," the old woman informed coldly. "He'll do better than you could, so just be off and never return here."

Wedging herself between them, Shahly stopped Nemlivv with her head and looked to him with pleading eyes, begging, "Please don't! Please! What must I do to convince you to leave him alone?"

The old woman slowly turned and folded her arms.

He smiled and patted the little unicorn's neck. "You just don't understand, and what we need of him is nothing you should be concerned with. We won't hurt him."

Backing away a few steps, Shahly half turned and countered, "Look at my haunch, Sorcerer. I'm bleeding! Is this what you mean to do to him, too?"

"Enough of this babbling. Nemlivv, get rid of this little beast and hurry with that spell while we still know where he is."

Shaking her head, the little unicorn's eyes were glossy with tears as she pled, "Please don't."

"I'm sorry," he offered softly. Looking away, he strode around her toward the stable.

Shahly's eyes danced around as her mind scrambled. The red unicorn they spoke of almost *had* to be Vinton, and she could not allow humans to take him again. "You don't need to have a unicorn captive," she heard herself say.

They stopped and turned around.

Pacing to the sorcerer and holding his gaze with hers, she raised her head, drawing a deep breath before she spoke. "You don't need him. I know I am not as strong as he is, but..." She closed her eyes. "I'll stay in his place."

"She's not strong enough," the old woman protested.

Looking away, Shahly softly argued, "I'm plenty strong. Promise to leave the other unicorns alone forever and I'll stay."

The witch and sorcerer exchanged looks.

"Promise!" the unicorn insisted.

Nemlivv released a sigh as he pretended to consider her proposal. "Okay, Shahly. I want your word. Promise me that you'll stay on your own, that you will break off ties with those who are coming for you, and I'll never hunt your kind again."

She closed her eyes again, tears streaming forth as she softly complied, "I promise."

"Done," he said in a low voice. "I'll see to it that your kind is safe from now on."

"Do you promise that?" the unicorn asked softly.

"You have my word," he confirmed just over a whisper.

Nodding, Shahly said softly, "Thank you." She took a stuttering breath, then paced around them toward the stable. Her ears drooped and her head was hanging low as she whispered, "I am so sorry, Precious One. Please forgive me."

"You don't have to stay in there anymore if you don't wish

to," he called after her.

She did not respond, and in a moment disappeared into the stable.

"There now," the old woman said flatly. "No more worries about having to guard it. Just see that it follows through to break those ties to those coming for it. If that dragon is on his way, it's best to stop him before we have to test our talisman against him."

He nodded. The unicorn staying of her own choice was indeed good news, but his heart remained heavy. Feelings for her were growing, and he almost felt as if he had betrayed her. "I'll be in my study," he informed softly as he turned toward the palace.

CHAPTER 31

Evening would come soon. The sun was casting longer and longer shadows outside of the castle wall and a slow breeze sent slow waves through the knee-deep grains that grew just outside. The forest had been cleared back almost five hundred paces in any direction, much like Caipiervell Castle, and grains and grasses grew freely and abundantly.

The taste was different, a little more of iron and sulfur, but not unpleasantly so, just different, just new.

Shahly chewed slowly, a few stalks of grain still hanging out of her mouth. She stared at a place in the field of grain a few paces in front of her, but really was looking at nothing. Blinking was slow, rhythmic and automatic. Her mind was finally at rest, though her heart was still heavy. She had cried all she could, now she would not allow herself to dwell over her new life of captivity, her lost friend Ellyus, or never seeing her Vinton or the herd again. She was just empty, and empty was the best she could do.

Many people had come to look at her since she had wandered outside to graze and she did her best to ignore them. Maidens wept, many pointed and made comments of how magical she was, and there were a variety of sighs and other sounds humans made that expressed emotions they could not put to words.

A few approached, but there were three soldiers who followed her about and kept onlookers at bay.

She would not know how many came and went or how many gathered at once to see her. Perhaps this is what Nemlivv really wanted, a curiosity to show off. She no longer cared. She had lost her freedom and now nothing else mattered.

She heard footsteps approach—again—and as before she ignored them as best she could, but she remained aware of them.

"Oh," yet another maiden drawled. "She is so beautiful!"

"Yes, my Lady," one of the guards responded dryly. "Lord Nemlivv has allowed you a few moments with her, but he does not want her disturbed long."

"I understand," she said dreamily. "Can I have a few moments alone with her? There are things a girl would tell a unicorn that a man should not hear."

He sighed, sounding a little annoyed, then he conceded, "Very well, my Lady. Just don't agitate her."

Shahly heard him back away, and turned away a little as she heard the girl's padding footfalls draw closer. A dainty, gentle hand slid across her back and she turned her eyes down, really not wanting contact with anyone. Her mane was stroked and the girl's fingers combed through it, then her arm slid over her neck and the girl drew close to her ear.

"Don't move," the girl whispered to her. Something about her voice was very familiar. "Just act like you are trying to ignore me."

"I am ignoring you," Shahly whickered back.

"We were good friends once," the girl informed softly, just over a whisper, "and I hope we are still."

Her ears perking, the unicorn slowly raised her head, her wide eyes trained in the distance as she finally put voice to face, and face to name. "Audrell?" She slowly looked toward her to see her friend in a yellow sun dress with her hair kept unrestrained behind her. The girl was smiling and there was much joy in her eyes.

Shahly found that she had to rein in her elation, lest she reveal that she and this girl knew each other.

Audrell stroked the unicorn's cheek and confessed, "I'd hoped that the next time we met would be under different circumstances."

"I did too," Shahly said straightly. "How did you know where to find me?"

"Your Vinton paid us a little visit, and I'm glad he did. Arden is trading pleasantries with Lord Nemlivv, telling him of our engagement and all that."

Shahly smiled. "So you two are to be mated, are you?"

Looking away, Audrell blushed and nodded, a tight lipped smile on her face.

"That is good news," the unicorn whispered. "I can see you are very happy. Perhaps you will..." She trailed off as one of the guards behind Audrell glanced their way. "What did Vinton say?"

"He told us what happened," Audrell reported just over a

whisper, "and where you are. We knew we had to do something, so Arden wanted to make a social visit to tell him of the engagement, that way Nemlivv would suspect nothing."

Shahly looked away, and her eyes widened. "Oh, no."

"Not to worry," Audrell assured. "We'll have you out of here before anyone can realize."

"Nemlivv knows about you and Arden," Shahly said blankly, her wide eyes staring into the distance, "and Arden and me, and you and me."

Audrell drew an uneasy breath, her eyes growing larger as she stared at the unicorn.

Shahly's gaze shifted to her friend. "You two should leave. I think you may be in terrible danger here."

Looking away, Audrell slowly shook her head and insisted, "No. Arden will find a way to turn this to his advantage. We'll find a way to get you out of here."

"I cannot go," Shahly informed grimly. When the girl's eyes snapped back to her, she explained, "I have to stay. It was the only way to protect the rest of my herd."

Audrell slowly shook her head again, her mouth hanging open in disbelief.

"Please understand," Shahly begged softly. "I had to promise him I would never leave, and now I must stay here. It was the only way."

"Shahly, you can't stay here!"

The unicorn closed her eyes and pulled away from her, turning to go back to the castle. "I have to." When the girl caught up to her, Shahly shook her head and insisted, "You have to understand, Audrell. You have to. The herd needs me to do this. At least this way you will always know where I'll be, and perhaps you will come and visit."

"Of course I will," Audrell assured softly.

One of the guards approached and said harshly, "That's far enough, my Lady."

Shahly turned and snorted at him and he stopped his pursuit, raising his chin. With narrow eyes, she looked to Audrell and informed, "I'm not exactly powerless here. Now we'd best hurry and find Arden before he says too much to Nemlivv."

***

Nemlivv would remain as polite a host as one would expect when a visiting dignitary was about. Knowledge of what Prince Arden's visit was really for was a strain on this, but he kept his features and his conversation pleasant as he offered his guest yet another glass of wine.

Sitting on the deep purple cushions of the chairs in the dining hall on the castle's ground level, the two men shared their pleasantries among the lavish décor and furnishings all around them. The table in the center of the room was easily seven paces long and a pace wide and covered with a long white linen. Vases of flowers were spaced out evenly about every two paces and plates and flatware were at the ready, accompanied by goblets and drinking glasses. Dinner time was hours away, but the table had to be ready at all times.

On each wall could be found deep cushioned chairs of ornately carved dark wood and small tables of the same wood with the same style carvings sat between the chairs.

Near the front entrance to this cavernous room is where the men sat, their chairs only half angled toward each other as they exchanged small talk, and three servants stood ready a few paces away with wine and plates of snacks for them.

Arden took his freshly filled goblet and looked down into it, smiling a little as he said, "I want to thank you again for allowing Audrell to see your unicorn. It is something she has always wanted."

"It is a pleasure to do so," Nemlivv replied. "We haven't had the opportunity to visit for many seasons, Prince Arden. I am happy you stopped by."

Arden nodded to him and took a sip of his wine.

Gazing down into his own goblet, Nemlivv watched it swirl inside for a moment before he smiled slightly and asked, "So how did you hear of my unicorn?"

"Word gets out," the Prince answered casually, clearly prepared for that question. "There is still the issue of what is happening to them at my kingdom. Audrell and I wanted to see one that is not destined for that horrible fate."

"Why don't you put a stop to what is happening?" the sorcerer asked, his eyes still on his wine.

"I will," Arden assured, "just as soon as I am crowned and

have the power to do so."

"That's good to hear," Nemlivv said with a nod. "We wouldn't want Shahly in that arena." His eyes turned to the Prince with a blink and he finished, "Again."

The game was up and Prince Arden knew it. With a slight smile, he took a sip of his wine, his gaze never leaving the sorcerer's, then he confirmed, "No, we wouldn't."

A long moment of silence passed between them, finally broken by the sorcerer who observed, "So, now we know the true reason for your visit. Now I just have to determine if you are here to protect her from that arena or steal her from me." His eyes locked on the Prince, he took a sip from his goblet.

Arden looked to his wine, swirling it around in the clear crystal wineglass as he organized his thoughts.

Nemlivv added, "I would only ask that you honor me with truth, Prince Arden."

With a slight nod, the Prince finally said, "I learned some time ago that the killing of unicorns was wrong. I also know that imprisoning them is just as wrong." His gaze shifted to the sorcerer again and he continued, "She will die if you keep her here."

"She stays of her own mind," Nemlivv corrected.

Arden raised his head. "Does she, now?"

The sorcerer nodded.

Raising his brow, the Prince announced, "Well, then, it would seem that the nature of my visit is one of social pleasantries after all."

His eyes narrowing, Nemlivv observed, "That was just a little too easy."

Arden shrugged. "If she stays of her own accord, then I simply must respect her decision to do so, especially with such a bounty being paid for her kind. It is honestly something of a relief to know that she is where she can be protected."

"Until your kingdom comes for her," the sorcerer countered.

Shaking his head, Arden took a sip of his wine and dismissed that notion. "No, not so long as I am Prince."

"Problem is you aren't King."

"True," the Prince admitted. "That being the case, we should keep her presence here a secret."

"I agree, Prince Arden. Does anyone at Red Stone know she is here?"

"Only Audrell and me. I wanted to be certain the unicorn hunters would be kept in the dark, and would not come for her."

The rapid clop of boots and hooves approaching drew their attention and they looked to the door to see Audrell and the Shahly run into the room. The marble floor was not well suited to accommodate hooves and the unicorn halted herself with some difficulty, sliding almost a full pace forward before she finally stopped.

For a long moment, Princess-to-be and unicorn stared at the two men who stared back at them, and clearly they were frantic in thought about their next move.

Arden finally smiled and greeted, "Shahly, it's good to see you again."

Girl and unicorn exchanged looks of concern and confusion.

The Prince stood and strode to Shahly, looking to her almost fatherly as he said, "Lord Nemlivv told me how you are under his protection, and I find myself glad of it. I recently heard that unicorn hunters are still prowling about."

Shahly stared back dumbly for long seconds, then hesitantly nodded. "Yes, he... He protects me from them." She glanced at the sorcerer, then looked to Audrell.

Looking to his bride-to-be, Prince Arden nodded to her. "Now we'll easily know where to find her when we want to visit. Did we ever determine the truth to that legend?"

She raised her brow slightly. "Legend?"

"Your first child being born a prince if you see a unicorn," Arden explained.

"Oh, that legend." She looked to Shahly and stammered, "I, um... I think it is. I'm marrying a prince after all."

The unicorn's eyes cut to her and she corrected, "I'm sure that's a coincidence."

"Not at all," Nemlivv assured as he also stood. "You are creatures of magic beyond what we can understand." He beamed a big smile to Audrell. "But I'm sure you already knew that of your little friend, right, Princess?" He looked to the Prince, then behind him as a palace guard approached and handed him a note. As he opened and read it, he set his jaw slightly and said with his eyes still on the parchment, "Your room should be ready by now if you two would like to rest for a while. You must be weary from that trip from Red Stone." He handed the note back to the guard and nodded to him, watching with tense eyes as the man turned and hurried out.

"Not at all," Arden assured. "I was hoping you would show me the legendary gardens about your palace."

A door across the room opened Nemlivv's sorceress apprentice strode in, her eyes immediately finding the Prince as she strode toward her teacher.

"I must apologize," the sorcerer offered, "but I have matters to attend." Looking to his apprentice as she reached them, he held his hand to her and suggested, "Perhaps my lovely student would show you around the palace."

She smiled as she looked to her master and nodded to him. "It would be a pleasure, my Lord." Turning her eyes back to the Prince, she subtly looked him up and down, then she bowed her head to him. "You must be Prince Arden. I heard of your visit. I am Deshett, your humble servant."

He nodded to her. "A pleasure to meet you. This is my fiancé, Audrell."

The sorceress' eyes were scrutinizing as they found the Princess-to-be, and she smiled a friendly smile laced with just a hint of challenge. Turning slightly toward her, Deshett made certain that Audrell got a good look at her larger size, her stature, and her more generous bust line, which she exposed a little more to the Prince, her cape opening to reveal her scant clothing beneath as she turned. "I am honored to meet you, Princess."

Audrell disapproved of the sorceress on sight as she looked her up and down, then nodded to her and did not answer otherwise.

"If you will all excuse me," the sorcerer said politely, his eyes finding Shahly, "I shall attend to this as quickly as I can and rejoin you. I'll have a banquet awaiting you around dinner time."

Arden offered him a smile. "Tales of the table you set are rampant throughout the land, Lord Nemlivv. I shall look forward to dinner tonight."

***

The dark of night was less than an hour away and Deshett was finally taking them back toward the palace. Her arm was wrapped around the Prince's and she talked casually and laughed with him as they slowly made their way down the path.

Audrell and Shahly followed about three paces behind them, and the daggers in Audrell's eyes could be seen clearly even by the blind.

Shahly glanced at her often, and finally observed in a low voice, "You don't seem to like Nemlivv's student."

"Not one bit," the Princess snarled.

"Arden seems to like her," the unicorn pointed out.

Her lips tightening, Audrell clenched her hands into tight fists as she said, "Yes he does, a little too much."

"I haven't felt this from you before," Shahly informed, "but I've felt this from others. Do you remember— "

"She'd better watch where she puts her grimy little hands," Audrell growled. "Oh, if she keeps hanging on him like that I'll break both her arms. Off!"

"You need to settle yourself down," Shahly whispered.

Audrell finally glanced at the unicorn and asked, "How would you feel if she was hanging all over your Vinton like that?"

Shahly looked to the sorceress, then back to Audrell and shrugged. She sensed Nemlivv's approach long before Audrell would have and looked behind her, seeing him walking at a brisk pace to catch up. Most of the time she would pause to let a friend catch up to her, but today she looked forward again and did not slow her pace, but she did murmur to Audrell, "Nemlivv is coming."

She grumbled back, "Maybe he can get his whore off of my fiancé."

The sorcerer trotted up to them and met their pace between them, offering, "Sorry. It seems that I have more visitors coming. Preparations to make and all that." He looked to Shahly and smiled a little. "They're coming to see you."

She glanced at him. "What if I don't want to be seen?"

"Then they'll have to await your convenience," he informed.

"I want Arden and Audrell guarded closely," she ordered,

turning narrow eyes to the sorcerer. "They are very dear to me and I will be very upset if anything happens to either of them."

He nodded and confirmed, "I understand, dear unicorn. Perhaps you would do me the honor of indulging my other guests."

Shahly sighed. "Perhaps. What are you asking from them to show me off?"

"I hadn't really thought to ask anything," he confessed. "Their visit is really to discuss an accord of non aggression. Seeing you could very well facilitate that much more easily." He looked to Audrell, offering her a friendly smile. "How are you liking the tour, Princess?"

"You have a beautiful palace and lovely gardens," was Audrell's polite answer. As she looked forward again, she added through clenched teeth, "And the people here are *so* friendly."

He glanced at Deshett, whose arm was still wrapped tightly around Prince Arden's, and he nodded. "Yes, very friendly." He raised his chin and summoned, "Deshett."

Still holding onto the Prince's arm, the sorceress looked over her shoulder, and when she saw her sorcery master she turned and pulled Prince Arden around with her, seemingly unwilling to release him. She beamed a big smile to the sorcerer and greeted, "Master Nemlivv. You didn't tell me of Prince Arden's sharp wit and silver tongue. I don't remember a more fond time with any of your guests."

He nodded. "Very good. We have more guests coming in the morning and I want you to personally see to their comforts."

"As you command, my Lord," She turned her eyes to Arden's and smiled seductively. "I shall look forward to spending more time with you, Prince Arden. Your charm equals Lord Nemlivv's."

He smiled a friendly smile back and nodded to her.

Reluctantly, she released the Prince and turned toward the palace, narrow eyes finding Arden's fiancé as she did.

Her hands clenching into tight fists, Audrell snarled a little as she watched the sorceress stride toward the door.

"Dinner should be about ready," Nemlivv informed as he half turned and extended his hand toward the palace door. "Shall we?"

"Sounds good," Arden said as he took his Princess' side, and as he did she grasped his arm with both of hers, holding it tightly, almost possessively. He raised his brow and glanced at her, then looked to Shahly.

She met his eyes and shrugged.

***

As Nemlivv had expected, the dining hall was ready and awaiting them, as were a dozen servants to attend them. They entered behind the sorcerer and Audrell was still clinging to her Prince's arm. Shahly also followed, as she wanted to be with people she actually cared about. No one would protest her presence in the palace, but everyone stopped what they were doing as she passed, and many of the servants in the dining room found themselves in a hushed reverence for the mystical creature in her presence.

Stopping a few paces past the doorway, Nemlivv scanned the dining hall, then he half turned and extended his hand toward the table, offering, "After you."

He watched as they strode past, then he looked to Shahly as she followed them and took her side. "I'm sorry we don't have a chair for you."

"Won't need one," was her curt answer.

"What can I interest you to eat?" he asked.

"Fruit salad," she replied.

Arden half smiled and glanced over his shoulder at her. "And some sweet wine?"

She smiled back at him. "Perhaps a little. Not too much, though. We don't want to repeat last time."

Nemlivv pulled Audrell's chair out for her, the one closest to his at the head of the table, but looked to Shahly. "The last time. When you were human, you mean?"

"Yes," was the unicorn's reply as she stopped beside Prince Arden.

Taking his place at the head of the table after seating Audrell, the sorcerer stood behind his chair and offered the other side to Shahly. As if reading his thoughts a servant quickly darted forth and removed the chair from that spot and Nemlivv watched as his unicorn paced around him with some reluctance in her steps.

When she was in place, Arden and Nemlivv took their seats.

A silent moment passed as everyone seemed to settle in. There was tension in the air felt by all, but it was Shahly, as usual, who would break it.

She looked to Arden as the wine was served, as a silver bowl was placed in front of her and filled with a red wine, and she smiled a little as his eyes found her. "Do you remember when you first found me and carried me into your castle?"

Normally jealous Audrell looked to him with wide eyes and barked, "You carried her into the castle?"

"She didn't have any shoes," he defended.

"And I was human and not as heavy as a unicorn," Shahly added. "Remember how I told you I used to be heavier?"

Unicorn and Prince shared a little laugh at the memory.

"And you eat like a horse," he added with a laugh.

She whinnied a hearty laugh, and everyone else laughed with her.

Shaking his head, Nemlivv observed, "That must have been a fine time."

"It had its moments," Audrell confirmed. "Shahly and I had quite the time fitting in with those other tr… Um, girls."

Arden nudged her with his elbow. "Be polite, now."

"I was about to be," she mumbled.

"What is a tramp, anyway?" Shahly asked.

The question caught Nemlivv mid-drink and he coughed and quickly raised a napkin to his mouth, slamming his glass down and almost breaking it. Between choking fits, it was clear that he was laughing.

Audrell buried her forehead in her hands, also laughing.

Ever the diplomat, Arden simply looked to the little unicorn and explained, "All of the other girls there but you and Audrell."

"Prince Arden!" Nemlivv laughed.

Shahly's eyes darted from human to human as she puzzled over what they found so amusing. "I still don't understand."

"Young women of loose scruples," the sorcerer explained.

"Oh," the unicorn said absently as she watched a servant fill her bowl with wine again. "Um, what are scruples?"

A fine dinner was served and the conversation never really strayed to anything serious. Generous food and wine would be served for a couple of hours as humorous stories were exchanged and remembered.

The sun was down and chandeliers and candles lit the dining hall before anyone realized how much time they had spent there or how much wine they had consumed. Shahly alone had her bowl filled six times during the course of the evening and watched with glassy eyes as a servant filled it for the eighth time. Raising her head, she looked to each of the humans in turn and slurred, "You know, I... I have to tell you all something. Can I tell you all something?"

"Sure!" Audrell declared, obviously feeling the same affects from the wine that Shahly did. "Tell us anything you want."

Shahly looked to her, her eyes wavering a little as she said, "I love you strange, crazy people. I mean, I really do." Turning narrow eyes to Nemlivv, she continued, "Even you too, Sor... Sorsus... Nemlivv."

His brow arched, he smiled at her and replied, "And I you, dear unicorn, enough to know you've had plenty of wine for this evening."

Arden took another sip from his glass and mumbled, "Not going to have too much wine. Remember last time."

Audrell leaned into him and turned a flirty look to him. "You might have to take me to bed soon, my love."

Clearing his throat, the Prince shot a glance at Nemlivv and agreed, "I think so, but Lord Nemlivv and I should talk for a while first."

Shahly backed away from the table. "Good. You two talk. I'm... I'm going outside."

They watched as the little unicorn turned and walked with unsteady steps toward the door from which they had entered. She stumbled a couple of times and once veered into the table, scooting the whole thing over a little.

Finally at the doorway, she looked over her shoulder and said, "I love you all!"

Audrell stood up and waved to her, almost shouting back, "I love you too, Shahly!"

Shahly paced out of the door, running into one of them on the way out, and everyone just watched the doorway as the clop of hooves echoed into the room. The unmistakable crash of a suit of armor hitting the floor was followed by stumbling hoof steps and Shahly whinnying to them, "I'm okay!"

"She is so magical," Audrell said dreamily.

***

Prince Arden's conversation with Nemlivv would have to wait until morning, not that the sorcerer minded one bit. With so much on his mind, he opted to say his good nights to his guests and take his leave of them.

On his way to the castle's front door, which would take him outside to the gardens and toward the stable where his unicorn no doubt slept by now. This was all he would allow in his mind, but he found himself intercepted before he could reach the door, and his annoyance was clear as he looked to the old woman who blocked his path.

Her eyes narrowing, she asked, "How did your meeting with the Prince of Red Stone go, Lord Nemlivv."

"It was fine," he growled, looking away. "I'll speak with him more tomorrow."

"He wants your unicorn, Nemlivv. You know it and so do I."

"I will accept his reason for his visit."

"And meanwhile what do you intend to do about it?"

He forced a hard breath through his nose, folding his arms as he considered, then he walked around her and growled, "I will work on an alliance with him, as I already planned."

"Nillerra already failed to secure your alliance, Nemlivv." When he stopped, she smiled slightly. "That plan did not work out so well, did it? Do you have another? One that will, perhaps, not rely on your cunning like the last did?"

He lowered his eyes.

She approached him slowly, sliding her hands up his shoulders. "That unicorn has robbed you of your strength, hasn't she?"

"She's given me more," he growled through clenched teeth.

"Of course she has," the old woman drawled. She turned him as forcefully as she could and glared up at him. "She's made you weak, my boy. Weak! Your thoughts are so consumed with her that you've forgotten your goals!"

"*Your* goals!" he countered.

Her eyes narrowed. "We've worked hard to make all of this

happen, Nemlivv. I have your brother in his place of glory and you are well on your way to yours."

"Glory," the sorcerer snarled. "He's a fraud and we both—" Her hand moved so swiftly across his face he did not realize he'd been slapped until his head snapped around and his cheek stung.

"You'll watch that tongue," she hissed. "I made you, I'll unmake you in a snap."

His eyes slid back to her, and he smiled just a little. "No, you won't. It's too late for that." He turned and headed toward the door again. "You'd best think about your own future, what little you still have."

"Your *magister* will be here sometime tomorrow," she informed, and when he stopped suddenly she smiled. "He should be here sometime in the evening, so perhaps you'd like to make the preparations that you should. Oh, and he'll probably want your unicorn for himself." Slowly, she turned and walked the other direction. "Perhaps you would like to tell him how she makes you stronger, and how he can't have her."

Her laugh echoed through the room and through his thoughts after she'd gone. He did not know how long he stood there, staring blankly at the door that would lead him outside. This new revelation was not a welcome one. He'd learned all he could from the man he had called *Magister* and was glad to be rid of him. That was a long time ago, and he had no wish to ever see him again.

Now, it seemed, he would have to surrender his unicorn to this horrible man, an immensely powerful sorcerer who lingered somewhere between life and death.

Sweeping the thought aside, he strode forward again, finally pulling the doors open as he reached them.

Not far outside, under the darkness of the sky, a crowd had gathered around one of his flower gardens. Many of the servants and soldiers there held torches to light what they were staring at. His eyes narrowed as he walked toward it, and a simple clearing of his throat made the people gathered there part in two directions to let him pass, and when he reached the garden, he folded his arms as he also stared down at the form that lay atop and among his flowers, his brow arching slightly.

Shahly lay on her side, her neck arched to bring her nose almost parallel with her back. Her mouth was ajar, her tongue lay on the ground between her teeth, and her eyes were gently closed as she slept soundly where she had fallen. From the look of how she lay, she was asleep before she actually hit the ground, passed out from all of that wine. But for her slow, rhythmic breathing, one might have thought her dead.

Looking to one side, he loudly announced, "I believe you have something else you should be doing."

The crowd dispersed quietly, taking most of the light with them. Only two remained, one a guard and the other a woman, a palace servant.

"My Lord," the guard said cautiously. "Should we, uh... Should we move her?"

Nemlivv folded her arms, staring down at his unicorn, then he slowly shook his head and replied, "No, she looks comfortable. We'll just have to tend the flowers in the morning. Keep everyone clear of this area until I say otherwise."

The guard bowed his head to the sorcerer before turning to go about his tasks. The woman with him followed closely.

Shaking his head, Nemlivv stepped into the flower bed himself and sat down beside her, gently stroking her shoulder and mane as he pondered how to keep her, how to protect her. As frustration mounted at the thoughts, tears came into his eyes for only the second time in many seasons.

CHAPTER 32

The black dragon rubbed his eyes with a thumb and finger as he stood in the morning sun just south of the Dark Mountains. He drew a breath, and released it slowly before he spoke. "Let me see if I understand you correctly. You want to go into this castle as visiting dignitaries, steal Shahly, and make your escape before anyone notices."

Looking up at the dragon with his arms folded, Prince Chail nodded slightly and confirmed, "It sounds very easy, I know, but—"

"But we both know how you have a way of botching things up," Ralligor growled. "*And,* you want me to give Plow Mule human form and send him in there with you."

"He is best able to find her and find her quickly," the Prince informed.

Gathered behind the Prince, Le'ell, Faelon, Jekkon and the other humans behind them anxiously stared up at the dragon. Vinton stood to Chail's side, his eyes also on the dragon, though less patience was there. Falloah stood in front of the black dragon, and raised her brow as he looked down at her.

Ralligor just stared at the dragoness for a long moment before asking, "How does this plan of his appeal to you?"

"It actually sounds reasonable," she replied straightly. When he raised his eyes, she continued, "If we assault the castle then she may be killed, and all of this would be for not. If they can get her out of there—"

"What is to stop him from taking her again?" Ralligor cut in, drawing nothing but silence from all around.

Vinton took a few steps toward him and suggested, "You can deal with him after Shahly is safe, and we all know how you want to. If you don't have to look out for her at the same time you are fighting him then you are more likely to be successful."

The Desert Lord growled again and looked toward the mountains. "Assuming you are successful, you would be pursued by the bulk of his army, probably Nemlivv himself."

"You just let *me* worry over Nemlivv," Rawl ordered as he emerged from the trees behind the dragon with Janees right on his heels. As the dragon turned toward him, he stopped some ten paces away and grasped his walking stick with both hands. "You are likely to have your hands full with Mettegrawr and his minions."

Janees saw Jekkon right away, and she pulled the hood over her head and tried not to be noticed.

Ralligor stared down at him for another long moment. He glanced away, informing, "Nemlivv will quite likely have to be killed to keep him from going after Shahly again."

"So be it," the sorcerer snarled.

Nodding, the Desert Lord observed, "We don't often agree, Rawl. I'm glad to see that we do today."

Smiling, the sorcerer just nodded.

Ralligor drew another breath, turning to look down at Vinton. "Okay, Plow Mule. You are sure this is what you want to do?"

Raising his head, the bay unicorn straightly answered, "Yes."

The black dragon loosed another breath, this one growling on the way out of him, and he bend down and held a fist over Vinton's head. As he opened his hand, a golden chain fell from his palm and over the unicorn's neck, falling evenly to both sides. A talon on one end grasped an emerald sphere on the other as they met and joined the chain in a flash of light.

Vinton turned his head and looked down at the amulet as the chain tightened itself around his neck, but not uncomfortably so. With a blink he turned his eyes back up to Ralligor's, eyes that sought instruction.

Standing fully again, the Desert Lord folded his arms and flatly said, "There you go, Plow Mule. The same incantation will work with that one, but you won't need our names, just the words. I'll tell you as I told her. Don't assume that all of your unicorn tricks will work in this form and don't trust everything you will see, hear and feel as a human. If you intend to survive the day, you'd best stay close to those you know you can trust, and out of the way of the hazards that await you there."

Vinton nodded once to him.

Ralligor turned his eyes to the Prince. "And make certain that nothing happens to him. If he gets killed trying to get her out of there then I'm sure I'll never hear the end of it when we finally do." He looked up toward the mountain peaks with eyes that were suddenly hollow. "For now, Falloah and I go no further. Once you are on the north side of the Dark Mountains you will be on your own and beyond my help. It's good that you remember that." He drew a breath and released it in a growl. "I will attack tomorrow at high sun, so be sure you have her out of there before then."

"What if we can't get her out before then?" Le'ell asked with a little frustration in her voice.

Slowly, the black dragon turned his eyes down to her. "Then just make certain she is safe. Nemlivv and his army will have their hands full with me so use the distraction to your advantage."

She nodded and assured, "I will do my best. We all will."

Ralligor looked to Falloah and ordered, "Head south. Tell Agarxus that I will be crossing here tomorrow at high sun."

She lowered her eyes. "I wish you would let me fight with you, *Unisponsus.*"

"Another time," he assured, "when we are not facing another landmaster. For now, just relay my message to Agarxus."

With a subtle nod, she assured, "I will, *Unisponsus.* Take great care tomorrow."

Ralligor watched her take flight and his eyes were on her until she disappeared over the horizon, and something empty was there in his eyes.

The old silver unicorn stepped forward, looking up to the black dragon with a trust that no unicorn should have had for such a dragon. He whickered to draw the dragon's attention down to him, and when he met his eyes he said, "You'll put your life at risk for a unicorn. I know of no other dragon who has even thought of such a thing."

Ralligor raised a brow slightly.

"That means you have my trust," the silver informed straightly, "and the trust of all I know. Be well, Desert Lord, and be safe."

Staring at the old silver for long seconds, Ralligor finally nodded to him, then he opened his wings and swept into the sky.

Vinton drew a breath, his attention straying to the North. Slowly, he released the wind that was within him and some of the nervous tension with it. Soon, he would see his Shahly again, and soon he would be in a battle for her freedom.

The silver approached him and whickered, asking, "Is this truly what you want to do, Vinton? Joining them in their world?"

"She did it for me," the bay reminded, still staring north. "I would give anything just to see her again."

"I'll head that way," the silver informed, pacing past him. "If we are to encounter danger, it is best to be prepared for it."

Finally turning, Vinton looked to Chail, to Le'ell, to Faelon.

All of the humans gathered around, nervously anticipating Vinton's transformation.

His eyes darted from one to the next, then to his unicorn brethren. Drawing a deep breath, he closed his eyes, lowering his head as he whispered the words in his own tongue. An emerald glow slowly enveloped him and a green mist slowly began to rotate around him in bands that turned in opposite directions, and they rotated faster and faster as the glow about the bay unicorn grew brighter.

A white light flashed and everyone turned their eyes away briefly, and the humans shielded theirs with their hands.

A long silence followed and everyone's gaze was fixed on Vinton.

His dark brown eyes darted from one to the next. There were only two kinds of reactions from the humans. Chail, Jekkon and the Enulam soldiers all looked to each other and nodded. The women, however, *all* of the women, stared wide eyed at him with their mouths hanging open. Even Pa'lesh wore this expression.

They all knew that Vinton would be quite a handsome human man, but all underestimated how much so. As humans go, he was perfect in all respects. His bulky, muscular build, broad shoulders and chest, his thick arms and legs were covered in a dark bronze skin that glistened in the sunlight. His was a face that most women see in their dreams. His jaw was a thick one, a solid one, and his face was free of hair. Deep brown eyes were unsure as they glanced about. The breeze gently blew long black hair that was much as his mane had been and dropped freely to his mid back. To someone who had not seen him a moment ago, he would have been thought a warrior from Enulam.

Another moment of silent staring back and forth passed.

Finally, Vinton asked, "Did it work?" His eyes widened a little more as he spoke in a voice he did not quite recognize. His black eyebrows dropped as he looked down at his hands in amazement. His eyes turned down further to examine the completed transformation into the strange creature he had become, and finally he looked to Prince Chail and raised his chin.

The Enulam Prince folded his arms and nodded. "You look good, my friend."

"Really good," Princess Faelon drawled absently.

One of the Zondaen soldiers added, "That is the prettiest man I have ever seen."

Dorell found herself unable to speak at all.

Le'ell murmured, "Goddess be praised."

Loudly clapping his hands together, Chail strode toward Vinton and announced, "Okay, Vinton. Let's find you something to wear and get— "

"Wait!" Faelon shouted, and when the Enulam Prince and former unicorn paused and turned to her, she looked Vinton up and down again, then nodded and said, "Okay."

Chail growled and turned back to Vinton, taking his arm as he led him toward his horse, grumbling, "That's enough, ladies."

Pa'lesh nudged Princess Faelon and offered in a low voice, "Thanks."

***

In short order, Chail had Vinton dressed in some of the finest clothing he had with him and another Enulam soldier offered up a spare pair of boots.

Looking over his work, Chail took a few steps back, and nodded.

Vinton found himself wearing a white swordsman's shirt and tight fitting black trousers. The shirt was unlaced halfway down his chest and stood open and a dark leather sword belt was wound around his proportionately small waist.

As the women in the group gathered around him again, and Relshee joined them, he looked over the garb he now wore, then looked around to everyone, asking, "Do you think I could pass as a man?"

All of the women eagerly nodded and Pa'lesh insisted, "I see no problem with that, my friend. I see no problems at all." She strode over to him and walked around him as if checking to make certain everything was in its place. His height was somewhere between her and Prince Chail, but his generous build filled out the Prince's shirt nicely. Looking down with a smile, she slapped his buttocks hard and nodded to him as he spun around with a surprised look on his face. "Yes," she observed. "You make a fine man. Almost a pity you'll have to go back to four legs."

He watched as she walked away and offered, "Thanks?"

Faelon approached next with Relshee on at her side and Dorell on the other side. Raising a hand to her chin, she pursed her lips and shook her head. "No, this isn't right."

"We haven't much else to work with," Chail informed.

"If he's a visiting dignitary," she went on, "he'll need jewelry. He'll need something showing off his status."

Folding his arms, Chail pointed out, "I don't use such things."

The Caipiervell Princess only glanced at him. "You carry a sword from Enulam and a dagger that is decorated to show your rank, and everyone knows that Enulam men don't go for adornments outside of their weapons. The Emissary of Rhine Keep should have a little more vanity than that, especially if he means to impress another kingdom."

Relshee leaned forward and sniffed, then she drew away and observed, "You even smell funny now, Vinton."

He gave her a sharp look and growled back, "I know. I'm right here and can smell everything."

Le'ell folded her arms as she walked up behind Chail and asked, "So where do we get him jewelry out here?"

"Might be a settlement nearby," a Zondaen soldier suggested.

Shaking his head, Chail assured, "We don't have time."

"Speaking of which," Rawl barked as he approached, "when do you plan to depart? And where's that girl who wishes me to teach her?"

Le'ell motioned behind her with her head. "She wandered into the forest with a couple of water bladders a while ago. I told her where the creek is down there."

The sorcerer growled and turned that direction.

"Wait!" Faelon bade, running up to him.

He turned and regarded her almost coldly.

"Vinton will need jewelry," she informed. "Can you help?"

Rawl glanced at the former unicorn and asked, "What's wrong with that around his neck?"

"That's fine," she assured, "but he'll need rings and other adornments. Can you help?"

He vented a sigh and looked to Vinton again.

Raising his chin, Vinton informed, "I can't go in there wearing this amulet. It's just like Shahly's and would raise suspicion."

Nodding, Rawl said, "Agreed. I'll find some gold somewhere and fashion you something."

"I have some," Faelon offered quickly. "Just use whatever you need. Oh, but not that broach with the ruby, and not the emerald earrings. Oh, and then there is—"

He raised a hand to silence her and interrupted, "Just pick out what you can spare and I'll do the rest."

She smiled and turned toward the horses and her waiting saddlebags, beckoning, "Come on, girls. Let's see what we can find."

Dorell and Relshee turned to follow.

Shaking his head, Rawl growled and turned toward the creek.

Vinton looked back to Prince Chail and admitted, "I can't say I'm comfortable with all of the attention."

Chail patted his shoulder and informed, "You're going to have to appear to be, my friend, and you're going to have to be cool and level headed. I'll do my best to instruct you before we get there."

Raising his brow, Vinton nodded and assured, "I'll do my best."

***

Janees was not hard to find, but creeping up on her like Rawl enjoyed doing was. Knowing that he was making too much noise on the loose rocks and gravel and the large number of dried sticks on the trail, he quickly gave up that endeavor and simply lumbered toward the girl.

She sat on a fallen tree, facing the shallow creek that ran swiftly over the moss covered rocks in front of her. Her hood was still over her head and her gaze danced on the fast moving water.

Rawl sat down beside her and also looked toward the water.

A moment later, she finally, meekly said, "I came down for some water."

"I see," he replied softly. "Those bags are empty."

She nodded.

He drew a breath and shook his head. "Just go and talk to him, girl."

"I can't, *Magister.* He needs to move on, and he can't do that if he thinks I will come with him. It's just how he thinks. It isn't his fault, it's just how things are."

"Perhaps that's how things are, Janees, but I think there is more to it. I think you just don't want to have to confront the lad."

Janees hesitantly turned her eyes to him.

He just stared into the water and continued, "Avoiding him is much easier than facing him and having to explain things. You wouldn't want to risk hurting the boy's feelings being honest with him, now would you?"

She asked in a timid voice, "But what if he doesn't understand?"

"Or even worse," Rawl countered, looking to her, "what if he does?"

Janees stared back at him for a moment, and tears filled her eyes. She finally looked away, back to the water, then she closed her eyes and nodded. Drawing a broken breath, she shook her head and sobbed, "I'm just being selfish, but he's all I have left." Raising a hand to cover her mouth, she leaned into him and cried harder.

Rawl growled a sigh. Slipping his arm around her, he informed almost coldly, "You realize that you see him as all that's left of the past, the same past you were supposed to have left behind."

Long seconds later she quit crying and pulled away from him, looking to his eyes as she informed, "He is one of only two people in the whole world I can trust anymore."

The sorcerer raised his chin slightly. "I see. Well then, perhaps you should trust the words of the other of these two people. Not all things that you should do are easy, girl. Those easiest of tasks are most often the easiest forgotten, and the least significant."

Her gaze danced away from his for a second, then returned, and she nodded.

***

When Rawl and Janees returned to the others, they found most of them ready to depart, and others still breaking down the camp. Walking behind the sorcery master as she always did, Janees' eyes darted about in a search for Jekkon and her nerves were pulled taut at the prospect of finding him. Rawl stopped and she did not notice as she was looking off to the side, and she ran right into him.

Slowly, he turned and looked down at her, an eyebrow held high.

Janees cringed and offered, "I'm sorry."

He motioned her away with his head and ordered, "Go find the boy. I think he's in that direction."

She nodded to him and hurried off in the direction she was instructed to go.

Rawl watched her scurry off, then he turned to the six mounted riders and approached, folding his arms as he had Prince Chail's attention. "I don't know about the wisdom of this visit of yours, Prince of Enulam."

"You aren't alone," Chail assured. "We'll be there in a few hours at a good pace, and I intend to have her out of the castle before you and Ralligor attack."

"I question his wisdom as well," the sorcerer informed. "Just make certain you are out of the way of that dragon tomorrow, and bear in mind that he will likely not be unopposed."

Nodding, the Prince agreed, "I intend to be. I have two garrisons that will be awaiting us at the end of the pass through the mountains. If he sends his army after us then he will have a nasty surprise awaiting him."

"Just take care, boy," Rawl ordered, "and take care that this unicorn man with you is kept from harm."

Chail nodded to him again, then he kicked his horse forward to start the procession north.

Rawl watched after them, then he turned as he heard

someone approaching from behind him.

Relshee's eyes were on the departing riders and she leaned her head a little, asking, "Do you think they'll be able to find Shahly?"

He just allowed himself to absorb this moment with a magical young unicorn, then he nodded and confirmed, "They'll find her. Let's just hope they will find her in good health."

CHAPTER 33

For once, Shahly had awakened before the sun, and had not been happy to do so.

With an aching head she started her day with a little grazing just outside of the wall, returned to the stable for some oats and clean water, then she had nibbled on some of Nemlivv's flowers, not really caring if he minded or not. The sorcerer had disappeared into the castle some time ago and she had not seen him for many hours, nor did she really care. She was most anxious to see Arden and Audrell again, but she was sure they would sleep late, especially considering how much wine Audrell had swallowed the night before.

With her promise to stay, she wandered the palace grounds unopposed and eventually into the palace itself, the loud clopping of her hooves echoing in the cavernous meeting hall just inside of the main door. Two big palace guards were with her at all times and kept close watch on her, and she ignored them as best she could. She was not sure if they were there to protect her or keep her from getting into mischief, but this did not concern her. Ever present in her thoughts was her freedom, and seeing her Vinton again. Also present was the immanent attack by her dear friend Ralligor, and what she was going to do when he did so. There was her word to keep, but Ralligor would likely not listen, and he was sure to kill Nemlivv and anyone else who tried to stop him from taking her. And that was something she did not want.

Leaving the palace again, she led her guards on a slow pursuit of her through the heart of Nemlivv's flower beds. At one point she thought about running from them to see if they would chase her.

Many soldiers on horseback, about twenty or so, charged to the gate and she turned to see what was causing the commotion.

They lined up on both sides of the gate, ten on one side and ten on the other, and they all faced each other from across the path that led to the palace.

Shahly leaned her head.

Six riders began to file into the gate in twos. They were led by two large men, one with long brown hair and a darker skinned man with long black hair. They were close to the same size, though the brown haired man seemed a little taller and a little bulkier. They were similarly dressed in white swordsman's shirts and high black boots. The black haired fellow wore an assortment of rings and a gold chain around his neck. Mounted on the saddle behind the bigger brown haired man was a menacing double bladed battle axe, one that he looked like he could wield with ease judging from the size of his arms.

Behind them were two women, a tall one with very long auburn hair and wearing a tan shirt and black trousers and a much smaller woman, a younger woman, with long brown hair, a white shirt with full sleeves and red trousers. Both wore black riding boots, but the smaller of the women more gold ornaments and jewels, rings and bracelets, long earrings and a diamond necklace.

Behind the women were two more, a tall, muscular woman with long blond hair that was restrained behind her head and a big fellow with short brown hair. Both were dressed in cleaned and oiled battle armor with form fitting plates over chests, arms and legs. Neither wore helmets and both carried broadsword, dagger and sword breaker.

Shahly cantered forward a few steps and then stopped again, studying them closer, and her eyes widened as she recognized the big man at the front of the procession, and the tall auburn haired woman, and the shorter woman beside her. Backing away a few steps, she watched them ride toward the palace, barely noticing the greeting party of well dressed soldiers that exited the palace to meet them.

Turning her attention upward, Shahly's eyes danced around the sky in the expectation of seeing a huge black dragon flying over to attack the castle, but he was not there.

Looking back to the procession, the black haired rider caught her eye. She knew most of them, even the Zondaen soldier at the rear, but this fellow... She did not recognize him, and yet he seemed familiar. As they drew closer, perhaps only fifteen paces or so, his eyes shifted to her, his brow lifting slightly and arching in the center. He was trying hard to suppress the elation he felt, an elation that was far stronger than that felt by the others who saw her.

Curiosity urged her to follow them, to find out more about the black haired one and to see those she knew, but Ralligor's warning about telling Nemlivv too much was still fresh in her mind.

Reluctantly, the black haired fellow tore his gaze from her, directing his eyes forward.

As Nemlivv's greeting party came out of the palace to extend the sorcerer's salutations, she took the opportunity of the black haired man's distraction to reach out to him with her essence and peer into his thoughts. Raising her head a little, her eyes narrowed as the essence she touched was not human. She gasped suddenly, her eyes widening as she backed away a few steps.

The essence she touched was unicorn!

Shahly raised her head and met his eyes as he glanced back at her again, and with that glance she knew him. He had come as promised, and she knew the rest of them were there to rescue her. She knew if she gave them away that the consequences would be horrible, and she could not allow that, so she would not reveal that she knew them.

Turning away, she paced toward one of the flower beds and sniffed at the flowers, then nibbled on one as she glanced toward the humans and her stallion now in human form. Her young mind was already formulating a plan, and Ralligor himself was unknowingly guiding her through all of his advice.

"I know they mean well, Precious One," she said, "but we have to protect them." She loosed a heavy breath. "I must keep my word to Nemlivv as well. This will be very hard, but it is something that must be done. I can't let them be in danger. I can't."

CHAPTER 34

Nemlivv's greeting hall was everything they expected and his guests looked around with a little awe at the ornate decorations and bright colors of this cavernous room as they awaited the arrival of the sorcerer.

And Nemlivv watched them from a slit in a doorway on the other end. Looking over his shoulder to one of the two guards with him, he ordered, "See to it that Prince Arden and his party do not come this way. Ask him if he would like to view the vineyard on the north side of the castle and take him there."

The guard nodded and hurried about his task.

Deshett's eyes narrowed as she glanced at her sorcery master, but she wisely said nothing. This was more a learning experience to her and she would not let it go to waste.

Drawing another breath, Nemlivv raised his chin and collected himself for the meeting ahead of him. Dressed in his formals, a heavy red shirt with gold embroidery, black trousers and high black boots with ceremonial gold greaves, he was not comfortable and hoped his unexpected guests would not pick up on this. Looking to his apprentice, who wore a black hooded cape, with the hood down, and a leather bodice over a long white shirt and her ankle high black boots, he warned, "I want you on your best behavior, Deshett. This could be very delicate."

"I am at your command, Magister," she insisted, "and all that I am is at your disposal. I shall do my best to ensure that all goes in your favor."

He nodded. "There are three rather big fellows out there, no doubt from Enulam, and three tall, well made women who appear to be from Zondae. Stay clear of the Zondaens and focus your efforts on the men."

"I will, my Lord."

"You prepared everything according to my commands?"

"I did, my Lord."

"Good." He drew another deep breath and pushed the door open.

As he neared his guests, he offered a big smile and opened his arms toward them, greeting, "I bid you welcome to Ravenhold

Castle. I am Lord Nemlivv."

Chail turned toward him first, his features like stone as he stepped toward the sorcerer and extended his hand. "Thank you for granting us an audience, Lord Nemlivv. I am Prince Chail." When he shook the sorcerer's hand, he did so very firmly, just to subtly exert his power. Turning, he extended a hand to the people behind him and introduced, "I bring with me Princess Le'ell of Zondae, Princess Faelon of Caipiervell, and, uh..."

Vinton stepped forward and extended his hand to the sorcerer, giving the appearance of someone who had done so hundreds of times. "I am an emissary from the Southlands and my name is Vinton."

Nemlivv took his hand and nodded. "From the Southlands, you say?"

Vinton raised his brow. "Have you ever heard of Rhine Keep?" When the sorcerer shook his head, he just smiled. "I've observed that nobody this far north has. Prince Chail mentioned that he was coming this way while I visited with him and I thought I would extend a hand in friendship here as well. I must say it's been quite a profitable journey." He looked back to Faelon and continued, "I've already struck some quick friendships at Caipiervell and my people have an invitation to return there."

Faelon smiled.

"Yes," Nemlivv recalled, massaging a hand that had been squeezed too hard one time too many. "We had some unpleasantness there that I had hoped to resolve."

Le'ell folded her arms and agreed, "Yes, that's one reason we're here."

Chail loudly cleared his throat and shot her an impatient look.

"Then we should discuss it," Nemlivv announced. "But, let's retire to someplace that is more comfortable." He half turned and extended his hand to the double doors that stood open. "This way, my guests. Enjoy my hospitality."

Deshett found herself consumed with Vinton and could not take her eyes from him. She reasoned quickly that he must be taken by one of the other women there, so she made herself look to Prince Chail, who was bigger and also very attractive, and she offered him a friendly smile as she approached and took his arm.

Le'ell grasped his shoulder and turned him, forcing herself between her prince and this sorcerer's apprentice as she slipped her hand around his thick upper arm. She said nothing. Her venomous eyes said it all.

Princess Audrell had been one matter as she was small, frail looking and Deshett knew she could be intimidated. This tall, well made Zondaen was a whole different story. She had a look about her that told Deshett quickly that this woman was not easily intimidated, and as she backed away from her, she reasoned that even a dragon would have its hands full with her.

Returning her gaze to Vinton, she found herself hesitant as she looked to the other Zondaen, an even bigger woman, and worried about approaching the striking black haired Rhine Keep Emissary for fear of her. But, at glance and silent command of her *Magister,* she approached him anyway and bowed her head to him, asking as the rest of the precession went toward the doors, "May I welcome you, my Lord?"

Vinton was not sure what to do, but he nodded and offered her a friendly smile, and allowed her to take his arm.

Behind him, Faelon covered her mouth and tried not to giggle as she watched this woman trying to flirt with a man who simply was not interested, and she would let her. When Vinton glanced over his shoulder at her, she waggled her fingers at him to wish him luck.

In short order, they were all seated at Nemlivv's dining table, enjoying a midday meal of several kinds of meat, fruits, vegetables and cheese. Four servants stood by with flasks of wine to refill goblets when they were low. Le'ell sat very close to Chail, her narrow eyes finding Deshett often, as she sat right across from her beside Vinton. As small talk was exchanged, she occasionally took a grape or some small food like that to offer him, and he would take it from her fingers with his mouth each time as a unicorn would do. Sitting beside Le'ell, Princess Faelon felt the security of her Zondaen bodyguard, Pa'lesh, sitting right across from her, right beside Vinton. Nemlivv, of course, sat at the head of the table with Pa'lesh on one side and Faelon on the other.

Pleasantries continued for some time, and as the meal ended,

Nemlivv's eyes found Princess Faelon yet again. He wiped his mouth with his napkin and laid it back in his lap, then he pushed his plate away from him and folded his hands on the table. "Princess Faelon of Caipiervell."

She looked to him and took another sip of her wine before replying, "Lord Nemlivv of Ravenhold."

He drew and vented a deep breath. "I would like to get this unpleasantness out of the way. Earlier this summer my troops were dispatched to defend your kingdom, and I only recently found out that I was going to the aid of the wrong man. I was told by his messengers that... Well, it isn't important. I wanted an alliance with your kingdom and I did not confirm his story before going to his aid, and for that I must apologize."

Ever the young diplomat, she reached to him and grasped his folded hands, a little smile on her lips as she said, "It was a troublesome time for us all. I came here to end any hostility and cultivate a friendship, not to demand apologies for the past. It is forgotten, my Lord, but if you insist on this apology, I shall graciously and humbly accept."

He smiled back. "I am glad to see the right person is finally on the throne of your kingdom, and you have started a friendship between us already." He took her hand and raised it to his mouth, kissing her fingers ever so gently. "You honor me with your very presence, my Princess."

She blushed a little and nodded to him. "The honor is mine, my Lord."

Turning his eyes to Chail, Nemlivv raised his chin and continued, "I am hoping you will accept the same, Prince Chail, Princess Le'ell."

Raising his goblet to his host, Chail insisted, "We are all here to cultivate that same friendship, Lord Nemlivv. I would be honored to be named among those in your favor."

"The honor would be mine, my Prince. When you return to your people, you may tell them that Ravenhold Castle extends a hand of friendship from across the mountains." Looking to Vinton, he added, "That same hand would be extended to the nobles of Rhine Keep."

Vinton nodded to him and accepted, "That hand would be graciously received, Lord Nemlivv." He drank with Chail and his host, then he set his goblet down, his eyes on it as, he observed, "I noticed that you have a unicorn wandering about your gardens." When all fell silent, Vinton coolly turned his eyes to Nemlivv's.

Tension thickened the very air all around.

Nemlivv looked over his shoulder and a servant was there in an instant to fill his goblet. Turning his eyes back to Vinton's, he asked, "Have you seen a unicorn before?"

"Many times," Vinton replied. "But, I've never heard of one seeking refuge within the walls of a castle before."

"That one has my protection for as long as she desires it," Nemlivv informed straightly, his eyes on his goblet.

With a slight nod, Vinton asked, "What would a unicorn seek protection from?"

The sorcerer's eyes slowly turned to Vinton's, stern eyes that bored into him, and he replied, "Protection from men."

Vinton's head rocked back a little. "Really. Men hunt unicorns?"

"Some do, Emissary, and some creatures do as well. I suppose you are aware that dragons will hunt them?"

"I've heard something about that," Vinton replied with a sigh. "I'd also heard that unicorns are deadly to dragons. It never made sense to me that dragons would hunt something that could kill them."

Nemlivv shrugged. "I've recently discovered that many things don't make sense. Where is your kingdom again?"

"Rhine Keep?" Vinton glanced at Le'ell, but looked anything but nervous. "My home is south and west of Zondae, and rather close to the lair of the Tyrant."

"And how do you keep his ire away from you?"

"Very simple. We do not have high turrets or a large, sprawling castle, no roads toward his lair or directly toward Trostan, and it helps that our home blends into the forest and cannot be seen easily from above. We don't attract his attention and he has no reason to show us his teeth."

"Interesting."

Vinton took another sip of his wine. "We don't even think about him most of the time. Being nearly invisible is just a way a life. Invading armies will not stray too close because of him so he unwittingly protects us from many such threats."

"And you would reach out for allies in the north."

"Always looking for friends," Vinton sighed. "You must bear in mind that large scale farming is not such a good idea with dragons about."

"More dragons than just the Tyrant?"

"Another is actually much closer. She is not quite as large and really the biggest threat from her is the raiding of sheep herds."

Nemlivv smiled slightly. "A small sacrifice for the protection of dragons."

"Quite true."

Le'ell and Chail slowly looked to each other, both astounded at the unicorn's tact and talent at making conversation, especially out of his element so. Both raising their goblets to their mouths, they looked back to the two as they conversed.

Smiling slightly, Nemlivv suggested, "Perhaps someday your king will grace Ravenhold with his presence."

"Perhaps," Vinton sighed, then he smiled a little himself. "We don't have a king, per say. The wisest of us make up a governing council that our people turn to in times of need."

"No reigning monarch. No nobles. Sounds like a dangerous way of life."

Vinton recognized that this sorcerer was probing him for weakness and he casually turned his eyes to his wine, swirling it unconsciously as he explained, "It has worked for many, many generations, and everyone from my home is responsible for its defense. An invading army that is large enough to succeed against us would attract the unwanted attention of the local dragons." His eyes were almost challenging as he turned them back to Nemlivv. "And there is no army big enough to stand against the Tyrant for more than an hour."

With a slight nod, the sorcerer raised his brow and asked, "And what of trade?"

A smile touched Vinton's lips again. "We trade with friends, with those we can trust. If you truly have the trust of a unicorn, then you sound like someone I would trust." He held his goblet to the sorcerer, who responded in kind, and they both drank.

"Your home sounds beautiful," Deshett said dreamily.

Vinton looked to her and offered, "Thank you. And might I

say I see much beauty here at Ravenhold."

She smiled at him and her hand found his thigh under the table. "I would gladly show you all of the beauty here if you like, my Lord."

Faelon knew what was happening and she raised a hand to her mouth, trying hard not to giggle, but trying unsuccessfully.

Nemlivv's eyes found her and he asked, "Something funny, Princess."

Tears poured from her eyes and she shook her head, finally managing, "No. I..." She wiped her eyes. "I just thought of something humorous."

Looking to the sorcerer, Vinton suggested, "Perhaps you will show us your unicorn, Lord Nemlivv."

Nodding to him, the sorcerer agreed, "I would be honored, assuming she wishes to be shown. We can go right after dinner." His eyes slid to Faelon and he informed, "Many of the men you did battle with a couple of months ago swore on their lives that you rode into battle on a big bay unicorn."

She looked to him and raised her brow.

He went on, "They say he was a big beast, a blood bay with a black mane."

Faelon raised her napkin to her mouth and giggled again, then she looked to Prince Chail and declared, "You were right!"

Nemlivv looked to the big Enulam Prince. "Right about what?"

He took a sip from his goblet before answering, "The headpiece on her horse has a long copper spiral horn like a unicorn. I told her that it would make people think she was riding one."

Hesitantly, Nemlivv nodded.

Princess Faelon took his arm and assured, "What unicorn would let a girl ride him into battle with her army? Besides, all unicorns are white. Everyone knows that."

"I suppose," he agreed. "Would you like to see her as well, Princess?"

Faelon gasped and grasped her chest, staring back at the sorcerer as she breathed, "Really? I can go see her, too?"

"Of course," he confirmed. "I would not deny you the opportunity to see such a magical creature."

She reached to him again, taking his hand. "Oh, Lord Nemlivv. I would love that! Thank you so much!"

***

Nemlivv did not want his prize under too much stress, so he would only allow his guests to visit her one at a time, and only for as long as she would tolerate them. Faelon, who was offered the first visit, could not seem to catch her breath and asked that she be allowed to wait until she could calm herself.

So, it was Vinton who was the first to approach her.

They found her right outside the gate, nibbling on some of the grain stalks that grew to the top of a human's waist.

Vinton's heart pounded as he approached her with slow, soft steps. His eyes were consumed by her and he swallowed hard as he stopped only three paces away. He was behind her, but enough to her side to see her absently grazing away. After so many days apart, he did not know what to say to her, or where to even begin. He knew he had to rein in his elation, lest he give them away.

Her ear twitched toward him and she raised her head, taking her time to chew a mouthful of grain before asking, "Do I know you?"

He dared to take another step closer, his eyes fixed on her as he replied, "You know who I was, and who I am still inside."

"I don't recognize you."

"I recognize you."

Her eyes shifted toward him and she turned her head ever so slightly. "So you think you know me."

"Better than I know myself," he said softly.

Shahly finally half turned and looked at him. "Really."

He nodded, tears glossing his eyes.

"And how would I know you?" she pressed. "Who am I that you think you know?"

Vinton raised his chin, struggling just to speak, but finally he managed, "You are the strongest half of my heart."

Shahly blinked, then looked back to the grass and nibbled some of the grain from the top of it. "I don't remember mating myself to a human."

His lips tightened and his jaw shook a little.

Looking back to him, she asked, "Sound familiar?"

Vinton's mouth opened slowly, slightly.

"Two hearts are two hearts," she whickered softly in the unicorn's language.

"Until they become one," he finished in a slight voice.

She chewed a few seconds more, and finally a smile touched her. "You really thought I would not recognize you, Vinton?"

He finally smiled, just a little. "I was hoping you would, Love."

"You should have recognized me," she scolded playfully. "Remember when I came to *you* in human form?"

"I remember," he confirmed, barely over a whisper.

Her ears lowered and she took on a look of despair. "I wish I could go to you right now, but I can't."

"I know," he whispered to her. "I want the same thing."

She nodded subtly. Looking away, she drew a hard breath and softly said, "Vinton, I know why you are here, but... I have to stay now."

He dared to take another step toward her. "Shahly, what are you saying?"

"I had to promise," she told him with tears in her eyes. "It was the only way."

"You can't," he insisted through clenched teeth.

She turned away from him. "Vinton, it was the only way. If not me, then he was going to go after another unicorn. He... He already had one selected and I couldn't—"

"Shahly," Vinton hissed, barely getting control of himself. Closing his eyes, he vented a deep breath and shook his head. "No, Shahly. You aren't staying. We are getting you out of here."

"I can't go," She insisted.

"Do you think Ralligor will accept that?" Vinton asked in a low voice.

"He has to. If I go he will find another unicorn to take my place."

"Shahly, we're getting you—"

"Vinton, he'll come after you!" she cried. "If I leave, he'll take you. I could never live with you being a prisoner again. I couldn't! Please understand. I had to promise him that I would never ever leave and I have to keep my word to him."

Raising his chin, Vinton finally folded his arms and assured, "We aren't just leaving you here. If Nemlivv means to come for me, then let him. He has meddled with forces he should have let sleep, and now it is time for him to face them."

"I don't want anyone to get hurt," she whispered.

"I know you don't, Love, but your captor may have made that an inevitability. Ralligor will not accept that you can't leave because he will just take another unicorn." Looking into the forest, he continued, "He intends to stop this sorcerer once and for all."

"I'm not the first unicorn he's taken, Vinton," she informed grimly. "Many seasons ago he had Bexton here."

Vinton's eyes snapped back to her.

Despair and pity were in her eyes. "He has the power to take the strongest of unicorns. No unicorn will be safe if I leave. I had to promise that I would stay forever, that I would break off ties to everyone, that means the herd, my friends, Ralligor..." She looked away. "Even you, my Love."

He took another step toward her, raising a hand to her as he breathed, "Shahly."

Tightly closing her eyes, she ordered, "Just go. Please, leave here forever and forget that you ever knew me."

Tears filled his eyes as he watched her turn and bolt to the tree line, and he slowly shook his head, whispering, "How could I ever forget you? How can I live with half a heart?"

CHAPTER 35

Little grew on a hill of dark stone not far away from their camp. This area was dark for midday and rarely received sunlight as it was on the north side of the Dark Mountains, but Jekkon took little notice. He stormed to the top of the little hill, one dotted with clumps of brush, then he strode with heavy steps down the other side, toward the trees.

He found what remained of a fallen tree at the bottom of the hill and turned to sit down on it. His elbow on his knee and his chin in his palm, his bushy brow was held low as he thought about his woes as best he could. Not thinking about the fragrant blooms of some of the trees around him or the cool breeze that blew off of the mountains, Jekkon found himself consumed with the problem at hand, and how to address it.

His eyes shifted about, then he raised his head and looked over his shoulder.

The white unicorn stared back at him from a few paces away, her blue eyes sparkling in the sunlight at the edge of the trees.

"Horsey?" he greeted hesitantly.

She paced toward him, raising her head as she asked, "Why are you so far north? I thought you were going to remain in the village."

"I'm with others," he replied, turning toward her on the log. "Looking for you."

She drew her head back. "Looking for me?"

"Took horsey," he tried to explain. "We go and get her." He slammed his fist into his palm. "Going to have to fight."

The unicorn leaned her head. "Took the horsey? Where did they take the horsey?"

His eyes danced about as he tried to recall, and finally he replied, "Ravenhold. Place is called Ravenhold. North somewhere."

Her gaze shifted that way. "I see. When do you think you will arrive to rescue this horsey?"

"Tomorrow, think," he answered.

Looking back to him, she leaned her head and asked, "Is that what you're upset about?"

Jekkon shook his head. "No. Found Janees."

Her ears swiveled toward him. "I thought that would make you happy."

He drew a breath and turned his eyes down. "Don't know. Janees will leave again. Did before."

"I don't think she will ever want to leave you," the unicorn corrected. "Sometimes destinies call and they must be answered."

"Can't go with her," he grumbled.

"If you did, I think Dorell would be lonely without you."

Jekkon offered her a shrug.

She took another step to him and nuzzled the side of his neck, and he giggled.

"People you know will come into your life and leave," she explained, "just as I must. But I know you, and so does Janees. You will always be in her heart and in mine, and when you least expect it, you will see us again."

"Promise?" he asked softly.

"Yes, Jekkon. I promise." Her head jerked up and she took a few steps back, looking up the hill. "Someone's coming and I must go. When your Janees finds you again, just remember how you love her and how she loves you. That's all that matters." She turned quickly and bolted back into the forest.

Jekkon stood and shouted, "Where going?"

"Ravenhold," the unicorn replied from a distance.

He stared after her for a moment, then he leaned his head and scratched his belly. Finally hearing the footsteps coming up on him, he turned around and saw Dorell and Janees walking toward him from the top of the hill, walking side by side. Turning that way, he lumbered toward them and they stopped as he reached them, and as he picked the sorceress up and pulled her to him she barked a scream and grasped at his big arms. Jekkon hugged her as tightly as he dared, and he smiled. "Good to see you. Missed you."

The girl was confused and patted his shoulders, assuring, "I missed you too. You seemed upset a while ago."

"Better now," he said straightly, putting her gently back down. "Horsey and me found Dorell. Horsey says stay with Dorell and you will visit. You will visit, right?"

Janees glanced at Dorell, then nodded to the huge boy and assured, "Of course I will, every chance I get."

Jekkon rammed his fist into his chest a couple of times, raising his chin as he growled, "I take care of Dorell and village. I work hard and protect them. I'm important now."

Looking to Dorell again, the sorceress raised her brow as if looking for confirmation of this, and she smiled when the other girl nodded. She turned her eyes back to the huge boy, smiling even as tears blurred her vision. "Jekkon, that's great. I'm very proud of you. I always knew that you would mean a great deal to many people."

"Still to you?" he asked.

"You mean everything to me," she confirmed. "One day, when I am a powerful sorceress, perhaps you and I can protect the land from the bad people."

He slammed his fist hard into his chest and assured, "I will be ready!"

Rawl emerged from the trees behind him and countered, "You look ready now, my boy." When the huge boy turned to him, he offered a smile and a nod. "You have great potential, lad, and I feel the eyes of the Fates on you. But now, we are ready to break camp and be on our way. Perhaps you will do me the honor of giving me an audience with Janees here and escort this pretty young lady back to the others."

Jekkon raised his chin, eying the sorcerer with the authority befitting his size, and he nodded. "I take Dorell back. You follow when done." When the sorcerer nodded back at him, he took the girl's hand and lumbered back up the hill with her.

Rawl folded his arms as he watched the ogre-boy disappear with the maiden he protected. "Now, what was so horrible about that?"

"He seemed really hurt at first," she informed, also watching him disappear over the hill. "It broke my heart."

"Your heart will mend," he assured. "So, are you still determined to learn from me?"

"Yes, *Magister*, I am."

"Then there is something for you to do, something very important."

"What is that, *Magister?*"

His eyes slid to her. "You made a challenge, and it is time for you to fulfill that challenge."

Distress took her features and she turned her wide eyes away from him. "You... You mean I have to face Nemlivv again? I can't!"

"You've learned a great deal from me, child, and now it's time to put it to use. Until you've overcome your fear of him and this defeat he dealt you, you will never advance further, and you'll learn no more from me."

Her breath came with some difficulty, her eyes dancing about as she nervously tried to respond.

"Confidence is your greatest tool here, Janees," he informed straightly. "Believe in your heart that you will prevail and nothing can stop you. Visualize what must happen and fight through your enemy, and never underestimate him."

"Are you sure I'm ready?" she breathed.

"Would I send you if I thought you weren't?" he countered. "This is the first of many tests you will face, and they don't get easier."

She nodded, and felt her knees begin to shake. "He told me that when sorcerers duel then one must die."

"Then if you're still alive, your duel is not over. It is time to finish it."

"Is it true? That one must die when sorcerers duel?"

Rawl laughed softly and took her under his arm, leading her back up the hill. "I have fought many a duel against other sorcerers, little girl, and not all of them are dead. One can fight to the death, of course, but what is the use in that?"

"Then why did he tell me that?"

"To frighten you. Come along and let me show you some things that will be useful in this duel."

She leaned into him, and nervously turned her eyes up to his. "What if he beats me again? What if I can't defeat him? Will you be there to help me?"

"There's no way I can be," he informed almost coldly. "This will be your battle and yours alone, and you should learn all you can from it. Just know that if you fail me then I will be finished with you and you'll have no chance to be my apprentice at all."

Nodding, she looked to the path before them and softly said, I understand, *Magister.*"

CHAPTER 36

The spacious room on the third level of Ravenhold Castle was one that was clearly meant to impress guests. It was decorated with ornate tapestries, large, wooden framed windows that stood open to allow the cool northern breeze to blow in. The furnishings were of the best craftsmanship and contributions from many artisans were everywhere, including busts of heroes long dead.

Le'ell stood beside Chail at one of the windows, watching Vinton pace back and forth with his gaze trained on the red and gold carpet before him. Pa'lesh stood beside the door, also watching him, and Faelon was huddled on a loveseat that was just down the wall from the door as she stared into the clear glass of wine she held. No one was speaking and the tension in the room was almost unbearable for most, and reaching its apex for one.

Looking to the table beside the loveseat, Princess Faelon gingerly set her glass down and then turned her attention to Vinton, and she assured, "This isn't over."

"Shahly would think otherwise," he grumbled, still pacing.

Faelon stood and strode to him, and when he turned she blocked his path and seized his shoulders. "No, it isn't!"

"You heard what she said. She's given her word to him and she has asked us to leave forever. She is unicorn and must keep her word even to her captor and there is nothing any of us can do to change that. That finalizes things."

Reaching up to his face, the young Princess gently framed his cheeks with her hands, shaking her head as she insisted, "No, Vinton. Nothing is finalized. Don't you understand? She's lost hope, but she still wants you to rescue her. You must have hope for her now."

He just stared down into her eyes for a time, then he looked aside as Pa'lesh grasped his shoulder.

The big Zondaen raised her chin as she met his eyes and assured, "None of us are going to give up, my friend. If I have to tear this place down stone by stone to get her out of here then I'll do it."

"He must release her," Vinton informed softly. "Her promise to him is binding even if he should lose this battle you are all planning."

Chail asked from the window, "Is this promise binding even in death?" When all eyes snapped to him, he continued, "We all know that the black dragon out there means to kill him and take her by force. In fact, I think he prefers it that way."

Vinton pulled away from Faelon and strode toward the other window. Once there, he grasped the wooden window sill and stared blankly out toward the forest, and finally he said, "The coming bloodshed is not something she could live with. I know I couldn't."

Faelon approached from behind him and wrapped her arms around his waist, laying her cheek between his broad shoulders and into the thick of that long black mane of hair as she hugged him as tightly as she could. "We'll think of something, Vinton. I promise we will get her out of here."

He nodded, lost in his thoughts. Venting a deep breath, he shook his head and complained, "I don't understand why you humans can't be more alike. You have those who are savage warriors with a bloodlust for battle, others who are evil enough to kidnap an innocent unicorn, and still others with compassion that makes you seem more unicorn than human." He grasped her hand, squeezing as hard as he dared as he finished, "You, my friends, have helped make this whole ordeal bearable, and I thank you for that."

Hugging him a little tighter, Faelon assured, "We shall always. I am yours, Vinton. I always will be."

A tear slipped from his eye and he nodded.

A knock on the door sent everyone's attention that way.

It opened and Nemlivv slipped in, closing the door behind him as he asked, "Am I disturbing you?"

"Not at all," Faelon assured as she approached him. "We have been taking in the beauty of your castle. I'm frankly a little jealous and I mean to plant hundreds of flowers when I get back to Caipiervell."

He offered her a smile and a nod, then he looked around to the others as they slowly approached him, all but Le'ell and Chail, who stood by the window, Le'ell in front of the big prince with his arms wrapped around her waist.

The sorcerer folded his arms, his expression a little less pleasant as he said, "I'm glad that you are taking in the beauty of Ravenhold. However, that is all you will be taking today." He saw them becoming uneasy and looked down into Princess Faelon's wide eyes. "Yes, I know why you are all really here, and I can assure you your plan has already failed."

Chail pushed off of the window sill and strode toward him behind Le'ell, who slowly crossed her arm over her body to grasp the hilt of her dagger. Pa'lesh also strode to him, but knew she needed no weapon in her hand.

Still holding his Faelon's gaze with his own, he slowly raised a hand before him and it burst into flames.

The Caipiervell Princess barked a scream and backed away, right into Vinton.

"Before you think too hard about doing anything foolish," the sorcerer warned, "I should tell you that I can kill everyone in this room with a thought, and if you do manage to get through me then you'll be dealing with the twenty of my soldiers who await you outside this door."

Pa'lesh stopped only a pace away from him and set her hands on her hips, her eyes boring into him. "Twenty, huh? They might keep me busy for a moment but you didn't bring any for Prince Chail to kill." When he turned his gaze on her, her eyes narrowed and she snarled, "I can snap your neck before you can get that thought out, little man."

He raised his chin slightly and a translucent yellow sphere exploded from the middle of his body, slamming into everyone with enough force to send them staggering backward a few steps. As they recovered their balance, he warned, "You should be careful about threatening a sorcerer, Zondaen. Very careful." His attention shifted to Vinton and he raised his brow. "I know who you really are as well, and what you really are. You did very well during our oratory sparring and anyone else would have been fooled by you. My compliments there, Vinton." When Vinton's eyes widened slightly, Nemlivv nodded and assured, "Yes, I know all about you. I've been expecting you, but you did surprise me showing up here in human form."

Vinton gently moved Faelon aside and closed the three paces

between him and the sorcerer, pleading, "Let her go and take me in her place. I will offer you that."

"I'm afraid that's impossible," the sorcerer declined. "You see, we are both bound by promises we made. She stays of her own will and all unicorns everywhere will be left where they are."

His hands clenching into tight fists, Vinton insisted through clenched teeth, "She cannot live so long a prisoner. She'll die! You *have* to let her go!"

"Let her go to what?" Nemlivv shouted. "Unicorn hunters who will eventually take you all? Dragons who would kill her on sight? What about all of the other dangers your kind face? She is safe from all of that here!"

"She is of the forest, sorcerer, and the forest is where she should be."

"This castle is surrounded by forest." Nemlivv turned away, back toward the door, and as he pulled it open he insisted, "You all must leave at once. Forgive my lack of hospitality, but I have much to attend to. You may come and see her again another time, but for now the guards will escort you to the gate."

As the sorcerer slammed the door behind him, silence took its icy grip on the room once again.

A moment passed, and Vinton turned his eyes down, slowly shaking his head as he softly said, "She cannot live long a prisoner. He just does not understand."

"She won't live a prisoner long," Pa'lesh insisted, her eyes narrowing. "He's going to release her, one way or another."

***

Nemlivv stormed out of the palace on the north side and finally grabbed the arm of a palace guard that he had assigned to his unicorn, demanding, "Where is she?"

The guard snapped to attention and replied, "She ran into the forest after speaking to that big black haired fellow. We were unable to follow her."

"Watch the gates for her return," the sorcerer ordered, "and have me notified as soon as she does." He continued on his way and was stopped by a messenger boy who had darted from the castle.

Turning to the boy, he folded his arms and growled, "What is it?"

Quick to catch his breath, the boy, about a twelve year old who was dressed similarly to the palace guards but wore no armor, snapped to attention and reported, "My Lord, word has come from Darkshadow Castle that *Magister* Coridrov will be arriving within the hour. He insists on a greeting party for him at the northern gate."

A breath growled out of the sorcerer and he shook his head, looking away. After a moment to consider, he ordered, "Have Deshett see to the greeting party and notify me personally when things are in order."

The boy bowed to him and hurried on his way.

Shaking his head, Nemlivv turned back toward the castle and grumbled, "I do not need all of this now."

Inside the palace, he was intercepted by another messenger, one who was about the same age as the first and identically dressed, who turned to meet his pace.

"What is it?" Nemlivv snapped.

"An emissary from Red Stone has arrived," the boy reported.

The sorcerer stopped in his tracks, his eyes forward and blank.

Stopping a pace beyond him, the messenger turned and continued, "He said he would like an audience with you at your earliest convenience to discuss the unicorn. The Crown of Red Stone is supposed to be here before dark."

Nemlivv's head began to throb and he raised a hand to his temple, massaging slowly as he asked, "How many in the Queen's party?"

"I believe the emissary said a garrison," the boy replied.

The sorcerer closed his eyes and drew a breath. Finally, he nodded and ordered, "See to the Emissary's comforts and have the castle steward see to sending a greeting party to meet Queen Hethan. Be sure she is given my apologies for not meeting her personally."

Nodding, the boy turned and hurried to task.

On the way to his study, he was met yet again, this time by a palace guard who summoned, "Lord Nemlivv."

"What!" the sorcerer shouted as he stopped.

"A girl is at the southern gate," the guard reported. "She says she will see you immediately or Ravenhold will be razed from the land forever."

Raising his chin, Nemlivv's eyes narrowed and he asked, "A girl?"

Moments later the sorcerer arrived at his southern gate, hardly believing what he saw as his eyes found a red clad Janees standing fifty paces beyond the gate, her black hood over her head and her cape flapping ever so gently on the wind. He approached slower after he saw her and motioned for his guards to stop at the gate. About five paces away, he stopped and folded his arms, raising his chin as he stared her down.

Slowly, Janees reached to the hood that was over her head and slid it back, her eyes locked on his.

They stared at each other for a tense moment.

Finally, he observed, "Well, here we are again, sorceress."

She nodded. "Did you think I would not find you?"

"I'm surprised that you even tried," he countered. "I'm also surprised to see you still alive, to be honest. How did you get away from the dragon?"

"I suppose you can ask him," Janees spat back. "I didn't come here for small talk, Sorcerer. I came here to finish what we started."

He raised his brow.

"If you have the courage," she went on, "then you'll meet where I say tomorrow morning, and if you mean to do battle with me honorably, you'll be alone this time."

Nemlivv folded his arms. "Sorceress, I simply haven't the time to— "

"Two leagues from here," she barked, "on this road. The forest opens and we'll both have ample room to wield the craft."

"And if I choose to fight you now?" he challenged.

Her eyes narrowed. "An hour after sunup. Don't be late, Nemlivv. I don't want to have to come looking for you again." She pulled her hood back over her head and spun around, storming the other direction into the forest.

Nemlivv set his jaw, then he shook his head and grumbled, "I simply haven't the time for this," as he turned back toward the castle. Hesitation found his steps and his brow lowered over his eyes. "Wait a moment. The *craft?*" He looked over his shoulder as she disappeared into the forest and a slight smile found his lips. "So. It would seem that a competent instructor has found you. A pity he lacks the foresight to forbid you from tangling with me again so soon." Shaking his head, he strode back toward the palace, and he summoned his own apprentice in his mind.

As he strode through the palace toward the stairs, Deshett caught up to him and met his pace beside him, asking, "You wanted me, *Magister?*"

His eyes slid to her and he confirmed, "Yes I did, my dear. There is something I want you to do tomorrow, something very important that I think you will really enjoy."

A smile touched her lips as stared back at him.

***

An hour or so later he stood at the window of his study and watched the visitors from the southlands ride slowly away from his castle. They were leaving as requested, but he was sure he had not seen the last of them.

New problems continued to swirl in his mind. Red Stone Castle was coming for his unicorn. His sorcery master, Coridrov, was coming for his unicorn. He could not risk denying either of them, and yet he could not give them what they wanted. Shahly was his unicorn, but more than that, he found that he cared for her, even loved her.

He pushed off of the window sill and turned to his desk, picking up the freshly repaired amulet she had worn. Even with the new emerald sphere in place, he knew he could not hope to match that dragon's power, but perhaps the amulet, intact anew, could do what he wanted it to do, and give his dear unicorn human form. Every particle of him longed to see her so, to have her so, and his heart refused to be denied the one thing in the world he truly wanted. He had quickly fallen in love with her, but it was love for the woman she could be, not the unicorn she was.

Slowly picking the amulet up by the chain, he looked it over at eye level, then he slowly slipped it into his pocket and turned toward the door.

He was a couple of paces away and reaching for the handle when it opened and the old woman strode in, stopping right in front of him. She held a glass orb in her hand, one that had a silver cap over an opening in the top. It was double the size of her fist and filled with a red liquid that he knew to be blood. Even in the light of day and the lamplight coming from the hallway, it was luminescent and he could actually feel the power it held.

Setting his jaw as he stared at the orb, he asked with irritation in his tone, "Why did you need that from her?"

"Come with me," she bade as she turned.

Nemlivv followed her toward the center of the palace and to the stairs that led to the highest tower. With her slow pace, it took them some time to reach the top, but when they did he first noticed that the round room that was eight paces across had been cleared of all but one table made of heavy timbers that had grayed over the seasons and the object made off gold and a mix of jewels that was in the center of it.

The Talisman itself was as long as a man's arm and made of nine golden rings that were in perfect alignment and graduated down from the largest, twice the diameter of a man's head, to the smallest which was only the diameter of a coin. Within the rings were webs of gold that suspended jewels, the largest holding a ruby, the next a diamond, the next a sapphire, then an emerald, and this pattern repeated to the small end of the device. Opposite the smallest ring and suspended within a ring of equal size to the largest was a golden cup about the size of the blood filled orb that the old woman held. The cup itself appeared to be a perfectly formed, semi spherical web of thicker gold wire and was held in place by even thicker gold wire that was pulled taut within the ring. Connected by gold brackets to the cup were two huge gemstones, one an emerald and the other a ruby, and these were in perfect alignment with the center of the cup and the jewels held in the center of the rings. The whole thing was held together by thick gold bands from one end to the other, bands with Latirus words scribed on them. Heavy iron rings were mounted on the sides that connected it on a swivel to the iron and hardwood base.

Nemlivv's eyes cut to the old woman and he asked, "This is what you brought me here to show me? I built the thing."

"And I've given it teeth," she added, gently settling the glass orb of unicorn blood into the cup. With slow movements, she removed the silver cap over the top of the orb and picked up a blue crystal that was suspended by a thin gold chain, then she looked back to him and informed, "I've sent a messenger to summon that dragon you forged such an alliance with."

The sorcerer raised his chin, his eyes widening as he stared back at her.

The old woman continued, "Now you can see what a dragon talisman can do when it is properly made, and with the right material and elements and spells."

"I mean for that dragon to be our ally," he informed harshly. "I have enlisted him to that end."

She laughed and held the blue crystal over the unicorn blood, looking out the window to a dark form in the sky that grew steadily larger. "You'll need no such alliance with him, not after you witness the power you will wield against his kind."

Nemlivv felt a little horrified as he watched the young dragon draw closer to the castle, and he glanced at the old woman several times as she corrected the position of the talisman to take careful aim at him, focusing the ruby on the end on the approaching dragon. He knew he dare not protest, though he found holding his tongue harder and harder as the dragon neared.

Linnduron's approach seemed almost casual. He was flying slowly and in a straight line, making him an easy target for the weapon

Nemlivv shook his head, insisting, "There is no reason to kill the beast."

"Of course there is," she countered. "You must see that this talisman works now, and we must know how well."

As the dragon neared, she made one final adjustment, then she lowered the blue crystal into the unicorn's blood. The blood boiled when it contacted the blue stone and a green glow enveloped the entire vessel. This glow was focused down the talisman and changed shades of green as it shot toward the end, and when it met the ruby at the end of the talisman, it erupted into many arching bolts of green lightning that enveloped a ruby beam that lanced out toward the unsuspecting dragon and slammed into his side right under his left wing. On contact with his skin, the power of the talisman exploded in an emerald flash and the dragon shrieked and floundered, finally turning and stroking his wings in an unsteady retreat. He trailed smoke from his wounded side and shrieked anew as he struggled to stay air born.

Slowly, the old witch turned her eyes to Nemlivv and smiled a wicked smile. "There now. That is how you kill a dragon."

"He flew away," the sorcerer pointed out, his eyes still on the wounded, retreating dragon.

"He'll not go far," the old woman informed. "In short order you'll be joining your brother in the ranks of dragon slayers, and perhaps you'll be the one collecting the bounty on the Desert Lord himself."

Nemlivv turned his eyes down.

"With the blood of a more powerful unicorn," she went on, "You'll be able to drop any dragon in the world, and I think with a little more tinkering this talisman could kill the biggest of them with the one we have."

"You mean the unicorn my *Magister* intends to come and take?" he asked, despair and frustration in his voice.

The old witch recognized that tone and nodded almost reluctantly. "Do you wish for her to stay with you?"

"Of course I do," he snapped.

"Perhaps we will figure something out," she said in a motherly voice. "Perhaps we could even find another for you."

"I want no other. And even if we do convince him not to take her, Red Stone Castle is coming for her as well." He shook his head, closing his eyes as he softly confessed, "I can't let them take her. I can't let anyone take her."

Slowly shaking her head, the old woman observed, "You've let the beast soften your heart, boy. She's made you weak."

He turned away from her, looking out the window as he corrected, "She's shown me strength I'd never even dreamed of, and many things you never did." He looked at her over his shoulder with narrow eyes. "I don't want her bled again."

She countered, "We'll need to take what we can from it before Coridrov comes for it."

"I said no more."

"And what will you do if you don't find another? How will you defend this castle against dragons without a talisman that can actually do something about them?"

He turned fully and reminded, "I have an alliance with Mettegrawr himself, and this— "

"You have that alliance so long as he does not tire of it!" she barked. Huffing a breath as he looked away from her, she sneered, "You are as simple minded as your father."

Nemlivv set his jaw and would not look back at her as he growled, "Perhaps I am. Perhaps that unicorn *has* softened my heart." His shoulders and neck tensed as he finished through bared teeth, "At least I will not end up the bitter, power hungry creature that you've become."

Her eyes flared and she hissed, "Don't forget who has given you life, boy."

"I remember, Mother," he countered, then he turned and strode toward the door as he added, "and I am ashamed of it every moment."

By now his head was throbbing and he massaged his temple to try and alleviate the pain, but to no avail. His chest hurt, tight from frustration. Shahly was *his* unicorn, and he would have no one else take her. No one!

"My Lord," a guard called to him.

Nemlivv stopped and turned an angry gaze to the ceiling as he growled, "What is it?"

Reaching him, the guard reported, "A runner has arrived from the Red Stone garrison. They have been unavoidably delayed and will not arrive until tomorrow near high sun."

Turning his eyes down, the sorcerer nodded as he stared at nothing and finally said, "Thank you." As the guard left, Nemlivv could only see this delay as his first stroke of good fortune for many days and he raised his brow and continued on his way.

Arriving out in the courtyard near the gardens and stable, he saw a group of guards leaving Shahly's stable, and his eyes narrowed. Behind them was that old fellow who was often seen in the company of his mother, and he was carrying that ornate, wooden box with him.

In a fury, he stormed that way, not to confront the guards and the old warlock, but to see his unicorn. *His* unicorn.

He arrived at her stall to see it closed and locked, and her trapped inside once again. She was lying in the hay in the middle of the stall, facing away from him, her head low and her ears drooping. For a long moment he just stared at her, not sure what to think or feel.

She turned her head slightly, her ear swiveling toward him, and finally she spoke. "I did what you wanted. I broke his heart. Perhaps you can rest your suspicions about me now."

He vented a shallow, silent breath and turned his eyes down.

Tears flowed from Shahly's eyes and she looked to the window. "That old woman thinks I should be locked away again, and I've heard people talking. Is it true that Red Stone Castle is coming for me?"

He nodded and softly confirmed, "It's true."

"Then you have protected me from nothing," she informed coldly. "They mean to kill me and use my horn in their talisman to turn on dragons. I saw that you have one also, one that uses my blood to kill."

He slowly turned his eyes to her.

"I know the dragon you hit with it," she went on. "He was fatally hurt, so I guess your talisman works with my help. That dragon had a good heart. I called him my friend, and it was part of me that killed him. I guess now you mean to turn it on the Desert Lord."

"If he attacks here," Nemlivv confirmed, his voice laced with shame.

"He's my friend, too," she said straightly. "I guess the blood they took from me tonight will be turned against him. He's also a dragon with a good heart, not that you care about that. You'll use my blood to kill my dear friend, and then Red Stone will come and take me to my death in their arena, and my horn will be used to kill even more. I wish you hadn't taken me. I wish I still knew nothing of you."

A tear escaped from Nemlivv's eye and he was quick to wipe it away.

"Please go," she asked softly.

He lowered his eyes again, and his gaze found the lock and chain that held the gate to her stall shut. He had no key to that lock and seeing it infuriated him. Reaching to it, he grasped it hard in his fist and it melted and fell to the ground to pool at his feet.

Shahly's ears twitched that way as the gate was opened, but she would not look back at the sorcerer as he entered her stall.

He strode to the far wall where she could see him and sat down, leaning back against the wall as he turned his gaze on her, and his heart grew heavier as she turned away from him again.

A long silence passed between them.

"Promise me something," he finally, softly insisted.

She turned her eyes to him, cruel eyes he had never seen on her before. Clearly she could not believe that he dared to ask anything of her.

Stretching his legs out, he looked down and picked at the hay beside him. "Promise me that you will find a day in the spring to come visit me. Just one day every season so that I'll know you are well. It is the last thing I will ever ask of you, dear unicorn."

Shahly slowly raised her head, her ears perking up as her eyes widened.

He would not look her way and just picked at the straw as he continued, "The wall I'm leaning against here will seem to fade. Just walk through it early in the morning before the sun and go directly to the castle wall across the compound. You will be able to see through it and walk right through it as well, then disappear into the forest."

Barely believing what she heard, she gasped, "You are releasing me?"

Hesitantly, he nodded. "Yes, dear unicorn, but only…" He shook his head. "You are free, Shahly. If you make me that promise or not, you are free."

She just stared at him for a moment, not sure if she should believe him or not, and finally she asked, "And Vinton?"

He smiled slightly, his eyes still on the straw he picked at. "Vinton. Yes, he can visit with you in the spring as well."

Shahly snorted. "That is not what I mean."

"You two belong together," he said straightly. "If you stay, then he must stay, but I promised you that he would never be a prisoner here, but he will be so long as you are, so if I am to keep my promise then you cannot be imprisoned here, either."

Looking to the window, Shahly considered, then she asked, "So, if I make you this promise, I can go? You'll really release me?"

"You are free, dear unicorn, promise to me or not. You are just free as you should always have been."

Her eyes narrowing, the unicorn suspiciously spat, "I think you are trying to trick me."

Nemlivv shook his head, assuring, "No, dear unicorn, not this time." He still would not look her way. "I have nothing left to trick you with. My heart belongs to you now and will no longer allow it."

Daring to peer into his mind and emotions, Shahly found what she sought within him. He was sincere, completely honest and open with her for the first time. She also felt pain from him, despair. One thing was certain, though. He wanted her to be safe. He wanted to protect her, and this was the only way he knew how to do that. In a soft voice befitting her, she asked, "What if Ralligor comes for me anyway?"

"I'll tell him where to find you," he replied straightly.

Shahly looked to the hay he was picking at, his heavy heart weighing itself on hers. Getting to her hooves, she paced over to him and lay back down beside him, and she gently laid her head in his lap and closed her eyes. As he began to gently stroke her head and neck, she whispered to him, "I've always loved the spring, and I think your flowers will be full and beautiful."

He removed the amulet from his pocket and gently slipped it over her nose and she raised her head a little as he put it back where it belonged.

"I wish I could keep you safe," he whispered.

"I know you do," she whispered back, "and you have."

CHAPTER 37

The sun would be down within the hour and eight travelers on horseback happened upon a grim sight just on the other side of the Dark Mountains.

Linnduron had nearly made it home. He lay on a barren piece of ground and from the looks of him and the dark rock and disturbed soil behind him he had landed rather hard. His wings were sprawled and half open, his legs extended on the ground behind him with his tail straight out between them, and his arms were folded under him. His long neck was curled half way and his head lay upright and looking with half open eyes toward his wing.

Jumping down from his horse, the Prince of Enulam sprinted the ten remaining paces to the broken form of the young green dragon, kneeling down beside his head.

"Chail!" Le'ell screamed, horrified that the beast would awaken and eat him.

"It's all right," Vinton assured, dismounting as well. "I know this dragon." He trotted over to the Prince and knelt down beside him, laying his hand on the dragon's neck. "He's cold already." Shaking his head, he went on, "Something doesn't feel right."

Pa'lesh walked around to the dragon's other side and caught a whiff of something, then she reached for his wing which was half outstretched and lifted it up, gasping as she saw his side. "Chail!" she barked. "Come take a look at this!"

Vinton and Chail sprang to their feet and jumped over the dragon's neck, rushing toward her.

Raising his chin as he saw the wound that was burned into the dragon's side, he took the wing from Pa'lesh and moved it over his back.

Approaching the wound which was burned all the way around and left a few ribs exposed, Vinton looked into it with his essence, slowly shaking his head as he found the remnants of what had caused the injury.

Le'ell and Faelon approached, and Faelon drew a gasp and

covered her mouth, her wide eyes locked on the wound.

Shaking her head, the Zondaen Princess asked in disbelief, "What could have done that?"

"Another dragon," was Chail's reply.

"No," Vinton corrected. "No dragon did this." He shook his head. "There is unicorn essence here, Shahly's essence."

"Shahly killed him?" Faelon asked, sounding confused.

"There's no way she could have," Vinton replied, "and yet her essence is here. I don't understand this. She's nowhere near strong enough to do this to a dragon, even if she penetrated his armor with her horn."

Pa'lesh looked to him. "If it wasn't her, then what did this?"

Ralligor landed on the other side of the smaller dragon, his eyes on him as he growled, "A talisman did this, one that used part of Shahly for its power."

He startled everyone and all looked up at him with wide eyes and backed away.

All but Vinton, who turned his eyes up to the dragon's and folded his arms. "Another talisman. Well, we know what he really wanted her for now."

The black dragon's eyes darted to him. "Are you enjoying human form that much, Plow Mule?"

His eyes narrowing, Vinton snapped back, "The amulet was left in Dorell's care so that I would not be discovered."

"But you were anyway," Ralligor observed. "I thought you would be." He looked back to the small dragon. "And then I heard him. He crashed here and was dead before I arrived. I was waiting up in the mountains for whoever did this to follow him and try to finish him off or collect trophies from him."

Pa'lesh looked to Chail and said, "That flash we saw as we were leaving, and that sound that followed it."

He nodded, still staring up at the Desert Lord. "Could have been the cries of this dragon in his death throws."

Ralligor looked over his shoulder and growled through bared teeth. "Very well, Nemlivv of Ravenhold. Now I deal with you personally."

***

They returned to their camp in a pass on the north side of the Dark Mountains. Little vegetation grew here and there were plenty of rocks found to make a fire pit, but finding dry wood turned out to be a chore, which Jekkon was all to glad to take on.

After dark, everyone sat around the fire, staring into the flames as they were all lost in their thoughts.

Finally, Dorell shook her head and mumbled, "I can't believe it ends this way."

Faelon clenched her teeth and looked to Le'ell.

The Zondaen Princess met her eyes and raised her chin. "It doesn't end this way."

Still in human form, Vinton corrected, "We still must follow her wishes, whether Ralligor agrees or not, whether he accepts that or not."

When someone approached from the darkness, walking up behind the Enulam Prince, everyone was on alert and reaching for weapons or ready to spring up and hide.

Stepping into the firelight was a man of average height with long black hair and deeply chiseled features. He was dressed in buckskin and carried a buckskin traveler's bag by a strap over his shoulder. His boots were simple in construction and lightly tanned leather. As he drew closer to the fire, his bronze skin glistened a little in the firelight and his face wore a stone-like expression. He really did not meet anyone's eyes, but he did wave his hand as he approached the Prince, and as Chail moved over closer to Le'ell, he sat down cross legged beside him and took the traveler's bag from his shoulder. Reaching inside, he produced a glazed clay flask that was almost the size of his head with a hand length neck that had some kind of wooden stopper in it. Pulling the stopper with his teeth, he took a gulp from it and handed it to Chail, looking up at him as he nodded.

The Prince hesitantly took the flask and drank a little from it.

"I have enough for everyone," the black haired man informed.

"I expected to see you before now," Chail said straightly.

"It's a long walk from where I was," the black haired man replied. He looked around him, his eyes fixing on Vinton, and he leaned his head. "You look different."

Vinton raised his head. "You know who I am?"

"You're her stallion," the black haired man replied. "I see you went to human form to rescue her. I also see you stay as one of us."

With a little shrug, Vinton said, "The amulet Ralligor gave me to change me to this form has been misplaced." He looked to Dorell and asked, "Did it ever turn up?"

Dorell looked to Pa'lesh, who narrowed her eyes, then she looked back to Vinton and shook her head.

A slight smile brightened the black haired man's features. "I see. Well, I'm sure it will emerge by morning. Try the mead. I have plenty here."

"And Shahly?" Vinton asked.

"We will speak of her," was the black haired man's response. "We must speak of how best to free her."

"She has given her word that she will stay, Traman," the unicorn-man grumbled, looking back into the fire. "We must respect that."

Traman looked to his bag and produced another flask, pulling the stopper out and taking a drink, then he passed it to Faelon, who sat on his other side. "Try that. I think you will enjoy it. Yes, my friend, we must respect her wish and her promise, but we must also respect the spirit of your kind. She must be freed, of his castle and the promise that keeps her prisoner."

Faelon took a sip and coughed, her eyes watering as she strained to say, "Wow! That is stout stuff!"

"Glad you like it," Traman said to her. "He must be convinced to release her if he hasn't been already."

"Who would convince him?" Pa'lesh asked.

He turned his steely eyes to the Zondaen Captain and answered, "You must not underestimate that unicorn. She has ways about one's heart that you cannot realize."

Vinton's eyes locked on him hopefully. "You think she could convince him to release her?"

"If she hasn't already, it is only a matter of time. But time is not working in her favor. Already there are people from Red Stone Castle there to take her, and someone of power has come from the Territhan Valley across the desert to take her as well, and he is of immense power. If he has her, she will be doomed for sure, and he will use her essence to unleash a great evil on the world."

An awful silence gripped the campsite, only broken up by the crackling of the fire.

Vinton shook his head as he stared into the fire. "How can unicorn essence be used for evil? That doesn't make sense."

"Her essence will not serve evil," Traman explained, "it will restore his life, what is left of it. Coridrov lingers somewhere between life and death and must consume the essence of the living to continue to walk among us. He is immensely powerful and cannot be killed by mortal means. It is said that once he consumes the essence of a living unicorn, he will not be tethered to the confines of the dead anymore, he will not have to seek living essence to sustain him, and he will be as immortal as any unicorn."

Vinton set his jaw. "Can a unicorn kill him?"

All eyes snapped to the unicorn-man.

Shaking his head, Traman replied, "I doubt it. Such evil cannot be undone by the pure. Only great power can tear him from the fabric of the living world and send him back to the realm of the dead where he belongs, and if he feeds on your mare's essence, nothing can stop him."

Pa'lesh turned her eyes back to the fire and snarled, "Then we're going to have to keep him from getting her." She looked to Vinton. "My friend, I will personally see to it that she is not taken by him or any other. If they get to her, then it will be through me."

"And me," Le'ell added.

Jekkon slammed his fist into his palm and shouted, "Not get horsey!"

Everyone looked to him, and an elated mumbling of agreement rippled among them all.

Traman raised his chin to the huge boy and ordered, "When it is time to attack, leave that stone in the care of someone you trust."

Dorell, sitting beside the ogre-boy, looked up at him and patted his leg. "I'll watch out for it while you go to free the unicorn."

Looking down at her, Jekkon took her under his arm and pulled her to him, nodding as he agreed, "Dorell will watch."

Pa'lesh stood and stretched. "Okay, people. I'm going to get some sleep. I advise you all to do the same." She looked to

Traman and called, "Hey." When he turned his eyes to her, a third flask of mead in his hands, she informed, "I want to share my bedroll with you tonight."

As she turned and walked toward her tent, Traman took a quick gulp from his flask before handing it off to Chail and standing, and he bade, "Good night, all."

No one else seemed to want to leave the fire or the mead and for some time they passed the flasks in a circle and each took a sip or a gulp, all except for Jekkon who had been told of the evils of spirits from a young age and stubbornly refused his turn at them.

Sometime later they were joined by someone else, whose silent approach sent a start into many of them.

As all eyes turned to him, Leedon offered them a smile and asked, "We are in good spirits tonight?"

"Good as can be expected," Chail assured. "The mead helps with that."

The old wizard sat down beside the Enulam Prince, where Traman had been sitting, and he settled himself down before he spoke. "I know of the woes with our little unicorn. Believe me, there are ways to work around them. When Ralligor attacks then we will have to act quickly to get her out of there."

Vinton grimly asked, "And if she refused to come with us?"

"I don't think it will be a problem, my friend," Leedon assured. He looked around at the group. "I was expecting Traman to be here by now."

Le'ell leaned forward to turn her eyes to him. "He and Pa'lesh have turned in already."

Nodding, the old wizard agreed, "We all probably should. Long day tomorrow."

Chail stood and pulled Le'ell up by the arm. "You heard him, woman."

She turned a sharp look up to him as he led her toward their tent and spat, "Do you mean to handle me so rough tonight, too?"

"Yes I do," was his reply.

Le'ell smiled and wrapped her arm around his. "I was hoping so."

CHAPTER 38

The sun had set and Nemlivv and his mother stood at the gate of the palace wall where he would greet his Magister. They were both dressed formally, as were the guards and all in attendance. His soldiers formed two walls of armed men from the gate to the palace door and more awaited outside the gate, all holding torches to light the way. Also formally dressed in sorcerer's robes similar to Nemlivv's were his apprentices, each standing a pace behind his shoulders.

The precession from Darkshadow Castle was moving slowly. Soldiers on black or dark brown horses escorted a dozen imposing black wagons that were each almost a height and a half tall, twice that long and pulled by eight huge black horses. They were difficult to see in the darkness even though each was lit by two torches at the front, two at the back, and each had stations for four archers on top. The armor worn by all of the soldiers was blackened steel plate that was adorned with brown or black horns along the edges of the shoulders. Helmets bore rows of pointed teeth from above the eyes all the way to the back and covered the entire head of each man. Heavy weapons, long swords, battle axes and halberds hung on the saddles.

Nemlivv drew a deep breath as he watched them approach, raising his chin slightly as the first of the soldiers and wagons stopped only twenty paces away, and the procession stopped behind them.

A door on the wagon opened and a tall, hooded figure in red robes and black boots stepped out, turning to retrieve a chest that was the length of a man's forearm about that square. It was trimmed in gold and held together with black steel strapping and hinges. As the tall figure in red strode to Nemlivv, the embroidery of gold along his robes became visible. These were ancient symbols that Nemlivv had only recently begun to study, but they clearly identified this man as a priest of some long forgotten order.

Stopping only a few paces away, the priest, whose face could not be seen, slowly set the chest down and with both hands opened the top of it. Within was a collection of ancient bones amid white and gray dust, a bleached skull in the middle of it all and tattered black and red fabric among it all. Some kind of gold amulet was half buried in the dust, one with jewels embedded in the gold.

From somewhere near the end of the procession, two soldiers forcibly escorted a man toward them. He was not a large man and was dressed only in the simple trousers of a farmer and appeared to only be in his twenties. Fear was in his eyes as he struggled against the soldiers, though he struggled in vain. As they reached the chest, one of the soldiers forced the man's arm over it.

The priest turned with a dagger and sliced the blade across the man's arm, and he screamed. His blood flowed freely into the chest, onto the bones and the dust within. Smoke began to rise from the bones and the dust, and a small flame burst from one eye socket of the skull.

Knowing what was about to happen, Nemlivv's eyes widened and he drew another breath, his whole body tensing as he watched. His mother smiled slightly in anticipation.

As more blood spilled into the chest flames erupted to consume it, growing higher but they produced no heat.

Terror took the man and he yelled louder and tried to back away, but was held in place by the two soldiers.

The fire from the chest grew higher and a horrible apparition emerged. It was a human skeleton, one that slowly rose from the burning chest to stand. It was enveloped in red flames and as it burned, flesh began to bubble up from the flames to cover the bones. When the man the soldiers were holding screamed in terror, the burning skeletal creature wheeled around, and when it saw him, it grabbed onto his bleeding arm.

The soldiers backed away.

Tortured cries of agony burst from the man as the red flames consumed him. Parts of his body tore away and were sucked into the whirling torrent of fire that was forming the body of the creature from the chest, giving the appearance that his body was liquefying and dripping sideways into the flaming bones. In seconds all of his flesh had been stripped away and all that remained was a bleached skeleton which fell from the flames to the ground, exploding to dust as it hit.

Changing color to almost a brighter red, the flames intensified, and from within them a tall, ominous form stepped from the chest toward Nemlivv and his party, and as he did the flames thinned and died. Dressed in the long robes of a Sorcerer Master that brushed the ground as he walked, he was a head height taller than any other man there. Gold embroidery along the cuffs of the sleeves, around the neck and the edges of the outer robe were Latirus words, spells that helped to sustain him as he walked among the living. He had a thin face that was little more than gray skin pulled over his skull, filled out with very little flesh beneath. Dark gray eyebrows were above his eyes, which were black surrounded by red and were pools of pure evil.

As his *Magister* stopped only two paces away, Nemlivv bowed his head and knelt, and his two remaining apprentices also knelt. The old woman was the only one who dared to step toward him, stopping only an arm's reach away as she bowed her head to him.

Coridrov regarded her coldly, raising his chin as he looked down on her, and finally he ordered in a deep and somehow distant voice, "Look on me, Allishira."

Slowly, she raised her eyes to his, her aged features showing her as completely vulnerable to him, and completely submissive. "Master Coridrov. My heart feels great joy in your presence."

He raised a long fingered hand to her, his gray skin and black fingernails looking as if they belonged on the dead and smelling faintly of death, and as he brushed her cheek with his fingers, fifty seasons of age washed away from her where she was touched.

Closing her eyes, she smiled and leaned into his touch. A shimmering ruby light emanated from beneath his hand to slowly envelope her entire face, and as he cupped her cheek in his ancient hand she looked like a woman who was only twenty seasons old.

Drawing a wistful breath, she whispered, "I have been so long without your touch, my Lord."

He nodded and slowly withdrew his hand, assuring, "You shall have it again at my convenience, slave." His eyes shifted behind her, cruel eyes that locked onto her son and he ordered,

"Rise, my unworthy apprentice." He watched Nemlivv and his students get to their feet and he demanded, "Where is this unicorn you have?"

Raising his chin to meet his Master's eyes, he nervously replied, "She has been put away for the night, *Magister*. I have prepared a ceremony for you at high sun tomorrow so that your rebirth can take place with the sun at its apex."

Coridrov's eyes narrowed. "I would have the unicorn now."

Nemlivv dared to take another step toward the undead sorcerer master. "*Magister*, please. I have made great plans and arrangements. Your rebirth should be witnessed by thousands and with great ceremony. It is something I have always wanted to give you. I beg you, allow me to return the kindness you have bestowed upon me with so many seasons of your teachings."

The ancient sorcerer's features were as stone as he corrected, "That was more charity than kindness, Nemlivv." He looked away and drew a long breath, then he looked to Allishira and asked, "Your thoughts on your son's ceremony?"

With the eyes of a very young woman, she gave Nemlivv a long look, then she turned her eyes back to the ancient sorcerer and replied, "I think the boy's heart is in the right place, my Lord, and he is right. Your rebirth should be with great ceremony."

Coridrov stared down at her for a long moment, then he drew another breath and conceded, "Very well. I will allow this ceremony. See to the needs of my escorts."

Allishira closed the remaining pace between them with a single step and reached up to grasp his robes, and when she did a light washed over her and she was the beautiful young woman of her youth again. "My Lord, I shall personally see to your comforts."

His eyes were locked on her as he slowly combed his ancient fingers through her hair which grew long and was suddenly a chestnut brown. "As you should, slave. As you should."

As Deshett grasped his shoulder, Nemlivv looked back at her, seeing that she was just as horrified as he was at the prospect of his mother spending the night with this monster. Their eyes met and he offered her a subtle nod, and she nodded back.

***

Some hours before sunup would find Nemlivv sitting in his tower study, staring out the window at nothing. He had not slept nor even visited his bed chamber despite the pleas of both Deshett and Nillerra that he join them for the night. Very shortly, his unicorn would be on her way and he would have to face the horrible creature who had taught him everything he knew about the *sortiri.* Also heavy on his mind was the imminent attack of the Desert Lord to free the unicorn. He knew of nobody who was foolish enough or powerful enough to challenge that dragon, not even his sorcery master, and perhaps that was the key to being rid of Coridrov once and for all. Perhaps a battle between the Desert Lord and the undead Sorcery Master could be arranged, with some careful maneuvering.

His mother had been right about one thing: The unicorn had softened his heart. However, he did not feel weak because of it. He felt great strength from it, and he felt a new light within him, one spawned from his friendship with a unicorn.

An early morning glow would mean that the sun would be up within the hour, but that glow was still an hour away itself. Everyone, even Coridrov, would be asleep at this hour, and now was the time to take advantage of the darkness and the absence of unwanted eyes.

Leaving his study, he hurried downstairs and through the palace, past the resting flower gardens and to the stable. The guards were on station and he glanced at each of them as he pulled the door open and entered. She should have already been gone and he hoped she was, and he hoped she was not.

Peering into the caged stall, locked anew, he saw her lying in the middle of it on a mound of hay. She was sound asleep and he shook his head as he watched her slumber. Opening the gate with a key this time, he silently entered and knelt down beside the sleeping unicorn, stroking her mane and whispering, "Shahly," to awaken her gently.

She woke with a start anyway and raised her head abruptly, her eye dancing around the stall until she found Nemlivv staring back at her.

"You are already supposed to be gone," he whispered.

The unicorn drew an awakening breath and whispered back,

"I guess I overslept." She got her hooves under her and stood, and as the sorcerer backed away, she shook herself violently, her mane flailing in every direction, then settling evenly to the sides of her neck as she was still again.

"You need to hurry," he insisted. "You must be many leagues away from here before high sun."

Unsure what to do or feel, she looked to him with eyes that betrayed a sense of reluctance, and finally she asked, "What if I'm caught?"

"I've seen to it that there are no patrols west and south of here so the way should be clear. Just be careful of the garrison from Red Stone. They are still out there somewhere. Make for that pass in the mountains and don't stop until you've found your friends there."

She nodded, then turned and paced toward the wall that was transparent now, only to stop three steps later and look back at him.

His lips tightened and he asked, "What is it?"

"Come with me," she urged.

Shaking his head, he insisted, "I can't. My place is here as your place is in the forest."

She just stared at him for long seconds, then she reluctantly informed, "I can't come visit you next spring. I can't explain why just now, but... Do you know how to get to the Spagnah River?" When he nodded she went on, "Go there this spring, late in the spring. Follow the river to where it meets the lake, and wait for me there. I will explain everything then."

"I'll try to be there," he said softly.

"If I don't find you," she warned, "I'll have to come here and give you a good scolding." She finished with a little smile.

"You will always be welcome here," he assured.

Shahly turned and he met her half way, hugging her neck as tightly as he dared. "I love you, Shahly. I always will. Be well, and if I never see you again—"

"You will," she assured. "You will."

He let her go and watched as she turned and disappeared through the wall. When she was through, it solidified again and he found himself staring at the stable wall. His heart had never felt heavier, but he knew he had done the right thing. Now, it was time to set his ruse in motion, and time to prepare for the mass chaos the coming day promised.

CHAPTER 39

The sun would be up within the hour and an early morning glow just barely illuminated the landscape north of the Dark Mountains. Where the land flattened out and was barren of all but a few hearty clumps of scrub brush, an ominous, black form raised his head, looking to the north with eyes that glowed crimson. This day, the Desert Lord would find himself challenging an old Landmaster yet again.

Hooves clopping on the ground drew his attention briefly and he turned his head to see the bay unicorn pacing up beside him, but the unicorn did not keep his attention long.

Also looking toward the north and the forest beyond, Vinton's eyes narrowed.

They stared that way for some time, their minds whirling around the battle to come.

"Won't be long now," Ralligor growled. "You up for this, Plow Mule?"

"I've never been so ready for anything in my life," the unicorn assured. Finally looking up at the dragon, he offered, "Thank you for this, Ralligor."

The black dragon's eyes shifted that way and he advised, "Don't thank me until we have her out of there and out of Mettegrawr's territory."

"I need to do it now," Vinton countered, "just so that there is no one around to hear."

Ralligor raised a brow and they both turned their attention north again.

After another moment, the dragon growled a sigh and observed, "It appears that our peace and quiet will end today."

Vinton nodded. "And we'll both be glad of it."

"I suppose. Just see about keeping her deep in the forest in the future and away from everything and everyone."

"I'm not sure how the herd would feel about that."

"They can be swayed, I'm sure. Perhaps after this she'll be less likely to get herself into trouble."

Vinton's ears drooped slightly. "One can only hope."

The dragon glanced at him and asked, "Is everyone ready to

move?"

"Yes," the unicorn confirmed. "They should be already."

Ralligor nodded. "Just make certain that you are able to get her out of there by high sun. I don't intend to leave that castle standing."

"And the talisman they use against your kind?" the unicorn asked.

With a soft growl, the Desert Lord replied, "I'll see to that if I can." He drew a deep breath, the glow fading from his eyes as he added, "If anything should happen during my battle— "

"See to it nothing does," the big unicorn barked, his eyes meeting the dragon's. "Take the castle down so that we can get her out of there and join us on the other side of the mountains when it's all over."

Vinton's sincerity for his well being was not something that Ralligor expected, and the only response he could muster was a slight nod.

The bay unicorn nodded back, then he turned and bolted back the way he had come.

"Take care of yourself, Plow Mule," Ralligor called after him. "I don't want to be on the receiving end of that crazy unicorn's wrath if anything happens to you."

Vinton whinnied back as he disappeared around the mountain.

His attention turning back to the north, Ralligor's eyes narrowed and he growled, "Have your affairs in order, Nemlivv. By sundown you will be relegated to history and this world will be rid of you."

CHAPTER 40

Confidence was not something that Janees held in great abundance as she strode into the sun bathed clearing. Facing down the powerful sorcerer again was not something she looked forward to, but with Rawl's assurance that she was ready she did so with all she could muster. With her cape flowing behind her and her hood pulled over her head, her boots found the road beneath her with purpose as her mind constantly reviewed the training she had received from her *Magister* from beginning to end, then she would start over. Little of it seemed useful in a duel, but he had told her she would need to adapt, and adapt she would. Her life depended on it.

Only ten paces or so outside of the tree line, she froze as her eyes found the caped and hooded form standing on the other side of the clearing.

Deshett stood near the center of the clearing, a wicked little smile on her lips as she stared back with predator's eyes. Her black cape and hood, trimmed in red lace, concealed her to the ground and shadowed her face. She knew her young opponent did not know what she was up against and she could feel the girl's fear, and liked it.

Striding forward a few more paces, Janees reached for her hood, slowly pushing it from her head as her eyes narrowed. "Where is Nemlivv?" she demanded.

Also pushing her hood from her head, Deshett regarded her challenger with amusement in her eyes. "You're a fierce one, aren't you, puppet?"

"I came here for Nemlivv," Janees spat, striding a few steps more toward the arrogant woman before her. "Where is he?"

Leaning her head slightly, Deshett smiled slightly and countered, "What makes you think he has time to waste on some little girl like you?"

"You mean the coward does not want to face me again."

Deshett laughed. "Oh, but you sound overconfident. That is simply scrumptious. Master Nemlivv sent me to deal with you, puppet, simply because he hasn't the time to answer challenges from barely trained little girls like you. I'm here because he thought I could use the exercise."

Her hands clenching into tight fists, Janees harshly informed, "I didn't come here to deal with his apprentice. I came for him."

"And to get to him," Deshett informed straightly, "you must come through me. Come now, puppet. Let's see if you are as worthy as you think."

Slowly, Janees reached to her throat with one hand and untied her cape, her eyes never leaving her opponent as she slowly pulled it from her shoulders. Deshett did the same, and her coy, hungry smile grew a little broader. They tossed the capes from them and squared off.

Deshett lowered her chin, her eyes locked on her smaller, younger opponent as she offered, "Well come ahead, puppet. Let's see what makes you so special."

Knowing that this confrontation had to be brief, Janees thrust her fist up over her head and a huge stone fist the size of a horse's body on the end of a long stone arm jetted up from the ground a few paces from the arrogant sorceress before her, and as Janees made the motion, the fist was brought down hard to crush her.

Deshett raised a hand to defend herself and her other palm quickly swept at the ground as she crouched down, then the fist came down on top of her and slammed into the ground, raising a cloud of dust as it sank half its size into the earth.

Janees watched for many tense seconds as the dust settled and she squinted as if to see into the dust and through the ground itself. Someone tapped her shoulder and she shrieked, spinning around to find herself face to face with her opponent.

Offering a little smile, Deshett informed, "You missed me."

Her eyes still a little wide, Janees backed away many steps.

"You went right to earth," Deshett observed, "just like a predictable, inexperienced little girl would. Do you know any other tricks, puppet? I'd love to see them. Oh I know! Try fire. I think you would be good at that."

Janees backed off further, her eyes narrowing as she said, "Okay, if it is fire you want, then I won't disappoint." She swept her left hand and a wall of fire exploded at Deshett's feet, and before her opponent could react, she thrust her right palm at her and a yellow light blasted into her chest, knocking Nemlivv's apprentice from her feet and to her back where she hit hard and the breath exploded from her. The flames disappeared and Janees spread her arms and the ground beneath Deshett opened and she barked a scream as she fell into the hole. When Janees clapped her hands together, the ground slammed shut, swallowing the arrogant apprentice. In seconds, no trace that the road had been disturbed remained but for a little dust that slowly settled.

Janees did not wait. She darted aside, off of the road and circled around the spot where her opponent was buried, stopping about ten paces away. Her eyes never left that spot and she squared herself and stood ready.

The ground exploded a second later, dust and debris erupting high into the air, and Deshett emerged from the dust cloud, her hands clenched into tight fists as she scanned the area where she had last seen the girl.

Wanting to keep her opponent off balance, Janees struck quickly, this time sending the ground under her foe forward like a catapult and sending her through the air.

Before hitting the road, Deshett thrust her hands down and the hard road transformed into something that was soft and spongy and she came to a soft landing on top of it. Rolling quickly to her feet as the ground solidified again, she raised her hands and the boulders and large stones that flew her way exploded before they reached her.

Janees yelled as she thrust both her arms.

Deshett crossed her arms before her and red met yellow in an orange explosion of light between them.

They each took a step back.

And Deshett actually smiled. "Well now, you seem to have learned from your encounter with *Magister* Nemlivv. He told me to expect that." She lowered her chin, her brow low over her eyes. "Let's see how you fare against someone who is twice as powerful as you."

Janees set herself and held her hands ready, cold yellow flames enveloping them as she awaited her opponent's strike. Rawl had told her that the best defense against an attack was not to be there to receive it and she slowly turned her palm down and commanded the ground beneath her to prepare to receive her, and the ground responded to her, but she could feel that it was under her foe's influence as well. Her eyes narrowing as Deshett raised her arms, Janees subtly changed her tactic, and she bent her knees.

A red light exploded from Deshett's hands and she thrust them forward and down.

Before the ground beneath Janees could open, she raised one hand and the ground she stood on lifted up like a trap door and she leapt backward, coming to rest in a crouch as she saw the ground where she had been standing collapse into a pit of raging fire. Raising her hand to shield herself against the intense heat of the flames, she realized quickly that she would be dead in that instant if she had not acted as quickly as she did. Rawl's training was emerging into her conscious and her actions more instinct now and she smiled a little as she stood. Still, this was a formidable opponent and she knew she dare not let her guard down.

Waving her hand, Deshett extinguished the flames and closed the pit before her, finding the other sorceress staring at her from fifteen paces away. She smiled anyway and set her hands on her hips. "Well, now. You are just full of surprises. I was hoping this would last long enough for me to enjoy you."

Janees folded her arms and smiled back, making a subtle gesture with her hands as she confirmed, "I have many surprises. Perhaps you would like to see more."

Five stone columns jetted from the ground all around Deshett and sharp, jagged spikes of varying lengths sprouted from them as they began to rotate, and as they rotated faster they began to slowly close in on her.

Shaking her head, Deshett thrust her hands up and the columns began to crumble to dust, but this only freed the spikes and they flew off of the columns and sprayed in every direction, and the sorceress barked a scream as she covered her head and dropped to the ground. Hearing the last of the stone fall to the ground, she abruptly looked up, her eyes dancing about as she scanned for her foe. Quick to get to her feet, she set herself and looked around frantically for the girl she had just been fighting, not seeing her anywhere. The turned fully a couple of times, expecting her little opponent to emerge from anywhere at any time, but it was not to be. "Where did you go?" she shouted. "Come on, little girl. You can beat me. Why are you hiding?"

"I'm not," Janees assured from behind her.

Deshett wheeled around, swinging her hand and spraying fire from her fingers as she did. The girl was not there and the fire simply burned itself out. Huffing an angry breath, she bared her teeth and ordered, "Come out and fight me, wretch!" A warning from her heightened senses alerted her and she swung around, raising her hands to shield herself from the flaming boulder that was streaking toward her, and she stopped it less than a pace from her. She stumbled backward a few steps, then set herself again as she stared back at her young opponent, baring her teeth.

Janees folded her hands before her and raised her brow, observing, "You don't look so confident anymore."

Deshett raised her chin and smiled a wicked smile. "Did you decide to stand and fight?"

Janees only offered a shrug.

They stared at one another for a moment, each waiting for the other to make a move.

"I'm getting bored," Deshett sighed. "It's time to end this." She held a hand toward her smaller opponent, then she turned her palm up.

Feeling something beneath her was amiss again, Janees started to leap aside, but was stopped by some kind of dark, metallic tentacle which lanced from the ground right in front of her and wound itself tightly around her wrist. It was as thin as a finger at the end where it had snared her and as thick as a man's leg near the ground where it had emerged, and was as strong as steel.

Deshett slowly raised her other hand.

Janees knew how to deal with such things. It was metal and would respond as any metal would. Grabbing it with her other hand, her power lanced into it. Crystallized metal was very brittle and could be broken with her bare hands, even steel if it was corrupted enough. Some of the thin end of the tentacle wrapped around her other wrist and brutally pulled them together. As it brought her arms together it became fluid and sticky, thickening instantly to the solid form it had been as her wrists were forced together, and its grip tightened. Janees tried to pull away, but it was far too strong and had her bound hopelessly tight.

Her eyes widened as she felt the *sortiri* within her drained to nothing, and Nemlivv's words assaulted her anew. With her hands bound together, she was not a formidable sorceress, just a frightened and helpless girl. Pulling harder, her young voice sounded in desperation as she struggled to get away.

Deshett folded her arms and strode slowly forward, her eyes on her little opponent as she neared, and she smiled almost hungrily. "Well now, puppet. It would seem that you've fallen for something you did not seem to know to watch for."

Looking to her, Janees' eyes were wide and full of fear as her opponent stopped only two paces away. She shrieked and looked down as another tentacle burst from the ground behind her feet and wound around her ankles, brutally forcing them together, and even as she struggled to keep her balance, the tentacle holding her wrists jerked downward, forcing to her knees and her hands to the ground.

With a little broader smile, Deshett looked over her helpless foe and leaned her head. "I think perhaps we can have some fun now, puppet."

Janees whimpered and jerked against the tentacle harder to free herself and she watched nervously as the other sorceress walked with sultry steps behind her.

This is what Deshett had come for and she leaned her head a little as she studied her latest victim. Slowly reaching to the girl's back, she pressed her fingernails to her neck, then slowly raked them down her back, and as she did the fabric smoked and burned through, and slowly slid from her skin.

"What are you doing?" Janees whimpered with shaky words.

Her hand gliding over the girl's pale, silky skin and her eyes following the motion, Deshett seductively asked, "Do you like how that feels, puppet?"

Unable to breathe easily, Janees looked over her shoulder, gasping, "What are you going to do to me?"

"Anything I want, puppet," was the reply, "and everything I want. Master Nemlivv doesn't have anything planned for me today, so I have all day to play with you. All day, puppet."

Looking forward again, Janees' eyes anxiously danced about. She looked to her bound hands and tried once more to wrench them free. The tentacle was solid now, solid and unbreakable iron. She could no longer feel the *sortiri* at all nor could she free her body. The little confidence she had managed to build was quickly drained away and replaced with horror. Her foe's touch was truly soothing, and yet it terrified her endlessly. Finally, she timidly asked, "What do you mean play with me?"

"Do you think a cat kills the mouse right away?" Deshett asked. "No. The cat craves the game, the chase, and even after the chase has ended, she craves the mouse's fear and its struggle."

"Okay," Janees announced with shaky words. "You've won. You've beaten me."

"I know I have, pet. I know. And now, I get to have you." She raised her head, her brow lowering inquisitively as she observed, "I like your voice, puppet. Now scream for me."

"What?" Janees cried. "What do you mean?"

A red glow enveloped Deshett's hand and she smiled as she pushed her fingernails into Janees' skin. "I mean scream for me." Red ripples were produced on Janees' back as if Deshett was pushing her fingers into water and she loosed her power and her will into the girl's body with horrible purpose.

Janees' back where she was touched felt as if it was being burned away, as if the sorceress' hand was hot enough to melt steel. Throwing her head back, she screamed as the agony overtook her and she struggled anew, frantically trying to free herself of her bonds and get away.

Deshett smiled and slowly moved her hand down the girl's back as easily as she would move it through water, and the red glow followed. Janees' screams grew louder and more tortured as her tormentor moved her hand, and finally she withdrew her fingers and allowed the girl to collapse to her side. The tentacles hardened again, and another emerged and wound itself around her waist to keep her down.

"There now," Deshett said in that seductive tone. "Wasn't that fun? I love your voice, pet. I want to hear more."

Crying, her eyes shut tightly against the pain that was fresh in her memory Janees shook her head and begged, "No more.

Please, no more."

"Oh," Deshett drawled, "but we have all day, and I have much more for you." She knelt down and stroked the girl's hair, smiling as she shrank away from her touch. "I do love your voice, little girl. I want you to sing for me. I want you to scream and lament and let me know how much you enjoy the gift of pain I have for you." She slid her hand to the back of Janees' neck and under her shirt, slowly sliding it off of her shoulder, and she eyed the girl hungrily. "Yes, I so love Master Nemlivv giving me new toys. Such a pity they don't live for more than a day."

Janees sobbed and she whimpered, "Mercy."

"You want mercy?" Deshett asked, almost a tone of sympathy in her voice. "Oh, very well, pet, but you don't get it until tonight when I'm finally through with you." She bend down and kissed the girl's bare shoulder, and when Janees turned a horrified look to her, she smiled anew and informed, "I'm going to have my fun with you, puppet. I'm going to play with you and torture you, and by dark I will have tortured you to death. But not to worry. I'll make certain to keep you alive until I've had my fun."

"Please," the girl whimpered, her eyes helpless and begging. "Please don't do this to me."

"Good girl," Deshett drawled. "You just keep begging. If I really like you then perhaps I will not let you die. I'll take you home and play with you for many seasons." She playfully pinched Janees' nose and asked, "Shall we begin?"

"No," Rawl answered from behind, "we shall not."

Deshett shrieked a gasp and sprang up, spinning around as she backed away, her wide eyes locked on the big sorcerer as she declared, "Rawl!"

He strode forward, his gaze locked on her in a predator's stare as he growled, "Yes, Rawl." Stopping, he looked down at his apprentice and folded his arms, then he made a simple gesture and the solid iron tentacles that held her bound to the earth shattered almost explosively. With Janees free and sluggishly pushing herself up, he turned his attention back to Deshett and raised his chin. "Janees, stand behind me where you belong." As she complied and struggled to shrug her shirt back on, his eyes narrowed as they were locked on Deshett, and he lowered his arms as he slowly strode toward her, snarling, "Your turn."

Backing away, Deshett's eyes widened further and she gestured with both hands.

Tentacles burst from the ground on both sides of the big sorcerer and lanced toward him, but they burst into thousands of brittle pieces as soon as they tried to wrap around him.

Deshett swept her hand and fire exploded from beneath the sorcerer, but he walked from it unburned. She thrust her hands apart and the ground beneath him cracked and tried to open, then was mended by his will. Swinging her hands forward, she summoned stones and boulders, and they streaked from behind her and toward him with a true aim, but each fell harmlessly to the ground before reaching him, rolling away from him as they slowed to a stop. Looking to the road at his feet, she directed her palms toward it and summoned fire from below the ground again, and as the ground opened to swallow him in its fiery breath a bridge extended as the big sorcerer stepped toward it and he passed unscathed again yet again. Through all of her volleys, he never even broke stride.

Deshett flinched as the big sorcerer casually gestured, and in a moment she ran back-first into a stone wall that was suddenly behind her. Startled, she spun around, slamming her hands into it, and too late realized that it was simply a distraction. Turning back to ready herself, she found she did not react fast enough and copper vines lanced from the ground and randomly wound around her legs, and before she could cast to stop them they had reached as high as her shoulders and quickly wound around her forearms and wrists, binding them tightly together. As she began to struggle, the vines around her forearms reached to her body, wrapping around her and forcing her hands to her chest. Those around her legs forced her to her knees and still more reached up from the road to wind around her. She cried out in fear, terror in her wide eyes as she glanced about at the vines of copper that bound her. Struggling hard, she discovered that she was hopelessly ensnared and robbed of her sorcery power, just as Janees had been.

Slowly, she turned her horrified eyes up to the big sorcerer as he neared, struggling to breathe past the fear that choked her.

Rawl approached slowly, his gaze locked on her, and he folded his arms again. "Well now, that's not so pleasant when it happens to you, is it? Nor is this."

A red fire burst from the vines that were woven around Deshett and she squeezed her eyes shut as she threw her head back and screamed in agony. This was the worst pain she had ever felt and it stabbed into her every nerve. No fire could hurt that bad, no lightning, no wound. Every part of her body was simply racked with every kind of pain she could imagine and many she had not known before and she felt as if she was being torn apart from the inside.

In seconds it was over and her body quaked, her head rolling forward as she fought to remain conscious. Breath came hard, but she slowly forced her head up.

"And I have all day to keep at you, puppet," the sorcerer mocked. "What say you to that, little girl?"

Her brow low over her eyes, she finally turned them up to his, something almost defiant in them, and yet a familiar hunger was there as her lip curled up in a snarl and she demanded, "More."

Rawl raised his chin slightly, his eyes narrowing.

"Please," she begged. "More. Hurt me, Master Rawl. Please hurt me more. I deserve it! I'll give you anything you want, just hurt me more!"

A smile touched his lips. Stepping toward her, he placed a hand on top of her head.

She watched him do it and smiled, anticipating the horrific agony that she knew he could torture her with.

"You do like the pain of others almost as much as you like your own, don't you, Deshett?" When she eagerly nodded, he went on, "You'd be just as happy being tortured nearly to death by me as you would torturing someone else, wouldn't you?"

"Yes," she hissed. "Torture me, Master Rawl. Hurt me!"

"Oh, I will," he drawled as a red glow enveloped his hand. "For so long as you crave the pain of others, you will feel nothing. Nothing at all. You will feel no pain, no pleasure, not the wind in your hair, the caress of a gentle hand, not the sting of a whip or the burn of fire. You will feel no satisfaction with the suffering of others, nor will you find the *sortiri* there to answer you when you call upon it for that purpose." He withdrew his hand and turned around, finishing, "Enjoy."

Her mouth fell open and the copper vines fell away, all but those that bound her wrists. True to his word, she could feel nothing, and as long as her hands were bound, she could not wield the craft of a sorceress. Clumsily getting to her feet as the big sorcerer just walked away, she screamed, "Rawl! You can't leave me like this! You can't!"

He turned Janees around by the shoulders and shook his head as he pulled her shirt back together, grumbling, "I had this made just for you and look what you've let happen to it." Running his hand along the tear, he mended it with the power of the *sortiri,* and once it was whole again, he ordered, "Come along, girl. Fetch your cape and let's go. We've much to do, and you need to pack."

Janees lowered her eyes and nodded. Deshett had beaten her, planned to kill her, and she had failed her *magister.* It would appear that her brief time as his student was over.

"Rawl!" Deshett screamed. "Please! Please don't leave me like this! I beg you!"

"Get used to begging," he called back. "Your craving for the pain of others will bring you no more joy. Have a nice, long life, Deshett."

Sinking to her knees, the sorceress screamed wildly, falling forward to her arms, unable to feel anything, not even the pain of her bruised elbows as they hit the ground.

And she wept.

CHAPTER 41

As the sun began to grow high, Ralligor was perched atop the tallest peak of the Dark Mountains as he scanned the area north. At some point after crossing the border into Mettegrawr's territory, one of his *subordinares* was sure to notice. They did not concern him, but the Landmaster did. Mettegrawr was a dragon he had tangled with before and he was sure he was still not a match for him. Growling a sigh, he looked up to the sun, now nearing its apex, and decided it was time to cross. Drarrexok and Falloah would be along in short order, but he hoped he could have the castle in flames, Shahly on her way home and be back over the mountains before the Northern Landmaster could react to him. And *quietly* destroying a stone castle was next to impossible.

Timing would be everything, but the Desert Lord found himself of little patience this day. Looking skyward, he could see by the sun that it was not yet time, but he was too anxious and ended up leaping from his perch and opening his wings, filling them with the wind as he soared northward.

To avoid unwanted attention, he flew low and did not announce his approach. He looked sharp and listened carefully, his eyes shifting in quick motions as he stroked his wings for more speed. He did not know the terrain here very well and as mountains yielded to forested rolling hills he stretched out his inner senses, the *wizaridi* to detect any threats that his eyes and ears missed. He could feel Shahly's unique essence a few leagues ahead and his eyes narrowed slightly as he prepared himself for battle. At this point he was many leagues inside Mettegrawr's territory and this knowledge made him more and more anxious.

Ahead of him the forest was cleared and grassland surrounded a broad, slow moving river. The ruins of an old castle were on the far bank, one that had been abandoned for what appeared to be a hundred seasons or more. Most of the high wall was still intact, but part of it on the up river side had crumbled many seasons ago and the forest was beginning to reclaim it. In the hollow of the stone structure, what had once been a huge meeting or banquet hall formed a man-made cave, one that looked ideal for a small dragon to inhabit.

And inhabited it was!

A young dragoness about Falloah's size scrambled out of the collapsed portion of the wall and turned dark red eyes up to him, baring her teeth as she saw him. Her scales were also a dark red, darkening nearly to black over her dorsal scale ridge that ran from between her black horns all the way to her long, thrashing tail. The scales from her throat to her belly and all along the underside of her tail were a much lighter red and the webbing of her wings lightened to pink between the fingers of her wings. An attractive dragoness, she was one who considered herself a force to be reckoned with, and she knew Ralligor.

Leaping into the air, she roared through bared teeth in a higher pitch to befit her gender and size and stroked her wings hard climb and meet the invader.

Ralligor growled, the irritation he felt evident on his features as he saw her coming. He had no wish to harm the little dragoness nor did he have the time to reason with her. Her roaring had probably already alerted Mettegrawr and this irritated him further. As she closed, he suddenly dove and arched his body to one side, and as they passed he slammed his heavy tail onto her back and sent her fluttering back to the ground.

She controlled her landing well and kicked off of the ground to fly up and meet the black dragon again.

Knowing she would not stop harassing him, Ralligor wheeled around and bared his teeth, and the two dragons met mid-air again, this time head-on.

The dragoness slammed into him and clutched at him with all of her claws, swinging her feet around to rip at him as her jaws went right for his throat. Ralligor grabbed her right behind the head and pulled his wings back and they fell ten heights to the ground. The breath exploded from the dragoness as she slammed into the earth below with the much larger black dragon on top of her. She was stunned and went limp, her head falling back to the ground. Now was an ideal time to kill her, but he did not feel the need.

Her eyes opened slowly and she raised her head, looking up at him as she heaved in each breath, and her brow lowered. Her lips sliding away from her teeth, she snarled, "Why are you here again, Ralligor?"

He also bared his teeth, his brow low over his eyes as he replied, "That is no concern of yours. I will not be here long and I will not tolerate any interference." He slammed his hand into her throat, curling his claws around her neck right below her jaw. "You can remain silent and live through the day or I can kill you right now. Choose wisely."

Even as she growled at him, defiant to the last, youth and inexperience conspired against her, and the black dragon raised a brow slightly as her eyes flitted to one sight ever so subtly.

"Not the right choice," Ralligor informed. He pulled her head from the ground, then slammed it back down with brutal force, burying her horns in the earth, then he stood from her and turned with gaping jaws. Fire exploded from between his teeth and slammed into the large drake that was diving on him.

Roaring in pain and anger, the other dragon shied away from the flames that scorched him, his dark blue scales flashing in the sunlight and the light of the flames as he lowered his talons to rip at his enemy as he passed. Nearly as large as the black dragon, he was just as long, just as tall standing, but clearly leaner in the body. His scales were light blue on his belly, fading to a darker blue on his back and his dorsal scale ridge was nearly black. His horns curled backward, like a ram and were thick and ideal for battle.

As Ralligor ducked down, sharp black claws ripped at the armor of his back but did not penetrate. As he passed, the other drake slammed his tail down onto Ralligor's back before wheeling around in the air to face his larger foe on the ground.

Spinning around, the black dragon faced off against an old rival with narrow eyes that glowed red.

The blue dragon's eyes glowed red as well and his teeth were bared as he slammed onto the ground and drew his wings to him. His tail thrashed violently behind him as his jaws gaped and he roared a mighty challenge.

Ralligor did not reply to his roar, but the glow in his eyes faded, though his brow remained low between them. As the two squared off, the black dragon informed, "I don't have time for you right now, Lorkryndo. I have business north of here and then I'm leaving."

The blue dragon smiled slightly. "You aren't leaving this time, Ralligor. I intend to finish what we started ten seasons ago."

"I beat you ten seasons ago," the black dragon reminded.

"You didn't kill me," Lorkryndo countered. "That was a mistake."

"That was charity," Ralligor corrected. "As I've said, I don't have time to teach you another lesson. Stand aside and attend to your dragoness."

"When I'm through with you," the blue dragon assured, taking a step forward. "And perhaps I'll attend to yours when you are food for the scavengers."

Baring his teeth again, Ralligor pointed out, "Your Landmaster isn't here this time."

Lorkryndo roared, "I don't need him for you!" He lunged and the black dragon responded with an outstretched hand. A burst of emerald lightning lanced from the black dragon's hand and exploded as it hit the blue dragon's chest, sending him backward where he slammed onto the ground and slid about ten paces before stopping in a cloud of dust.

"As I said," Ralligor snarled, "I don't have time for you."

Another roar from behind and above alerted the black dragon to the approach of others and he turned to see two more bearing down on him. One was a dark brown drake, the other a light green dragoness, and both were smaller than the Desert Lord. Frustration left him in the form of a long growl and he swept his hand, calling upon a high wind which swept down from above, pulling a cloud apart with it only seconds before hitting the two dragons from the side and blowing one into the other. Dropping quickly, they struggled to separate again and fill their wings with the wind and Ralligor acted swiftly, bringing his hand down and calling upon a powerful downdraft that sent the two careening into the forest below.

With most of the local threats down, Ralligor turned and swept himself into the air, turning toward Ravenstone Castle and Shahly once again. He was not very high when he heard something cut the air and he looked behind him just as a massive copper and bronze colored form slammed into his back. He crashed into the ground hard and instinctively pulled in his wings as he bounced a little and rolled to one side, finally sliding to a stop just short of the tree line. Raising his head, he shook it to clear his wits and blinked the dust from his eyes, then sprang up as he felt the presence of yet another dragon. With fluid movements, he wheeled around, firmly setting his feet as he prepared to do battle with the huge dragon who slammed into the ground only fifty paces away.

The scales on his throat and belly were a dark bronze; those on his sides and back were more of a copper. His wing webbing was almost black. Bronze horns were thick and curled outward from his head, similar to those of a ram. Eyes of amber were locked on the Desert Lord as he squared off against this old enemy.

Ralligor's eyes narrowed and the words of his own Landmaster surfaced from his memory. He would face Mettegrawr alone this time, but he would have forty seasons of wizard training to call upon that he did not have before.

The huge copper and bronze dragon smiled, his jaws parting slightly, and he observed, "I finally have you on the wrong side of the border, Ralligor. You'd better pray you can fly faster than I can."

His eyes locked on the big Landmaster's, Ralligor growled back, "I don't intend to retreat from you, Mettegrawr. I have business a few leagues from here to attend to and then I'll be on my way. You'll be wise not to interfere."

The bronze dragon huffed a laugh. "Oh, you must mean the unicorn that is being held at the human castle called Ravenhold."

Ralligor raised his head slightly.

"You thought I wouldn't know about that?" the Landmaster asked with an amused tone, slowly stalking toward the smaller black dragon. "I am aware of all that happens in my territory. Nemlivv has given me all kinds of tributes for my favor and has kept me apprized. And I've been waiting for you."

"I see," Ralligor snarled, his brow growing lower. "And now I suppose you mean to fight me."

"I mean to kill you," Mettegrawr corrected, "and then I'll

throw your broken carcass back over the mountains for Agarxus to find."

"You're forgetting something," Ralligor warned as the bigger dragon was almost within reach.

The bronze dragon stopped his advance and almost laughed, "This should be amusing. What have I forgotten, vulture fodder?"

Ralligor simply replied, "Lightning." He thrust his hand and blasted the huge dragon in the chest with a white-hot bolt, one that exploded so violently it sent the bronze dragon staggering backward. Fire exploded from the black dragon's gaping jaws and enveloped the Landmaster's head and he retreated further, roaring in pain and rage. Jetting his wings out, Ralligor stroked them hard and lifted himself into the air, kicking with both feet and slamming them hard into the bronze dragon's chest.

This time, Mettegrawr stumbled and fell.

Raising his hands, Ralligor's eyes began to glow emerald as he called upon the clouds above to gather and strengthen, which they did with unnatural speed and rumbling thunder. Looking down at the huge dragon, who was scrambling to stand, the Desert Lord shouted over the winds he had summoned, "Contrary to what some say, lightning does often strike the same place twice, and sometimes it strikes over and over." The light in his eyes flashed with new intensity and the clouds responded by spitting lightning down at the big Landmaster, striking him over and over and sending him back down.

The blue dragon swept in over the trees and slammed into Ralligor's back, knocking him to the earth and then landing on him. With the Desert Lord down, the clouds began to dissipate and the volley of lightning stopped.

Ralligor lunged up and turned as the blue dragon slammed his jaws shut at the base of his neck. His heavy armor did not yield to his enemy's teeth, but he roared and turned his head fully to bite back, his teeth finding a wing and plunging into the dense muscle there. The dragons engaged in a fierce wrestling contest as the blue dragon fought to remain on his enemy's back and Ralligor fought to remove him. This was a contest of speed, strength and skill. Claws and teeth ripped at armor that would not yield to them. Finally, the black dragon rolled from under his foe and stood, finally bringing his full strength to bear and in a maneuver that Lorkryndo did not anticipate, Ralligor slammed his jaws shut around the blue dragon's snout and bit down with all of the force he could muster. As the blue dragon shrieked, Ralligor wheeled his bulk around and hurled him into the charging Landmaster.

Even as they stumbled and fell, Mettegrawr's three other *subordinares* regrouped and descended upon the formidable black dragon, attacking him from the air in a group. Before they reached him, Ralligor waved his hand and emerald explosions blasted them backward and they trailed smoke all the way to the ground. Fire exploded on the black dragon's chest and he was knocked backward, stroking his wings for balance. Another burst slammed into him and he was blasted into the trees, knocking one over as he crashed into them. Before he could get his bearings, Mettegrawr was upon him, his jaws slamming shut around his chest and shoulder, and this time his armor yielded.

Roaring in pain, Ralligor swung his head over, ramming one of his horns into the side of the Landmaster's head, then again, and again as his claws raked at the huge dragon's seemingly impervious armor.

Finally withdrawing his teeth, now stained red with the black dragon's blood, the Landmaster grabbed the Desert Lord by the throat and arm and hurled him toward the castle ruins.

Ralligor hit awkwardly and rolled to a stop, but was quick to get himself righted and he staggered to his feet, facing the huge dragon who charged him again.

Stroking his wings, Mettegrawr leapt into the air and brought the claws of his feet down at the black dragon.

Spinning away, Ralligor slammed his tail hard into the bronze dragon's knees, and Mettegrawr fell forward very awkwardly, catching himself with both hands before he crashed all the way to the ground.

The Desert Lord wheeled around to face the Landmaster and thrust a hand at him, and this time thin beams of emerald light lanced from his claws and ripped into the Landmaster's scales, and Mettegrawr stumbled back and roared in pain once again.

Lorkryndo was already upon the black dragon and Ralligor was unable to respond quickly enough as the claws of the blue dragon's foot ripped into the side of his head and neck.

Stunned, Ralligor crashed hard to the ground this time, bleeding from a gash just behind his eye as well as two others halfway down his neck, and many holes punched through his armor by the big Landmaster's teeth. He was slower to push himself up this time and as he tried to stand Mettegrawr's foot slammed onto his back and crushed him back to the ground.

Grabbing for the black dragon's neck, Mettegrawr found himself just a little too slow and the Desert Lord snaked his long, thick neck away, turned his head and clamped his jaws shut around the Landmaster's forearm—and this time his teeth sank all the way in! The bronze dragon roared in pain and backed away as he tried to wrench his arm free, and Ralligor took the opportunity to scramble to his feet as he shook his head violently to work his teeth in even deeper.

The blue dragon struck again, slamming both feet squarely into the Ralligor's back. He grabbed onto the black dragon's nose and tried to pull his jaws away from his Landmaster's arm as he clamped his own jaws down onto the Desert Lord's already wounded shoulder.

Mettegrawr finally freed his arm and slammed the other clawed hand hard into the side of Ralligor's head. Lorkryndo pulled him backward and twisted his body to throw the black dragon to the ground with all his strength.

Rolling to a stop, Ralligor growled with each breath and slowly opened his eyes. He found himself surrounded by the smaller dragons, and Mettegrawr stood right in front of him. Slowly raising his head, he looked up at the big Landmaster and snarled, "Do you give up yet or do you need me to beat you down more?"

A thunderous growl rolled from the bronze dragon's throat and he slowly shook his head. "Defiant and callous to the end, aren't you Ralligor? You don't deserve to be killed by me. You simply are not worth the effort."

Ralligor pushed himself up a little, his eyes locked on the Landmaster's as he struggled to recover his strength and his wits, and he allowed the *wizaridi* to surge up within him. "I don't agree, Mettegrawr. In fact, I'd be beating you right now but for your *subordinares* interfering. I think you are afraid to face me alone."

The Landmaster's eyes narrowed and he looked to the blue dragon, who stood behind Ralligor, and ordered, "Kill him. Slowly."

Tensing to spring up, Ralligor started to turn that direction, seeing the red dragon raise her claws to strike at him first, but something else caught his eye, a glint of scarlet over the treetops, and he smiled and lowered his head, digging the claws of his feet into the ground.

Falloah slammed hard into the red dragon's back and Ralligor lunged at her at the same time, catching her low and wrapping his arms around her legs. As the red shrieked, the Desert Lord stood with her and spun around, slamming her into the dragons behind him and knocking them backward.

Falloah turned in the air and stroked her wings hard, her jaws gaping and fire belching from between her teeth right at the big Landmaster.

As Mettegrawr turned to engage the small scarlet dragon, Drarrexok swept down and kicked him with all his strength high on the back, and the big Landmaster staggered forward.

Ralligor retreated out of the circle of dragons who surrounded him and held his ground twenty-five paces away. Falloah landed on one side of him and Drarrexok on the other.

Squaring off against them with his *subordinares* at his sides, the Landmaster half spread his wings, baring his teeth as he observed, "You are still outnumbered, Ralligor."

Falloah also opened her wings and stepped toward him, roaring back, "And you are outclassed, Mettegrawr!" She raised her snout and let loose a high pitched call, one that echoed from the castle ruins and reverberated throughout the forest all around. Her call ended in an eerie silence and she looked back to the big Landmaster, her eyes narrowing as she warned, "Withdraw."

Drarrexok's lips slid away from his teeth and he growled.

His eyes sliding to the scarlet dragoness, Ralligor mumbled, "What are you doing?"

Mettegrawr's scaly lips rolled away from his teeth and his fingers curled over his palms. "I've heard enough of this foolishness. Kill them."

A deep, horrifying roar answered Falloah's call and the Landmaster and his *subordinares* turned their eyes skyward, and they all backed away a few steps.

Sweeping in fast, Agarxus drew his wings to him and slammed onto the ground, dropping to all fours with bared teeth and red glowing eyes. He was a nightmarish sight as he had his gaze locked on the smaller Landmaster. Slowly, he stood, towering over all of the other dragons.

"Oh," Ralligor mumbled, his eyes on his Landmaster. "*That's* what you're doing."

Backing away a step, Mettegrawr pointed a clawed finger at the larger dragon and roared, "This does not involve you, Agarxus! We have an accord!"

"Yes," the massive dragon agreed, his voice like thunder "we do. And I am not interested in your territory."

Ralligor and Falloah took his one side and Drarrexok took the other, their gazes locked on Mettegrawr and his *subordinares.*

His brow lowering over his eyes, the bronze dragon demanded, "Then why are you here?"

A rare smile curled Agarxus' mouth and he answered straightly, "Today, I simply wish to fight."

The four dragons with Mettegrawr backed away, giving each other doubtful looks.

"I have no quarrel with you," the bronze dragon growled.

"I know," Agarxus assured, "so I intend to make one." He looked to the black dragon and snapped, "I believe you have business elsewhere, Ralligor."

"I do," the black dragon confirmed, his eyes locked on the other Landmaster, "but my place is at your side." Without awaiting instruction from his Landmaster, Ralligor opened his jaws and fire burst from them, slamming hard into Mettegrawr's chest.

The bronze dragon roared as he stumbled backward and before his minions could respond, Ralligor swept his hand and an emerald wave crashed into them, exploding in brilliant light and sending them to the ground, leaving only Mettegrawr standing. With the smaller dragons down, the Desert Lord launched himself forward and slammed his body into the Northern Landmaster

Far stronger, Mettegrawr twisted around and threw the black dragon from him, roaring to his *subordinares,* "Kill him!" Before he could turn back, Agarxus was upon him, and before his minions could attack Ralligor, the Tyrant's *subordinares* were upon them. Numbers did not seem to matter. Here, strength was called upon, and the experience of many battles.

Falloah inflicted a deep bite to the wing of one dragoness and as that dragoness retired she turned on the red, meeting her with claws and teeth. Drarrexok slammed himself into the blue, his hind claws scraping at the other dragon's back but not penetrating his armor. When the dark brown drake tried to go to the aid of the blue, Ralligor roared to distract him, then he met the brown head-on. Both dragons' jaws gaped as deadly teeth looked for an opening to rend flesh. Claws swiped toward enemies and would occasionally glance off of armor scales. Experience and strength favored the larger black dragon and as the brown dragon lanced his head toward the Desert Lord's belly to seemingly exploit an opening and a mistake by his enemy. However, this was a ploy and Ralligor turned his body sharply, slamming his jaws shut around the brown's snout and clamping down as hard as he could, his teeth plunging through armor and into bone. The brown dragon shrieked and tried to retreat, and Ralligor opened his jaws and allowed the smaller dragon to back away. Bleeding from the snout, the brown looked to Ralligor, and backed away more.

Falloah spun around and threw the red dragon from her, slamming her into the brown's back and sending them both to the ground, then she met her mate's eyes only briefly before turning on another dragoness.

Turning to the Landmasters, Ralligor's eyes narrowed as the blue dragon and another dragoness attacked Agarxus from behind, drawing his attention from the retreating bronze. His eyes narrowing, the black dragon snarled as Mettegrawr set himself to attack the Tyrant, and he acted quickly, springing into the big bronze dragon and slamming his jaws shut around his neck. Less than two thirds Mettegrawr's size, Ralligor did not intend to fight a clean fight and he called upon the *wizaridi* with a horrible intent, sending it into the claws of his right foot as he kicked up and dug his claws in, raking them down the northern

Landmaster's side and easily tearing through the bigger dragon's armor with the fiery glow that surrounded his claws.

Mettegrawr roared in pain and anger and turned to respond and Ralligor twisted his head to sink his teeth into the big dragon's armor scales, and slowly wrenched them in. The bronze dragon spun around and Ralligor's fire-enveloped claws found his thigh, tearing into him there as well and burning deep into the thick muscle. Now the northern Landmaster's roars were higher pitched as he began to succumb to the pain of the injuries inflicted on him and he sent his gaping jaws toward the black dragon's back. Before his teeth arrived, emerald fire enveloped Ralligor's dorsal scales and quick shots of lightning lanced forth and popped all over the bronze dragon's head, and the Landmaster shied away.

With all of his strength, Ralligor planted his feet and drove into the bronze dragon, forcing him sideways and off balance, and finally he let go with his jaws, slammed his palms and claws into the Landmaster's side and pushed with all of his might.

Stumbling only a few more steps, Mettegrawr was robbed of his balance and fell, and Ralligor forced him down onto his side where he crashed onto the ground. A shroud of dust rose all around the dragons and the Desert Lord leapt clear before it could settle.

This was a tremendous victory for any dragon, felling a Landmaster, and Ralligor threw his head back and roared through bared teeth to celebrate. Looking back down at the bronze dragon as he tried to struggle to his feet, Ralligor thrust a hand at him and blasted him with deadly emerald lightning and Mettegrawr roared in pain and went back down.

Agarxus grabbed one of Ralligor's horns and turned his head to meet his eyes, baring his teeth as he warned, "You ever do that to me I *will* kill you!"

Ralligor raised his brow and countered, "That's why I don't do that to you."

Throwing the black dragon from him and watching him stumble sideways, the Tyrant ordered, "Go find the unicorn and leave this fight to me."

Meeting the Landmaster's eyes, the Desert Lord nodded once to him, then he looked back to the bronze dragon and gave him a good blast of fire that exploded on his wounded side before he turned and strode to Falloah.

Agarxus lips slid away from his sword sized teeth and he growled, "Impudent cur."

Falloah had found herself downed by the brown drake and Drarrexok was already upon him, and as the two drakes rolled to the ground, Ralligor strode over to his scarlet mate as she pushed herself up and he took her arm, lifting her to her feet.

She offered him a smile and cooed tenderly to him as she met his eyes.

"You going to be okay?" he asked.

Falloah assured, "I'm having a wonderful time, *Unisponsus.*"

He nodded and informed, "I'm going after Shahly. Be careful here."

"I will," she replied, then she stepped toward him and brushed her snout to the bottom of his jaw. "Bring our unicorn home safely, my Love."

He smiled a rare smile back and stroked her face with his hand, then he turned and walked the other way, opening his wings and casually taking flight.

He did not look back as he heard the sounds of the battle behind him continue. He did not need to. Even with greater numbers and Mettegrawr right there, the northern dragons were simply outmatched by Agarxus and his *subordinares*. Nor did he fret over his Falloah being in the fray. The red dragoness with the black back was well known to his mate. They shared parentage and were sisters and both had fled the West in search of freedom from that Landmaster, though many seasons apart. They were rivals, but only so far as their bloodlines would allow them to be and they would not fight to the death.

Only a few leagues ahead was Castle Ravenhold and he projected his dragon born senses and called upon the *wizaridi* to search for his little unicorn friend. Flying low, he hoped to avoid any unwanted eyes, and especially that talisman that he knew could potentially bring him down. It would have to be located and located quickly, and first.

Sweeping only a couple of heights over the treetops, his eyes narrowed and began to glow emerald as he channeled his wizard enhanced senses through him and directed them forward, looking beyond his own dragon born sight.

And there it was, in the highest tower of the dark stone castle. A growl rumbled from him and he shook his head slightly, realizing that two other such talismans were also in the highest towers of those castles, and he almost laughed at how predictable humans could be.

He flexed muscles in his chest, putting the crop full of brimstone and gems within his chest under enormous pressure. Spreading his arms, his open hands were engulfed in emerald fire that trailed behind him. His first strike would be a devastating one that would announce his presence with a horrible purpose.

The people on the walls and in the compounds of the castle never saw him coming and did not know of his presence until it was too late.

Fire lanced down from his jaws and bursts of emerald light bombarded the wall and compound of the castle. He killed scores on his first pass and abruptly climbed, blasting the highest tower with flames that caused the very stone to explode, but he did not manage to destroy the talisman so quickly.

Ralligor disappeared over the trees on the other side and turned sharply to the north and east. As the humans tried desperately to regroup, the black dragon re-emerged to strike at them again, this time from a direction they were not watching. Calling upon all of his power as a dragon and as a wizard, he left devastation in his wake once again. Fires burned from within the palace and towers, all over the compounds and stone walls yielded to his power and collapsed, but once again he failed to take out the talisman, and as he circled and soared low toward the western wall, the talisman flashed to life and an emerald light lanced forth, barely missing the big dragon.

Ralligor turned sharply, looking back at the tower as he stroked his wings for speed and altitude. The talisman fired again and he barely avoided its power once more, this time retaliating with a burst of emerald fire from his palm, which blasted a huge hole in the tower just under the highest window of the tower.

It fired again and this time a glancing shot struck his shoulder and then his side, burning a deep gash through his armor and into his flesh, and he roared in pain and stroked his wings hard to control his flight, but lost the wind and ended up crashing into a stable that collapsed under his weight and bulk. A huge cloud of dust was raised and debris fell to the ground for a few seconds after.

Lying on his back in the rubble of the stable, he was slow to reclaim his wits and sluggishly raised his head, looking up at the top of the tower with eyes that glowed red, and his lips slid away from his teeth. A green glow grew brighter from within and he knew they were about to strike their death blow, and he already prepared to receive it with the best defense he could muster against the essence of a unicorn.

He never got the opportunity.

A powerful burst of red light lanced from behind his shoulder and perfectly entered the highest window, and the top of the tower exploded brilliantly with a thunderous thump in fire and multi-colored lightning. Debris rained down from the fire and smoke cloud, many of the pieces trailing smoke as they fell.

Turning his head, Ralligor looked to a corner of the stable that was still standing, to the dirty and well dressed human who occupied it.

Nemlivv was dressed as he had been the night before and stared back at the dragon.

A moment of silence passed between them, the sorcerer staring dumbly back at the huge dragon who was lying on his back with his neck twisted around to see the human who stood only a few paces away amid the rubble of the stable and some kind of cage that had been built within it.

Finally setting his hands on his hips, Nemlivv complained, "You almost killed me when you came through the roof!"

Ralligor nodded slightly, his eyes never leaving the sorcerer. "Well," he finally replied, "it seems I missed. And you are?"

"I am Nemlivv," the sorcerer replied straightly, "the man you came here to kill."

Turning his head, Ralligor looked up at the remains of the tower, then back to the sorcerer.

"If you're looking for Shahly," Nemlivv went on, "you're a few hours late. I sent her on her way before sunup. I worry over her sense of direction and it did not occur to me until too late that I sent her right toward the garrison from Red Stone Castle. I beg you hurry to her before they can get her."

Ralligor's brow lowered over his eyes. "You abducted her from the forest only to release her? Did you fear what I would do to you if I found her here?"

Nemlivv shook his head. "No, Desert Lord. I feared what others would do to *her.* She can't be more than a few leagues from here. Please hurry. I've repaired the amulet you gave her so perhaps you can use it to find her."

"You are an odd little man," the dragon observed.

Nemlivv shrugged. "She has a way of changing hearts. If you mean to kill me anyway, please get her to safety first."

"And you?" the dragon asked.

The sorcerer shrugged again. "I'm most likely to face dire consequences for destroying the talisman that was meant to kill you."

"Assuming they know you did it," the dragon countered.

"I'm sure they'll figure it out, dragon."

Ralligor growled. "I hate being in someone's debt, so I'll repay it now. Do you have a spell that will soften the ground?"

"Of course."

Rolling to his feet, the Desert Lord grabbed the sorcerer and stood, his hand engulfing most of Nemlivv's body. He turned and hurled him across the compound and toward the flower beds, then stepped from the debris of the stable in pursuit.

Nemlivv found himself yelling in fear and quickly thrust his hand at the ground where he was about to hit, and when he did the ground collapsed under him as a huge pillow would, then reformed and hardened. Staggering to his feet, he turned and faced the dragon who stalked toward him, and was quick to raise his hands as a storm of fire exploded toward him.

Nemlivv easily warded off the fire and retaliated with a thrust of his hand that sent fire back, striking the dragon hard in the chest.

Ralligor stopped as the fire hit him, but he only growled and then roared, "Is that the best you can do?"

Backing away, Nemlivv realized that the dragon could already have killed him. An attack of fire on a sorcerer was a losing proposition, as fire was one of the elements controlled by the *sortiri,* and the dragon no doubt knew this.

Archers from the palace windows loosed their arrows toward the dragon in a futile attempt to repel him but the arrows all disappeared into puffs of smoke before they hit him, not that they would have done any good against him anyway.

Looking to the palace, Ralligor bared his teeth, his eyes glowing red. His jaws swung open as he raised his head and fire exploded from between his teeth once again.

Those archers who did not retreat quickly enough were incinerated in seconds.

Nemlivv took advantage of this distraction and turned to his palace, running as fast as he could to one of the entrances and the waiting guards who rushed him inside and closed the doors.

Ralligor turned his eyes to the doors as they closed and nodded slightly, saying under his breath, "We're even now, Nemlivv. See to it we don't cross paths again."

He turned and started to open his wings, then he froze and looked down to another entrance of the palace, a crimson glow overtaking his eyes as he bared his teeth.

Coridrov stared up at him with his brow low over his horrible eyes.

They stared at each other for only a moment before a crimson fire burst from the sorcerer's hands. An emerald fire overtook the dragon's eyes and his claws glowed the same color.

Ralligor knew that this creature lingered somewhere between life and death. The best weapons forged could not kill him. The most powerful mages could not kill him. But the Desert Lord's power was so vast that he could rip the living essence away from even an undead body and tear it apart, and Coridrov knew this.

Slowly shaking his head, the ancient sorcerer backed slowly away, warning in a deep, distant voice, "Not today, Desert Lord, but soon."

Leaning his head, Ralligor demanded, "Why not today? We both know I will send you back to Hell sooner or later."

"Perhaps," Coridrov drawled. He smiled, his bleached teeth showing brightly against his gray skin. "One of us will die when next we meet, Desert Lord. Beware your own power." He bowed his head and crossed his arms before him, then was engulfed in fire.

With a snarl, Ralligor thrust a hand at him and sent a blinding emerald light toward the ancient sorcerer, but too late. The blast hit the ground behind the burning form and blew a sizeable hole in the earth it struck. As the fire quickly burned out and was gone and the sorcerer with it, the black dragon growled, his eyes narrowing, then he looked to the top of the castle wall and opened his wings again, this time making it air born.

His thoughts were consumed with finding the bothersome little unicorn, and how to do that in dense forest. As that emerald glow overtook his eyes again, he reasoned that the amulet she wore was indeed the key.

CHAPTER 42

Shahly had most of the Abtont forest put to memory, specifically where the paths were, creeks, what grew where and how, cliffs, hills, grass fields and the like. By instinct and reflex, she knew where she was and where she was going by what she saw. The elders had taught her everything they could and she remembered most of it, but not what to do when she was in unfamiliar territory. Little things like the position of the sun were different here. It was further south and did not rise as high as she was used to, and this confused her. She knew it stayed more to the south than the north and she knew it was about high sun, but she had difficulty remembering what to do. There were mountains on two sides and she simply did not know which to follow.

With her mind scrambling and her senses alert for anything familiar to her, she wandered the paths in the forest for many hours, twice realizing that she had gone in complete circles.

She snorted and tried to pick yet another direction toward one of the mountain ranges she saw.

The path widened and she was grateful for this. For a while longer she paced down the wider path, her head low and her eyes fixed before her. Once again good judgment was ignored and she just wandered and did not pay close attention to her surroundings. She was happy to be free again, but frustrated that she could not find her way home.

When the path turned sharply and emptied into a larger path, she absently followed it. She was already weary, her ears drooped and her thoughts were a frustrating whirlwind of confusion. Sounds were reaching her, but she barely noticed.

A horse snorted behind her and she finally realized that she was on a human's road, one that was a good ten paces wide. She heard many hooves behind her and the mumbling of humans, the clanking and clicking made by metal equipment, and the rattles of wooden wagons.

Finally raising her head, she looked over her shoulder and saw humans on horseback, many humans riding four abreast and in long lines. They escorted three wagons and she recognized the uniforms as those of Red Stone Castle. Many eyes found her and several of the soldiers pointed to her and shouted, and she heard "Unicorn!" several times.

"This isn't good," she mumbled to herself. Looking forward again, she quickened her pace slightly, not wanting to bolt as she would draw more attention, but she was sure this was an inevitability. A chase was coming, and this was a rare time she did not want one.

Glancing back at them, she noticed that the soldiers at the front had quickened their pace. They were pursuing, drawing closer, and meant to capture her.

Even as her mind scrambled around figuring out what to do about them, she launched herself into a full gallop and ran as fast as she could, but did not know where she was going. Looking back again, she saw almost a score of them in pursuit. She did not feel fear, but she did feel that certain excitement coupled with surges of frustration. She wanted to go back home and see her Vinton and start a new life with him, one that did not involve these foolish chases anymore.

The road turned, then suddenly opened into a wide field where humans grew grain. It was huge, almost half a league long and nearly that wide and surrounded by dense northern forest. The stalks were tan for the most part with just a little green lingering about in most of them. They were fairly tall, coming up to her shoulder, but not tall enough to hide in. The road she was on was an almost perfect straight line right through the middle of the field and she could not see the end of it as the land rose right in the middle of the field and obscured much of the forest on the other end, but she was sure she could put some distance between her and them in the field and then disappear into the dense forest when she reached the other side.

Kicking her stride longer, she easily opened the gap between herself and the big horses behind her and in short order was over the top of the hump in the middle of the field and suddenly she locked her hooves and dropped her haunches nearly to the dirt road, stumbling a little as she brought herself to an awkward stop.

Just emerging from the forest about two hundred paces ahead of her was another group of humans on horseback. About forty in number, she recognized them as soldiers of Ravenhold Castle and puzzled for a moment as to why they would be coming this way. Quickly concluding that they were coming to meet the soldiers of Red Stone Castle, she turned and saw the soldiers behind her closing in on her from just over a hundred paces away and began to feel cornered. The grain could slow her if she ran through it but that seemed to be the only way out.

No. She turned to the soldiers of Red Stone and planted her hooves, her essence channeling into her eyes and horn. She had never pulled off a broad deception of so many minds before and did not know if she was even strong enough to do so, but she would try it anyway. At the very least she would spook some of them and cause enough confusion for her to make it to the forest and disappear.

She lowered her head and drew an image from her memory, a memory of Ralligor when he was angry and on the attack. With this image fully in her mind, she thrust her essence at them and the mental image with it and she raised her head and whinnied as loudly as she could.

They just kept coming and did not even break stride.

Snorting at this failure, she called upon all of her strength of essence and tried again, thrusting the image of the black dragon at them will all of her might.

Ralligor landed hard right behind her and fell to all fours, bringing his hands to her sides as he opened his jaws and roared through bared teeth.

To the humans he was something of a nightmare and they abruptly stopped and turned their horses, many of them shouting in terror.

Shahly looked up at him as the soldiers fled.

He craned his neck around and looked down at her with one eye.

Staring back for a few seconds, she finally greeted, "Hi."

"You're going the wrong way," he snarled.

"I *was* going the other way," she informed straightly, "but I ran into soldiers of Red Stone Castle and came back this way."

"That's the wrong way as well," he countered. Rearing up, he stood and folded his arms as she turned to face him. "How long have you been away from the castle?"

"I don't know," she admitted in a sigh. "He snuck me out before sunup and I got lost right after that. How far did I get?"

He raised a brow. "In about half the day you made it less than a league. Did it occur to you to just turn south and head toward the mountains?"

"Which mountains?" she spat back.

Ralligor replied through clenched teeth, "The only mountains to the South!"

"How am I supposed to know which way is south in the dark?"

"So much for you instinct of direction."

She snorted. "Maybe I don't..." Looking up and behind him, her eyes widened and she whinnied, "Ralligor! Look out!"

He wheeled around and barely got an arm up before the blue dragon slammed into him and knocked him to his back.

As the black dragon crashed onto the ground, Shahly backed away, watching the other dragon as he circled for another pass.

Ralligor rolled to all fours, his teeth bared and a growl rolling from him as he slowly stood to face his old nemesis.

Seeing movement behind him again, the unicorn shouted, "There's another behind you!"

He turned to see the red dragon bearing down on him. She was a battered sight, clearly from her fight with his own Landmaster, but her resolve seemed undeterred. With Lorkryndo bearing down on him from the other side, he raised a hand to each of them and loosed green bursts of light that struck true and downed them both.

Rising first, the blue dragon faced the Desert Lord with bared teeth and a deep growl. The red dragon was slower to rise and was dazed and off balance when she did.

"I see Agarxus didn't kill you," Ralligor observed.

"Nor will he," Lorkryndo snarled back.

As the two larger dragons closed for battle, the red dragon slowly rose from the ground, her eyes locked on the Desert Lord's back. The two bigger dragons locked in a contest of strength, wielding their claws and teeth against one another, and Ralligor clearly had the advantage here. This appeared to be a ploy as the blue dragon was not fighting to win, rather he was just keeping his foe's attention on him to allow the red to attack from behind. Spreading her wings, the red dragoness crouched to leap onto the black dragon, but she was seen.

Shahly bolted forward, whinnying and snorting as she charged to the defense of her big friend.

The red dragon shied away, backing up a step as she saw the unicorn charging her. Sensing that this unicorn was not a powerful one, the dragon's lips slid away from her teeth and her brow was low over her eyes as she arched her neck back and backed away a little more, slowly opening her jaws.

Shahly knew that meant fire, and she remembered Ralligor's warning about dragons using fire and unicorn's inability to defend against it. She was not looking for a victory over a dragon, she only sought to keep the odds from tilting out of the black dragon's favor, and she would call upon a seldom used cunning to that effect. Raising her head, Shahly whinnied, "Behind you!"

The dragoness hesitated, drawing her head back, then her eyes narrowed, her lips slid away from her teeth and she snarled, "Do you think me a fool?"

Shahly's ears swiveled toward the dragoness. "You *do* know that my kind doesn't lie, don't you?"

Again the dragoness found herself gripped by apprehension and her teeth were slowly shrouded in thick lips again. She backed away a few steps, her eyes never leaving the unicorn. Indecision dominated her features.

Shahly leaned her head, just staring back up at the dragoness.

Something hit the ground behind the dragoness and she wheeled around, angling away from the unicorn as she backed away—and found herself face to face with the scarlet dragon.

Her brow low over her eyes, Falloah hissed through bared teeth.

Lorkryndo slammed into the ground not far away and rolled to a stop, quick to scramble to his feet and face the larger black dragon, who pursued with heavy steps.

Ralligor glanced at the unicorn and shouted, "Shahly, go! Get out of here!"

"Which way?" she asked desperately.

"Pick a direction!" he roared.

Shahly turned away from the fighting dragons, galloping as

hard as she could down the road toward the forest. She had put considerable distance between herself and the fighting dragons when she locked her hooves and came to an abrupt, awkward stop on stiff legs. Her wide eyes filled with the riders before her, soldiers dressed in polished metal armor with red and black tunics, black riding trousers and ornate helmets. She could see a decorated wagon in the middle of the procession, one drawn by six horses with two men at the seats, one of whom held the reins to control the animals.

The Garrison from Red Stone Castle stopped, and they all looked as surprised as the unicorn felt.

One paced through the halted soldiers, one whose gaze was fixed on the white unicorn.

Shahly's fear finally overwhelmed her hunger for excitement and she drew a shrieking gasp, slowly backing away.

Ralligor slammed onto the ground close behind her, dropping to all fours with the little unicorn right beneath his chest. He roared through bared teeth, his eyes glowing red, then emerald as all of the power he had surged through him and he faced an old enemy yet again.

For a moment, time itself appeared to stop and everything around was deathly quiet as black dragon and black unicorn stared each other down.

His eyes glowing violet, Bexton backed away a step, his dull black coat of hair showing the tension of the muscles beneath. The size of most of the horses that the soldiers rode on, he was an imposing sight, and his horn burst into violet flames. He also wore polished plate armor over his back and neck and hinged plates draped over his haunches and shoulders and neck. A form fitting helmet protected his head from most human threats, but he seemed to know that such armor would be useless against this dragon.

A deep growl thundered from the Desert Lord's throat and the black unicorn answered with an ominous and deep whicker. The two did not seem to fear each other and they both took the moment to size up the circumstances that were.

Back on his feet, Lorkryndo roared a challenge to his old rival.

Ralligor stood and swung around to answer, emerald fire enveloping his hands.

Shahly also looked.

The blue dragon was battered and bleeding. Ralligor had inflicted many wounds, many deep bites, and still he did not seem to want to yield, though they both knew he was too weak to fight on effectively.

Quick to turn his attention back to the black unicorn, Ralligor wheeled that way, raising a hand to strike a killing blow with his power of wizardry, but he hesitated, his eyes widening slightly.

Shahly also looked, her eyes darting about.

The black unicorn was gone, and so was his army of humans.

"You're wise to slip away," the black dragon snarled, "but I'll have my day with you." He looked to Shahly and suggested, "Try another direction. Do you know which way south is?"

She shook her head. "I'm afraid not. I'm not familiar with this part of the land."

He motioned behind him. "Go that way back toward the castle and look for a road that will meet this one and turn right. It will take you directly to the pass where everyone is waiting to take you home."

Shahly nodded. "Will you be okay?"

"Quit worrying over me and get home! I have things well in hand here. Now go!"

"I'll see you soon," she assured. Bolting around him, she ran as hard as she could the other direction. The other dragons knew that she meant something to the black dragon and the blue turned to cut her off. Staying on the road, she kicked her stride longer and tried to outrun him, but he was closing fast. He was forty paces away, his focus on her unwavering when Ralligor slammed into him hard enough to send them both back to the ground. The red dragon was engaged with Falloah and Shahly made it safely to the protection of the forest.

The sounds of the fighting dragons grew more distant and she ran with everything she had toward that road that Ralligor had spoken about. After a while her steps became hesitant and her eyes darted about again. He had not mentioned how far that road to the south was and she began to wonder if she had missed it.

She continued on at a canter, still debating if she should turn around and see if she had run past it or if she should trek on and hope it was still ahead of her.

Not knowing how long she had traveled, her canter turned to a hesitant trot, and she finally looked behind her. Ralligor had never really sent her astray and had, in fact, worked pretty hard to keep her on the path she needed to be on. While he had her absolute trust, that trust was not to be found with her own sense of direction.

The road turned, then, to her relief, it forked! Whickering a big sigh, she almost smiled as she veered to the right and quickened her trot. Others were waiting for her and she could not wait to see them. There was wonderful news to share!

Something slammed into her shoulder on the left side and she whinnied as horrific pain and shock tore through her. Stumbling, she managed to stop before she fell, her eyes closed tightly against the pain, and finally she looked back to see what had gotten her. Standing on that leg was suddenly very painful and she drew a gasp as she saw a human's hand length of an arrow sticking out of her shoulder.

"Oh, no," she breathed. Looking forward again, she tried to run away, but the arrow was deep in her shoulder and hurt terribly every time she tried to take a step.

Another struck her side, crashing through ribs and plunging into her lung and she whinnied in agony, stumbled, and finally fell as her other front leg collapsed. She rolled to her side on the hard road, heaving for each breath as she laid her head down as gently as she could. Just breathing was painful now, each breath stabbing into her side. Tightly closing her eyes, she tried to get her wits about her and struggled against the overwhelming pain she felt. When footsteps approached, she opened her eyes, and a chill swept through her.

Wearing black riding trousers and a loosely fitting white shirt with full sleeves that was open all the way down her chest, Nillerra's polished black boots found the dirt road beneath them with slow and steady steps, one right in front of the other. She wore a smile and held a crossbow in her hands with a bolt in position and ready to shoot.

The black haired girl stopped only four paces away, looking down at the wounded unicorn as if she was a hunter who had just brought down prized game. With a little nod, she informed,

"I knew you would come this way. It's a road that is not well traveled and is out of sight of the castle." She reset the crossbow in her hands and raised her chin. "I saw you leave last night. You looked lost. You just stood there for who knows how long. Were you just trying to get your bearings in the darkness or were you reluctant to leave him?"

"I..." Shahly started. "I didn't know which way to go."

Nillerra shook her head. "Silly little unicorn. I told you I would not let you leave alive, didn't I? I told you I would kill you before I let you go. You should have run farther when you had the chance. I've been waiting for you here all morning and was just about to give up and return to the castle. Isn't it fortunate that you are slow witted and you don't know your way around here?"

Shahly turned her eyes away, and a tear rolled down her nose.

"Oh," the black haired girl drawled. "Does it hurt?"

Her breath coming a little harder, the unicorn softly asked, "You mean to kill me, don't you?"

"I already have," Nillerra replied. "Now I shall just wait for you to take your last breath. And believe me, Shahly, I shall enjoy watching it."

"Then tell me why," Shahly demanded, still not looking at the black haired girl. "Here at the end, you owe me that at least."

"Why what, Shahly?"

"Why you hate me. Why you would wish to cause me such pain."

"Oh, I'll tell you, but be honest with me first." Nillerra leaned her head. "Are you really a woman or really a unicorn?"

"I am unicorn," Shahly answered with a labored breath.

"Then maybe that's why," the black haired girl snarled. "You never came to me when I was a girl. You never came to me in my greatest need. If you are truly a unicorn then that means you abandoned me when I needed you the most."

"So that's why you are so cruel," Shahly observed softly. "I suppose you think killing me will make things better for you, but it won't. Your bitterness will remain, and you'll never know happiness."

"Oh, I'll be happy enough, Shahly. In fact, I'll be just giddy as

I watch you take your last breath." She sat down on the road, crossing her legs with the crossbow in her lap as she smiled at the stricken unicorn before her. "Do you mind if I sit here and watch you die?"

Closing her eyes, Shahly whispered, "No, I don't mind."

"Good!" Nillerra declared in a girlish voice.

Three men, castle guards from Ravenhold, approached from behind the black haired girl, their eyes locked on the unicorn. One was armed with a crossbow, the other two with swords, and they wore their full combat armor.

Looking over her shoulder, Nillerra ordered, "Stay sharp. I think someone down the road there was expecting her, so go down that way and find them, and when you do, kill them!"

They nodded and turned that way, but the man with the crossbow barely got turned before an arrow slammed into his chest, through his armor and he fell straight to his back.

Standing ten paces down the road, Pa'lesh lowered her bow and reached for another arrow.

The other two guards froze as they saw her.

Nillerra sprang up and shouted, "Guards! They're here!"

Pa'lesh loosed one more arrow, slamming it right between the eyes of the next guard, then she tossed the bow aside and pulled her sword, glaring at the one remaining Ravenhold soldier.

Ten more burst from the trees, drawing their weapons.

Princess Faelon and Dorell ran up behind the big Zondaen, but stopped when she gestured with her other hand for them to do so.

Looking over her shoulder, Pa'lesh ordered, "Run back to the others." When they did, she turned back to the eleven men who slowly stalked toward her, and she began to back away.

Nillerra would not wait around for the fight. She dropped the crossbow and approached the unicorn, leaning her head as she stared down at her, then she smiled and offered, "I should help you before I go, Shahly. It's the least I can do." She grabbed onto the arrow that was sunk deep in the unicorn's ribs and wrenched it out.

Shahly bayed in agony, her eyes closed tightly against this new and excruciating pain. Struggling to catch her breath, she finally looked toward the black haired girl, but Nillerra had already slipped into the forest and was gone. She looked toward the guards as they pursued Pa'lesh around a turn in the road, and when they disappeared, she finally felt alone. This was how she wanted to die, without anyone else around to share such sadness, but for one.

Drawing a breath, she stared blankly into the forest on the other side of the road. A tear rolled from her eye, and softly she offered, "I'm sorry, Precious One. I'm so sorry."

Silence claimed the forest around her again but for the wind in the trees and the doves somewhere that cooed as if to mourn the coming and tragic loss to the world.

Closing her eyes again, Shahly whispered, "I love you, Vinton."

Nearly asleep, she was alerted to approaching hooves on the road and the heavy steps of human footfalls, and she half opened her eyes as a shadow fell over her.

CHAPTER 43

Pa'lesh had run enough and wheeled around to stand her ground against the charging Ravenhold men. Her teeth bared, she raised her sword before her to make her stand against them and get back to the wounded unicorn.

They stopped only about ten paces away, their weapons ready.

Faelon, a little out of breath, ran up behind her and took her side.

Glancing at the little princess, Pa'lesh growled, "I thought I told you to get back to the others!"

The Princess caught her breath and nodded, confirming, "You did, and I did, and I brought them with me."

Chail took her side, his axe in his hand as he glared at the soldiers before him. Le'ell, her scimitar in her hand, stopped beside him, and Traman on her other side, his expression as blank as it always was.

Nodding, Pa'lesh conceded, "Okay, you did well. Now get behind us."

The Princess complied, backing away with her gaze locked on the dozen men before her.

One of the Ravenhold soldiers, the best decorated of the lot, stepped toward them and raised his chin, announcing, "We have you outnumbered three to one. Surrender with honor and I am sure that Lord Nemlivv will spare your lives."

Prince Chail took a step toward him and offered, "Surrender to us and I shall spare yours."

"We outnumber you!" the soldier shouted. "You've no chance against us all!"

Looking to Pa'lesh, Chail grumbled, "I'm already tired of this."

"So am I," Le'ell agreed.

Nodding, Pa'lesh snarled, "Let's spill some blood."

The four of them yelled in horrific fashion and charged the Ravenhold soldiers, and steel met steel in a fierce battle. Le'ell held her own against two of them, Traman took two more and Pa'lesh fiercely engaged three. Chail killed one with his first blow and three backed away from him as he pressed his crushing onslaught.

Even over the sounds of battle, Faelon heard a sharp, high pitched whinny in the distance and she gasped, her wide eyes looking beyond the combatants as she breathed, "Shahly!" Darting around the battle and careful to avoid flailing weapons, the Princess ran toward the unicorn, desperate to go to her aid. With a look over her shoulder, she saw that her four friends had things well in hand, and when she turned back she found herself confronted by three more Ravenhold soldiers who were suddenly right in front of her. Shrieking a gasp, she stopped quickly and tried to back away, still desperate to reach the little unicorn.

Striding toward the fray, two of the three soldiers drew their weapons while the third locked his eyes on the small woman before him.

Faelon tried to dart around him but he caught her by the throat and pushed her back. She tried to push his hand away and get past him, but she did not see his hand come up into her. Her eyes flared, her mouth gaping in pain and surprise as his dagger plunged into her belly. The shock had not entirely set in as he threw her from him and she collapsed to the ground.

He watched her fall and sneered as she lay on the ground, then he gestured to the men still behind him to join the battle.

Vinton's head slammed into his chest, knocking him back four paces where he slammed onto the ground on his back, blood erupting in a brief red fountain from his chest as he hit.

The other two men backed away as the unicorn slowly turned his attention to them, and as ruby flames engulfed his horn to burn away the traces of blood still there, the big unicorn bayed and thrust his essence into the men's minds with a horrible purpose and they screamed and dropped their weapons, running back the way they had come as fast as they could.

Faelon lay curled up on her side and was quickly bleeding to death.

The battle was all but over except for one that Le'ell still engaged and Pa'lesh's eyes found the stricken girl immediately. Drawing a gasp, she ran to the girl's side and dropped to her knees, gently rolling the Princess to her back. She shook her head, trying to regain her thoughts, then she ripped Faelon's shirt open and reached for anything that could be used as a bandage.

Princess Faelon's eyes half opened and turned to her eyes to her Zondaen bodyguard. There was little color to her face, but she did not look afraid.

"Just lay still," Pa'lesh ordered as she ripped a piece of Faelon's shirt away to press into the wound with shaking hands.

Chail, Le'ell and Traman approached, their eyes locked on the girl.

Vinton paced to her and nudged Pa'lesh backward with his nose, a ruby light enveloping his horn as he ordered, "Go for Shahly."

Looking at the unicorn as he lowered his horn to the Princess, the Zondaen Captain informed, "Shahly's been injured. She's been shot with a crossbow."

"Go," the stallion ordered calmly. "Keep her safe until I get there."

Chail pulled Pa'lesh up by the arm and barked, "You heard him!"

As they ran toward the stricken unicorn, Faelon raised a hand to the stallion's face and weakly breathed, "No. You have to go to her."

"You won't be left here to die," Vinton informed straightly.

Galloping hooves neared and Faelon turned her eyes that way, seeing the old silver and the little blond mare stopping quickly as they reached her, and the little mare drew a gasp as she saw the Princess lying on the road.

"Vinton," the silver whickered.

"Shahly is injured," the bay informed. "She's down the road behind me."

Without responding, the silver launched himself into a full gallop that direction.

Relshee was hesitant as she watched after the old silver, and finally she looked to Vinton and asked, "What should I do?"

"Follow your instincts," the bay ordered.

When the silver arrived where Shahly had fallen, he only found the humans there.

Looking about, Pa'lesh shook her head and insisted, "She was right here! She had two crossbow bolts in her and..." She clenched her teeth, her eyes still darting about.

Traman knelt down and looked to the ground where Shahly had been lying; his eyes narrow as his fingertips touched the ground there. "She was here. She was lifted from the road where she fell." He looked over his shoulder. "Only one set of tracks."

"Someone took her?" Le'ell asked as if she barely believed.

Dorell finally caught up to them, out of breath as she reached them and she looked around herself. "Vinton sent me to help. Is she here?"

Looking to her, Chail asked, "What happened to Jekkon?"

"He followed Rawl to go and help Janees," the girl answered. "Princess Faelon is hurt back there but Vinton looks like he's almost through healing her. He said Shahly would be here."

"She isn't," the Enulam Prince growled. "Traman, can we follow the tracks and find whoever took her?"

Traman stood and strode to the other side of the road, his eyes on the ground before him. He stopped at the road's edge, his eyes glancing about in the forest, and he shook his head. "Trail ends here. I've never seen the like before."

Chail set his jaw and ordered, "Everyone pair up. We're going after her."

Pa'lesh turned desperate eyes back down the road, toward the injured princess who was in her charge. "I need to see how Faelon's doing." When the big Prince nodded to her she turned and ran that way.

***

Shahly was not to be found. There was no trail to follow and no clues as to where she might have been taken.

Vinton did not receive the news well and continued to search for her even after dark.

Having rendezvoused at their camp from the night before, no one spoke as they awaited the arrival of the Desert Lord and of Traman who had also stubbornly continued to search for her. His ears drooping, Vinton had joined them many hours after sunset and now lay some distance away as he stared into the forest to the north as if still searching for his lost love.

Still feeling drained after her ordeal, Faelon finally

approached the big unicorn and sat down beside him. Slowly, her hand glided over his mane as she also looked that way. She did not know what to say, what to do, so she just sat with him in silence.

When the stallion's ears perked up and swiveled toward the forest and he raised his head, Faelon also looked, and she stood as she saw Traman striding toward them.

Vinton slowly got to his hooves, his eyes on the bronze skinned man in both hope and despair.

Traman would not look at the bay unicorn, but he paused and dropped a crossbow bolt on the ground before him. It was covered with dried blood. His mouth tight and shaking slightly, Traman strode past, his head bowed as he softly informed, "It's all I found."

Vinton lowered his head and sniffed the bolt, then he turned away, tightly closing his eyes as he confirmed, "It's Shahly's blood."

"No," Faelon breathed. "Vinton..." She sank to her knees and covered her face with her hands, and she wept.

Others from the camp, including the silver and blond unicorns, slowly approached, knowing that something was horribly wrong.

Pa'lesh knelt down and picked the bolt up, slowly shaking her head as a rare tear escaped from her eye.

Turning to Chail, Le'ell clung to him and shook her head as she buried her face between his neck and shoulder, and she cried shamelessly.

"This can't be," Chail whispered.

The old silver unicorn slowly paced up behind the Zondaen Captain and sniffed the bolt himself, then he loosed a hard breath and closed his eyes, softly saying, "Even as the sun rises tomorrow, the world will be darker."

Relshee lay on her belly beside Faelon and leaned into the girl, and the little princess wrapped her arms around the young unicorn's neck and buried her face in her mane, crying even harder. Dorell joined them there and wept with them.

Ralligor finally landed, Falloah behind him, and as they approached the humans and unicorn the black dragon's eyes were uncharacteristically wide as he stared down at them. With a snarl on his mouth, he demanded, "Where is she? I told her to..."

Pa'lesh stood and turned toward him, holding up the crossbow bolt as she looked up at him with tears streaming from her eyes.

Lowering a hand to the ground, Ralligor bent down and sniffed the bolt, then he drew his head back slightly as he stood and backed away.

Falloah's jaws parted as she looked down at the bolt herself, and finally she tore her eyes away and crooned in sorrow.

Looking to the North, Ralligor bared his teeth, his eyes glowing red, and finally he raised his head and roared a horrible challenge. The very ground trembled and thunder rolled through the sky. A growl rolled from him as he finished and he backed away a few steps. His rage was just starting and he breathed in deep, angry breaths. His eyes fixed on some point to the north of them, he roared, "You've brought this misery, and now you will pay for it!" The big dragon's wings jetted out. "Ravenhold is soon to be no more! I will hunt down and kill everyone responsible for this, everyone who— "

"No you won't!" Vinton whinnied as he wheeled around. When the black dragon looked down at him, he raised his head and shouted, "You'll not disgrace her memory with vengeance. The land will have her back, and in her absence you and I will settle this thing between us once and for all!"

Ralligor drew his head back, his wide eyes locked on the big stallion.

His horn glowing crimson, Vinton took a few steps toward the Desert Lord and insisted, "I'll meet you at Falloah's lair in three days, on the cliff side that overlooks her cave. Three days, Ralligor, and you and I will finally finish what we should have this spring."

The black dragon just stared back at him, not knowing what to say or do.

Vinton raised his nose slightly, and a tear rolled from his eye. "Three days. Please, Ralligor. I would do it for you."

Setting his jaw, Ralligor finally bared his teeth and growled back, "Three days, Plow Mule. I'll be there, and we'll finish this once and for all."

The big stallion just stared back at him for a long moment, then he turned and ran south toward home, and toward his final confrontation with the Desert Lord.

Falloah took the big dragon's shoulder and breathed, "Ralligor, you can't."

Watching after the unicorn, the black dragon countered, "I have to. It's the least I can do after failing them both. And I know he would do the same for me."

***

The sun had just set and an orange glow illuminated the sky to the west before Rawl and Janees returned to the camp, and the big sorcerer found his companions silent and staring into the fire. The old silver unicorn had followed Vinton south, but Relshee remained with the humans, lying between Faelon and Dorell as she also stared blankly into the fire.

Rawl stopped behind Prince Chail and grasped his shoulder, his eyes glancing from one of the people to the next. Their expressions said what they could not and he knew their mission to rescue the little unicorn had failed. He turned his head and ordered, "Janees..."

She sheepishly turned her eyes up to his.

The big sorcerer drew a breath and finished, "Go and... Go sit down. Rest a while."

"We were so close," Le'ell whimpered, clinging to the big Enulam Prince beside her.

"Did Jekkon not return?" Rawl asked.

Chail half turned and looked up at him. "We thought he was with you."

Shaking his head, the sorcerer informed, "He babbled about having to talk to someone and ran off before we got a hundred paces. I thought he had returned here by now."

"He should be easy enough to find," Traman said dryly. "I'll head that way and track him down in the morning if he does not return tonight."

Venting a deep breath, Rawl patted the Prince's shoulder and said, "I suppose we start the long journey home tomorrow. How did Ralligor take the news?"

"Not well," Pa'lesh replied, "about like the rest of us."

The sorcerer nodded.

Relshee's ears perked and she raised her head, looking toward the forest to the north as she informed, "Someone's coming."

As she sprang up and headed that way, everyone turned that way and slowly they got to their feet as they heard someone approaching.

CHAPTER 44

The journey back into the Abtont forest was long and lonely and Vinton's heart felt heavier than it ever had. With Shahly no longer in his life, his heart could see only darkness. For two nights he had stopped to sleep only after exhaustion had claimed him, and for two nights he had seen the little mare he loved so much, but only in his dreams. Haunting him further was the man he had killed. He was unicorn, and yet he had joined the heat of battle and killed someone. Perhaps it was justified, but his heart would not allow him to rest or dismiss it so.

He would be at Falloah's lair after another day's travel, but kept his pace quick to be there as soon as he could. The pain in his heart only grew worse as he traveled toward home, toward the confrontation with his old enemy and Shahly's dearest friend. Only when he arrived there would the pain in his heart come to an end, and only then would he be able to join his beloved Shahly in the life beyond and answer for the death he had brought to another.

Rain fell on him in a gentle shower as if the land and skies grieved with him. He paced down the lonely, human's road without fear, without thought of consequence as he always did, and without awareness of his surroundings.

As evening drew near, he found himself standing on that grassy cliff side that overlooked Falloah's cave. He stared into the blackness of the cave for a while as the sun set, and his eyes glanced around at all of the green things that grew all around it. This was a beautiful place and Falloah had chosen well when she had decided to live here. Fresh again in his memory was how Shahly had repeatedly hurled herself from the tall cliff and into the deep water below, just for fun, just to live all she could and experience everything that her life would offer, and a smile finally touched his mouth.

With his beloved Shahly warming his broken heart, he lay down to his belly and slowly lowered his head to the ground. After a while, as the sun descended past the treetops, he closed his eyes.

He found her there yet again, playing and frolicking as she

always did. Even in his dreams he had always looked to protect her, to warn her away from danger, but this night he was at her side as they ran and climbed to the top of the highest mountain they could find. Once there, she gave him a smile and beckoned with her head for him to run with her, and he did, and they hurled themselves off the mountain and ran on top of the clouds. He did not think about the danger, only the soft clouds beneath his hooves, the wind in his mane, and the playful and perfect young mare at his side.

Shahly stopped and looked to the side and Vinton stopped just beyond her, looking back as she stared off into the distance. The sun was rising over the clouds and bathing her in a bright golden glow. When he turned and tried to approach her, she moved away from him, backing up toward the sun.

Her eyes showed reluctance and sadness and she softly told him, "I have to go now, Vinton."

Shaking his head, he whinnied back, "I'll go with you!"

"You can't," she informed sadly, still backing away from him.

Vinton stopped, pitifully calling, "Shahly!"

"Goodbye, Vinton," she said from a distance.

Vinton raised his head and whinnied, "Shahly!" Squinting against the rising sun, he turned his eyes away from it, a tear rolling down his cheek as he realized she was not there. Looking to his other side where she always slept, he found the same emptiness there that was in his heart, and his hopes that he would be reunited with his lost love were dashed for the last time. He closed his eyes, squeezing new tears out of them, then he looked down to Falloah's lair, seeing the black dragon sitting catlike just outside of the cave with the scarlet dragon beside him.

This should have been a terrifying sight for any unicorn, but Vinton felt only relief. The pain in his heart would stop with his death, and that was all he had to look forward to.

Something seemed amiss. Falloah did not look as distraught as he thought she would, and the black dragon's eyes looked like he was almost smiling. Perhaps he was looking forward to this battle as well, and Vinton would not disappoint him. He raised his head, wanting to give the big dragon a challenging glare but he could only manage a blank look this day.

One of Ralligor's eyebrows cocked up.

A unicorn tenderly nuzzled his ear and he quickly turned, his eyes wide as he whickered, "Shahly?"

She smiled back at him.

Springing to his hooves, Vinton whinnied, "Shahly!" as he reared up.

The white unicorn did as well and they lunged into each other with unbridled joy, kicking their forelegs, and they tumbled over and hit the ground on their sides.

Ralligor looked to Falloah and they shook their heads.

Tears streamed from the stallion's eyes as he rolled his body and looked down at his little mate, who lay there smiling back at him with tears streaming from her own eyes. Neither could speak, though there was so much to say. Remembering what she had done to surprise him a few days prior, the stallion kissed her mouth, then got to his hooves and ran away from her.

Shahly watched in a little confusion as he ran from her, then she smiled and scrambled to her hooves, running after him. A moment later they galloped to the cliff side and hurled themselves off and into the deep water below, crashing into the surface at the same time.

Falloah looked to the black dragon and asked, "Do you remember when we used to do that?"

His eyes slid to her and narrowed. "It was a month ago. Of course I remember."

Side by side, the unicorns scrambled ashore toward the dragons, and Shahly paused to shake some of the water from her, and as he was pelted by little droplets, this time the stallion did not mind. When she finished, he shook and pelted her back.

"Ahem," Ralligor growled.

They looked up at him.

He raised a brow again as he looked to the white unicorn, scolding, "Are you sure you should be doing that in your condition?"

"I'm fine," she assured with a laugh.

Vinton looked to her and said, "I have so many questions! Wait a moment." He looked up at the dragon. "Her condition?"

Ralligor informed, "Your life is about to get a whole lot more complicated, Plow Mule."

Vinton drew his head back.

Shahly nuzzled him and smiled when she had his attention, tenderly informing, "I'm going to have a baby."

His eyes widening, the stallion took a couple of steps back, and he could not tear his gaze away from the little mare.

"Congratulations," Ralligor snarled. "Now go home."

The unicorns looked up at the big dragon.

Vinton took a few steps toward him, his eyes on the black dragon's a he stammered, "Ralligor, I..."

The Desert Lord responded with a nod to him, then, "It wasn't all my doing. Someone played a much larger part than I did. Now go home." He turned his eyes to Shahly, his brow low over them. "With two of them we are going to have to enlist half the land just to keep them out of trouble. Rejoin your herd and keep a close eye on her."

Shahly lowered her head, her ears drooping as she reminded, "We can't rejoin the herd. I've been banished."

One of Ralligor's eyebrows cocked up. "Just go, little unicorn. Let them know you are carrying their future." He looked to Vinton. "Take her home. I'll see you in a couple of days."

Vinton nodded once to him, then he looked to Falloah and nodded to her, smiling a little as she nodded back. Turning toward the thick of the trees, he led Shahly away from the scarlet dragon's lair, not speaking for some time. His heart was in turmoil, and something told him he was still dreaming.

Almost an hour later Shahly butted him with her nose and summoned, "Vinton?"

He gave her a long look, then turned his eyes forward again, mumbling, "This is too perfect."

"What is?"

"You. Our foal. Rejoining the herd." He closed his eyes. "I know it isn't real. I know you are a dream again. When I awaken... I can't lose you again."

"You aren't dreaming, Vinton."

"I wish I could believe that," he said softly.

She turned her head and raised her nose to nuzzle his ear, then she unexpectedly bit his ear hard.

Whinnying, he shied away and stumbled a few steps away from her, shaking his head.

Shahly whickered a laugh as he turned bewildered eyes to her and she asked, "Is that part of your dream, my stallion?"

He stopped, watching as she paced on. His heart thundering anew, he asked, "So... I'm not dreaming? You are alive and you're... You are pregnant?"

She did not stop, but she did look back at him and smile. "Our Precious One will need her father to have his wits about him, Vinton."

Vinton cantered forward and caught up to her, his eyes staring blankly ahead of them.

"Are you okay, my Love?" she asked softly.

He nodded.

"You are happy to be a father, aren't you?"

He nodded again.

"Some call this shock," she informed. "I'll just be quiet and let you sort your feelings out."

Vinton finally looked to her and smiled just a little. "I have too much joy all at once, Shahly. Too much joy. And yet..." He stopped and lowered his head, closing his eyes tightly.

Shahly turned toward him, giving him a look of concern as she gently summoned, "Vinton?"

He drew a breath, one that stuttered out of him, and finally he confessed, "I killed someone."

The little mare drew a gasp and took a step back.

Looking away from her, he stared into the forest and shook his head. "I can't be forgiven for this. I shouldn't be."

Her eyes narrowing, Shahly barked, "Wait a moment. I spoke to Traman and Chail and Pa'lesh and they told me about this. They said he hurt Faelon and was going to kill her. They said you saved her from him."

"I could have done that without killing him," the stallion insisted.

Leedon strode to him and patted his back. "My friend, hindsight is the sharpest and most regretful of all."

Vinton's head swung around, surprise on his features as he did not even know the old wizard was approaching them.

Shahly looked to the wizard and admitted, "I don't know what to say, but the others tell me that Vinton was protecting an innocent."

"That's no excuse," the bay insisted. "I am unicorn. We're not supposed to kill."

Offering the big unicorn a little smile, Leedon patted him again and said, "Do not try to justify your actions or condemn yourself, my friend. What happened happened and an innocent girl is still alive thanks to you. Sometimes we do things that we feel regret for, and sometimes we feel regret even for those things that are justified."

"I still killed someone," the stallion grumbled.

"Give yourself some time, my friend," the wizard advised. "At some point you will come to grips with this. In the meantime, it is best that you are a mate and father."

Vinton finally turned his eyes to the old wizard.

And Leedon responded with a smile. "Be who you are, my friend. Be her mate and your child's father, and don't let this lead you to more regret."

The stallion just stared at him for long seconds, and finally he nodded.

"Absolution will come in its own time," the wizard went on. "Don't rush it."

"I won't," Vinton assured softly.

Shahly finally approached and asked, "Will you come with us?"

Shaking his head, Leedon replied, "I have something that requires my attention, but I'll surely visit you when I can." He smiled again. "And I'll want to see that little foal this spring. You two be well."

As he turned to leave, Vinton quickly said, "You have my thanks for your help rescuing Shahly. I shall always remember."

The wizard stopped and half turned, smiling back as assured, "You have honored me with your friendship, and I shall always remember that."

The two unicorns walked on, side by side for some time, and deep in the forest, Shahly finally observed, "You're very quiet again."

He glanced at her and nodded. "My heart's in turmoil. Even as I push the death I caused from my mind, I have all of the joy of having you back building up. And more builds up when I think about our foal. I didn't think this much joy and happiness was possible all at once. I suppose I just don't know what to do with it all."

"Easy," she said. "We run." She launched herself into a full gallop and he followed.

Hours later they were deep in the tall, ancient trees of the forest, walking a path that humans and their kin did not know about.

However, something else did, something that knew the white unicorn very well.

They sensed the forest cat a hundred paces before they reached him and Shahly raised her head, drawing a breath as she observed, "Well, he's waiting for me again."

They closed three quarters of the distance and Vinton stopped, Shahly stopping at his side. Something was in the stallion's eyes that she had never seen before, something challenging and almost mischievous.

Looking to her stallion, she suggested, "Perhaps we should go around."

"No," Vinton corrected. "I'll take care of him. Wait here."

Shahly watched as a red glow illuminated his horn, then she felt him fold his essence around himself as he turned and paced into the forest. A few moments later, up ahead where they knew the forest cat to be, she heard the cat scream in anger and Vinton whinny in joy, and she shook her head as she watched the furious cat chase her stallion across the path before her. With a deep sigh, she paced toward them and mumbled, "This can't be good."

Silence followed.

For long moments she watched the path, expecting some movement any time. Surely the cat had not gotten her stallion! Concern took her and she paced slowly forward, her eyes darting about as she whickered, "Vinton?"

"Yes?" he answered from beside her.

She snorted in surprise and danced a few steps away.

Vinton paced on, smiling as he said, "Welcome to my world, Love."

***

Dusk was near when they reached a familiar clearing with tall, soft grass, a creek nearby, berry covered bushes, and the remains of a dead Grawrdox in the middle of the field.

"Just know," Vinton went on, "that where you go from now on I will go. Even if you get up in the night for water, I'm coming with you."

"Vinton," she protested, "I don't think he's going to try to take another unicorn."

"Perhaps he won't, Love, but I'm certain others will try."

She snorted. "You were overprotective before, but I think you are becoming unbearable now!"

"He has a right to be," Dosslar informed from behind them.

Shahly wheeled around, her eyes widening as she whinnied, "Ahpa!" She bolted to him, then stopped halfway there and raised her head as she saw the unicorn who paced at his side.

The other unicorn was as snow white as she was with sparkling gold ribbons in her horn and golden hooves. Blue eyes found Shahly's as the other white unicorn raised her head and was barely containing the joy she felt at seeing Shahly.

A big smile overtook Shahly's lips and she bolted the rest of the way to them, and as they nuzzled the expected mother to be, Vinton paced up behind his little mate with wide eyes as he looked upon a unicorn he had not seen for many, many seasons.

The blue eyed unicorn looked to Vinton with a smile and slowly paced to him, nuzzling the side of his neck as she reached him. "It is good to see you again, Vinton," she greeted. Stepping back to look into his eyes, she was clearly very proud, very happy.

"I see your wanderings have finally brought you home, Shawri," the bay stallion observed.

"They have," she confirmed. Looking back to the other white unicorn who took her side, she added, "And just when I needed to be here. Dosslar found me a few days ago and our reunion was a troubled one when he told me about Shahly." She looked back to Vinton and continued, "I had been watching over a large boy with ogre bloodlines before my stallion found me, and when he told me that he and others were going to rescue a white unicorn..." She glanced at Shahly again. "Well, it was not much trouble to figure out which one."

Shahly snorted and looked away.

Vinton raised his head. "So, when she had been shot by the

humans..."

"Dosslar and I found her, and Jekkon carried her to safety so that we could heal her. We covered his tracks so that the humans would not find her again." She looked to the big tan unicorn with loving eyes. "While we healed her, that's when the great and joyous news was revealed."

Raising his head, Vinton looked as proud as any unicorn could and he turned his eyes to his little mate.

"Well," Dosslar started, "come along, all. Let's eat something and bed down, then we can talk about Shahly rejoining the herd."

As her parents paced on toward the creek, Shahly had despair in her eyes once again as she cantered to catch up to them. "But I've been banished! They won't want me to be within smelling distance of the herd again."

Vinton took Shahly's side and assured, "You just leave that to us, Shahly. The elders now have four other elders to contend with."

"And," the blue eyed white unicorn added, "you seem to have made quite a powerful friend. I *never* thought one of us would actually befriend the Desert Lord himself and I want to hear all about your story with him."

***

A full day later, the circle of the elders was convened again, but not at that magical spot that was so sacred to the unicorns. This time it took place right beside the Spagnah River, the place where Vinton had first tried to approach Shahly to be his mate. This was the place most special to them and the elders would just have to accept it.

But, it was not chosen simply for that. Vinton and the old silver unicorn had already formulated another plan that would require a wide open space, and they would require the whole herd there, not just the elders. News of the blue eyed white unicorn's return to the forest had already reached the herd and many were anxious to greet her, not knowing that she would have a banished member of the herd with her.

The circle was there, but incomplete. Three elders were missing and the circle of elders and the whole herd watched as four unicorns paced toward them.

Shahly glanced about nervously. Made to pace ahead of Vinton and her mother and father, she felt uneasy with the eyes of the elders who had banished her watching with such scrutiny. She hesitated at the gap left for Vinton and her parents and looked back as her father whickered to her.

With a proud smile, Dosslar motioned her on with his head and prodded, "Go on, Shahly."

She took a deep breath and paced through the gap and paced on toward the center of the circle as the gap closed behind her. Looking to the left as she reached the center, she saw a familiar and friendly face and smiled at the old silver unicorn as he nodded to her. Slowly, Shahly turned to meet the eyes of each of the elders, seeing quickly that most of them disapproved of her presence among the herd again. When she had greeted the eyes of all, she gently laid down to her belly.

A stirring was caused among the elders. There was only one reason a mare would come before the elders to do this and a few of the elders danced restlessly, glancing about as this banished member of their herd announced that she was with foal.

The old silver stepped from his place in the circle, his eyes proudly on the little white mare as he observed, "Well, now. This changes everything, doesn't it?"

The old brown mare also stepped in, her eyes on the silver as she countered, "This changes nothing. She is known to be a danger to the herd— "

"Enough!" Dosslar whinnied as he also stepped in. "Banishing Shahly is the worst mistake this herd has ever made. She is with foal and carries the future of our herd within her."

The black unicorn with the silver mane shook his head. "No, Dosslar. She must leave. We cannot be sure that her old habits will not return despite her pregnancy."

Shawri stepped in and raised her head. "I thought when I returned that I would come home to see a united herd, not one that would banish a young mare in her greatest need." Her eyes scanned the ranks of the elders and she informed, "The decision is made, my friends. Shahly is to return to the herd and that is that."

Raising his head, Vinton announced, "Seconded."

Also stepping in, the old gray countered, "The decision was

made days ago and will not be rescinded by four of you. Shawri, while we are all happy to see you return to the herd..." He turned his eyes skyward and danced backward a few steps.

All of the unicorns looked.

From the treetops directly behind Vinton, Shawri and Dosslar, an ominous black form swept over the clearing.

With Falloah behind him and to the side, Ralligor swept his wings forward and landed softly near the trees about seventy paces away, trotting off the last of his speed as he slowly folded his wings to his sides and back. The scarlet dragon took his side. As all of the unicorns turned fully toward him, many with their essence channeling into their horns, Ralligor raised a palm to them and announced, "Just calm down. I'm only here to observe."

The old brown mare's eyes narrowed and she shouted, "And again she brings enemies of our kind into the middle of the herd! You would have us take her back in now?"

The old gray raised his head and assured, "The presence of the Desert Lord among the herd will not sway our decision."

Vinton turned and walked to Shahly, assuring, "It isn't his presence that should concern you. And, yes, your decision will be swayed today."

Dosslar and Shawri followed him and the old silver stepped from his place in the circle and paced right to Shahly.

Panic struck the rest of the unicorns as the Tyrant himself glided in from behind the other dragons and slammed onto the ground only forty paces away from the circle. Standing fully, he did not close his wings as he towered over all in his presence, a deep growl rolling from him as he watched most of the unicorns flee toward the trees on the other side of the clearing.

A few of the elders stopped and turned, their wide eyes on the giant dragon as they channeled their essence into their horns to make a stand and defend the other unicorns.

This was ignored by the huge Landmaster as he turned his attention to the five unicorns before him, especially to the little white one who still lay in the grass staring back at him. With slow, heavy steps, he strode forward, lowering his body and reaching to the ground with his huge, clawed hands.

As the giant dragon's nose and teeth neared, Shawri

swallowed hard and gave Vinton an uneasy look, saying to him in a low whicker, "I hope you know what you're doing."

Only five paces away, with the bottom of his jaw about a man's height from the ground, Agarxus' attention turned to the four unicorns who stood behind the little white one, his eyes boring into them.

The old silver was first, slowly bowing his head to the Landmaster. Vinton and Dosslar followed suit, and finally the wide eyed Shawri, who never took her gaze from him.

The Landmaster grunted back, then looked to the little white unicorn who lay before him. He took one more step toward them to close those last five paces toward the little white unicorn with that single step and lowered his nose to her, sniffing a few times.

Shahly smiled and licked the end of the giant dragon's nose.

He did not regard her coldly as he had before. Drawing his head back slightly, he boomed, "Have you learned your place in the natural order?"

Nodding, Shahly assured, "I have, Landmaster."

Agarxus briefly turned his attention to the four unicorns standing behind Shahly, then he rose up until his head was some four heights from the ground, his eyes narrow as they found the seven elders who stood their ground only thirty paces away. Another growl rolled from him and he bared his teeth, informing, "This unicorn is in my favor, as is the offspring she carries within her. Humans have thinned your numbers and decimated your kind elsewhere. Guard well this next generation and replenish your numbers to where they should be."

The old gray unicorn dared to pace forward a few steps. "We are your enemies, and you would have us—"

"My enemies," the huge dragon thundered, "are those that pose a threat to my territory and my hunting ranges. You are part of the natural order and should remain so." His eyes narrowed. "Remember my words this day and guard well the life that grows within this one. I would be greatly annoyed if anything should happen to either of them, and that might make me rethink your place in my territory." His eyes darted from one to the next. "Her safety is in your charge now. Do not fail me."

As horrified unicorns watched, the giant dragon stood fully and turned, sweeping his wings to lift himself into the air and over the treetops.

Ralligor looked to the herd elders and raised his brow. "Well now. Looks like you unicorns have a problem, doesn't it?" He leveled his body and strode to the little white unicorn. With his nose only two paces away, he raised a brow and snarled just a little.

Staring back at him, Shahly assured, "I promise I will do my best to stay out of trouble and not torment forest predators anymore."

"And?" the black dragon pressed.

She turned her eyes away. "I promise I will not put myself at risk or embark on any more crusades without your permission *and* Vinton's."

"And?" Ralligor growled.

Huffing a hard breath, she stared across the field and added, "I promise I won't try to befriend any more wandering dragons or drakeniens or ogres or humans or anything without permission." She finally looked back at him with narrow eyes. "But I *am* going to still have fun!"

"Under the watchful eye of everyone you know," Vinton assured.

Ralligor's eyes snapped to the bay stallion. "If that foal she carries is anything like her—"

"I'm trying not to think about it," Vinton grumbled.

The black dragon stood, his eyes darting from one elder to the next. "You appear to be in the position of reinstating Shahly to your herd. I won't keep you. Just remember that if anything happens to her while she is in your charge you will not have just the Landmaster's wrath to contend with. I'll be watching as well." He looked down to Vinton and bade, "Be well, Plow Mule, and best of luck to you. You're going to need it."

Falloah strode to them and smiled at the bay stallion, assuring, "We'll help how we can, my friends. Shahly, I am happy for you beyond words. I can't wait until spring to see your baby!"

Shahly smiled and offered, "Thank you, Falloah. Thank you Ralligor."

The scarlet dragon reached to her and gently stroked her back with her clawed hand, then she ran the backs of her fingers tenderly down Vinton's neck. Standing fully, she took the black dragon's side.

A tear slipped from Shahly's eye as she watched the dragons fly over the treetops, and she softly said, "Thank you my friends. I love you both. Please visit soon."

Dosslar and the old silver unicorn turned toward the herd elders and paced a few steps toward them, both holding their heads up. Vinton took the silver's side and Shawri took Dosslar's.

The other elders approached, walking shoulder to shoulder.

Shahly got to her hooves and walked around the four who protected her and met the other elders only a few paces away. As they stopped, she looked to them each in turn and begged, "Please, no more conflict. The herd must be one again. I promise I will behave and not be a danger to the other unicorns anymore. I promise."

The old brown mare paced to her, looking to her with authority as she announced, "You are out of place, Shahly. Take your place at the center of the circle of elders. We each owe you an apology."

"You don't," Shahly assured softly.

The black unicorn with the silver mane approached and butted Shahly with his nose. "You have the favor of the Landmaster, and you've brought that favor and his protection to our herd. Now take your position in the circle." He paced by Vinton, asking, "Have you thought of a name?"

As the circle was reformed and Shahly lay in the middle, the rest of the herd emerged from the forest to receive the news of an addition to their herd and to rejoice over that. Three more pregnant mares joined her and Shahly, for the first time in her life, was not regarded as a child. Her life had finally opened a new chapter.

CHAPTER 45

The cabin was as dark and forbidding as it was the first time Janees had seen it, though it was a little cleaner. She entered behind the big sorcerer and looked around her. Trying to anticipate what he would want, she leaned her walking stick on the wall near the door and strode to the fireplace, picking up the metal pail and the little shovel as she knelt down to clean out the ashes from the last fire.

"That won't be necessary," Rawl barked as he sat down at the table with that book he always wrote in. "You won't be here that long. Pick those books up on the table here and put them back where they go."

She stared into the fireplace for long seconds, trying to fight back tears that tried to emerge, then she slowly put the pail and bucket back in their places and stood, turning to the table where the big sorcerer sat. As she collected the books and hugged them to her, she would not look to the sorcerer as she walked around him and went about the task of finding where they were supposed to go on the shelves.

Rawl scribbled away and seemed to ignore her.

Janees put the last book where it was supposed to be and lowered her eyes. A hard, unsure future awaited her. With nowhere to go and Jekkon now in someone else's charge, there was nothing left for her.

Turning back to the fireplace, she walked over and knelt down again, picking up the shovel and pail to clean it out.

"I said you don't have to do that," he reminded.

"I heard you," she replied softly, scooping some ashes from the fireplace, "but I should leave it as I found it." She labored for a moment, and halfway done she bowed her head and closed her eyes, offering, "I'm sorry I failed you."

"How did you fail me?" he asked in a hard voice.

"I lost the duel," she replied softy. "I used all of your teachings, but I just was not good enough. I was not strong enough or quick witted enough to match her."

"And how did losing like that make you feel?" he prodded.

She slowly took another scoop of ashes and answered, "Like a nothing. I couldn't match her no matter what I did. I just wasn't powerful enough."

"Hmm," was his response.

Janees continued with her labors, and a moment later was almost done when she stopped and raised her head, staring at the stone before her as she breathed, "Humility!"

Rawl slowly turned his attention to her and laid his pen down.

Still kneeling by the fireplace, Janees turned to him and repeated, "Humility. *That* is the first lesson a sorcerer should know!"

He smiled.

Dropping the shovel, she stood and strode to him, smiling as she stopped a pace away. "That... It was so simple!"

"And yet you could not see it for many days," he observed, "and I had to prod and shove you down that path the whole time. It's like being in the forest, girl. You cannot see it when the trees obscure your view of it. Sometimes you don't look hard those things you most need to find, you just need to find them."

She drew a deep breath, raising her chin as she nodded. "Yes, *Magister.*" Something more solemn took her face and she turned her eyes down. "I still failed you. I'm sorry."

"How did you fail, Janees?"

Janees took a deep breath and let it out slowly, finally answering, "I lost the duel."

"Did you learn from that defeat?" he pressed. When she nodded he informed, "Then you didn't fail."

Her eyes snapped back to him.

"You were there to learn," he informed with a smile, "not to win. In learning the lesson I presented to you, you won the duel within you. I knew you were no match for Nemlivv as I knew you were no match for Deshett. It was important for you to know as well."

"I understand, *Magister,*" she said softly.

His eyes narrowed and he shook a finger at her. "Now don't think I'm taking you on as my apprentice permanently, little girl."

Shaking her head, she assured, "I won't, *Magister.*"

Rawl stood and slammed the book closed. "I've many things

awaiting my attention and I'm a busy man."

"Yes, *Magister.*"

He strode around her to the door and took his walking stick from beside hers. "Come along, girl. We've somewhere to go. There is much you still need to learn before I can unleash you upon the world, and the world is where you will learn it."

She followed him out, taking her own walking stick as she asked, "Where do we go?"

He stopped and turned to her, his brow low over his eyes as he countered, "Just where do you *think* we go?"

Faelon looked around her and turned a few times, finally pointing to the other side of the cabin and announcing, "That way."

"Why that way?" he asked.

She offered him a smile. "If I am to learn, then I should take a path I haven't already walked."

"Very good," he commended. "At least I know now you can be taught. Okay, little girl, lead on. While we walk, you will tell me what you learned from Deshett."

The new path Faelon was on would prove to be the hardest of her life, and yet it was the most natural, the most rewarding, and as she walked with the big sorcerer and told him of her battle with Nemlivv's apprentice and what she had learned, her heart filled with the joy of new learning, of the guidance she had always craved but never truly had, and with the companionship of someone who she could learn from, and could trust with absolution.

But her journey was only beginning…

Made in the USA
Columbia, SC
25 May 2022

60764284R00265